It is 1941. Europe is a … e of committing its for… …ng on the edge of commitment is Daniel Lawrence, a rootless Englishman, sent to Japan to spy for the Americans, and caught by the attractions of Ayako, his lovely young interpreter. Then comes Pearl Harbour.

This story follows the fortunes of Daniel, Ayako, and the child born from their encounter, through the war, inside Japan and across the Pacific. We see the brutality of the Japanese concentration camps, the appalling devastation wrought by the Tokyo Firestorm, and, finally, the pain and paradox of the plutonium bomb dropped on Nagasaki.

Bernard Clark's wide-ranging scholarship and carefully-researched eye for detail brings vividly to life the individuals caught up in one of the most devastating of global conflicts, their interlocked humanity and their intractable differences. We follow the crew of *Bock's Car* on their harrowing flight to drop the world's most powerful atomic bomb, and discover that the dropping of *Fat Man* on Nagasaki was, perhaps, the most humane act of the war.

Detailed, devastating, and deeply respectful, NAGASAKI grips the reader every step of the way from first encounters to the dropping of the bomb – and beyond.

NAGASAKI

嘉数の子守唄

今夜の月はお悔やみの月
それというのも夜空は花火のように
赤や白や青の炎が天の星まで舞い上がっているから

Mrs Okunaga's Okinawa lullaby

The moon is in mourning tonight.
Because the sky is alight with firecracker trails,
Searing flames of red, white and blue into the stars of heaven.
I have nothing to live for, save this tidy bundle...

NAGASAKI

A NOVEL

BERNARD CLARK

GREAT CUMBERLAND PUBLISHING

First Published by
Great Cumberland Publishing Ltd 2025

Registered UK Office:
18 The Glasshouse Studios, Fryern Court Road, Fordingbridge,
Hampshire SP6 1QX
infogreatcumberland@gmail.com

ISBN: 978-1-0682610-2-2

Cover Design: Mark Peters
Layout: IdleWilde

DEDICATION

Yoshihisa Hayashi, NHK
Winner of the Peabody Award
for
'Two Hours that Changed the World' (Pearl Harbour)

1

SEPTEMBER 1941, NAGASAKI

SPARKLES. That was Dan's first impression of Nagasaki from the sea. Sparkles flickering across the choppy waters of the bay; flashing sparkles from the tiny tin-and-tile *minka* tenements, terracing up the steep streets; sparkles glittering from the starred epaulettes of the menacing military uniforms on the dockside below.

Daniel Lawrence was leaning on the salt-caked port-side railing of the *Akagi Maru*, looking away from the harbour, because, as he'd been told several times – threatened, even – that curiosity by a Westerner would be seen as spying in Japan in 1941; that he should keep 'eyes below;' he learned the furtive sideways glance of the Orient – how to see without looking.

He was conspicuous, of course. 'Six-foot-one-inch-thin', rather than 'tall', the Brazilian Embarkation Officer had called out in Portuguese to his assistant, with a sardonic grin, because Dan, although wide- shouldered, had no visible muscle, and precious little flesh – very different from the short, brawny, deckhands hauling the mooring ropes at the stern of the boat.

The day after departing Santos, as the ship left the protected waters of Brazil, he had been brusquely ordered to remain in his oily cabin without being given a reason. When allowed out after an infuriating and claustrophobic fortnight, his large feet sticking out from the end of the bunk, the crew had repainted the deck in provocative naval camouflage, and bolted four 152mm/50 calibre low angle naval guns to the fore-and-after-decks. So, from leaving Brazil as a forty-year-old peaceful cargo transporter, the *Akagi Maru* was transformed into an attack ship as it butted through the South Atlantic, the Indian Ocean and into the Sea of Japan – to join the ranks of the increasingly powerful Japanese Imperial Navy.

When the ship bumped onto the Nagasaki dockside, a cascade of fighting seagulls swooped along the deck, allowing Dan to take mental snapshots of the harbour as he shooed them away. At last he could begin. He felt a thrill. He had a task – risky, to be sure, but one he was determined to accomplish – the prize he'd been promised meant so much, and would open the gateway to so much more.

The port was crowded and vibrant, and guarded not only by soldiers but by armed military police – the feared *Kempeitai*, the Japanese equivalent of the Nazi Gestapo, who were standing by each cast-iron mooring bollard, looking as stiff and immovable as the bollards themselves.

High above everything, in the hills away from Nagasaki city, on a crystal blue-sky day, the Catholic Church at Urakami, once the biggest Cathedral in Japan, looked down majestically, though somewhat incongruously in such an Oriental panorama. Looming ominously round the coast towards Fukuoka, the endless corrugated roofs and clapboard barracks of the Mitsubishi Naval workshops and heavily fenced armaments factories – although Dan most certainly knew not to be seen looking in that direction.

A Korean cabin-boy came to his aid, swatting the gulls with a bamboo broom, while making an effort to bow, saying 'Mister Lawrence, you go', leading him down a rusty ladder to the embarkation deck, where his metal trunk was waiting with a porter. The crew, mainly Indo-Portuguese from Goa, half saluted and patted his shoulder, as they said goodbye to this gangly Westerner, one who had tipped them well on the seven-week journey.

A welcoming party – if you could call it that – was lined up on the quay, a dozen officials, some in military uniform, some in khaki *kokumin-fuku* – the drab, civil uniforms encouraged by the authorities as Japan edged towards war – encircled Dan as he approached in his off-white, slightly crumpled linen business suit, with his purposely battered Panama perched jauntily on his head. The crumpled suit and the scruffy hat were elements in Dan's armour, deliberately donned to fool the opposition into thinking him weak and of no account. The Japanese officials moved forward and corralled him, using hand gestures, into an echoey, covered warehouse.

There, a small, rotund official, wearing a pristine uniform with a curved sword hanging low on his hip, and surrounded by a gaggle of deadpan subordinates, looked Dan up and down, before slowly spit- ting out two words – 'you wait'. The official nodded to a younger assistant, who thrust his arms out and presented his superior with a large sheet of heavy paper that had been expertly folded down to foolscap size.

The crowd went silent for a moment. This document had accompanied Dan from the Japanese Consulate in Sao

Paolo – in a word, it was the *deal* agreed between the Americans and the Japanese to allow the ship to avoid sanctions and, given that pedigree, it was not to be welcomed.

Ignoring his assistant, the official opened the document and flattened it out on a rickety cloth-covered table. He leant a heavy hand on each of the top two corners, and carefully read the details as several of his colleagues held the other corners. Every inch was covered in column after column of carefully penned kanji characters, with the occasional box bordered in red. The party gathered around, leaning over the table, reading, gasping, muttering, nodding, '*Hai*', or '*Naruhodo*', or '*So-ka*'.

Dan smiled gently and shook his head. Was this theatre, or the way Japanese always do business?

And then he saw her.

At the back of the group of muttering men, slightly to one side, wearing a plain, dark pair of loose-fitting trousers and a neatly pressed white summer shirt with short sleeves bunched around her upper arms, stood a slight woman in her early twenties. Her shiny jet-black hair had been carefully fastened at the nape of her neck and she was nervously clutching a pretty cloth bag to her midriff, while staring vaguely in his direction.

Their eyes met briefly before she shyly looked away with a slight bow of the head, a daughter of the Imperial Empire, obedient, detached, her ivory cheeks glowing a faint red. Somehow, this slender woman exuded a sense of curiosity that no-one else did, and was immediately of interest to him.

Dan towered above the group bent over the huge official document and watched with interest as they became increasingly agitated, their shouts echoing around the warehouse. One after another they were pointing at sections, glancing at each other, waving at another section, before repeating the same gestures and catcalls. Finally, the older official, who had a face like a hornet, held up his delicate hands, sniffed with disdain at the obviously 'corrupt' document, and then inexplicably bowed to Dan.

Unsure what to do, Dan bowed back then held out his hand to shake, which the official angrily dismissed with a flick of his wrist. All eyes now on him, Dan shrugged, and watched as the official spat out his words while gesturing to the document, as if Dan had brought shame on them all.

Turning round, the official shouted an order at the wide-eyed girl at the back, her tightly- gripped bag squeezed firmly against her chest.

To Dan, already feeling protective towards this innocent-seeming, doll-like girl, it appeared as though the official was unfairly blaming her for some mistake in the document, but he held his tongue and watched as she stepped forward, her head down while she fumbled in the bag for a crisp new writing pad and carefully sharpened pencil.

The whole warehouse fell deathly quiet. Mumbling an apology, she gave a little bow to the official and drew alongside him.

'Hello. My name is Ayako Okunaga,' she said nervously. 'You can call me Okunaga.' She looked down at her notepad. The sheet was blank. She hesitated. 'You have coffee on your... trade ship?'

Having been living a monk-like existence surrounded by leather-skinned reeking men for seven weeks while crossing half the world's oceans, Dan could not resist a beaming, boyish grin. 'I do, indeed, Miss, Oku... Miss, er, Ayako.'

She turned a cheek modestly down and away from him, feeling in the bag for her wire-rimmed spectacles, looked towards the official, nodded and gave a shaky, '*Hai*.'

'How much coffee you have?' Hornet-Face asked, oddly in English. 'Four thousand tons, as agreed with your consular in Sao Paolo.' All eyes turned to Ayako as she finished scribbling on her pad and carefully translated. Then she turned back to the official who flicked disdainfully at the document and spat out a series of phrases in Japanese.

'*Hai*. Mr Hayashi says, this all is paid. So, why you come Japan?'

Dan took his time, aware that every face was watching, knowing the importance of controlling the pace. 'Because I have to guarantee that five hundred tons goes to embassies and foreign delegations in Tokyo. That was the deal negotiated with the United States so the coffee could pass through the embargo.'

Ayako frowned as she wrote, and then translated back, creating a burst of outrage from Hayashi at the impudence of this young man, and a flurry of whispers from the seemingly flustered lower-ranked officials next to him. Hayashi stood and, turning towards Dan, jabbed a finger at the document as though the paper itself had the final say.

'You no go Tokyo. No go.'

Dan shook his head, holding his ground. 'Then the coffee goes back to Brazil, and no more will be sent.'

'Coffee not back Brazil. Stay in Japan.' The official stared resolutely into the distance and fell silent.

During a secret briefing, before leaving Brazil, Dan had been told to expect this; an elderly, boss-like hard man, furious, demanding, explosive, unbending. The Japanese, he was informed, have a word for it. *Tetsujin* – midway between Samurai and bully. But he'll be a 'put-up job', they said, 'to get you riled, check the young '*gaijin*'s spirit.'

Time to flush out the real boss, Dan thought, enjoying the transparent intrigue.

So, he deliberately turned away from Hayashi and spoke directly to his interpreter. 'Would you tell Mr Hayashi, Miss, that perhaps he's misunderstood. If there isn't confirmation of delivery to the embassies in Tokyo, the embargo will be enforced, and there won't be any more coffee.'

Ayako gave a single nod and, abandoning her notepad, rattled off the translation, hesitating slightly before she reiterated Dan's threat of 'no more coffee'.

Hayashi's shoulders shuddered, but otherwise he didn't react. He simply clasped his hands together defensively. After a collective gasp, the whole group fell silent again, now seemingly more hurt than outraged.

As if on cue, a dark-eyed officer in shiny jackboots and an immaculately pressed black suit – with conspicuous white and orange *Kempei* armband – who had been sitting on a tea chest to one side, stood up and slowly, deliberately, ominously, brushed himself down.

The room held its breath. He walked over, heels clipping on the concrete, bowed to Dan, and simply said, '*Wakarimashita*.' Hayashi lowered his head in submission while the military police officer turned to Ayako and spoke for some time, ending with raising his chin in Dan's direction.

Ayako replied with a short, sharp, '*hai*' and then turned back to Dan. 'He says we Japanese always honour agreement, not like Americans.'

'"He"?'

'Ah.' She looked towards the officer but he slowly shook his head, so she turned back to Dan and waited for him to speak, hoping he might not push it any further.

'I like to know who I'm dealing with.'

Ayako blushed and looked down at her pad, but while she care- fully turned to a new page the officer crisply said, 'Saito.'

Dan swung back to the military man, staring him in the eye, while Ayako scribbled furiously on her pad.

'Ah. Well, I'm Daniel Lawrence. Sent by my company, Amparo, to ensure fair dealing with the coffee, and to employ a local manager for a regular supply. Once that's done, I will take the train to Tokyo, where I will board a ship to Singapore, and get out of your hair.'

As Ayako translated, Saito listened blankly, looking bored, while slowly twisting a gold wedding ring round his thin, bony finger. No clues there. But Ayako was shivering with nerves, glancing down at her notes, hesitating, afraid to say in Japanese what she knew would be seen as impertinent, almost arrogant – her voice faded to a whisper as she said the final word, '*Shingaporu*.'

Saito looked up at Dan with pursed lips and murmured, '*Yousu o miyou*, Lawrence-san.'

Dan stared back at him, declining to look at Ayako as he asked, out of the corner of his mouth, 'What did he say?'

The two men continued staring at each other as she replied, '"We will see, Mr Lawrence."'

Finally, Saito sniffed at the papers, and gave them a dismissive flick. 'You go Nagasaki Grand Hotel. Wait.'

He straightened the jacket on his suit, spun round and marched stiffly to a drab military staff car, where his driver opened the door. He climbed in, bowed once more while sitting, and was driven away.

At his departure, the tension in the warehouse dissipated. Ayako took a huge breath and gestured to a waiting rickshaw. 'Please.'

'There's room for two.'

She fanned her face with the little pad and looking at the rickshaw replied, 'No, thank you. I will walk.'

After three years of doing all kinds of business deals in Brazil, some shadier than others, Dan was accustomed to the decaying smell of mouldering vegetation in the midday sun; but as the coolie trotted out of the port towards the city, past the rows of tiny family-run restaurants, the stink of salted fish mingled with unfamiliar scents and was comparatively perfume-like in its sweetness

With the coolie effortlessly dodging handcarts piled high with baskets and wooden crates, Dan sat back under the shade of the canopy, exhilarated by the busy-ness of it all. And, equally enthralling – he caught a glimpse of the young woman, Ayako, in the reflection of a shop window, slowly losing ground but gamely running along behind with as much grace as she could muster, while her bag swung in the humid midday air.

Dan grinned to himself. Maybe trading a few weeks in

Japan for that coveted US passport wouldn't be entirely wasted after all.

The bumpy journey took them to The Bund – a dilapidated stone dock-cum-promenade running alongside Nagasaki Bay, and as they rounded a corner, he caught a sudden sight that took his breath away.

The old, careworn, almost deserted Nagasaki Grand Hotel.

Three stories high, with a blue tin-tiled roof, the crumbling frontage was two stories of eighteen symmetrical stone arches, patched up by yellow bamboo spindles, creating terraces overlooking the Bay. A large sign by the entrance proclaimed in English *'Tariff Moderate – Special Terms allowed for a prolonged stay.'*

The coolie hauled the rickshaw to face the front, dropped the handles to bow, and then scurried round to provide Dan any help he needed. With a jolt, Dan realised he had only pounds and dollars in his wallet, but started reaching into the inner pocket of his tropical jacket anyway.

Having taken a few shortcuts along the steep narrow paths running up between the closely packed houses, Ayako finally caught up, breathless, and waved Dan's awkwardness away. 'Already pay,' she said, as if it should be obvious that coolies weren't tipped.

Dan climbed from the ornately embroidered seat, as a second rickshaw pulled up with his metal trunk. *Pretty organised, these Japs,* he thought, and stood back to take in the crumbling beauty of the hotel.

'Magnificent,' Dan murmured to himself.

Ayako stood a foot or so behind him, horrified that a foreigner had been sent to this creaky old wooden hotel rather than a smart new one. 'It is very broken,' she said, fanning herself with a neatly folded square handkerchief and gazing up at the faded indigo and ochre pastels of the peeling paint.

Dan turned to look at her properly, noting with a little guilt the oily beads of sweat that had gathered along her hairline during her rush to the hotel, threatening her face powder.

She bowed slightly under his gaze and dabbed nervously at her forehead with the handkerchief. Perhaps she should have stayed quiet about the state of the hotel.

'The *world* is very broken,' he said, detached, as if it was a foreign planet that had nothing to do with him.

They stood for a while watching the oversized bamboo in the neglected garden rubbing against the cedar veranda, as the plants swayed in the breeze, rattling, creaking, whispering – as if imparting worldly secrets to their new guest. Dan didn't need an interpreter: the bamboo was saying, as voices always said in his wary mind, 'don't get too friendly, you're better alone, don't show your... Don't show anything.'

Ayako had been told time and again that she thought – and spoke – too much. In her mind the chattering bamboo was goading her: 'this man is everything you hate, yet has everything you want. Yes, he is from Britain, the land of Shakespeare. He has travelled all over the world, has mysterious ways and big, colourful eyes, blond hair, he's tall and likes to smile, but he is not helping his country fight its war, maybe a rat, a coward... be especially careful...'

Interrupting Ayako's thoughts, the coolie barked at her, unhappy that he had been kept waiting in the hot sun when he could be resting in the shade watching for his next fare. He nodded at the heavy metal trunk that he had lifted off his rickshaw and wanted to know what to do with it.

Ayako pointed to the top of a wide flight of wooden steps, where a young, waifish porter wearing a black bowtie had appeared and limped down the stairs towards them, careful of the flaking paint and loose treads. He paused at the bottom and bowed at Dan, a little too low to be sincere, his bright white gloves standing out against the stiff, dark cloth of his neatly buttoned overcoat.

INSIDE THE HOTEL, behind the shield of the high mahogany counter, a tiny receptionist stood almost to attention, a fountain pen in his right hand, hovering over a sheaf of official-looking papers. He eyed Dan suspiciously, with an air of forced courtesy, but rather than address his foreign guest, he turned to Ayako and reeled off a list of questions, as if rehearsed, noting the answer to each one in the ledger. He then turned back to his guest and addressed him without a smile in French. 'Visa, *s'il vous plait*,' he said curtly, holding out a gloved hand.

'I have a Special Dispensation, not a Visa,' Dan replied.

'He means passport.'

'Oh.' Dan handed the battered and frayed booklet over, everyone noting the British royal crest emblazoned on the front – a powerful object in global travel.

The receptionist took it with both hands and, bowing especially low, as if to the passport itself, opened it on the counter, placed an antique brass paperweight in the shape of Mount Fuji across the top of the photo page, and began to fill in a form. He then came to a halt, puzzled, confused, uncertain what to do, and turned to Ayako.

'It says "place of birth, Sarajevo". What is this?' Ayako was equally puzzled. 'Sarajevo?'

Dan shrugged, recognised the word, used to this. 'Now Jugoslavia. I was born there before the First World War. My parents were refugees, took me to England as a baby...'

The receptionist was not satisfied. '*Shosho o machi kudasai,*' he said, with an air of disapproval, more towards Ayako than Dan, and went to the office immediately behind, returning with an elderly man, tall, dressed immaculately in tie, tails and striped trousers – clearly the senior manager.

'Please,' he said, bowing with a friendly smile, took up the pen, examined the passport and as a world-weary hotelier who'd seen it all, methodically continued to add to the ledger.

At that moment a siren began its slow ascending wail, from an initial low hum to a higher howl, then a shrieking wail, screaming across the whole of Nagasaki.

Dan was mildly alarmed. 'What's that? An air-raid?' he asked Ayako.

'Lunch,' she said, not entirely the whole story.

But the brash receptionist couldn't resist contradicting such a forth- right young girl, especially one he'd just been embarrassed in front of, pointing at Dan, challenging, man-to-man. 'You *gaijin,* yes. Japan prepare *war.*' To people like him, the siren was also a rallying call to create nationalistic zeal across Japan, as the military government sought to cement its control.

The older manager glanced up apologetically from writing, dismayed at the impudence of the receptionist to a guest, but seemingly powerless. 'Perhaps it is both.'

'Oh.' Dan dismissively shook his head at the smirking, petty little runt, then smiled up at the manager. *Tricky people, these Japs*. 'Any chance of a cup of tea?'

While Dan went up to check out his suite, Ayako visited the bath- room, looked in the mirror, and nearly fainted. She had failed to notice how the journey from the port had smudged her usually immaculate powder and simple make-up. What must the hotel and Dan, think of her? She slid the carefully folded handkerchief out of her blouse and dabbed her face gently, then tidied her neck, hair and face. A wave of emotion and self-doubt was rising up inside her. Had she done her duty in the meeting, had she made a good impression...?

Ayako closed her eyes and took a deep breath for courage – as her mother suggested if things threatened to overwhelm her. She smiled inwardly and looked in the mirror again. No, she could do this. Through her father's academic friends, she was no stranger to foreigners, no stranger to their brash behaviour and forthright ways. And, she wanted to make her family proud, do her part for the war effort and her country. And, Dan Lawrence.

Though rather tall and thin, he didn't seem too bad...

Smoothing down the collar on her white blouse, Ayako sighed. Of all the pretty clothes she loved, her first encounter with a foreigner for afternoon tea and she was stuck in a plain white blouse and a drab knee- length skirt. She toyed with the top button as her mother did seductively before visiting the Foreign Ministry, then stopped herself.

When Dan came down after checking into his suite on

the second floor, he found Ayako sitting nervously at a small, low table with tea for one, tucked in a corner of the cavernous, empty ballroom under two groaning ceiling fans. As Dan sat in the chair opposite, he nodded at the teapot. 'Bet you don't have sugar.'

Ayako stared at him, suppressing a burst of anger. So it was true what they said about Western men; demanding everyone was their servant, ungrateful, impolite. 'No sugar,' she replied with suppressed venom.

Dan hadn't meant to annoy her. She seemed too delicate, too innocent, for him to be brutal, so he offered a tiny apologetic bow, with a mild admonition to himself. 'You mean because of sanctions.'

She waved away his platitude. 'The coffee you bring. Not for cafes. Not for people. Only for American Embassy, England, Australia and Japanese government. Coffee taste is Japanese fashion, very popular, but only for officials, military and the Emperor. That is who can buy.'

They fell into silence. She hadn't meant to blame him, seemingly a lonely man, lost – so un-Japanese, so alien – he was, yes, mysterious, and mysterious is always dangerous, because it drew a woman in, beguiled her. But Ayako decided, there and then, with the resolve of a fledgling Bushi – that she wouldn't, shouldn't, ever... think about him anymore.

The tea tasted bitter, without sweetness. But Dan smiled to himself, he was willing to bet his beloved Waltham field watch that there was sweetness hiding somewhere within this bitter-seeming young woman.

As if reading his thoughts, she tried to create a gulf between them. 'Japan is powerful country. Japan Empire is very strong now. I think Japan will win war,' She paused and thought carefully about her next words, as if they were partly about her. 'Japan has never been *conquered*.'

After too many past experiences with difficult women, this made Dan want to smile, though he didn't. *Guess she likes me quite a lot*, he mused, hopefully.

THERE ARE many different kinds of sleep and over the previous year, Dan had experienced most of them.

The half-hour cat naps, during interminable business meetings in Brazil, while the Germans and Portuguese went to a separate room to argue amongst themselves, and calm down, and reluctantly accept the terms of a ruthless, twenty-seven-year-old English 'brat';

The half open-eyed sleep, at his flat in Rio, with a Luger under the pillow, where he'd wake up tired – but happy to be alive;

The insomniac sleep, when he didn't have enough to occupy him, and his loneliness and ambition pressed in on him, keeping him churning all night;

The pre-embarkation dully exhausted sleep, because there were too many secret training sessions, and too many briefings, three long nights in a row;

Followed by the never-ending monotonous sleep, because there was nothing better to do but look out the salt-caked cabin window at the sea, and count the seventh wave, the forty-ninth wave, the three- hundred and forty third wave, the...

And then there was last night's sleep at the Nagasaki Grand Hotel, the most refreshing he could remember in a long time, between perfectly laundered, starched linen sheets, with the ceiling fan gently caressing the evening heat away, a *'miruku se-ki'* milkshake on the bedside table, and blissful dreams of sweet, juvenile Japanese love – well, more like lust – while on the frontline of duty.

He had woken to sounds of the long, low shipping horns echoing round the harbour, and was so relaxed that he worried he might lose his edge. 'Must be what they mean by the sleep of the righteous', he giggled, not ashamed to revert to being adolescent when alone and considering the adventures that had shaped his life. He had been root- less and ruthless for so long, making deals, making love, leaving one place after another, one woman after another. How he ached to build a proper life for himself within the thrusting, hustling United States. Where he could build his own fortune and prove those entitled idlers back in England wrong. Meantime, though, there was a job to be done, and, perhaps, a rather delightful Japanese woman to be discovered.

While Dan was bathing, the first proper bath for seven weeks, there were two very loud knocks from outside and a note slid under the bedroom door, causing a grip of anxiety. It felt like the end of peace.

'Please attend car at ten hour.'

Um, Dan thought, *that wasn't written by Ayako,* and he grimaced, surprised at his disappointment. *Careful, Dan* he thought to himself, looking out at the bay from the terra-cotta tiled terrace, *don't get too involved.*

There was a smart black staff car waiting outside, with bright red leather seats and heavy white lace curtains in the back windows, so the appointment must be with someone important. The gloved military driver bore an expression of absolute loathing towards Dan, but he still bowed while opening the rear door – only then did Dan notice the passenger in the back, who reached across for an actual handshake.

'Mr Lawrence. My name is Kado. Doctor Kado, doctor of physics, not medical, I'm your translator today. Hope that ain't too much of a disappointment.'

Dan noted the Australian accent. 'Doctor,' he replied, shaking Kado's hand. 'Well, it will be easier to keep my mind on business...'

Kado laughed, mocking the obvious attractions of a pretty young girl, the international language of male bonding, especially if you went to school in Darwin.

Before leaving Rio for Santos, Dan had also been told about the Japanese Military-Industrial-Academic establishment – not unlike the way lawyers were running espionage in the US State Department. 'The academics aren't in charge, but they are the brains.' he'd been told; 'Anything you say to them, you're saying to Hirohito.'

'So, where are we going?' Dan asked breezily.

'You'll see, Mr Lawrence,' Kado replied, the same dismissive phrase from Saito yesterday, as the car pulled jerkily away. Then he laughed. 'I think our driver is more used to driving a tank. Was in Manchuria, eh.'

Who is the cat here, and who is the mouse? Dan wondered, as they raced and swerved along The Bund, scattering pedestrians, following the road round the bay, away from the city, passing an endless procession of bicycles, street hawkers and door-to-door salesmen hauling their wares in boxes, wooden tubs, baskets hanging from yokes. Some were chanting as they trudged through the streets, housewives in day kimono protected by neat white aprons shuffling quickly in and out of the tiny shops, until the car swung inland, overtaking crowded trams, and heading uphill towards

Urakami, the commercial offices and houses thinning out.

For a moment, Dan wondered if Kado was taking him to the Cathedral, but the car suddenly turned and took a bridge over the Urakami river, coming to an abrupt stop outside a low office building on Sanno Street.

'We are here,' Kado announced, a little shaken himself from the jerky ride. 'The Fukuoka Chamber of Commerce and Industry.'

Kado almost looked like a caricature of a Japanese man – buck teeth, a smiley mouth, suspicious eyes, and a chunky build, almost as wide as high, fitted perfectly into a well-tailored western suit from Hongkong, the wartime uniform of the senior academic. He gestured Dan up the steps where another aged man waited, wearing a similar suit, somewhat less well tailored, hands behind his back, bobbing on his heels rather than bowing, and looking down on their approach with an assumed authority.

'Oshimizu-san,' Kado called out as they reached the top step, at which point he did bow, curtly.

Dan now knew better than to try a handshake, so he simply replied 'Daniel Lawrence...' Whereupon Oshimizu reached out and shook his hand limply.

So much in Japanese life seemed to be about ritual and status. Dan understood little about the former, and, as a slight, young-looking, twenty-seven-year-old, felt he would not score too high on the latter. Still, the Japanese would surely reason that there was business to be done, and if the Americans had sent a boy, then that was their mistake.

Unusually, there were no further formalities. Oshimizu simply led them through a wide marbled lobby, past half-a-dozen middle aged men idly standing round a waist high metal ashtray stand, one of whom opened a wood and glass door into a boardroom, where another dozen older men were already sitting stiffly at a conference table, each with a lined pad and pencil. They neither stood up nor acknowledged Dan.

Oshimizu took the armchair at the top, Kado the armchair to his right, and Dan was offered the hard metal chair on the left. It reminded Dan of the 'Prefects Forum' at his elitist grammar school in Henley, a star-chamber-style court of punishment for the older boys to exert their power on 'upstarts', especially the son of immigrants. Dan was painfully caned for no reason, the psychological scars remaining until he had secretly exacted a myriad of different humiliating vengeances on each of the perpetrators, privately, one at a time. In the best British tradition, nothing was ever said – but he was never bullied that way again; and in any case, he left school before his fourteenth birthday.

Now, Oshimizu, as if the head prefect, cleared his throat. In front of him was a single sheet of paper and he began reading from it in Japanese. This went on for two minutes, during which Dan pretended to listen intently, although he understood very little. 'Coffee', 'America', and 'Tokyo' were the few words he recognised.

At the end of this monologue – silence. The dozen men around the table sat like waxworks, motionless, unblinking, until Oshimizu took his speech formally in both hands, turned it over to Kado and sat back.

Kado put his fist to his mouth and he too gave a little cough before starting the same speech in English, translating confidently as he read.

'Japan is a friendly nation. She wants to live her own life interfering with no one...' On and on. Dan had suffered many similar meetings in his short, but illuminating, time in business, 'ceremonial' he called them, 'softening you up', but he knew that the real horse-trading would take place one-to-one, in a cramped, smoke-filled late-night hostess bar, pretty well the same the world over. This was, perhaps, more surreal than usual because of Kado's Japanese-Australian nasal twang, and the relaxed body language of a quasi-Westerner, until reading ahead to himself, unexpectedly he paused, then continued in a serious, more threatening, nasal monotone.

'Because of the Western Powers' continuing trade embargoes, and because the American President has announced the freezing of all Japanese assets in the United States, the Imperial Government has retaliated by freezing all Western accounts and payments in Japan. Henceforth, Mr Lawrence can only be paid 50 yen a month.'

Dan knew that was just $120. He didn't physically flinch as Kado droned on for a few more sentences, but when the Doctor finished, there was only one thing to say. He deliberately ignored Oshimizu because as the supposed boss he'd engineered an impossible negotiating position and he wouldn't understand English anyway, so he answered Kado directly, who now had the expression of an apologetic, sad, 'it-hurts-me-more-than-you' torturer.

'Thank you, Doctor. So I will take the next boat to Singapore.' That said, Dan stood up, nodded blankly to Oshimizu, and began to stride quickly from the room. The waxwork men around the table were astonished – this had never happened before.

Kado shouted, 'Mr Lawrence, please, sit down. You cannot go anywhere.'

As Dan squeezed past the back of the conference chairs, he called back, 'Are you arresting me, Doctor?'

'Maybe...'

Dan lifted his hands, gesturing that he'd done nothing wrong, and continued out of the boardroom and into the lobby while Oshimizu shouted shrilly to the men there to stop this impudent *gaijin*. So the suited middle-aged men bounded across to the entrance and formed a chain, locking arms, meaning that Dan could not pass without violently pushing them aside. Kado had galloped after him, and slid in front, his back to the human barrier.

'Mr Lawrence, please, this needs better discussion.'

'Not on that basis.'

'It is not of our making.'

'Tell that to the Marines.'

'What?'

'You know what it means.'

At which point Kado, defying expectations, threw his head back and howled with laughter. At which point also, Dan knew – just knew – that Kado was the real boss – the rest was yet another elaborate act.

Yes, tricky people, these Japs.

'If you join me for lunch, I can get us *real* coffee, Dan. Round here it's like Mount Boppy gold dust.'

'You got sugar?'

'Wasanbon, from Tinian – tastes like mud, but sanctions...'

The Doctor clicked his fingers and one of the board members appeared bowing extravagantly with his brief-case. Kado put an arm round Dan and, winking, said, 'We go.'

Dan couldn't help liking Kado. But... as the Americans had said, 'underestimate those little Japs at your peril. It's the ones who seem the most friendly, amenable, Western, they're the ones to watch. They may seem fifty per cent English, fifty per cent French, but in their hearts and minds, they'll be two-hundred per cent Japanese, and planning to plunge a dagger in your guts.'

The restaurant was top-of-the-range, of course Japanese, but even with war on every horizon, the fish was strikingly fresh, the noodles made in-house, the vegetables in the miso soup from local fields, and Kado was treated like a dictator-king, the bowing staff showing them to a private room, with a low, square lacquered ebony black table, *tatami* mats, ornate *zabuton* cushions and a 20-page *saké* carte.

Kado, glasses perched on his crew-cut head, put down the carte and smiled. 'Our Emeritus professor inherited his late father's *saké* brewery,' he stabbed a stubby finger at the page and puffed out his chest, 'this will be very pleasant.'

Rough and smooth, hard man-soft man, both men pretended to be building a friendship, to be finding fellow feeling, greasing the wheels of commerce, all the while looking for the soft parts of the other's back. The bonhomie was subtly false, not only because of their different cultures, but also because of the different sides of the combative worlds they came from; yet they played the game of ignoring any issues, ignoring even that Dan was being marooned without any funds – but there were rules. Such as that 'entrapment' was an absolute no-no, in the world of business.

Kado waited until the plates were cleared away and the *saké* almost finished, before attempting his clumsy, treacherous ploy.

'There is a little thing about which I would be grateful

for your opinion, Dan-san.' He reached for the battered brown briefcase, paused as if in thought, then nodded to himself, as if to make it seem he personally had just decided.

'As you may know, my PhD is in fluid displacement, kinetic flow, underwater ballistics. My own father ran a pearl-diving company up towards Thursday Island, off the north Australian coast – beautiful place, but very dangerous currents – we lost many pearl divers. All Japanese. And as a boy I would join Pa from Darwin, and began a life-long interest in currents, and how craft move through water.'

Kado hugged the briefcase to his stomach, looking past Dan, remembering. 'In 1929, I was invited by your Royal Navy to visit Portland, on the south coast, to advise on their new torpedo – became the 21-inch, very good. Similar to what we have here at Mitsubishi, not exactly the same, good development, but let me show you.' He reached into his briefcase...

Dan turned his head, pushed the low dining table away. 'Doctor Kado, please. Do not continue.'

But Kado was already sliding out a drawing... breaking faith.

For the second time that day, Dan stood up sharply, this time shouting, 'You stupid old fool!' He swung his arm, knocking the briefcase and drawings across the private room.

'You have no business showing me such sketches. If they now found their way into the hands of a foreign power I would be implicated as some kind of spy.' Dan pulled on his jacket – he was leaving. 'I am a simple businessman, solely here to trade with Japan.'

Kado was unapologetic. He shrugged and bowed

farewell at the same time, a gesture that made him seem a hunchback. 'I tell you, Dan, all businessmen are also spies.'

'Maybe in Japan, Doctor.'

'Everywhere, Lawrence-san.'

AFTER JOGGING AWAY from the restaurant, doubling back several times to lose any hidden followers, then walking vigorously for an hour to get the anger out of his system, Dan sat down on a parapet, feet dangling over the River Urakami, and simply had to laugh. What was it that Abe Ford said in Rio after he flew down from Washington to see Dan, about how they would try to trap him? 'Innocence is no defence in Japan, only the clever avoid jail.' Now he understood. They were all treacherous bastards.

But it was difficult to think badly of Nagasaki, especially now he was alone, even if the locals did initially look at him with surprise, followed by suspicion, seeing a Western man allowed to wander unsupervised. Dan enjoyed being free in a beautiful city, a beautiful country, on a beautiful sunny afternoon, surrounded by fascinating – and dangerous – people.

He was charmed as he watched random strangers scurrying by, small in stature but full of purpose, their faces etched with determination. It appeared that they were content to be moulded into a singular, national will – to make Japan the best country she could be, respected everywhere for her burgeoning success and, yes, maybe being warlike.

Dan was reminded of soldier ants, seemingly disorganised, chaotic, scurrying this way and that on some unfathomable mission, but ultimately working in harmony and achieving unimaginable feats together.

What was the word? Umm – regimented, *through birth, through upbringing, through instinct – is that the way of the Japanese?* he wondered. *A regimental mindset, is that what will win this coming war? A national purposefulness?* Dan shook his head. *Or will imagination, enterprise, individuality and drive, pull England and America through?*

He threw stones into the river, and reflected on Dr Kado and the seemingly innocent Ayako. Are they a double-act perhaps? The thought made him snigger again and he aimed a stone at a bobbing twig. It missed. Although only average height for a Japanese woman, maybe just five-foot two, Ayako was still taller than Kado, and would look down on his tanned bald patch. Dan's snigger became a laugh. Maybe it was the *saké*, or just the fun, the joy, of being among real people again, rather than salt-caked, half-crazed sailors. If Ayako was part of a conspiracy, well, it could be a whole lot worse. What species was it where the female eats the male after mating? A spider, the black widow. He laughed again, then looked at his Waltham field watch, a present from Abe Ford on his briefing visit to Brazil. It was time to go to church.

THREE MILES AWAY, in her stuffy six-mat *tatami* room above a small *shokudo* restaurant bustling with locals, Ayako had unfolded her futon mattress early and lay staring at the ceiling, frowning, annoyed with herself. Why did she keep thinking of *him*, when she had resolved not to? Why had the *Kempei* summoned her to their offices first thing tomorrow? And why did she suddenly feel so isolated, worthless, and anxious?

She thought back to the time before she left home just six weeks ago after the Ministry had sent for her father, Professor Junichiro Okunaga, who taught literature at the University. He had returned from that meeting and surprised Ayako with a box of her favourite sweets, much to her younger sister Michiko's chagrin. When he announced that the school where Ayako taught had relieved her of her duties and that she would be leaving their house near Hosei University in Tokyo for an important interpreting assignment in Nagasaki, she was both honoured and excited.

Each night during the time remaining before she left, she would stay up with her father practising English with him, repeating incessantly the pronunciation of every single word on his wind-up gramophone record, to the point where her mother and even Michiko started to join in. Any free time in the school staff room or after work, had been spent with the English language *Japan Times and Advertiser* – poring over articles, including the advertisements, and noting any unfamiliar vocabulary with care. With each new word, she was making her own personal contribution to the war effort, to Japan.

Although a distinguished professor, her unworldly father, as with many internationally renowned academics, was considered 'soft, unreliable' by the military Government, and had not been furnished with the details of the assignment, so said little about the task allotted to her, other than to stress, 'it will not be a straight river,' but, such was Ayako's respect for him, she refrained from pestering him further.

As he kissed her goodbye on the forehead at Tokyo

railway station, before calmly placing her small brown suitcase on the net carrier rack overhead and while her mother fussed over her already spotless first-class seat, he looked at his daughter and nodded.

'Beauty, fidelity and strength, that is your calling, beauty, fidelity and strength.' He nodded again, more for himself than Ayako, and then fell silent.

Ayako had pondered the significance of those three words all the way to the ferry terminal in Kyushu, where she was met by one of her numerous aunts, this one on her father's side, who had been tasked with chaperoning her on the stopping train to the lodgings in Nagasaki that had been arranged by the ministry. Her aunt was quick to confirm that Ayako's father was strongly making the point that she came from a decent family and should therefore be treated with the utmost respect and kindness.

On her first night in Nagasaki, tired and homesick, yet resolute and firm, she had ink-penned her 'calling' in three-inch kanji onto some of her precious sheets of calligraphy paper, and put it next to her pencil and pad which she had placed on the low table by the window.

Such an unusual calling – maybe it was from Shakespeare, a writer her scholar-father often quoted – and early each night, she would take a slow, deep breath and repeat her little mantra over and over, sometimes in English, sometimes in Japanese – 'Beauty, fidelity, and strength' – until her eyelids grew heavy and she would sigh, slip below her coverlet, slide the buckwheat pillow under her neck, and enjoy the untroubled sleep of the truly innocent and purposeful. But that was before she had met Dan. This night was different.

What was it about that man Lawrence, what was it about him, that drew her in, while at the same time making her wary? Was it that he was the enemy? Or that she didn't – never would – understand him? Or that – oh, no, don't think this – that he reminded her just a little of her father? Sincere, but subtle, tricky but funny. Or – even more unthinkable – was she too, like her distant, controlling mother, drawn to powerful men, regardless of propriety and convention? Ayako shuddered – she would much rather be like her sweet, lyrical father, than like her heartless, ambitious mother – but she felt, deep in her core, that perhaps there was more of her mother in her than she wished to acknowledge.

THE CHURCH of Our Lady of the Immaculate Conception was a fifteen-minute rickshaw ride through the restaurants, tea-shops, geisha- houses and the all-night *joroya* brothels of the Gay Section of Nagasaki, into the scrappy industrial suburb of Urakami. Dan kept the curtains open to catch the gusts of man-made breeze as the rider pedalled furiously up Motohara Hill.

A promise of rain hung in the heavy, humid air, which would still not ease the clammy atmosphere. But the cool, dark, marble interior of the Church provided space to think while Dan knelt as if at prayer. They had said, 'wait outside the confessional in the early evening, Father Luigi will know you are there, and summon you inside with a tap on your right shoulder.'

After only a few minutes, a tall statuesque man, dressed head-to- toe in black, except for a crisp, starched dog-collar, tapped Dan's bicep firmly, and quickly disappeared behind the wooden engravings around the rear compartment of the ornate confessional and closed the door. Dan waited a minute, went into the penitent's front compartment, closed the door, knelt, and made the sign of the cross.

'Forgive me, father, for I have sinned. It is many months since my last confession.'

'Please go ahead, my son.'

'I confess to sins. Lewd thoughts, and some dishonesties. I lost my temper today, with a Doctor of Nautical Physics on secondment from the Imperial University in Tokyo. Should I tell you about it?'

'If you feel it is proper, my son,' came the murmured reply through the iron lattice grille.

Dan leaned back; Father Luigi suffered from garlic breath. 'I believe he is supervising the testing of a new weapon of war, father, and attempted to trap me into showing interest. I am here in an effort to provide coffee, but the Japanese believe all Westerners are agents of some kind. His name is Dr Kado, and his research is for the Mitsubishi works here in Urakami. He attempted to show me the sketch of a shell which is, I believe, a ridiculous copy of a shell for a German gun. Anyway, not the sort of thing to be manufactured by the Ordnance Factory .'

Dan paused for a second, listening to the echoing hush of the Church. Was someone moving out there? No, just the beginning of rain.

'Father, am I wasting your time?' Dan whispered.

'You must speak as you see fit.'

'My talk could be dangerous.'

'It is secret between you and your priest, unless you indicate otherwise.'

'Thank you, Father.' Dan fell silent again.

Father Luigi prompted him. 'You were talking of a Physicist...'

'Yes, Father. Dr Kado said he is an expert in marine propulsion; in 1934 he wrote a paper on wave flow and fluid drag, so I am sure he's working on naval developments – probably an underwater device. My guess is a small submarine or torpedo.'

Both men were breathing heavily in the cupboard-sized cubicle; to Father Luigi this Anglo-American was a complete mystery. He was here without warning, although a Bishop visiting from the Philippines had briefed him on 'possibilities.'

'My son. You said "lewd thoughts".'

'There is a lady interpreter, Father, it may be difficult.'

'Ah, that can be God's way. Temptation.' Luigi pretended to understand, then cleared his throat. 'Are there any sins of the flesh?'

'No, father.' Dan sounded almost sad. It might have bolstered his often lost sense of self if there had been.

'Have you observed Mass?'

'In my way, Father.'

The session was winding up. The priest spoke in Latin, blessing his penitent, ending with the ritualistic, traditional words. 'Say three "Our Fathers" and three "Hail Marys" and try not to lose your temper again.'

Dan finished with specially chosen words, too. 'I shall try, father. Thank you for allowing me *to share my burdens with the Church of Rome*.'

In the rickshaw, splashing along the deserted streets on his way back to the hotel, Dan peered through the metal struts of the canopy at the shuttered shops and occasional sliver of dim light slipping out from behind the black-curtained windows. How would Father Luigi feel if he fully understood? Used? Would they be guilty of some kind of sacrilege, a mortal sin against God, bringing the wrath of the Devil down on his shaky soul? Probably. But such heavenly scruples could not be allowed to scupper the will of man. As Abe Ford said, the evening before he flew back to Washington.

'Japan is a completely closed society. Pigeons won't work, short- wave radio's too darn open and dangerous, all post is read and censored. But what you tell the Catholic Church, you tell the Vatican; and what the Vatican hears, filters to the State Department. We've got a guy inside St. Peter's.'

———

BACK AT THE Nagasaki Grand Hotel, rushing through the warm rain from the rickshaw into the lobby, Dan saw too late two stubble-headed black-suited men ahead, lurking in the shadows. He hesitated, wondering whether to turn around, but they had seen him. An evasion would now seem suspicious.

They bowed and presented an envelope, stepped away backwards, and bowed again, then ominously sat down like guards by the entrance. The elderly manager politely averted his gaze, so Dan went upstairs before reading the handwritten letter.

'Please be present for an interview at Hongkong and Shanghai Bank building at 9 a.m. tomorrow.' The royal-blue writing was florid, feminine, perhaps a hopeful sign, but the two red seals planted squarely beneath the text crushed any intimacy. He put the terse note on the walnut desk, before wandering out onto his private terrace overlooking Nagasaki Bay.

The lights of ships in the port blinked lazily in the misty, humid haze, and the *banza katydid* crickets were at full shrill, overpowering the gentle sound of the waves lapping against The Bund. In spite of the turmoil of a country set on conquest and violence and aggression, Dan was enchanted by the peace, the serenity of this semitropical paradise, on the very western edge of Japan, on the road to nowhere. He closed his eyes and sighed, breathing in the sultry midnight air.

What is the point of war? Why would any nation, prosperous or not, allow its leaders to risk the stability and prosperity, the comfort, of family life for a national adventure with an uncertain outcome. Ambition? Anger? Pride? Stupidity?

'Ah well,' he said to himself, the adventurer, the fatalist in charge. 'Maybe Ayako will be there tomorrow, I can't imagine Jap Gestapo cops speaking English.' The thought was uplifting but also made him shudder – what was he getting into? But, at least there were diversions.

After a long celibate voyage across half the world, as he switched out the light, the lewd thoughts began to creep back. He'd surely have to visit Father Luigi again.

———

NOT SO FAR FROM the Nagasaki Grand Hotel, lying on her thin futon mattress, lamenting the heat and the incessant buzzing of the mosquitos outside her bleached net, Ayako turned first one way, then the other way. Did she feel hatred – he was, after all, an enemy, wasn't he?

She let out a short, sharp groan. No, he wasn't. That was unfair. In a way, she felt deep down that he was, in fact, lost – neither British, nor American, with no particular place to call home... The *Kempei* had said his family had fled their homeland as criminals, refugees. Odd, then, that he seemed so sure of himself. If only she could find such certainty.

For the seventh time that night she stood and repositioned her futon on the tightly woven *tatami* mat in the hope of locating a cool draft, glancing at her little mantra before she lay down. ‘Strength. If I count to one hundred, I will forget this strange man who is invading my thoughts, my life.’

Then she inwardly bowed to the Emperor, but still didn’t sleep.

2

DAN'S first concern the next morning was, 'just how many stubble-headed, menacing men do they have in Japan?' Because two of them were in the otherwise empty lobby when he clambered down the wide, creaking staircase, a little before seven a.m. – but not the same two as the night before. Subtly different, although on the surface identical – pale, muscular, alert, with the same crisp uniform-like-suits, military bearing, and dead, flat expressions.

When he wandered apprehensively out to the bay and strolled along The Bund with its sweeping view of the city harbour, they followed him, not from a distance, but closely behind, making a point of being there. Intimidating on purpose – under someone's orders, *meant* to be threatening.

As he walked, he felt uneasy. When Dan stopped to take in the view, they would stop twenty yards behind him. He crossed The Bund, they crossed, too. Even more personal.

'What are they trying to say? That you are the enemy, and we are watching you, waiting to pounce.'

When he got back to the hotel there were two more. Again, almost identical to the other four, perhaps a little taller, slightly more confident, with marginally smarter suits, more important, yet sitting in the same seats, halfway between reception and the entrance.

The elderly manager was on duty and stood with his gloved hands placed firmly on the counter, nervous. Dan tried to catch his eye, in expectation of his usual over-polite old-fashioned greeting, but the increasing unease was heightened as the manager averted his gaze. Dan sensed the fear caused by the all-powerful, disciplined, ruthless Military Police.

Desperate not to show his own rising anxiety, and keen not to be seen cowering in their presence, Dan turned to the four of them, politely, impudently, 'Gentlemen. Would you join me for breakfast?'

They stared back blankly, either not understanding or, just as likely, unable to respond due to lack of instructions from above on how to deal with such a direct approach. So Dan shrugged and turned to the friendly manager now cowering behind the reception desk – 'I will take breakfast on my terrace, today, please,' and strode away.

At nine a.m., Dan was coldly escorted to a small car that took him to the Hongkong and Shanghai Bank building – now a security station – less than five hundred yards along The Bund. The two later arrivals were sitting behind a wide metal table, with Major Saito in the middle. There was a single hard-backed chair in front, with an ashtray on the seat, signifying the prisoner-to-interrogator dynamic.

But Dan hardly noticed the three men, because, thank God, to the side of the table sat Ayako, impeccably dressed and with head bowed, clutching her pad and pencil, avoiding looking in his direction. He considered greeting her, but this meeting was too sinister to allow any human warmth.

Dan placed the ashtray on his side of the table, sat and folded his arms across his chest, his body language defensive. Over to them.

Saito stared intently at a document he had placed on the table directly in front of him, which he harangued for almost half a minute before looking in Ayako's direction. She gave a gentle nod, said, '*Hai,*' and began reading from her pad without looking up.

'Major Saito said it is not safe you walk in Nagasaki City without other people... without supervisor. He is very unhappy that yesterday you disappear and walking alone. There are robbers and bad people who would especially attack foreigners. It is not safe you to leave the hotel without bodyguard protect you.' Dan watched as she almost stabbed at each noun on her pad, while stuttering nervously through her robotic delivery. She kept her head lowered as if uncomfortable about being caught in the middle of the two parties. 'This will be'— she paused, uncertain of the exact word—'*always* enforced.'

Dan could think of many replies, but knew it was pointless. Like a jail, he thought, and given his chequered life, it would not be for the first time. 'I do not want you to have this burden,' he said. 'If I could just receive confirmation that part of the coffee I brought has gone to the embassies as agreed, I can leave.'

Ayako finally glanced up. She knew his request was pointless, but she translated anyway.

On hearing Dan's reply, the Major spent some time

lighting a cigarette, took a long, grunting draw, and then fiddled with the smouldering end, tapping it on his ashtray, while narrowing his eyes to glare accusingly at the glowing tip. Then he looked up and spoke directly to Dan in Japanese, eye to eye, leaving Ayako to translate as best she could. As she did so, with a tremor in her voice, Dan tried to keep his gaze steadily on the Major.

'Major Saito said you are not prisoner of Imperial Japanese Army. If you need go out from hotel during the day, you must always have one bodyguard soldier. You cannot leave hotel at night. That is my order.'

Dan shook his head, as if he disagreed, but understood the stage was being set, with him piggy-in-the-middle, while they decided what to do with him. Abe Ford in Washington would have poured himself a whiskey in celebration if he had known how Dan was in their lethal sights. The coming war was not only about valour, blood and guts, but also about using people to tie the enemy in a myriad of knots, while they tried to do the same to you.

Dan was where he never wanted to be – in the front line.

How could he have been so stupid as to let a silver-haired and silver-tongued, tricky American lawyer in the State Department appeal to the foolhardy, adventurous side of his character, to go on this journey of bravado, while they had been gossiping on the safe, sandy beaches of Rio? OK, there was the bribe of US citizenship, but that wouldn't matter if he had a Jap noose around his neck when the trapdoor snapped.

But then, rising up through exasperation at his own idiocy, came the businessman, in the ethereal voice of Kalmár, his corrupt, Austro-Hungarian trading mentor. 'Even if the other side have all the cards – all the cards –

never leave a meeting without some kind of concession from them,' a mantra he'd heard many times. Kalmár was probably now languishing in some foul faraway prison, but the principle still stood.

Dan sighed, and for the first time uncrossed his arms, changing his body language, no longer defensive – the interrogation had become a negotiation. 'Well, as there will be nothing for me to do...' He leaned forward, still eye-to-eye with Saito, but now with a twinkle, as if closing a deal, 'I would like to learn Japanese. Can this be arranged?'

Suddenly aware of Dan's intentions, Ayako fiddled with her glasses before almost biting off the words as she translated.

Having finished his cigarette, Major Saito lit a fresh one to give himself time to think. A ruthless man with a sense of innate wickedness, the Major had felt, rather than observed, a frisson between Dan and Ayako. He saw a game-plan taking shape in his mind. 'That might be difficult,' he said hesitantly, to the ashtray. Then he flicked his head up as he drew deeply on his cigarette and glanced over at Ayako, caught Dan's eye and gave a humourless smile. 'No. I think – perhaps possible,' he said, nodding in Ayako's direction.

Partly because she knew Dan had understood, Ayako decided not to translate Saito's words, but tightened her lips in open, petulant annoyance at the Major, the way she did when her mother insisted that she fetch more coal in on a cold, wet day. 'You might need an interpreter for more important tasks than teaching Japanese to a foreigner,' she said directly to Saito.

The major raised his eyebrows and gave Ayako a look of powerful rebuke. It didn't pay to defy or show annoyance to a senior *Kempei*, especially when he was relishing formulating a rather delightful plan. He batted her feeble suggestion away and said, with an air of superiority, 'You'll teach him... daily. Until it is not convenient.' Ayako sighed inwardly, begrudgingly replying with her usual '*hai*' before looking down and mumbling the English translation for Dan.

Although his cigarette was only half smoked, Major Saito stubbed it firmly and decisively into his yellowing glass ashtray, straightened his back and stared ahead with a glimmer of paternalistic satisfaction and anticipation. The meeting was over.

———

AYAKO WAS OUTRAGED, and raced furiously back to her tiny room above the *shokudo* restaurant. Barging through the restaurant, pushing the dining chairs aside, she shouted, '*Kempeitai* are BRUTES,' at Mrs Matsuo, before climbing the stairs three at a time. Perhaps a little spoiled by her professor father, maybe even more so by her status-oriented mother, and not accustomed to being scolded by authoritarian men, Ayako went straight to bed – pulling the coverlet over her head to make the world go away, even though it wasn't even noon yet.

Mrs Matsuo shook her head at Mr Matsuo. Having agreed with Ayako's aunt to be a 'watch-over', and knowing the *Kempei's* well-earned reputation, she put aside her cloth and climbing the narrow steps, knocked gently on Ayako's paper-thin door.

'Go away,' came the reply.

'I always say – the best cure for anger is miso soup with some of your "uncle's" *fu*. I can bring some up.'

'They have no heart. If they did – I'd rip it out.'

'How about some milk bread? The baker has just been.'

When Mrs Matsuo returned with the mini-feast, Ayako was sitting cross-legged, dabbing her eyes with the handkerchief, sketching Dan on her pad, and jabbing the pencil at his face. 'I hate him, too,' she said.

'Eat, and then sleep. You will feel better. And then we must talk. Because they will come to find you.'

Ayako shrugged – she didn't care – took the soup and, stabbing the *fu* with her chopsticks, slurped on it extra loudly.

'And they will send a message to your father.'

Ayako waved Mrs Matsuo away. It was all her father's fault, anyway.

Three days later, they did, indeed, come for her. Two soldiers and an officer, slightly later than the regular lunch-timers. Mrs Matsuo knew immediately who they were, and put them on the table furthest from all the others, directed them to the handwritten menu on the wall and, with a shaking hand, brought them some tea.

The other diners also understood and finished their lunch quickly with hooded looks, until only the trio were left. Mr Matsuo looked out over the empty room with a heavy heart as the officer pointed upstairs – 'fetch her'.

When she came down, Ayako went to sit, but the officer gestured for her to stand, looking around so that Mr and Mrs Matuso also scurried away, out onto the other side of the narrow street.

'Explain,' the officer said.

It was on the tip of her tongue to reply defiantly, 'Explain what?' but her nerve failed. 'I have been unwell.'

The soldiers looked at each other and shook their heads.

'Also, I have been working on a course of learning.'

The officer nodded. 'I expect it to be complete by tomorrow morning.' He reached into his tunic and pulled out a handwritten note. 'Major Saito instructs that you teach the foreigner, and you make him a very close friend. Your parents will be so proud that their daughter is performing an important task.'

'I am not here to make friends with this Englishman,' Ayako murmured in a low voice, almost sobbing.

But the *Kempeitai* officer simply gave a narrow smile and replied, 'Not yet,' while his colleagues giggled knowingly. The *Kempei* were not asking, they weren't even ordering politely. They were threatening her. Openly. And, worse, in the coded world of wartime Japan, they were threatening her respectable parents, too. It all suddenly fell into place. The daughter of a Tokyo university professor she might be, but down here, away from her family circle, she was nothing. Or worse. A stuck-up, spoiled, Tokyo *prima donna.*

At the top of the tree, there was The Emperor, of course. Next: Japan; next: *Kempeitai*; next: her parents; next: their duty; next – there wasn't a next. It certainly wasn't her. People like Ayako didn't register on the scale. They just did as they were told.

MEANTIME, Dan had been spending far too long on his terrace, anxiously watching the coasters chunter by, wondering if there was a way to escape by sea. As a rule, Dan enjoyed being alone, but this enforced isolation felt more like solitary confinement. There was not one person in the whole of Nagasaki, in the whole of Japan, that he could consider a friend, or even an acquaintance. Except, Ayako, and he hardly knew her.

His minders never spoke, not even to each other. They just sat, glowering, staring angrily at their charge like coiled snakes ready to strike, while Dan lounged around glumly in the hotel picking at bento boxes and, for the first time in his life, ate slowly – before finishing off his meal with a flaky Japanese cigarillo and sour green tea.

Then on the fifth day, on a morning of scattered, heavy, tropical raindrops, when it would have been a pitiless act to take the minders' thin, crumpled suits on a walk along The Bund, Dan made his way down the sweeping staircase for breakfast and was greeted by the tinkling sound of a grand piano.

After what seemed an absence of forever, Ayako was on the far side of the ballroom, her back to him, tentatively playing with one hand, while using the other to hold up the piano dust sheet.

Quite an entrance, Dan thought, smiling for the first time since he'd last seen her.

Knowing that she was now aware of his presence, he listened for a while to the poignant notes of *Clair de Lune* from the untuned piano echoing around the stately, dilapidated salon.

She played until she reached the crescendo where the player simply must use two hands, and she had to give up. Ayako closed the lid, let the dust cloth fall and turned to face him, head held high.

'I love the moon.'

In that moment, only half-dressed in a cotton breakfast robe with Nagasaki Grand Hotel embroidered in large, blue kanji, Dan's heart did a triple somersault. Entranced by Ayako's sudden return and revelation, Dan shook his head in wonder, grinning, and walked towards her, his footsteps echoing off the bare walls. 'I'm a sun man myself.'

She shrugged. Of course, he would be. Her smile faded, there was a price to be paid for his earlier 'arrogance'.

'You did not ask.'

He leant casually on the stage and looked up. 'Ask what?' 'Japanese lesson.'

Dan frowned. 'I did ask. You were there. You translated my request. Anyway, you're here now.' He gestured to the empty ballroom.

'A Japanese would... enquire privately. Polite asking. Of the person. *Not* sudden request in front of superior officer.' She shrugged dismissively, getting her sense of annoyance out – condemning him as an ignorant foreigner. 'To speak Japanese, you must think like Japanese.' She tapped her temple. 'Up here. *That* is first Japanese lesson.'

Despite the air of vanity that accompanied her rebuke, Dan was caught by the wistfulness of the moment: the music with its poignant melody, the sad, forgotten ballroom with its creaky wooden floor, the loneliness of the past few days. He looked around to check no one was watching, as Ayako stood up from the piano stool and sat on the edge of the stage where she prepared to lower herself down, but he dropped to one knee, and put his palm out, almost as if proposing, '*Okunaa-ga sama.*'

Ayako's head jerked up on hearing him attempt to use her surname complete with correct use of the respectful honorific.

'Please would you oblige, and teach me Japanese.'

Now their eyeline was level, she shrugged indifferently, as if to say 'Maybe', while he, surprised by his sudden sentimentality, smiled and said suggestively, 'Now, may I help you down from there and we take breakfast on my terrace?'

She unlocked eyes, turned modestly away in reproach, and leaning her head to one side, declared assertively, 'That would be difficult. We will eat in the dining room and have lesson in the garden *tatami* room.'

Listening obliquely from across the lobby, to the flirting tone of their voices, without being seen, the *Kempei* guards nodded to each other at this verbal embrace. 'The Major – he'll be seriously pleased with his handiwork.'

As if all this was planned, the rice and egg and pork and green tea, which Dan always had for breakfast, was already laid out on a round wooden table covered with a neatly ironed white tablecloth and set by a window in the deserted ground floor lounge, close to the deserted Japanese garden room with its *tatami* mats, low chairs and small, rectangular table for two.

Kneeling on the *tatami* mat, looking up towards Dan, Ayako began her first lesson, teacher to pupil, enunciating clearly, and exaggerating the movement of her lips, to draw out the correct pronunciation. 'We start with "hello". *Hajimemashite.*'

'*Haji...*' stuttered Dan. Despite her intention to insist on proper Japanese, Ayako suddenly felt bad for tripping her pupil up on the first word but stuck with it. '*Ha-jime-ma-shi-te.*' Dan gave it a second try and failed.

'I thought "*konnichi wa*" was hello.'

Ayako's heart sunk. '*Hajimemashite* is for first time hello. After this you can "*konnichi wa*".' She paused, desperate to claw back the upper hand. 'But *you* can say "*konnichi wa*".' She had no need to add 'if you find it too hard'. The look of pity on her face said it all.

'*Ha-ji-me-ma-shi-te*,' he said, with an effort. 'I don't like easy.'

The young maid who cleaned Dan's room brought in a tray with a small teapot and handleless cups and, kneeling next to him, set it on the table. Dan grinned and instead of thank you, tried out his improved pronunciation. '*Konnichi wa*.' The maid giggled and shuffled off. Dan liked making her giggle, though it wasn't hard to do.

Ayako decided to ignore the encounter and, looking first at her pad and then across at Dan, straightened her back. 'Now "goodbye". *Sa-yo- na-ra*.'

'*Sayonaaa-ra*.'

THE LESSONS BEGAN at ten every morning and finished just before lunch, leaving Dan's head spinning. He was by no means a natural linguist, but he had no trouble enjoying the attention of this attractive young woman who seemed to be warming to him with every day that passed.

Ironically, it was Ayako who suggested that he learn about shop- ping with a walk into town, followed, of course, by Dan's minders. Dan noticed that they, too, appeared to be more relaxed, staying further and further back, and on occasion talking to each other. One day, when Ayako took him to a fish market to teach him the words for different foodstuffs, Dan noticed that only one minder followed, rather sulkily – presumably the war effort had diverted the other minder to duties elsewhere.

In the deserted ballroom of the hotel one afternoon,

after a terrific rainstorm had delayed their usual morning start – it was one word that did it.

The word for 'wife.'

'"Wive" – *okusan*.'

'*Oka-san*," he repeated dutifully.

'That is mother. Wive is *Okusan*,' she corrected.

'*O-ku-san*.'

'You have "wive" and child, Lawrence-san?'

He paused. Her first personal question. His instinct was to avoid, to hide, to mislead, to escape. Ayako enjoyed the uncomfortable pause – her ornithologist uncle, the one she most admired, was like that, running from anything private.

'No *wife* at the moment, Ayako,' he replied eventually, emphasising the corrected pronunciation, dropping the honorific, 'and too much of a wanderer to be weighed down by children.' The usual guard had come up in Dan, there was no need for her to know. It didn't go unnoticed.

'But you are rich, handsome man,' she carried on, subtly pricking at his reticence, his pride.

Dan twisted his ankles out from underneath him and stretched out across the *tatami*, leaning back in the little legless floor chair as he did so.

'I like children – was once one myself.' He chuckled, as if to dismiss any chance of sincerity. 'Mine wasn't a happy childhood, parents were too...' He stopped; this had gone far enough. 'What about yours?'

'Very lucky. My father is a professor, always busy, funny, crazy – and my mother...' Now she stopped.

They looked at each other – she frowning, wondering if her talking like this was somehow unprofessional; he with an encouraging smile, waiting for her to continue. But Ayako changed direction.

'I liked that, when you saying about yourself.'

He pulled out one of his Japanese cigarillos and placed it casually between his lips. Her heart thumping, Ayako picked up the lighter and leaned in. Dan nodded his thanks almost casually and turned to the little garden window. Perhaps it was something to hide behind, Ayako wasn't sure, but he continued anyway.

'Yeah, parents too strict. Too *nothing*.'

'No one can be nothing.'

'They are. Mr and Mrs Do Nothing. Get up, Dad does *their* gardens, Mum cleans *their* house, Lord and Lady, high-and-mighty Stevens. Then have supper go to bed early. Same next day, serving the Stevens, same after that... don't know why I'm telling you this...'

'It's interesting, Dan-san.'

'They are Do Nothings – I want to do *everything*...' He gestured with the cigarillo around the empty ballroom, as if it was the world. 'Everything.'

Now her heart was thumping even more, thinking – *this man is like my father. Never happy to sit, to relax. Always active, even after Dad's knees became sore.*

Deep inside, Dan was split. Although he avoided talking about himself, he also knew that – for a certain kind of woman, the intelligent, the attractive ones – being open, sincere to them, was seductive. Like racing clouds with their emotions, he'd found women are enchanted by it. And, anyway, talking about his parents, putting them in a kind of front line from 6,000 miles – what harm could there be in that?

And then he shifted gears and drew her further in. 'You didn't finish about your mother.'

'My mother?' His eyes were burning into hers, she had to continue. 'She is – very strong. Very strong woman...'

'Like you?'

'I am more like my father.'

'Really?'

Why didn't she have some tea to pour, or another cigarillo to light, there was nowhere to go. 'I admire them both, Papa is funny, she is...' at least she could remove her glasses, look at them as if needing a clean, but they didn't. So, she put them back on, pushed the ashtray towards Dan, but he was twinkling – maybe he's a good guy inside, but this is agonising – and he's still waiting her out.

And now, to cap it all, he's offering her his cigarillo, which she looked at and declined with a nod of very absent-minded, distant thanks.

'People all say I am like him, but maybe...' *Oh, I'll just have to say*. 'She has more energy. Not in Man's World, not allowed, but for women's groups she is powerful, has medals, so, yes, that I admire.'

Although he knew it was completely off-limits, Dan was thinking *My God, how attractive she is*, with flashing, uncertain eyes, modest, yet fiery, and breaking Japanese etiquette rules – halfway between a grow- ing-up daughter and tantalising woman. Oh, how he was enjoying himself. And then, as Dan could sometimes do, he nailed it.

'Do they love each other – your parents?'

Ayako was shocked. No Japanese man would ever ask that, it was a step too far, her hand went up and began fanning across her now perspiring face.

So he let her off, another Dan trait, knowing when to retreat. 'Because my parents do, love each other. Forever and ever, 'til death – do you know that?'

She shook her head.

'Marriage service. 'Til death us do part, together forever – in monotony .'

As Dan found the Japanese lessons mentally exhausting, he suggested to Ayako they went on what he called 'word trips', to parts of the city that provided new word opportunities. The single minder hung further and further back, but always within eyesight. It was when they were down at the old fishing harbour, now more like a museum than a bustling port, that she touched him for the first time – just a fleeting hand brushing against his shoulder as they sat on a pair of rusting cast-iron mooring bollards to watch the seagulls swoop and cry.

'My uncle said seagulls marry for life,' she said quietly, probing. 'They never divorce. Only divorce if they don't have babies.'

Dan shrugged, his mind still on the brief touch of her hand on his shoulder. 'Can't see that.' He pointed upwards at the fifty or so flocking around them. 'They don't look like couples to me. Just dozens of brutal predators.'

'Seagulls like to live in groups, but they love in couples.' She stared ahead with a faint smile playing on her lips. She was enjoying goading this hapless man. 'Maybe like we Japanese.'

Dan felt hot, tired and grumpy. He'd finally had enough, so he went on the attack. 'Well, I did hear they're treacherous, and fight among themselves...' and let it hang.

He expected an admonition. Instead, he got the best laugh he had ever heard from a woman – joyful and natural, low and endless – and loud – a laugh to drown out the raucous cries of the seagulls, however aggressive and noisy and treacherous.

He sat on the bollard shaking his head – what had he said?

IN THE AUTUMN OF 1941, messages in Japan were often relayed in sealed envelopes, or verbally, by trusted messengers rather than the post. Telephones and telegrams were rare, and treated with suspicion, especially by the senior *Kempei*, whose headquarters in Nagasaki were in the old Hongkong and Shanghai Bank building further along The Bund from the hotel.

However, because the hierarchical military authorities still wanted to control the minutiae of even the most trivial issues – through endless processes of consultation – they had roomfuls of fit young orphans eager and willing to jump and run to any assigned task.

When Dan asked his minder after breakfast if it would be alright if he and Ayako went for a picnic up Mount Inasa one day, he had presumed the answer would be a long time coming. However, as he sat on the veranda thumbing an old phrase book the friendly hotel manager had dug out, a furious process of consultation was taking place just a few hundred metres away along the harbour.

A couple of twelve-year-old boys went haring along the dusty Bund from the *Kempeitai* HQ, first to an all-day massage parlour in the backstreets of the entertainment district, then to a bordello nearby, then to a *Geisha okiya* in Maruyama and finally to a restaurant in Inasa – before racing back to the old Bank building, and finally to the Nagasaki Grand Hotel, all by the end of the morning.

Dan, of course, knew nothing of this nor of the subtle, treacherous thinking behind the reply to his request.

All he knew was that the senior minder came to him later the same afternoon and said simply, in English: 'Lawrence-san. Hiking. *Hai*. You go. Take her.'

Dan could only presume his mundane trudgings with Ayako around the city centre had bored the authorities so much that he was no longer of much interest to them.

Ayako, though startled by the swiftness of the reply, looked forward to escaping her dreary routine for a day. She ordered a picnic box for both of them from Mrs Matsuo and took care choosing her outfit, regretting that the sturdy European hiking boots her father had bought her were in Tokyo, but she'd manage.

———

AND THEN AN EVEN GREATER SURPRISE. On the morning they were leaving, the sardonic receptionist wasn't just pleasant, he went out of his way to be helpful. But when she asked if the hotel had a map, he became confused, flustered, opening several drawers before going back to the office and returning with a small box.

'Please, Miss, here are the maps for your expedition to Mount Inasa. This one – is in English, but many years old.' He unfolded the map and ran his stubby finger over the route, all the way to the top of the hill, glancing knowingly at her as he did so. 'You must be careful, because I hear a storm is coming.'

After so much haughtiness from him, Ayako was confused, and almost overcome. 'Thank you, thank you for your concern. We'll. Be. Fine. I've been hiking many times.'

The receptionist seemed unsure as if there was more to say. Their eyes met – both knew something they weren't telling the other.

After several seconds hesitation, he handed over the map and bowed deeply, as if praising her for doing a patriotic duty.

Next, it was Dan's turn to be confused. He placed his lunch box on top of the hotel's borrowed binoculars and the towel he'd packed in the rucksack the hotel had lent him, and turned to the young-looking junior minder who had replaced their usual stooge.

'We're off, then.' The minder didn't move, not really sure how to react. '*Hai. Itteirashai.*'

Dan turned to Ayako. 'What does that mean?'

'We go and come back.'

'I see.' Dan didn't really, but something else had piqued his interest. 'Are you not coming?' He looked at the young minder, who stiffened in an attempt to regain his authority.

'You go... now.' The minder turned and sat, obviously finished for the day. Astonishing. Are they trusting him at last? Or is this another trap?

Dan picked up his rucksack and Ayako strapped on her little homemade one that she had stuffed with a thin cloth sheet to sit on, the sun-blanched English map, her little picnic box, and took the dainty sun umbrella foisted on her by Dan's overly-concerned room maid.

Ayako was oddly nervous – but perhaps it was just the fact that it felt strange to leave the hotel without being tailed by the obligatory minder. Perhaps.

As they set off through the narrow streets and out of

the city towards the mountain, neither of them mentioned their unexpected freedom, what it might mean, or what was happening. Unusually they didn't even talk, until Ayako said out of the blue, 'That receptionist. He's strange. Doesn't even seem to know his own hotel.'

Struggling for breath in the heavy heat, Dan just nodded and let it go. As the climb ahead suddenly became steeper, Ayako had to pause for breath too. 'The manager said we must take care. There is a storm, going Kokura, Japanese typhoon, so it may...' She waved in the direction of the harbour below. 'It will become windy.'

Dan didn't care. He was simply exhilarated to be out in the wilderness, away from the relentless bustle of the crowded Japanese city, but also troubled, though uncertain why. As he had left breakfast, the elderly manager carefully placed the Panama on Dan's head like a men's clothing shop tailor, shook his hand, holding it in his two hands, while looking at Dan directly and said, 'Lawrence-san, please, please take care,' as if he could not bear to see his guest in danger, but couldn't say what. In response, Dan frequently looked behind, unobtrusively – but no one was following.

They passed neat but tiny farm-workers' cottages, with peasants in thick baggy *monpe* pants standing outside, watching them with suspicion, whispering to each other, the word '*gaijin*' hanging in the air. Now, on the steep, overgrown, rocky hiking trail, peering through the wall of trees he could see the whole green, brown and blue patchwork of Nagasaki Bay spread out below them. Apart from a couple of boys far below them flying kites in the strong sea breeze, they had the world to themselves.

After two hour's walking, then climbing and finally

clambering, they reached the summit – and the picnic lunch.

'Here good?' Despite the heat of the sun, Ayako smiled, her cheeks glowing, feeling strangely close to him in this wilderness, wondering what they were to each other? Friends, a couple, or just two strangers, alone with one of the great views in all Japan.

Dan nodded his approval before turning his attention to the bay below. Taking the hotel binoculars from the knapsack, he peered over the trunk of a fallen tree and inspected the small fishing boats bobbing gently in the wild, craggy inlets along the surf-washed coast, before zeroing in on the naval activity on the far side of the bay, away from the city, out towards the islands in the Sea of Japan.

Ayako, however, seemed more interested in quizzing him about life in the West, than paying attention to what he was doing.

'Dan-san. How is America?'

'I am English, not American.'

She pretended not to know. 'Oh? So, if you English, why you're not soldier? I think you very good-looking in uniform, very noble. Why don't you fighting at war – for your country?'

Dan continued looking through the glasses. In the distance, a group of naval officers were standing on a floating platform, signalling across the bay to a motor patrol boat.

'Honestly Ayako, what difference would it make to the war if I returned?'

Dan didn't bother to go on. No doubt the concept was alien to anyone Japanese, especially with the newspapers, the cinema, the radio all calling the entire nation to arms.

She probably didn’t under- stand, *could* not understand. ‘Anyway, I’d rather be here with you, much more fun.’

Ayako didn’t take the bait. She put her tea cup down and looked up. ‘How can you say that? Every citizen have *duty* to fight for coun- try. If all men think this way – England lose the war.’ She shifted on her knees, trying to catch his eyes, but he continued to look through the binoculars.

‘So, what if England does lose? All it does is bully other countries.’

Dan's words confirmed what all Japanese propaganda had been saying for several years. The Colonial West is pacifist, lazy, in decline, incapable of properly fighting a war. Ayako studied this tall, vague man with pitying sympathy. How sad, how decadent, she thought. He does not love his country. Or, probably, his family either...

At that moment Dan didn't care what she thought. A splash of spray had billowed from the patrol boat, and a silver streak was flashing through the waves; he counted silently to himself – one and two and three and four and... fifty-one and fifty-two and fifty-three and... crash! The silver streak collided with the floating wooden platform, rocking it up and down, throwing several observers into the water – maybe one was Dr Kado. Dropping the binoculars from his eyes, Dan estimated the distance from patrol boat to platform at about 2,000 yards. Then he turned back to Ayako, pretending to be engaged in their conversation.

‘Ayako, I am a twenty-seven-year-old businessman with good prospects. Why should I want to die for the old men who rule the world?’

While Ayako set about her detailed explanation, Dan resumed watching.

'I can't believe you care so little for your country – my father says England is great, very civilised, we learn much, but you won't go be soldier to save her...'

The dummy-torpedo was about ten feet long – a hell of a size, and clearly very accurate.

'...and we do not think ourselves as individual people. The Nation, the Empire, is more important, and we are honoured to give our lives for our country Japan!'

As the officers bobbed in the water, they raised both hands repeatedly skyward with glee; the experiment appeared to have been a success. '*That* is why Japan will soon become leader of all Asia. My country is strong and Britain and America cannot stop her!'

Usually, such a monologue would have annoyed Dan, but it had acted as camouflage. A gust of wind blew dust through the trees as Dan turned back towards her with a ruthless smile and tapped his forehead. 'This is where I fight my wars.'

Ayako shook her head. 'Then, you lose.' She held out a cup of green tea to Dan and, smoothing out the sheet, waved for him to sit, watching to ensure he didn't dirty it with his shoes.

'That's another thing,' he said, 'why, when we're up the mountain wearing climbing gear, surrounded by dirt and earth, do you put down a sheet to keep our clothes clean?'

'It's Japanese way. Clothes must be clean.'

He shook his head. 'Crazy.'

'OK. I don't know. Maybe it *is* crazy – but it's rule.'

They laughed, then sipped in silence, until Dan threw a rock at a small flock of seagulls. 'I'm surprised to see seagulls this high,' he said.

'Seagulls go everywhere,' she replied. 'See, that one, there – reminds me of receptionist.'

Dan turned to her, delighted at this playfulness in such a serious- seeming young woman. He felt so happy to put down for a moment all the burdens of war and masks and secrets, and simply be a man and a woman, alone together on a mountainside. He wanted to hear her laugh again.

'Look over there,' he said, pointing at a rather portly seagull sitting preening himself slightly apart from the flock. 'Doesn't that look like the hotel manager?'

And howl she did. Loud and long and joyful.

The wind was gusting around them as they pointed and giggled. Dan's Panama hat was blown off, and tumbled away down the mountainside. They laughed together at that as well, but inside Dan felt a sudden chill. Had he lost part of his armour?

Then later, after an increasingly blustery picnic lunch, a dreadful thing happened.

A shrill, slow-moving aircraft droned across the bay from Takashima Island. In the gathering wind, the biplane weaved and shook, descending through the darkening sky until its flight path took it directly towards the floating wooden platform. About a mile from its target, an explosion of spray plumed up below the aircraft, which immediately began to climb.

Dan tried to ignore this unwelcome side-show, but Ayako demanded the binoculars and took Dan's place by the fallen tree. Half a minute later, Dan watched in horror as the platform rocked once again, though this time its tiny occupants were holding on more tightly.

Ayako put down the binoculars, saying nothing for a while, bowing her head in thought. Finally, she spoke to the ground.

'Now, I see. I understand how you fight wars.' That she sounded betrayed did not surprise him. Dan smiled; though uncertain how a smile might be interpreted – it just seemed the thing to do.

'Don't be stupid,' he said, his mind racing. 'I was watching the fishermen.'

He should have known she was brighter than that. Now he had a situation to deal with. Should he attempt to push her off the mountainside? – but these Jap women know a thing or two about self-defence. Anyway, an unplanned murder was always a stupid risk.

Perhaps he should just laugh out loud and continue to bluff ignorance? But then Ayako would feel insulted, become angry, and would be more likely to report him, even if the report was solely based on the flimsy evidence of her own eyes. But maybe any evidence would be enough in Japanese eyes.

Or should he beg for mercy? But pleading would be anathema to the proud Japanese spirit, and cause her to despise him completely.

Which left blackmail or bribery? – no, she wasn't the type.

Or... Should he tell her the truth, whatever it is? – absolutely not.

A terrifying irony crossed Dan's mind. Spies were hanged; and in spite of all his self-serving cynicism against war – it seemed he might have inadvertently blundered onto the frontline and an executioner's noose.

Ironically, Ayako became protective – her voice cutting through his thoughts. 'Lawrence-san, the sky is becoming dark. We will leave.'

But now 'Lawrence-san'. Suddenly formal. Cold. Threatening.

Dan looked across Nagasaki Bay. The men on the platform were hurriedly packing up. The leaden tobacco-coloured sky had taken on a deep purple glow and the atmosphere felt increasingly heavy. In the absence of anything else to say, while folding the thin sheet and watching Ayako hurriedly pack their things, Dan asked her what was happening to the weather.

'I thought the storm was heading to Kokura.'

'Maybe wind direction changed. Typhoon coming this way,' she replied with a slight tremor. 'I think it will very heavy rain.'

He took the binoculars and was about to stow them when he looked back downhill at the track they'd come up and almost cried out. Five men in fatigues were climbing the hill in their direction. Zooming in, he recognised one as the officer from his first meeting with the *Kempeitai*, and another the hotel receptionist. An arresting party. He was trapped. The noose was tightening. So, now – who was betraying whom?

Then the storm punched into the mountain like a fist.

The squad of men below held onto each other, then began to scatter, until the officer pointed downhill and they swayed and slid down-wards, disappearing in a lashing blizzard.

When the tornado reached further, up and up, it smashed Dan and Ayako hard – blasting them off their feet. Ayako grabbed his arm, staggering and stumbling on the loose stones, as the howling storm and rain whipped and tore at them. And when a second, stronger, blast of hot heavy wind thundered up the side of Mount Inasa, he found he could hardly breathe.

'How long do these things last!?' he shouted at Ayako, already drenched and increasingly frightened.

'One hour! Or two hours! Maybe a day!' Ayako picked up her pace.

Christ, thought Dan. *And we're still near the top of the mountain.* Concern for their survival now added to his fear of discovery.

TYPHOON BOCA SHOULD HAVE MISSED Nagasaki and hit Kokura, two hundred miles further up the coast. But at the last minute the storm centre swung inland, looming over Nomozaki Point, and funnelling into the V-shaped Nagasaki Bay. At the centre, the winds were over a hundred miles-an-hour, ripping up Mount Inasa from the sea, with no land buffer in the way to slow it down.

Dan was learning at first hand that the speed at which a typhoon goes from being a purple cloud out to sea to a whirling, pounding full- force storm is literally bewildering. Apart from the terrifying blasts of wind that continuously threw both Dan and Ayako off their feet, the most frightening aspect was the explosive sound, like the very Devil screaming from hell.

Huge branches from large trees crashed around them, cracking like whips as they fell, blocking the crumbling path as they struggled downwards. Dan, taller and heavier, gripped Ayako's shoulders from behind, his fingers digging into her skin as he desperately tried to stop her from being blown away.

Next came the torrential rain – so intense, and so hard to breathe against, it felt as though they were drowning in a tidal wave. The deluge almost instantaneously turned the rocky path into a raging torrent that tore away at the flooded ground, leaving Ayako and Dan slipping and sliding down the mountain, cutting their arms and legs on the rough stones as the frenzied wind whipped up leaves and gravel and sandpapered their exposed skin.

Dan lost track of time. It felt as though hours had passed since they had set off. The eye of the storm swept over them with an odd calm, along with a feeling of exhaustion Dan had never encountered before. At the moment that the wind dropped, they reached a small, dark forest clearing in the centre of which, under a thick canopy of camphor leaves, sat a tiny, wooden shrine with a neatly tiled roof. The shrine was raised slightly off the ground, so it was not water-logged. Although dilapidated it would offer shelter.

Grabbing Ayako's hand, Dan pulled her towards it and fumbled with the door, desperate to get away from the torrential rain, but Ayako hesitated, unsure if it was sacrilegious, even in this situation. Dan was past caring. Ignoring her reluctance, he shoved her inside, almost throwing her down, before yanking the door closed and collapsing in a breathless heap beside her on the bare wooden floor.

They lay in the gloom facing each other, trying to get their breath back, while the eye moved on and the storm exploded again, the gales howling, bringing back the creaking and cracking of tree branches and a continuous thunderous roar. Ayako finally worked her way into a sitting position and, unstrapping her sodden little backpack, formally spread her wet sheet on the floor.

Dan could see her lower lip quiver in the gloom but she refused to cry. Instead, she dug out a couple of handkerchiefs and, handing one to Dan in silence, set about wiping the blood off her arms and legs. Safe from the screaming wind and rain outside, and having tacitly agreed to wait the storm out, Dan now had time to calculate his options.

Clearly there were two: persuasion or, well, murder – in that order. Firstly, he must dispense with formalities. 'Ayako, when you said "I see," is it because you really believe I'm some kind of spy?'

His pleading voice, though gentle, surprised her in the cosy confinement of the little shelter, but she did not reply. He lowered his voice as though speaking to a child.

'Ayako?'

He heard her sigh. 'My father said. Everyone is spy. Everyone spies.' Marooned in a small shrine, almost touching, she raised her head and looked at him, straightening her back and, taking extra care with her annunciation, quoted. '"For now sits expectation in the air." My father teaches William Shakespeare. Very popular in Japan.'

Dan could not believe his ears; he almost laughed. Shakespeare, a man he'd hardly heard of – in these surroundings. From the mountain- side, he heard a loud wooden crack, like a gunshot, as another wind- blown pine crashed down. 'Do you like William Shakespeare?' she asked.

'I... I don't know him,' Dan answered lamely.

He could sense Ayako grinning to herself. 'I hear his plays from my father, Junichiro.' She paused with an even deeper sigh, sad that their easy companionship was now broken. Yet, with the mention of her father's name, a paradoxical sense of duty, to him, to Dan, to learning, took hold, and she just had to tell the truth, Japanese-style, obliquely, subtly. And to her this was so important, she almost massaged the words with her tongue as she spoke.

'"Suspicion always haunts the guilty mind." You know?'

This is when Dan's truncated education let him down. Her subtlety left him confused, unable to understand the hidden meaning of what she was saying, albeit through Shakespeare.

Instead, Dan was still selfishly calculating angles. Certainly, this could not be a manoeuvre to trap him, because there was no point now. Or had she read his ruthless mind and decided to placate him until safely back at the hotel with the *Kempeitai*? Dan weighed up the evidence, coldly, with little emotion or compassion, the boy in the playground wondering whether to start a fight, deciding on the best course for his own safety. He examined his fingers, and pictured them around her beautiful throat. A breath-taking thought, literally.

Outside, the howling wind and thundering rain reached a crescendo. The back of a typhoon was usually the most violent, Dan knew. He gripped the wooden support next to him as the little building shuddered. There was a deafening resonant twang from outside, a whipcrack louder than all the others, followed by the splintering sound of breaking timber all around. Before he could reach her, the roof and walls of the shrine crumbled on top of them – and all went blank.

CONSCIOUSNESS CAME and went in waves.

If I can move my little finger, my thumb, my hand – yes! It's free... Dizziness. Being numb. Pain. *The tile on my arm is so heavy. I can't...* Ayako screwed up her face and gave one final heave... *Ah... Good. Tingling.* She flexed her fingers and squirmed onto her side, feeling down to the heavy weight resting on her trapped leg. Pain shot through her and she gasped. She closed her eyes and concentrated, trying to clear her muddled thoughts. *Why am I wet? Where is here? What's holding me down so firmly?*

She started feeling tentatively around her. A beam, several rocks, the leaves and branches of a camphor tree lay across, pinning her firmly to the floor of the shrine. She tried to wriggle out from under them, but the pain in her leg screamed every time she made the slightest effort. She twisted it a fraction, and the heavy stone roof tiles fell away, enough for her to slide fully onto her side, push against the fallen wall with her right foot – kick, kick, kick – and drag herself free.

She rolled onto her back and gasped. How could she get help if she couldn't walk. *Where am I? Mountain... Earthquake?* She closed her eyes and forced herself to focus. *Typhoon. Shrine...* 'Lawrence-san!'

She turned her head and felt blindly around her. 'Lawrence-san? Lawrence-san!' She gingerly put her hand on his arm and shook it gently. 'Mr Lawrence-san?' She shook it again, harder, almost as though she were shaking off the fear that he was dead. She thought she heard a groan but couldn't be sure. 'Mr Lawrence...?' She chewed hard on her lips, desperate to stop the tears welling up in her eyes. *I need to get help. I need to get help, or Lawrence-san will die.*

If it had been the other way round, and Dan had come to, her head would have been conveniently crushed by the weight of the roof tiles, or by a rock wielded by Dan. But Ayako had no thought but for her duty.

So she crawled from the demolished shrine into the downpour and, dragging a badly cut and swollen left leg, began crawling, slip- ping and sliding down the deeply rutted trail towards the city. In places, she almost swam through the mud and debris where it had pooled; elsewhere, fallen trees blocked her way – causing her to have to clamber over them, gasping at the effort and the pain.

She gave up several times; once, rounding a bend on the rocky path, the misty lights of Nagasaki seemed so very far away. *How can I possibly crawl such a distance?* she asked herself, tears merging with the sweeping rain. She gasped and lay back against the steep trail bank. But, on coming to, Ayako raised herself again on battered elbows, and continued clawing her way downhill.

In the early hours of that Wednesday morning, by a blown-over wooden fence on the outskirts of the city, her sodden and bleeding body finally gave out and she collapsed onto a public road, but as she fainted a weak smile crossed her lips. Someone would surely find her.

Twenty minutes later, Constable Harada, patrolling the area for damage and avoiding the puddles along the Mount Inasa Road, chanced across a crumpled figure lying face down in the mud. He swore to himself. 'Another hit-and-run' – a common occurrence along this narrow coast-road without pavements, on the outskirts of the town. He stooped down and shone his torch on the face of a young girl.

She's still breathing, he thought, feeling the warmth of her cheek through hard-skinned hands. Without a moment's hesitation, he draped his waterproof cape over the body, grabbed his paper loud- speaker and shouted at the top of his voice in the direction of the darkened farm workers' houses. 'Oi! Oi! Someone! Help me out here! Oi!!! It is the duty of all citizens to come to the aid of the police!'

Within a few seconds, lantern-light and chattering voices filtered through the paper-thin walls and a babble of half-dressed men clattered out of their flimsy wooden front doors, as if rehearsing a fire drill.

'Over here!' shouted Constable Harada. They gathered round, gabbling noisily, making suggestions, scouring the road ahead and behind as though there was a perpetrator lurking to watch what would happen, until Harada took control and barked out a series of instructions. A dozen pairs of arms were linked under Ayako's body, the order to 'raise!' was given, and Ayako, limp and badly grazed, was lifted from the street and carried onto the hastily cushioned floor of the nearest tenement house.

Someone held her head on their lap and pressed a cup of strong *shochu* to her lips. She spluttered and looked up through tear-filled eyes into a circle of curious yet suspicious faces.

'At the shrine, at the shrine on the mountain. He's dying...' In her mind, the faces just stared and the voices fell silent. But in that tiny, crowded front room, Constable Harada turned to face the group of expectant faces and gave further orders.

By the time they'd organised themselves and fought up the mountainside through the lashes of the tail of the typhoon, a dark grey dawn was leaking from the sky. The gusting wind had rendered their lanterns useless, and the dwindling batteries of Constable Harada's torch had given up completely, so by the time the talkative group arrived at the demolished shrine, they assumed Dan was dead.

'*Araa* – Look at that big, old tree...'

'Right across the middle...'

'*Yaa* – Crushed like a pea-shell...'

'Flattened to a wafer...'

'However did the girl crawl out?'

'*Oi!* Over there!'

First, they saw a large leather boot poking from the ruins of the entrance. Presuming the man to be dead, no-one hurried. Two of them leant back against a fallen tree and lit cigarettes, hesitating at the thought of touching a holy shrine destroyed by an act of God.

'Come on,' growled the Constable, handing one of the heavy tiles to the nearest idler, 'we've work to do.'

Following his lead, they heaved the tiles off the roof, stacking them neatly to one side, and found another foot.

'*Wah,* he's a big man!' exclaimed one. The group peered over his shoulder and mumbled its agreement.

'You don't think...? It's not that foreigner...?' suggested another.

'A foreigner?' They all began chattering at once, as the mood changed – a westerner? So, as more of the body appeared from under the debris, the rescuers became more deliberate.

'Careful, careful...' Harada was well aware that the rescue might be investigated – and, if so, would conceivably be written up in the newspapers. Japanese life might be cheap, but if it was a Western body, it would be big news.

Groaning with the strain, a group of rescuers held up the remains of the wooden wall, while Constable Harada bravely slid underneath on his belly and reached through the soggy ruins towards the man's head. He struggled as he repositioned himself and then paused before touching the body.

Still warm! He shoved aside a few heavy splinters of wood and squeezed his fingers through the camphor tree branches, feeling for a face. Now he could see in the gloom. It was a westerner, which made him peer more closely. The mouth was open, lips still moist.

'Hold it!' he yelled. 'Everyone quiet!' They all stopped.

The Constable's hand slid down the bristly chin, slid down the smooth long neck, slid across the shirt and felt towards his heart.

The rain seemed to stop in mid-air, the wind held its breath, as a strong, confident, elated cry rang out across the mountain.

'He's alive...'

3

For a while, Dan thought he was dreaming.

He could hear the murmuring of female voices, the rattle of some sort of small carriage, then there was the sweet, sickly smell of soy and overcooked vegetables, of carbolic, of disinfectant. He could feel a sheet across his chest, a heaviness on his arm, a tight band around his head. His body was either numb or excruciating, but detached – somehow, not part of him.

Then he opened his eyes.

A trio of girlish nurses in short-sleeved white dresses, with white stockings and shoes and starched hats, were in a huddle gossiping quietly. One noticed him move, and the other two turned around, and for a moment they were uncertain. Then the tallest of the trio swept away, leaving the other two watching him.

Dan tried to twist onto his side, to see them more clearly, but he seemed to be pinned down, and trying to move was painful anyway, so he gave up and continued just watching out of the corner of his left eye.

The tall nurse came back with a small, elderly man,

who was wearing a long white coat, with the obligatory stethoscope around his neck – obviously a doctor.

'Where am I?' Dan asked, interrupting the examination, but the doctor ignored him and gesturing with a wrinkled, freckled hand at the reports on the clipboards behind Dan's head spat out '*Kinshi*!' and banged on the board with his fingers before turning to Dan. 'I cannot say.' And with that, he was off.

Over the next week, while slowly recovering from a coma-inducing heavy whack to the head, a hairline fracture to his arm, crushed ankle, and a large number of cuts and lacerations, Dan was told nothing – neither about his treatment nor where he was nor what was going to happen to him. Nobody, not even the medical staff, would make eye contact, let alone talk to him. All he got was blank faces – and no people in the world, he thought to himself, do blank faces like the Japanese.

So, the few words and phrases he had learned from Ayako were useless, save at mealtimes – which was all the more frustrating because he was desperate to find out about her. What had happened to Ayako, where was she, was she even still alive? The questions nagged at him obsessively.

The wider world, especially the world according to Japan, knew all about Ayako Okunaga, and how she had saved the 'American' who had fallen off a mountain during a typhoon, and was now recovering at Nagasaki College Hospital. The censors had made absolutely certain every Japanese newspaper headlined the story.

'Englishman saved by heroic Japanese girl'
'American businessman in Japanese lifesaving rescue'

However, there were ‘problems’ caused by this ‘unknown Westerner being too weak to be interviewed personally’, but now that was changing.

Dan knew nothing about these stories, until he had begun hobbling around the hospital corridors on sticks. A man in a black suit, who he vaguely recognised as one of the original *Kempei* minders from his hotel days, arrived and, without speaking, dropped several recent copies of *The Japan Times and Advertiser* onto his bed, then strode away. Dan read the articles greedily and with amused relief that he was so useful for propaganda. Such glowing reports were unlikely to be followed by *‘Rescued businessman was foreign spy.’*

But still, the carefully written stories continued to gloss over that one irritating mystery. What had happened to the girl?

‘Did she survive?’ he asked. The answer always came with a shake of the head – ‘*Kinshi*’ – forbidden.

He also pondered the reason why? *Why* had a minder, one of the *Kempeitai*, helpfully provided the newspapers? And, later that after- noon, why had the seriously ill man in the bed right next to him suddenly, and unceremoniously, been carted away, and a younger man, who seemed fine to Dan, been stretchered in to replace him?

Both mysteries were answered the next day when an official from the British Embassy arrived from Tokyo.

‘A charming town, Nagasaki, don't you think?’ The diplomat, Lewis Seale, greeted Dan, smiled benignly, and sat on a seat strategically placed so that they could be heard from the next bed. Dan shrugged. Perhaps Mr Seale could help with a mystery. ‘What happened to the girl? Ayako Okunaga, who saved my—?’

Before he could even finish the question, Seale shook

his head, seemingly uninterested and moved across, to perch on the edge of Dan's bed, 'Where was I? Ah, yes, Nagasaki. Quite important to their Navy, I gather.'

The patronising superiority of this sweating, unworldly Foreign Office official took Dan back to the mid 1920s, to a time when his father, the third assistant gardener on the Steven Estate, was treated with contempt bordering on cruelty. His mother, Scara, with her guttural Bosnian accent, would chide Dan when he mimicked their plummy arrogance. 'We know our place and are 'appy 'ere, better than Austrian secret police...'

Now, faced with Lewis Seale, Dan frowned. Bugger Nagasaki, bugger the Navy, bugger everyone and everything. He just wanted to regain his strength and get out of this bloody hospital and Japan as soon as possible. He emphasised to Seale that they obviously needed the space. The patient in the next bed had been seriously ill the day before, but early that morning they had carried him off and rushed in that other young fellow 'sleeping' there now.

The pompous diplomat dabbed at the perspiration on his brow with a primrose-coloured handkerchief. 'Quite, quite, walls have ears, that kind of thing – perhaps we could stroll around the grounds.'

Dan shook his head, wouldn't be allowed. He was just a business man, hoping to leave Japan soon. End of story.

''Fraid not, my dear fellow. In fact, a dickie bird told us you were for "the one-way drop",' he slid a finger across his throat, 'but Tokyo preferred the propaganda angle. For the moment at least. Now, as to the point of my little trip. The Japanese Home Ministry wrote to Sir Robert Craigie, His Majesty's Ambassador, to say that "for commercial and technical reasons" you won't be allowed to leave.'

He undid the button of his tweed suit jacket, leaning forward to whisper in Dan's ear. 'The fact is, old boy, we've been wondering what it is you know...'

Almost immediately, a nurse appeared, busying herself plumping up the pillows, haughtily gesturing to the diplomat to 'get off the bed' and 'return to the chair provided.' Dan watched the diplomat's humiliation without expression.

'Perhaps you ought to go,' he suggested.

The diplomat threaded his fingers together, waggling them up and down in schoolmasterly admonition. 'As you wish,' he sighed staring at the wall, 'it's just that if you tell us what it is, presumably they'll no longer have cause to detain you.'

The incredulous dumb scowl on Dan's face did not really require words as well.

'I'm sorry, Mr Seale, I simply do not know. Now, would you kindly leave, please.' Within three hours, the original patient was back in the next bed.

———

AS DAN RECOVERED, he noticed little things that in wartime Japan provided big clues.

Orderlies and porters began looking at him, partly out of curiosity at seeing a *gaijin*, partly due to his 'celebrity' status. His whole ward was wakened early for a thorough spring clean; flowers sprouted in vases, and new sheets were tucked into beds. A gang even arrived to clean the windows. Finally, the rubber soles of the hospital principal squeaked along the newly polished floor, before coming to a standstill, at the bottom of Dan's bed. With him, the young man who had been in the next-door bed just the day before, having made a miraculous recovery, resurfaced as a somewhat hesitant translator.

'Everything is well?'

Dan shrugged and nodded. 'Except, what happened to the girl, Ayako Okunaga, who saved my life?'

Hearing her name, the principal sucked air through his teeth. He followed this with a short, sharp '*So ka.*'

He then spun on his rubber heels and, offering a brief nod in Dan's direction, strolled away, leaving the flustered translator to deal with it. 'I cannot say.'

After lunch an invasion proper began.

A huge arc lamp on casters rattled through the double swing doors, followed by an entourage of technicians, who seemed to gabble at least ten opinions on everything.

The nurses gawped at the controlled chaos while giggling quietly, their territorial instincts having been trampled by the assumed superiority of the invaders. Dan sat in bed reading a *Teach Yourself Japanese* book, affecting not to care or notice though, clearly, he was the centre of this particular attraction.

The blinding, humming lights burst into life at the end of his bed; an enormous, even noisier, camera whirled; the director yapped for silence, that ridiculous black-and-white board clapped, and the ward waited for action.

Whatever should I do now? Dan thought, still pretending to read.

In the corner, the double doors creaked jerkily open – and in she floated, treading carefully, eyes directed ahead of her, towards the floor. She was dressed in a light blue silk kimono, bound with a beautiful *obi* belt and clasping a delicate silk purse to her midriff. When she neared the bed she looked up. The feigned shyness was made untruthful by the twinkle in her eyes. Dan finally put down his book.

'Well, hello there, Miss Ayako,' he said.

In every cinema in Japan, audiences warmed to the touching scene, which played after the reports of war in Europe and international tension, at the end of the newsreel:

'The Young American businessman Daniel Lawrence recovering from his ordeal on Mount Inasa, meets the brave Japanese woman who saved him.'

'Now fully recovered, Okunaga Ayako Sensei, the young teacher from Tokyo who risked her life crawling down Mount Inasa at the height of Typhoon Boca, while fetching help for trapped American businessman Dan Lawrence, meets him once again. The meeting with Okunaga Sensei took place at Mr Lawrence's request and our cameras were present at Urakami Hospital for the glad occasion. Speaking with his saviour, Mr Lawrence said, "Without the perseverance, spirit, courage and generous help from this brave Japanese, I would not be alive today." Yet more evidence that the aggression of the United States government will not harm the brave spirit and generosity of the people of Japan!'

At the back of the 'Central Kinema' in Nagasaki, Ayako translated the overenthusiastic commentary by whispering intimately in Dan's ear, her perfumed breath overpowering the thick smoke and stuffy smells of the oriental cinema. Having felt so isolated, lonely even, in hospital, Dan took the opportunity to move slightly closer, on the pretext of stretching out his legs, and brushed against Ayako's hand as the hammed-up nonsense spewed once into the auditorium then, in English, out of her tantalising, kissable mouth and into his ear.

But Ayako failed to appreciate the irony of the story, or the humour of their being used as two more victims sacrificed to satisfy the voracious appetites of war propaganda. She simply sensed his male desire and politely edged away.

Given the anti-American fervour, perhaps an even greater irony was the main film, with the Hollywood idol Buster Keaton creating belly-laughs. The house gasped as Buster slipped, then roared as he pitched and rolled and walked away from what yet again should have been certain death. For a brief moment Ayako forgot herself and her polite schoolgirl giggle and, throwing her head back, laughed from the back of her throat. Dan loved to hear her laugh. He loved being out of the hospital and close to this rather lovely young woman. He tried to move closer – to be politely rebuffed for the tenth time.

They left the main film early, deciding to make the most of Dan's special night out, before he had to return to the college hospital by his ten-o'clock curfew. He limped awkwardly alongside his slender companion as they made their way across the Gay Section for supper at a little family run restaurant.

The waitress came to the table and, glancing at Dan with a faint look of disdain, turned to Ayako and took their order.

'How is Japanese, Lawrence-san? Did you study in hospital?'

Dan looked up with a frown. *Was she serious?* The dim light cast by the blackout shade around the single lightbulb above their table suited her features as she played host, carefully positioning the vegetables and tofu in the simmering broth which bubbled and boiled between them. The way she looked after him so solicitously melted his annoyance. He leaned across and, breaking strict Japanese protocols, helped himself to a gristly piece of octopus directly from the seething stew, and guided it – rather amateurishly – into his mouth.

'There's been no one to teach me, so my Japanese hasn't improved much.' His voice was edged with accusation – where had she been while he had been recovering? He then lowered his voice in frustration. 'Anyway, I want to leave, go back home – as soon as possible.'

Ayako ignored his crass *gaijin* table manners. She put her chop- sticks down, slowly and decisively teased a strand of hair from her eyes and sat back on her heels with a fierce glare. As she did so, the kimono sleeves fell in feminine folds onto her lap which, in Dan's eyes, only made her more attractive.

'It is difficult.' She looked down and smoothed out an invisible crease running the length of her long silk sleeve, unsure whether to continue. Dan waited her out, not asking why, but staring at her pouting mouth rather than her eyes, a technique he often used as an unasked question. Now she had to tell him.

'You cannot leave... because of information you might know.' Her answer was very direct, far from the way most Japanese girls had been brought up, to be submissive, modest, reticent, secretive. As always, the rebel, pushing boundaries, her mother's acerbic daughter.

Dan continued chewing on the rubbery piece of octopus, wondering nervously if she knew about the 'one-way drop?'

As if reading his mind, Ayako leant over the pot, slipping a selection of meat, vegetables and noodles into her little bowl, and murmured down towards the tabletop, softly, 'I did not tell them.' She sat back again, took several mouthfuls, then still holding the bowl in front of her chest, looked him in the eyes with reproach.

'They ask me many questions. Many questions. But I said you had *spied* only on the seagulls, looked at the trees, and were not interested in the Bay.'

'Spied.' She'd emphasised that word.

'And, I say to them – maybe you liked me.' She giggled, then modestly tilted her head and looked down, quite innocent in Japan, but in what Dan, reluctantly celibate for many months, hoped was an act of seduction.

'And what did they say to that?' Dan murmured, completely at a loss, trying to smile.

Her hand waved backwards and forwards – that give-away sign of 'no'. 'They were very angry. They say, "Japanese woman should not like Western men".' Another tilt of the head, and a little laugh, ridiculing him, oddly out of place; whatever did it mean this time? He was thinking, *these Japs must have some kind of magic code for understanding each other.*

Dan finally gave up chewing – the octopus was still a solid lump of rubber. He took a deep breath, and miserably swallowed the offending morsel in one gulp.

THE NEXT MORNING, two of the minders turned up at the hospital to escort Dan back to the Nagasaki Grand Hotel. Ayako wasn't with them, so there were a lot of misunderstandings, and pointing and arm waving and confusion before he was bundled into a car, which bumped painfully across the tram tracks and stone paving, and finally along the dusty unmade Bund.

The elderly hotel manager greeted Dan with a smile, as he had been distraught that one of his guests should have been injured while at his hotel. The young porter seemed equally pleased and made a movement like pedalling a bicycle with his white-gloved hands, mimicking a movie camera. Only the tricky receptionist avoided catching his eye. *This is almost home,* Dan thought, and gave an exaggerated deep Japanese bow that, too, was met with a grin.

Unimpressed by the behaviour of the foreigner, the jollity was savagely interrupted by the senior 'supervisor' in a uniform black suit, now with a conspicuous *Kempei* armband.

'You! Go out only with patrol,' he barked, staccato style, as if reading from a script. 'You go Police Station ev-e-ry morning.'

Once finished he stood stock still and glared. Wondering who had taught this fierce *Kempei* those words, Dan threw back a short, sharp '*hai*' and ostentatiously limped up the wide staircase to his second- floor suite, realising he was under a kind of house arrest. What devious scheme were they planning now?

Sitting on his private terrace in the early evening as an increasingly chilly gloom descended on the bay, Dan wasn't sure if he felt exhilarated or terrified, and it all came down to whether he could trust a twenty-two-year-old, really rather attractive, but fiendishly unknowable woman.

The last of the autumn mosquitoes swirled around, trying to avoid his cheroot smoke, while the bay lights came up and the sun went down, and he thought to himself, *are you kidding yourself, you bloody idiot?*

He poured the dregs of the house *saké* the hotel manager had sent up to him, with a shaking hand. *She's a woman, a good-looker, a Jap. Of course they know what she knows. So, what are they waiting for?* Then he nervously sniggered to himself, unleashing *saké*-fuelled gallows humour. *They want another Newsreel moment, catch me red-handed.* Not for the first time did he deeply regret ever agreeing to this perilous adventure, the vanity project of a clever lawyer in Washington. He shuddered.

'Ah well, here I am,' he murmured to the twinkling, lapping bay, unsure if it was now the frontline or a backwater.

'FORGIVE ME FATHER, for I have sinned. It is two months since my last confession.'

'I know, my son, we have been waiting.'

In the cramped confessional box, Dan's hand fanned back and forth in front of his nose like Ayako had the night before, and he made a mental reminder not to attend Father Luigi after the priest had his garlic supper. He knelt on one knee, the other knee still painful.

'Father, I have told lies, many lies – perhaps, I've betrayed innocent affection. And there have been self-serving thoughts of, yes, breaking the sixth commandment. But only thoughts, father.'

'You are forgiven, for that which must be done.'

Christ, thought Dan, *someone's been having a word with Father Luigi.*

'I was followed here, father.' Dan was whispering. 'They are waiting outside.'

A slight intake of breath – thank God – and a murmur of reassurance.

'My lie is to the Japanese people. They are testing a torpedo out in the bay.' Dan paused, he could hear Father Luigi writing, and spoke slowly. 'A large torpedo, twice the size of others. It has a range of over 2,000 yards, and is accurate to within a few feet. Its speed through water is 75 knots, just below the surface, and can be launched from the belly of a plane. Obviously, it's to be manufactured at the Mitsubishi Ordnance Works here in Nagasaki. Is it a sin that I betray, to notice these things?'

'What you confess is no longer a sin. Are you unburdened fully, my son?'

'Yes father.'

'No lewd thoughts?'

'Well, yes, father, some lewd thoughts.' 'Or acts of the flesh?'

Dan sighed – if only. 'No, father.'

'Say three "Our Fathers" and three "Hail Marys" and try not to think such thoughts again.'

'I shall try, father. Thank you for allowing me to share my burdens with the Church of Rome.'

'Come more often, my son, it is most important that you do.'

For the first week, after moving back into the hotel, Dan found it part frustrating, part frightening, to be closely followed everywhere again. In truth, life became intolerably dull. Every morning he would check in at the police station, limp round the crowded city streets with two minders stuck to him like glue, perhaps have his light brown, straight hair cut by a meticulous barber, or sit in the deserted lobby reading and learning from his growing collection of Japanese text-books, maybe go out for lunch, decide to get a shave, sleep all afternoon, fret away the evening and lie awake half the night.

His parents at their tiny tied-cottage on the Steven Estate, his ex- business partner, Dubos, in Sao Paolo, even an old gold mining pal, Robert Weaver in Australia, must have been amazed at the rambling letters he sent – if they ever made it through the notorious Japanese postal system, or were passed by the censors and reached their target.

This inaction was akin to torture. Dan needed to be busy, needed to be achieving. He had never taken holidays – 'What's the point of them?' he'd say. If a week went by without a deal, a contract signed, a sale concluded, he would become depressed, once telling a long- suffering girlfriend 'the problem with religious countries is them closing for the Sabbath. I have an identity crisis every Sunday afternoon.'

But now each day was like an empty Sunday.

He would lie back on his bed, staring at the ceiling and let memories play out like theatre in his mind. He could see the characters, smell their smells, hear them talking, almost touch them.

Like Saphia Maria, a darkly sensuous Brazilian girl, in love with him, but about to be someone else's bride. Saying to him:

'You are one-dimensional, yes?'

And him replying, 'Two.'

She had shaken her head. 'Only business.'

And he laughed. 'Business and women. So two, in that order.' Then she took the cherry from her brandy, sucked it briefly, transferring it as she kissed, allowing him the taste that he soon would lose. 'To love you is to be in a line, I need devotion.'

And then she fled. To what he thought of as ordinariness.

Then there was his ex-boss, Sergei Collumbo in Brisbane, who wore leather from head to toe even in a tropical heatwave, and was more like a gangster than company director, but a business wizard, with scars and bruises from being born, like Dan, in a 'not-one-of-us' foreign gutter.

'We both immigrant, yes, and I tell you, Daniel, a lot of best businessmen are. And we have to learn patience, deals take more time for us. And have to try more hard, but also to be on outside is to see things from a different way, to be independent, not part of the crowd. Remember that phrase, "The Emperor don't wearing any clothes"? Home-grown big guys on the inside, they don't see it, but we do, really useful.'

Dan would even mimic Sergie's accent, and his anecdotes – acting to the ceiling fan.

'My father, God rest his soul, was good businessman but put family first, and you can't do that and shoot the heavens, so he only bit successful, he once said – "Hey, son, don't you go sleeping with different women, in case talk in your sleep, might give family secrets away." Yeah, he really said that. And for years I would leave at midnight, or throw them out – and one day Papa said – "was a joke. No one says any sense in sleep", which saved me packets because I didn't have to book two hotel rooms no more.'

Lying on his hotel bed, Dan laughed at the craziness of

the weird and wonderful characters from his past, but some of the advice was profound.

'One more thing. Stick or twist. Yeah, that's blackjack and all businessmen should play – not for big bucks, 'cos the banks always have better odds, but to understand what's in your spirit, negotiating way. Say you been dealt 16 – you stick or twist? That's always the question. And I tell you – no one knows. No one. But there it is – Queen and six, in your hand. Whatcha gonna do? And though there ain't no answer, there is a tip I can give you, Daniel – might save your fortune, maybe even your life, one day.

'Only twist if you can afford to lose. Otherwise HOLD. Will be less exciting, but let the other guy, or the bank, take the risk. You be thinking for weeks – "What if I had got a five?" but that's loser talk. Loser talk. Because when the bank has sixteen too, they gotta go for twenty-one or bust. But we don't. We can survive until tomorrow, and hope for Ace-Jack. And that what real patience is.'

However much Dan brought these apparitions back to life, played with them, it was only an illusion. He yearned for the real thing. Trapped as he was, there was no work, no deals, to divert his constant anxiety. Although he didn't realise it, business was his displacement therapy, what held him together on lonely, dark nights, but right now – no business. So he was close to falling apart.

And even worse, during all that time, no sign of Ayako.

Dan had caught himself looking out of the window so many times as a car or rickshaw drew up that even the old gardener, resting on his rake handle, had started to look up at him with a sad shake of the head. Was it that obvious?

It was around this time that Dan noticed the ordinary

Japanese he passed in the street were treating him in a different way.

Until late November 1941, they had been curious, might nod in an attempt to offer a friendly acknowledgement; some would stare, little children might even run alongside him calling out a jocular 'hallo'– because he was Western, exotic, different, strange. However, that, too, like the balmy weather, changed to an atmosphere of frosty hostility, of fear, as if his face, his wan colour, his pointed nose, his round blue eyes, his height, even the purposefully battered Panama, was a provocation, and his mere presence a personal threat.

So, now, when he tried to relieve his loneliness by seeking the company of the crowded streets, he felt despised, hated even, for what he represented – more isolated, and nervous, as if taken hostage by this strange and beautiful land. And, as always, where was Ayako? An inveterate, suspicious loner, Dan the ambitious upstart was discovering introspection, and doubts in himself. Maybe he could even tell Saphia Maria, he'd found a third dimension – vulnerability. Because now, for the first time ever, he needed a friend.

LESS THAN A MILE AWAY, Ayako was even more in despair.

Ever since that first morning at the docks, she had desperately tried not to think about Dan as anything other than a duty, and mostly it had worked. Instead, she forced her thoughts to focus only on her role in the war, her work with the Ministry, her country, and, of course, her family – even, unexpectedly, her remote mother Shizuko, who had been only interested in working for the nationalist women's group, Aikoku Fujinkai, winning the Special Merit Badge and the Distinctive Service Medal from the Foreign Ministry, but who now came into her thoughts more and more, along with her jealous sister Michiko. Although like many Japanese young women, Ayako had always hero-worshipped her father, Prof Junichiro, who now seemed too liberal, too old-fashioned for such warlike times, and was becoming... oh, she couldn't say it, even to herself... irrelevant.

She would kneel for what seemed like a hundred hours at the tiny window in her little room above the *shokudo* restaurant, looking out over the children, housewives and handcarts scurrying about in the busy street below, wondering why she was not being asked to 'associate' with Dan. Why did the military no longer need her help?

Instead, for at least a little purpose, she would use the daylight to read and reread the book, gilded and leather-bound, that her father had presented to her that day at the railway station. *The Complete Works of Shakespeare* in Japanese. But that made her even more home- sick for her family, pining for ordinary life at the school, though not the head teacher, Yamamoto Kocho – why did she miss them so? But... no, she wasn't complaining, that wouldn't be appropriate.

After dark, by the light of the dim lamp she had been given, Ayako would give up on Shakespeare and read herself to sleep with the cheap and cheerful women's magazines that had managed to remain in print, especially her favourite advice columnist, Sakamoto Kyoko, who answered letters from readers in 'sadness pits', because the war in China had cut them off from loved ones, especially sons and husbands. Sakamoto Kyoko wrote that good effects would come from good efforts:

'Try not to let your thoughts wander when you have an idle moment. Instead, find things to do that will calm the mind. Write letters to those loved ones you so dearly miss and spill your heart out to your family. However, be mindful of waste and instead of sending these letters, keep them safe in a drawer. The secret drawer of your heart.'

Ayako's first letter was to herself:

Dearest Ayako,

She smiled to herself. She shifted on her knees so that her back was straight and her ink brush was held in the correct position, as her mother had taught, and continued.

She enjoyed the tranquillity she felt as the long, thin brush slid over the delicate paper and wanted to carry on. But then she checked herself and returned to the task in hand. Swapping out her ink brush for the Ministry's pencil, she abandoned her beautiful paper, and let her emotions run free as she scratched wildly with the pencil at her translation pad.

This situation makes me so angry. I have been sent here to work but all I am doing is waiting. Everyone says I must be patient because it is my job and my duty, but patient for what? I explained to them that Lawrence is not only a businessman but someone looking for Japanese secrets. Do they not understand he is a spy? Instead, they tell me he is American so that is to be expected but America is not yet at war with Japan so suspicion is not enough and he must be caught doing it.

She underlined it twice and almost broke the lead.

Doing what? Anyway, now his coffee has been accepted I don't see why they can't send him away so I can return home. I don't want him to be imprisoned or hurt. He is like a naughty best friend. Sometimes he is like Uncle Tanaka and tells jokes and it is difficult not to laugh. He is funny and...

文子へ

この状況は本当に頭にくる。仕事があるからここに来るようにと言われたのに、待てと言うだけで何もすることがない。お務めだから辛抱しなさいと周りは言うけれど、一体何のための辛抱なの？ロレンスは実業家ではあるものの、我が国の極秘情報を探っている男だと説明したのに、スパイだということが彼らにはわからないのだろうか。米国人だから当然秘密情報を漁っているだろうが、米国はまだ我が国とは戦争状態にはないから容疑だけでは逮捕できない。現場を押さえないことには、と彼らは言う。

現場を押さえるって、一体何をしているところを？とにかく、コーヒー受入の件は決着したのだから、彼をここに留めておく理由はないはず。彼を帰国させれば私もうちに帰れる。彼が投獄されたり傷つけられるようなことは嫌だ。彼はやんちゃな親友みたい。三郎叔父さんを思い出させる時があって、彼の冗談にはつい笑ってしまう。面白い人で…。

Her mind drifted off and, with a sigh, she gave up and folded the paper away carefully. It hadn't exactly ended up where she had intended.

THE NEXT LETTER was to her father, in reply to a letter from him, bemoaning the coming war, and questioning if they should respect each other and the family more than the increasingly militaristic state. However, he was sure that censors were opening correspondence, so his writing had to be oblique, with the likelihood of misunderstanding…

My dear Papa,

You taught me to forebear rather than complain and I have learned not to say 'it is wrong' when things cannot be changed. Instead, I react with patience and duty, and treat the situation with respect, as I learned from you. However, I have read your letter a thousand times and still cannot find a way to truly understand.

You quoted Othello and said I must NOT think like Desdemona and make the nation my husband. So I have been reading and reading this passage – there is nothing else to do here – but what I read did not give me comfort.

'My noble father,
I do perceive here a divided duty.
To you I am bound for life and education.
My life and education both do learn me
How to respect you. You are the lord of my duty,
I am hitherto your daughter.

'But here's my husband,
And so much duty as my mother showed
To you, preferring you before her father.
So much I challenge that I may profess
Due to the Moor my lord.'

Do you mean I should not be making Japan the 'lord of my duty', 'preferring' my country before my father?

And who is 'the Moor'? Is he Tojo?

Is that what 'preferring you before her father' means, Papa? If so, I don't like it very much. I liked our peaceful life in Tokyo and Grandma's house in Okinawa.

I think the military people who are in charge of Japan have good intentions but don't understand learning, don't read, don't have culture. Maybe the Englishman does; he's strange. Not educated like you, but not shallow. He says he does not care about his country, but that is a lie. It makes me afraid for him. And also for me. I know what duty is, but what if another part of me has different…?

Again, Ayako veered off the point, towards Dan, becoming incoherent. Anyway, she rarely finished the letters she was never going to send, sometimes because her mind wandered and sometimes because the tears started flowing, not tears of self-pity – although she did feel that way – but tears of utter hopelessness. Mostly, however, she didn't finish because she did not want to face her true feelings. They scared her – worse, they left her ashamed. She was determined, she was not going to be like her mother, with her not-so-secret 'friendship'.

お父様へ

不平を言うよりも耐え忍ぶようにとパパは教えて下さったので、物事を変えようにも変えられないときには「間違っている。」と言わないようにしています。その代わり、パパから教わったように、忍耐強く、お務めを心して対応し、状況を受け入れます。それでも、パパのお手紙は、何回も何回も、繰り返して読んで、読み返しても本当に理解する道が開かれません。

シェイクスピアのオセロを引用して、「絶対にデズデモーナのように考えてはいけない。この国があたかも私の夫であるように考えてはならない。」とおっしゃいました....。ここでは他にすることがないので、この一節を何度も繰り返して読んでみました。でも、心の平和は訪れません。

「お父さま、わたくしの義務は、こゝでは二つになつて居るのでございます。 生《うみ》の御恩、養育の御恩のあるお父様はわたくしの義務の主でおありなさいます。 ですから、それに對してはお父様を第一に尊敬せねばなりません。 これは女《むすめ》としての務めなのでございます。けれども、 今はこゝに夫がをられます、お母様が貴下《あなた》を其お父様以上に大事になされましたと同じに、 わたくしも夫のムーアどのに務めを盡さねばならんと存じまする。」

おっしゃりたいのは、祖国を「わたくしの義務の主」にしないほうがいいですか。代わりにお父様を「大事に」したほうが良いということですか。

「ムーア」は誰になるのでしょう。東條大将でしょうか。

「お母様が貴下を其お父様以上に大事になされました。」とはそういう意味なのですか。パパ、そうなら、私にはあまり良いとは思えません。東京や沖縄のお婆様のおうちでの平和な生活は好きでした。

日本を支配している軍人は、学問に対する理解がないのです。読書もしない教養のない人達です。あのイギリス人は違うかもしれませんね。変わった方です。パパのような学識はないけれど、浅はかでもない。自分の国などどうでもいい、と言っているけれどあれは嘘。あの方の先行きがどうなるかと考えると怖くなります。私の将来も不安です。お務めとは何かはわかっています。もしも、私の中にいる別の私に違った考えがあったら....。

She found a more cheerful correspondent, one who – at least in her own mind – would be more sympathetic.

Dear Uncle,

I am dreadfully sad living here in Nagasaki. People are nice to me, of course, especially the owner of my room, but I'm an outsider and I get lonely. To cheer myself up I think of the fun we would have when you would come to visit us and today I decided to write you a letter. Sometimes I remember you smoking a cigarette the wrong way round, with the burning end in your mouth, and I laugh. I remember you taking me to see Enoken at the cinema and laugh when I remember you knocked the hat off the lady in front and pretended it was the man on your left. And I thought of you the other day when I was talking about seagulls with the English man I have been translating for and told him that they stayed in couples for life but he didn't understand because they were in big flocks, swooping down and attacking people. Are you still doing your Magic tricks? I like the one where you pretend not to hear when someone speaks, like Buster Keaton. Do you still juggle with knives?

Ayako paused her unpunctuated ramble and re-read the scribbled lines. Her heart sank as she realised that the little girl who used to play with Uncle was now grown up and she should be focusing her correspondence on the more important things. She poured herself a little cup of green tea and started a new page.

Uncle, Father said in his last letter that you had joined the military coding team. It sounds like a terribly important job, hiding people's thoughts from others. Fancy! I dream of work like that, but instead I am stuck in this tiny room, suffocated by the acrid factory fumes, and waiting on the Kempeitai *all day who never ask me for…*

三郎叔父様へ

今、長崎にいるのですが、やりきれなく寂しい思いをしています。勿論、とても親切な大家さんをはじめ、皆さんに親切にしていただいています。けれども、私はよそ者なので寂しいばかりです。自分を元気付けるために、叔父様が遊びに来て楽しく過ごした時のことを思い出しています。そこで、今日はお手紙を書くことにしました。

タバコを逆方向に、火のついた方を口にくわえて吸っていらしたことを時々思い出しては笑っています。映画館にエノケンを観に連れて行って下さったことがありましたね。前の席にいるおばさんの帽子を振り落としてしまいましたね。隣の男の人のせいのように見せかけたことを思い出すと笑ってしまいます。この間、私が通訳をしているイギリス人とカモメのことについて話した時、三郎叔父様の言ったことを思い出しました。そこで、「カモメは一生、同じつがいで連れそうのよ。」と言ったら、彼はカモメは大群で生息していて、突然飛んできて人を攻撃するからと、私が言ったことを理解できなかった。

今でも手品をしていらっしゃいますか。人が話しかけているのに、バスター・キートンみたいに聞こえないふりをする。三郎叔父様のあの芸当が好きです。今でもナイフでジャグリングをなさいますか。

お父様の最近のお手紙に、叔父様は暗号部隊に入隊されたとありました。ものすごく重要なお仕事のようですね。考えていることを他の人にわからないように隠すなんて、想像もつきません。私もそんなお仕事ができたらと思っているのに、この三畳部屋にとじ込められて工場の煤煙が鼻に突くようで息もできないありさま。しかも、一日中憲兵が来るのを待って、そのあげく…。

Ayako put her pencil down and lay back on the *tatami* mats, watching as the pale moonlight caught the bare branches of the tree outside and cast hazy theatrical shadows on the paper *shoji* window. Still only eight p.m., maybe she would try to sleep. How her life was being wasted, why was she stuck in this backwater city, why couldn't she do important work, why couldn't she help them deal with *him*?

As she watched the shadows jigger and flit, like the lurking baddies in a silent Chaplin movie, she could see a figure, a shadow boxer, it was almost hypnotising her. First a plane, swooping, then a dancer, then a—

Her thoughts were interrupted by a commotion from downstairs, inside the restaurant, shouting, banging, furniture crashing, a *saké*-induced fight maybe? *How…?* she thought, *how do I know where my duty lies?* She stood, pulled the mismatched curtains firmly closed and lay back. Somehow the dark made it easier to hear.

'You leave her alone!' The muffled voices of the restaurant owners worked their way through the thick *tatami*.

'The girl has been unwell!' A shrill, middle-aged voice, undoubtedly the owner's wife. 'Anyway, hasn't she done enough of this now?'

A guttural scream rose up in response and was followed by a stinging slap, then a sound like smacked meat, tables overturning and a pleading yelp from the owner, before a deeper voice of authority put a crashing end to the affair.

The last few words were mumbled and Ayako heard the wooden door slide open then shut, more loudly than usual. The restaurant went deathly quiet for a few minutes, before the usual banter resurfaced, although with an undertone of outrage. But as the familiar murmur and clatter of boxes and bowls lulled Ayako into a fitful sleep, she turned over with a sigh of excitement. That was most definitely the *Kempeitai* coming for her. For the first time in weeks she might be needed.

The next morning, when Ayako entered the restaurant for breakfast dressed appropriately again in her dark knee-length skirt and white blouse, her face scrubbed and her hair drawn back tightly over her head, the whole room fell quiet.

Glancing at the owner's wife, who had a wide yellow bruise across her cheek, she lowered her head and walked to her spot at the busy end of the counter. Behind her sat the tall young *Kempei* and his older boss, who had spotted the chance of a good breakfast and insisted they come in early.

The few locals who had dared return simply watched. They felt no need to talk as they'd already gobbled up all the gossip, not to mention the embellishments, that had flown round their little community the night before. Comments and speculation could come later.

Ayako's only words that morning, as she forced herself to remain calm and to eat every last grain of her breakfast, were 'thank you' and 'sorry'. When finished she straightened her back, walked slowly to the *Kempei's* table and bowed.

The senior *Kempei* said, 'You must come and see the Major. He has a plan from Tokyo concerning Lawrence. It is very important.'

Ayako bowed again, deeply. She stared at the floor, careful to show none of the excitement she felt as she considered his words and glimpsed the possibility that she might just have purpose again, and through that purpose, status.

AYAKO ASKED HIM, 'Have you ever been in love?'

Dan teased her with a cryptic answer. 'To an extent.'

'What does that mean?'

He was sitting on the harbour wall, feet dangling over the bay, sideways from her, enjoying talking without the distraction of her beautiful face, the high cheekbones, the soft lips and the dark, dark eyes.

'Never been head-over.'

'Head-over?'

'Heels.'

'"Heels"?' She was confused, though this was obviously important, because he was being honest – well, maybe.

Dan laughed, apologetic, realising he was confusing her. 'What I mean is never completely in love. Don't think I can. Get hurt, you know.'

'You would not die for love?'

He didn't reply because they both knew the answer. Of course not.

'And you?' he asked, still looking out at the bay.

'It would be selfish,' she replied, 'much too selfish, but I will die for love.'

'Really?' Then he picked her up on her grammar. '"Will"?' She smirked to herself, and he noticed, because he was now turned to her, watching her hesitate, staring out at the bay, mouth softly opening, her tongue licking her top lip, paused in thought. 'I... would die for Japan, my country.'

Of course, he knew that. Or it's what they say, but she'd changed the tense. 'Before you said "will",' he pushed, then immediately regretted it.

Ayako looked down at her fingers, twisting, fiddling, picking. She wished he would not be so relentless. A single tear welled up in her right eye and rolled down to her mouth, which she licked sharply away as if it, too, was traitorous.

'You *will* not know, not care,' she said staring into the distance, out across the bay – he was nothing, without beliefs, without a home… She had changed the tense again, and with that, the whole meaning. 'It is best way to die. For love.'

Enough, he thought. 'I just want to live.'

'So, you will die inside.' Then she changed tense yet again. 'Already dead.'

At last, she turned to him. Dan had the slightest hint of a smile. 'It's not going to be easy, your love affair,' he said.

She frowned. 'What do you mean?'

'Your love affair with Japan. Your guys aren't kidding, you're looking for war. Was in *The Japan Times and Advertiser*. Japan feels left out, with the rest of the world fighting each other. Want your share.'

Ayako turned back to the bay, folded and then unfolded her arms, unsure whether she should let him into her thoughts. They were so different, yet so similar. How could that be? She sighed, what was it about him? Such self-possessed judgement, so little doubt. The world would always be his, not hers. She dipped her head slightly and looked away from him like a *geisha* – thinking of herself like a *geisha*, or a tiny fragile porcelain doll, to be picked up, and used by others.

She looked further into the early evening sky and mouthed silently, in English, 'fragile.' She frowned to herself again. Of course she was not fragile, except… except…

She turned back to find Dan staring at her neck, and she blushed. Then he broke all the rules. Unable to control himself in the moment, Dan reached over and took her hand in his, and lifting it up to his mouth, he kissed it.

From their vantage point high on the roof of the old

Hongkong and Shanghai Bank building, the *Kempei* observers put down their binoculars and nodded to each other. *The Major will be very pleased.* They must inform Tokyo immediately, by coded message.

WITHIN A MATTER OF DAYS, that message had been intercepted by two code-breaking operators, separated by five thousand miles, and a universe of culture, with very different attitudes to the couple.

The first led to a meeting at a little bar on the outskirts of Hosei University, Tokyo.

Uncle Saburo Tanaka had asked to visit his brother-in-law, Junichiro Okunaga, saying that Ayako was wrapped up in a fiendish, dangerous plot.

Professor Junichiro Okunaga was breathing air into a mouthful of Johnny Walker, a blatant indulgence in 1941 Japan. 'I am not surprised, but what is there to do? I asked for them to release Ayako, they said they'd think about it. Got Baron Mitsui to write – remember him at Hosei? – the coal king of Fukuoka, but even his authority hasn't worked.'

Saburo expected his brother-in-law's cynicism, but was not there to be sensitive. 'You could talk to her mother. I hear she has influence at the Ministry of Foreign Affairs.'

Junichiro laughed sardonically. 'Influence? Is that what they call it these days? You don't need to use code with me.'

They shrugged at each other. Saburo now had permission to discuss the usually undiscussable. 'Well, Shizuko has "direct access" to the Deputy Minister… or is it the other way round?' He laughed at his own joke.

Junichiro cackled back, 'So I hear.' He swilled another slug of Johnny Walker around the glass. 'I have talked to her, husband to wife, father to mother. And explained the dangers. But it makes Shizuko proud to have a daughter working for the military police. Perhaps she also might receive a medal one day. Damn it.' His empty glass hit the bar table a little too hard.

'And you, my brother-in-law the esteemed professor?'

'The coming war is an abomination. A tragedy worthy of Shakespeare. I had thought only sons would be sacrificed to stupidity, but fate is not like that.'

'It is not like you to give up.'

'I am of no consequence any more, likewise the University, or our faction. I used to hope, but now even that is gone. All we have left is that mercy will prevail. Otherwise, there is nothing to be done.'

Prof Junichiro raised his empty glass for another Johnny Walker. 'So, to you dear Saburo. Are you still persecuted for being what you are?'

'Not so much. Out of our section of twenty-two, at least three are likewise. The best three. It is our joke. Having to live a coded-life has trained us to see so many hidden meanings, to know where every coded secret is buried. Especially with the Bolsheviks, where fear of deviant discovery is the only currency.' He giggled. 'So much of warmongering is about old men's hidden perversities. What they can't do must be forbidden to others, through unspoken ways. In the West, it's religion; in Russia, it's the Party; here – it's jealousy of what they do in the west.'

'And you've got a ringside seat.'

He nodded. 'And you, dear Jun, the mutinous professor, must never let them hear, or see, or read, what you think, about how wrong and stupid they are.'

Junichiro shrugged. 'They already know what I think, and I don't care. Nor do they.'

FIVE THOUSAND MILES AWAY, the Head of Naval Intelligence in Washington, the code-breaker, Admiral Byron Pearce, paid an urgent visit to the President's intelligence gatekeeper, Abe Ford.

There was virtually no ceremony. Both were busy men. Admiral Pearce came straight to the point.

'Abe, your man in Nagasaki is in danger. Can he be warned?'

Abe Ford didn't ask how this was known – Ford was one of fewer than twenty people who knew the Japanese Imperial code had been broken.

'He cannot.'

'Could you not *pray* for him?'

'Not even that, Byron, the Vatican goes only one way.'

They sat in silence for perhaps half a minute. 'In my experience, praying doesn't work anyway. Faith? Ah, that's a different matter, and not in the church. I have faith in *our man*.'

Byron Pearce seemed entirely unconvinced.

'Tell me why.'

Ford held up his fingers, and began to count. 'Born survivor, no scruples, no morality.'

Now Pearce nodded. 'Perfect agent.'

Ford shook his head. 'No loyalty. Not to country or creed. But…'

Pearce could hardly wait.

'Smart as a whip, and desperate for success.' Ford reached into his pocket, and pulled out a five-dollar note. 'This is what he's loyal to, why he's gone, and why he'll make it back.'

After the Admiral had departed, Ford sat for a long time staring out of the blast-proof windows that faced onto the reflecting pool and the side of the Lincoln Memorial. The threat to Lawrence was yet another sign that the Pacific war was coming real soon. As the US embargo and sanctions had bitten deep, Imperial Japan had gone from sulky, to persecuted, to fanatical, to preparing, to warlike, to committed – past the point of no return. From defensive to attack mode.

'It's a-coming, sure is,' Ford said to himself. 'Only question is when? And where?'

4

THERE HAVE BEEN millions of words, many books, many theses, written about whether President Franklin D. Roosevelt knew about the Pearl Harbour attack in advance, that he allowed several battleships, cruisers and thousands of sailors to be bombed as a matter of political expediency.

The Japanese attack came at 7:48 a.m. on Sunday 7th December 1941, local Hawaii time – 12:18 in Washington, just as the politicians in the White House were beginning to think about lunch. In all, 353 fighters, dive bombers, torpedo bombers and five submarines, damaged or sunk all eight US Battleships, three Cruisers, three Destroyers, and killed 2,393 Americans.

The Japanese had not declared war in advance, perhaps due to a series of deceits by the Imperial Navy and Army, who wrote at the time, 'Our deceptive diplomacy is steadily proceeding towards success.' The day after the attack, Roosevelt addressed Congress, describing December 7th as 'a date which will live in infamy', mainly because of the treachery of such an act while still engaged in diplomatic negotiations, and without declaring war.

But the Americans had broken the Imperial code, using a decryption process code-named Magic, and were able to read all messages sent by Tokyo to their Embassy in Washington DC. The question therefore is – was the Japanese Embassy warned?

It is known the warlike Imperial Government had sent a 14-part communiqué to their Embassy on the Saturday afternoon before the attack, holding two parts back, and that the bellicose language should have alerted the US code-breakers; but did the Defence/State Department urgently pass the decoded messages forward on that fateful Saturday evening, or was it bureaucratically buried to allow Roosevelt a full night's sleep?

Theories that the President *did* know in advance are based more on the politics of treachery, or perhaps the treachery of politics, than any historical evidence: Roosevelt wanted America to enter the war – he saw it as inevitable – however there was no consensus in Congress for such a defining step. But a 'cowardly' attack on the US Navy at Pearl Harbour, without warning, would sweep away the doubters once and for all, and Roosevelt would have his war.

Given that's what happened, the conspiracy theorists point to the inevitability that the Japanese would have informed their DC Embassy, and that using Magic the US cyphers had cracked the code and therefore Roosevelt *must* have been warned – QED, and there was treachery on both sides.

But – was Roosevelt warned? We will never know.

These historic events had not quite come to pass by the end of the first week of December 1941, when the lanky Japanese bellboy unexpectedly knocked on Dan's door very late – in fact almost midnight – and enticed him down to the deserted Nagasaki Grand Hotel reception, smiling and gesturing the whole way.

Even the usually caustic receptionist bowed with a friendly smile and handed over a small parcel wrapped in a thin, patterned fabric, fastened at the top with a neat knot.

'Some medicines… I think your leg?'

From the wrapping Dan didn't need to guess who it was from, and though surprised, he smiled back, bowed, and limped up the stairway to open it in the privacy of his room.

Sitting on the bed, he held the small, elegantly-prepared package, and pulled gently on one of the ties. The silky material drifted away from the contents, falling into his lap in the same way Ayako's kimono sleeves had fallen and folded in the restaurant – almost like a bird unfolding its wings.

In the centre, a tiny, carefully wrapped slice of Castella cake lay snuggled next to some packets of powder tied with a bow, accompanied by a thin slip of paper on which she had written from top to bottom in ornate, beautiful calligraphy a single line of flowing text for the most common sentiment in the history of the world, and one which Dan recognised from his Japanese textbooks:

(愛してます) – *Aishitemasu* – I LOVE YOU

He drew in a ragged breath, trying to steady himself, then shook his head – this was too much.

Underneath the love-note a turquoise, unsealed envelope, which he opened nervously.

It is very dangerous for you to stay Dan-san, I told them this was medicine for the pain in your leg.

Do you remember the little restaurant, Namihei, where I sleep? Eat lunch in Namihei tomorrow.

The owners are friendly – they do not like your bodyguards – what they say, you must do. I will be nearby.

Dan put down the note and stared out at the bay. 'Stick or Twist?' That eternal conundrum of blackjack. If he stays, she's right, it could be very dangerous – and more dangerous every day. If he accepts her offer and twists, she'll be in danger, too.

Stick or twist?

Then, from somewhere in another universe, the clock on the old Hongkong and Shanghai Bank tower clunked midnight, Sunday 7th December, a ridiculous sign of normality in the crazy, gathering storm of war.

THE NAMIHEI *SHOKUDO* restaurant was bustling as usual. No sooner had one person left, than another two seemed to enter and, while Dan's arrival was noted, his presence seemed to be more of a nuisance than anything.

He looked over the low tables, packed with customers, heads bowed, shovelling their food down at breakneck speed. Every now and again a shout would go up, the owner would throw back a loud '*hoy*!' and briefly tear his attention from the stove to acknowledge their thanks. Downing chopsticks, the leaving customer would swap out with the next arrival, giving the owner's wife the almost impossible task of receiving payment, taking an order, clearing the table and delivering the next order all at the same time. Dan stood by Ayako's spot at the end of the counter watching the spectacle, waiting for a break in the flow, increasingly aware from the furtive glances in his direction that something was afoot.

The biggest change, Dan noted, was that the scowling *Kempei* minders had gone, replaced with a slightly more pleasant-looking municipal policeman, who seemed to know the owners of the *shokudo*, and happily plonked himself down on a bench outside the entrance door with a packet of cigarettes, rather than ostentatiously bullying his way inside and onto the table next to Dan's.

As soon as Mrs Matsuo got a minute, she directed Dan to take a seat by the stairs, where the outside minder couldn't see him. Having grown used to the fracas, he opened his well-worn Japanese phrasebook, painstakingly worked out what was on the hand-written menu – and waited for Ayako to show.

Finally, when there was a lull in the comings and goings, and the lunch crowd were head down in rice and noodles and vegetables, Mrs Matsuo walked over to Dan with two large black bento lunch boxes stacked one on top of the other. Without a word, she nodded to Dan, and, shuffling down the endless side-corridor, launched herself breathlessly up the narrow wooden stairway. Without hesitating and, as unobtrusively as possible, Dan grabbed his book, slid off his shoes at the little raised entrance to the corridor, and followed.

On the first floor, away from the monthly rental rooms

running the length of the corridor to the front of the building, they passed the family apartment, then a tiny alcove on a landing crammed with bowls, old bento boxes, cleaning equipment and piles of noodles and rice. Then finally they came to a halt by a door leading to the room over the restaurant that her son used to occupy.

The lady put the boxes on the floor, opened a flimsy door which led into a tiny room, and gestured Dan to pass. Her face was void of emotion as she handed across the tray, and stepped back before melting away, unnoticed by Dan, who had glimpsed inside the room, and couldn't take his eyes off the beauty before him.

Ayako was kneeling on the *tatami* mat, wearing an ornate silk robe tied in a bow under her bust, open at the neck. Most remarkable, though, was her hair, lit from the brittle early-afternoon sun flickering through the small window, black and straight and luscious, flowing down to her waist, the first time he had seen it free.

Without looking at him, she placed a little table into the middle of the room, took the boxes and got out some tea cups. Dan, uncertain where to sit in a confined space, which was obviously nothing more than a lady's bedroom, finally knelt down, wincing at the pain from his leg as he did so.

'Please,' she said, giving him her thin, square cushion and gesturing to him to sit on her folded futon bedding, 'I am used to.'

As he sat, their eyes met. Dan reached across the table and took her hand, not wanting to look away.

'Not sure I want to eat,' he croaked, almost unable to speak.

She was more confident, serene. 'You must. Because you should be strong.'

He found his voice, partly through anger. 'For what? To stay in a God-forsaken hotel, with nothing to do? Waiting around for some goons to arrest me?'

She slipped her hand out from his and resumed fussing over the lunch arrangements, using the chopsticks as a distraction, to give herself time. 'I agree, we must escape.'

Now it was said. 'We' must escape.

'Escape where?'

'To my grandmother's house. She lives in Okinawa. Very quiet.'

'When?'

'Tonight. One hour after midnight. There is a tuna boat leaving.'

For a while he didn't answer, sitting awkwardly, trying not to slide off the large, sloping wad of bedding pressed up against the wall. There was too much to consider, too many questions, and it wasn't his idea.

Ayako dropped some noodles into the miso soup, stirred it with her chopsticks, and moved it towards his mouth, as if feeding a baby, unexpectedly intimate. He tasted, tilted his head backwards and swallowed.

'Thanks,' he murmured, overcome, again unsure what to say.

'I am good *mama-san*, no?'

'The best,' he grinned back, as she continued stirring, ready for the next mouthful.

He put his hand up for her to stop, gently, not wanting to offend. 'Ayako, why would you risk everything – even your life – for me?'

Ayako bowed her head, still looking at the miso soup, a frown surfacing on her silky skin. 'I wrote you why.' She meant the message on the parchment paper. He felt his heart twisting in his chest. He folded his arms and shook his head, and to her surprise and his, closed his eyes to hide the tears.

'Sorry, it doesn't feel right. Putting a girl – you – in danger.' His tears were flowing, so unexpected for both of them.

She put down the chopsticks, leaned over to him, slid the table from between them, and kissed his cheek, his mouth, his ear, his neck. Backed against the wall there was no room to retreat, and didn't want to even if he could. The initiative changed as lust took over, and he reached for her, kissing her face furiously, tenderly, deeply until, whimpering, she quietly surrendered. But then her turn to pull back, to seem uncertain.

'Promise me...'

'Promise what...?' Dan was now beyond easy self-control, trying to sweep the bento boxes and food aside with his knees, opening the bow of her robe, edging on top of her.

'Promise... that you will come tonight... for make our escape... at the harbour... where the seagulls sleep.'

'If that's what you want...'

'Say *yakusoku*. "Promise"...'

His hand was inside her robe, her eyes were closed. Maybe she couldn't stop now, either.

'*Hai*,' he grunted, opening her robe completely, cupping her breast, astonished at how beautiful and soft and silky and open she was. 'Where the seagulls sleep...'

And the last thing he remembered Ayako gasping as he arched tenderly above her, among the lunch boxes was, 'I never did... before...'

As Dan made his way along the darkening, crowded streets, back toward the hotel, the atmosphere had changed, yet again.

Firecrackers were being thrown into the air, groups of people were dancing in circles, shouting and singing, pointing to the sky happily, fists raised militaristically, shouting '*Shinju-wan*.'

'Shinju-wan*?' What's that?* he thought, trying to weave through the throng, while cute Japanese children began aggressively chanting at him – '*Paaru Haabaa, Paaru Haabaa, Paaru Haabaa*.'

He smiled at them, and repeated back, confused, hoping to fob them off by joining in their little game. *'Pa-haa-baa'* - and they laughed raucously before forming a ring, spinning round, and chanting louder and louder, '*Paaru Haabaa, Paaru Haabaa, Paaru Haabaa*.'

The old municipal policeman grinned and laughed along with them, throwing himself into the role of body-guard, gesturing to them not to be excessive. But still Dan had no idea what was going on, what or why they were celebrating, and why he was not just involved, but the centre of the street's whole exalted attention.

He turned a corner into the marketplace, where the party was even larger, with a procession of men wearing the usual mish-mash of loose-fitting kimono, western hats and clattering along in wooden *geta*, parading Japanese flags, while a small band played and replayed Kimigayo, the Japanese national anthem.

He walked on, feeling more and more alien with each step, pausing frequently to stop and check his beige cotton jacket, Panama hat and dark trousers, in a shop window, in a bid to quell the increasing feeling of paranoia brought on by their pointing, jibes, cheering and leering.

But then an exuberant teenage paper-seller waved a fresh-off-the-press single page *go-gai* extra in the air, and thrust the special edition of the *Nagasaki Shimbun* at him with such excitement that Dan started fishing in his pockets for a coin, but the boy just shook his head and passed the sheet over with a hoot of triumph. The banner headline was 戦争 – War – and underneath *Shinju-wan*, above photos and maps from Hawaii of American battleships in ruins.

'Paaru Haabaa' the newspaper vendor shouted triumphantly as he walked off, and although Dan still didn't understand, he knew that somehow everything had changed – from skulking in the shadows he now seemed to find himself caught in the limelight, bang on the front line. Bizarrely, his minder, the old municipal policeman slapped him on the back, a friendly gesture, and shouted '*ikimasho*,' – let's go – shepherding him out of the square before the crowd's joy turned *gaijin* ugly.

Back at the hotel, smoothing out the single sheet, Dan laid the paper on his bed and tried to pick out some familiar kanji, but the densely packed text was almost indecipherable. If his understanding of the detailed map was at all accurate, and if it was to be believed, the news was terrible. In the end he gave up and slunk back downstairs to seek the help of the ever-present senior manager, who might be able to offer a basic translation and, if his suspicions were true, some hint of sympathy.

'I can only say, Lawrence-san, that *Shinju-wan* means "Pearl Bay".'

Twenty minutes later, having worked their way painstakingly through the single page article, Dan had learned that, 'The American fleet had been destroyed, several battleships had been sunk, and an aircraft carrier or two, Japan would rule the Pacific Ocean, the US could no longer bully a peaceful nation with sanctions.' Japan was now at war with America and his adopted country Britain.

Dan was an enemy alien, in a country at war.

Trudging back to his room, he threw the crumpled paper onto his neatly-made bed and flopped down beside it, staring at the ceiling. *Christ! What a day!*

He was being enticed to take the biggest personal risk of his life; Japan was now at war with his own nation; and he had experienced the greatest passion and love-making of his life with the most attractive, exciting, entrancing woman he had ever met. *Jeez.* He sniggered. 'Lewd thoughts' had vividly become 'sins of the flesh'. In spite of everything, this final thought made him snort. He'd already decided it was time to visit Father Luigi again, although not for God's purpose. For a moment he became almost hysterical at the juxtapositions, and then calmed down.

Was he really going to take the greatest risk of his life?

Dan looked at his watch, then went back to staring at the ceiling.

Yes, he was.

There was a mountain of stuff to get through before the hour-after-midnight deadline down at the docks, 'where the seagulls sleep'. He smiled. Time for action, time to go…

AYAKO TOO WAS STARING at the ceiling, as she lay, dressed in sober khaki, on the *tatami* mats. She felt somehow that what had happened that afternoon had changed her, but she was not sure how, nor did she know what had become of her country, or what would follow. The only thing for certain – she was now a woman, no longer a girl.

It was not how she expected. Dan was insistent, but tender, too. He held her with love, more kisses than could ever be imagined, and how he talked, in between the passion, about his hopes for the future, about wanting a family when he would settle down. Maybe that was a lie, said to all the girls, but wasn't she lying, too? This thought made her groan at the untidiness, the inconvenience, of life.

After Dan had gone, Ayako gradually became aware of the growing commotion outside and of the shouts of '*Shinju-wan*' from the streets below. She had wandered down to the kitchen to discover the owner's wife in tears, clutching a photo of her son to her chest and mumbling. Her husband, meanwhile, matter-of-factly relayed the news of the Imperial Navy's attack on the American fleet and of the declaration of war as he busied himself with preparations for the evening influx.

Overwhelmed, Ayako started to cry. Her body still resonated from Dan's touch, while her mind now pictured him as one of the dead sailors, driven helplessly down below the merciless waves of *Shinju-wan*. Or perhaps – the thought shot through her – perhaps Dan *was* the enemy, *her* enemy, now, and he deserved to die. She was so confused. Did she feel shamed, or fulfilled? Was she betrayed or was she betraying?

There was only one thing Ayako knew for certain. For better or worse, she had done what she had been ordered to do.

She straightened her shoulders, and walked over to her spot at the counter, grabbing a handful of chopsticks so she could refill the boxes on the tables. Mrs Matsuo had dried her eyes, restored her son's photo to its place next to the family shrine, and returned to doing the accounts. She glanced over at Ayako with an expression of – 'So, did the plan work?'

Ayako may simply have been a lodger, but as she was the same age as her only son, it seemed natural to Mrs Matsuo to offer her maternal support. She certainly didn't agree with the situation, but after the violence of the *Kempeitai*, she had resigned herself to it and felt the same concern a mother would the first night after a chaste daughter's arranged wedding.

Ayako nodded in reply, but more in common politeness than in acknowledgement of the unspoken question. She slipped out of the restaurant and looked up and down the street. It was calmer now, with men in groups in the shadow of shop fronts talking to each other sombrely, perhaps beginning to come to grips with the fact that there would be a reckoning with America.

Why did I cry? Ayako wondered, shivering slightly as she stood in the open doorway. She watched a gaggle of schoolchildren going by, all talking at once, and she knew the answer. There are some things about a person, about life, that should be too valuable to be given away, to be traded, even on behalf of the nation.

But those were the feelings of the innocent girl she had once been – the girl moulded by her liberal father's delight in the love spoken of so beautifully by his darling Shakespeare. But the woman she now was knew – however much it broke a little bit of her heart – that this world was too hard, too cruel for such sentiments.

Two ragged old men staggered past, arms around each other, sipping from bottles of meth-style spirits, which they raised to her as if a toast, and shouted '*Kampai.*' She returned their pleasantries with an empty smile, grateful they were unaware of the thoughts and feelings battling inside her. She leaned back in the shadows and felt the tears dry on her cheeks. No more crying. What was the use?

'I will think what I have to; must weigh the good and bad, my own beliefs, my family, my country, my Emperor – and then must do what I am told.'

WHEN DAN CREPT down to the lobby the old municipal policeman was slumped forward in a lounge chair, head resting on his chest, snoring gently, a stone bottle of *shochu* on the floor by his side. The reception counter was unmanned – but he could hear the muted sounds of agitated voices in the back office, so he tiptoed quietly outside.

The firecrackers had stopped, with only the occasional ship's horn hooting in celebration as he walked down to the rickshaw station at the end of The Bund.

'I'll hire you for the evening,' he told the lone runner, who smirked as he bowed too low for it to be sincere. America had just been defeated, their navy destroyed, he might take Dan's money, but the *gaijin's* honour was gone. However, he was also too conditioned by a lifetime of service to be impolite.

'*Kashikomarimashita* – at your service,' he mumbled.

'Tour the town awhile. Anywhere you feel like going.'

The rickshaw runner hesitated, then turned and headed down a gentle slope to the river and towards the eastern temple area – an easy jaunt. Another confusing

Westerner! – but then their navy lies at the bottom of the Pacific…

Dan checked the rear window several times as the rickety carriage lurched along, but the street was empty – his minders were busy elsewhere, celebrating. Leaning through the musty curtains he tapped the runner's ragged shoulder. 'Now up to the Church of Our Lady in Urakami.' The runner sighed at the thought of the steep hill, and turned. *So much for 'anywhere'.*

On their arrival at the church, he handed the breathless driver ten sen, and spoke in pigeon Japanese. 'Will be ten more when I return. Bad news, I will pray – Return in some hours.'

The driver understood and almost smiled at Dan's discomfort. 'I will wait.'

The deserted church felt eerie and winter cold as Dan pushed through the heavy bronze doors. Instead of turning to a pew and kneeling in prayer, he walked briskly down the wooden aisle, veered left before the marble altar, and marched immediately out through a side door, across an overgrown terrace on the far side, hidden from the front. Then, down the rounded grassy slope and onto the path which would take him back towards the blacked-out city. Not only was he free, he had an alibi.

The wire fences and watchtowers of the Mitsubishi Ordnance Works stood out harshly against the lighter dark of the cloudy sky, but three hundred yards to the left, the two-storey wooden buildings of the Research and Design department were completely deserted, summing up for Dan the bureaucratic nature of Japanese security in this closed society – they'd keep an eye on suspicious people, but not guard important buildings. While the authorities insisted on half a dozen men to 'supervise' a single Westerner, a crucial centre of military research was not being monitored. *Tonight,* thought Dan, *might be their undoing.*

The third set of neglected wooden shutters groaned open on rusty hinges, and the thin wire-mesh behind was designed for repelling insects rather than burglars, so the bottom left corner peeled back easily. Dan scrambled inside. The break-in was so ridiculously easy that he became suspicious – had 'they' out-thought him, and laid a trap?

He stood panting for several seconds, identifying all the regular creaks and bangs of the deserted building. Anything different from that pattern would stand out immediately. Turning back to the window from inside the building, he closed the shutters and flattened back the mesh.

The thin beam of his pen-torch flicked around the store room, hitting cardboard boxes, piles of stationery, startling a spider or two. *No clues here.* Across to the door. *Ah-ha! A long, low- ceilinged corridor… but, not too fast.* He found he was sweating in spite of the chilly night air. It was time for another long listen. *Good, not a sound.*

Across the corridor the flash-light found a paper name plate, 'Room 19, secretary to Dr Nomura' – whoever he might be. Dan began searching on the ground floor, unravelling the Kanji name-plate on each without luck, but up the creaking wooden stairs, the fifth door yielded the name he sought. 'Dr Kado, Head of Wave Motion and Fluidity.' Dry mouthed, he squeezed the handle… 'Damn! It's locked!'

A choice – force the door or search for a key? *What's the time? Five past ten. Allow ten minutes.* A nervy, creaky walk down to the reception desk in the bare entrance lobby, where the right-hand drawer was an Aladdin's cave of personal keepsakes, but, in the left, a jumble of keys and labels, impossibly mixed. *No choice, try them all.*

Upstairs again. First a listen – all still quiet. The keys were counted, forty-one in all. Then the laborious process of trying each one. Some didn't fit, others, almost – but not quite – clicked round. Then, number twenty-nine turned, and the door swung open. The discarded keys were replaced in the reception desk before the office search began.

Hmm, he thought, *what am I looking for?* In truth, Dan did not exactly know – so first a ransack around the austere office to see what was available. Two four-drawer wooden filing cabinets – locked by a bar along the side. A main office desk – unlocked. And, yes, inside – the keys to the cabinets. A drawing board with several sheets of sketch paper. A six-shelf plan-chest – unlockable. Yet another listen. Still eerily silent. *Good.*

On the second shelf of the plan-chest he struck gold – sectional drawings of a long tube- shaped object which could only be the design of a naval torpedo. The sketch was incomplete, but on the bottom in pencil was a Japanese name and number. Now across to the cabinets, to unravel the filing system.

The first bulging blue file which he chose, solved the problem. The entire drawer was devoted to one subject – the No. 93 Torpedo. Dan rifled through, then sat and thought for a while. Doctor Kado was an academic boffin, so most of his work would be theoretical research. What Dan needed, the actual dimensions and production, would be designed elsewhere. However, in the great tradition of Japanese team efficiency, a copy would certainly be stored in these files. In fact, as he discovered a few minutes later, Dr Kado had several copies of the full design plan. Dimensions, power, explosive capacity, manufacturing manifest – in fact everything knowable about the No. 93 Torpedo, each fifteen-page document updating the last.

Dan unclipped the second most recent full set of plans, slipped them under the elastic at the back of his underpants, put every item in the office back to its original position, locked the door, jumbled up the keys in the reception desk while stealing a large buff envelope, then calmly let himself out by the automatically re-locking front entrance.

It was nearly eleven o'clock; he must return to the deserted Cathedral and the confessional for a final solitary visit.

The driver was dozing on the seat of the rickshaw with his feet up. 'Back to the hotel,' Dan shouted, rousing him with a start. As the sleepy runner pulled away, it started to rain.

ON DIFFERENT SIDES of the city, as Nagasaki headed towards midnight on the most momentous day in Japanese history, two very different people, who had been bound together in passionate love-making just ten hours earlier, each contemplated the next few hours with extreme anxiety and suspicion.

Ayako looked at her watch every five minutes as she paced up and down the quayside, watching the little wooden fishing boats raise their heavy off-white sails in the moonlight, wending their way slowly out of the harbour, as they left for another long night of fishing.

Dan packed his few possessions in the metal trunk,

chucking them in at haste, and slammed the lid shut with a satisfying clack. He went out onto the terrace to watch the rain sweep across the bay for the last time, no lights on the ships, now the war with America had begun.

As midnight beckoned, Ayako sat on a bollard near the seagulls, remembering when she'd been there with Dan before, thinking of her mad uncle Saburo working now for the Government's code service, her mind awash with fears of treachery and aggression. Would the authorities have accepted 'the deviant personal life of her uncle' if he wasn't so clever, so useful? She sighed, uncertain about that side of him anyway.

They each heard midnight chiming. The Prefecture clock proclaiming the hour down by the docks, the Hongkong and Shanghai bank clunking its way into a new day up by the hotel. No longer the day of *Shinju-wan* – it was now the day after, and there were dues to pay, the hangover had begun. Ayako sniffed in the gloom, aware of many eyes watching her.

That night, timing was everything.

At exactly half-past twelve, Dan limped down the wide staircase for the last time, stuttered a sudden goodbye to the hotel staff, and requested in pigeon Japanese that the tricky receptionist send his trunk on later.

He gave a curt bow, as if this was to be expected, and disappeared into the back office. The elderly manager, still wearing his immaculate morning-suit, appeared and went to great pains to stress in slow but impeccable English that he understood, of course – however inconvenient the hour, that in the circumstances his guest had to check out. But 'despite the troubled times, the Nagasaki Grand Hotel would be delighted to welcome him back, should he be presented with the opportunity.'

They bowed to each other, genuinely sorry to be parting, and the manager went back into his office.

The receptionist and Dan looked over at the old municipal policeman, who had moved to the garden room earlier in the evening and was now lying flat on his back on the *tatami* mat with the sliding door wide open. Both instinctively knew he was only pretending to be asleep. The snoring was too peaceful, regular, and there was none of the dribble, or the disgusting rattle that had accompanied his previous, genuine slumber.

'Umm,' Dan grunted, with a knowing smile.

The receptionist shrugged inscrutably, and waved at the exit, encouraging, meaning – 'if Dan just wanted to leave the hotel secretly, unseen, it was alright by him.'

But confounding as ever, Dan walked over to the garden room and, sliding back the door a little, slammed it, forcing the policeman to pretend to snap awake, with a fussy, exaggerated air of grievance.

'Would you escort me to Kanko-dori Police Station, please,' Dan said in excellent Japanese, because he'd been rehearsing it all evening.

For a fleeting moment the policeman's deadpan expression deserted him, and the confused, gaping mouth returned, but then it was '*Hai*,' and business as usual – except for an almost imperceptible exchange of confounded glances with the young receptionist.

Dan realised that the municipal policeman and the receptionist were in on some kind of tricky game together – no matter what the circumstances, both were team-Japan first.

Having dispensed with the annoyance of attending to

the *gaijin* so late, the policeman beamed as he laced up his boots. This unforeseen change of plan would make his Sergeant's night.

———

WHERE DO *the seagulls go to sleep?* Ayako wondered, her heels kicking against the massive iron bollard, as she glanced at her watch for the tenth time in as many minutes. She looked about. Where was he?

The skipper of the tuna boat was now impatient and wailed at Ayako in his slow, whiny drawl, berating her and the damned, meddling police for yet again disrupting his work.

The drizzle persisted and Ayako started to worry. She had always been one for punctuality, a trait that had been hammered home by her mother, and this was far too late. Was he lost? A dreadful thought stabbed her heart. *He knew*. She pressed her fingers to her lips in humiliation and alarm. She had failed. He had known all along. She breathed in very deeply, trying to keep control of the growing panic clawing at her chest. This was too much to bear.

She closed her eyes, swaying slightly in the cool harbour drizzle. It was impossible to know what to feel. When he had kissed and caressed her, she felt they were together, that they were making love – yes, she had been ordered to seduce him, but she had kept secret from them the knowledge that Dan really cared for her – and that, deep in her secret self, she cared for him. He was so handsome, so tender, so special. She knew it had been real, she felt it, and yet – was she being a foolish girl? Perhaps it hadn't been lovemaking, perhaps it had been a treacherous seduction on his part. Like an assault? Was it true? Had he not cared? Or was it the foul Major who had abused her, by ordering her to sleep with an enemy? She shuddered, knowing that all around her she was being watched and judged.

———

A LITTLE AFTER ONE A.M., with the old municipal policeman in a state of heightened excitement, Dan gingerly climbed the slippery concrete steps of Kanko-dori Police Station, asking for the duty sergeant. A tiny grey-haired Japanese stepped forward, introducing himself with a polite bow as Sergeant Hanazono.

Dan stuttered along in very poor Japanese; he'd just heard about *Shinju-wan*, how Britain and Japan were now at war, and decided as a citizen of Britain to ask the police for protection. Hanazono was most amused. 'You already have "high-level" supervision, Mr Lawrence.' Dan fanned a hand across his face, pretending not to understand.

Hanazono let out a yelp of laughter, joking over his shoulder to colleagues at the top of his squeaky voice about the difficulty they were having dragging in the few foreign sailors left in Nagasaki, who had dissolved into the Joroya district of the town for a final night of fun. And yet here stood a Westerner whose whereabouts were well known, giving himself up. He roared at that, as did his squad, pleased to see their sergeant happy.

Then a constable mentioned the *Kempeitai*, and the laughter really exploded. 'A special operation!' ... 'weeks in the planning!' ... 'cleared at the highest levels!'

Their shrieks carried out onto the street, because the

powerful, elitist military police were bullies, arrogant and not popular with the ordinary municipal cops.

'Protections? Most certainly,' hissed Sergeant Hanazono, wiping the tears from his eyes. 'Stay here until morning if you like; we've only got a cell…'

'That'll be perfect.'

They slapped Dan's back, and wondered if he'd like some *saké*. After all, Japan was celebrating.

By 3 a.m. Ayako knew without a doubt Dan wasn't coming. Neither the hotel receptionist nor the Municipal Police had sent a runner to alert them of Dan's no-show because no one wanted to give bad, humiliating news to the *Kempeitai*. So, the tuna boat was waved off and the senior watchers gathered around the bollard that Ayako was miserably perching on.

All eyes were on Major Saito, what was he going to say? He sniffed the night air. Although the operation had been a failure, he was looking forward to this.

'Okunaga! Maybe your love skills aren't so good, eh?' He threw back his head and laughed.

She stopped crying in an instant. Such vindictiveness, such a personal accusation, actually made her feel better, the victim of a corrupt system, rather than the victim of a traitorous Englishman. And there was no hint that she had conspired with Dan, or had given their murderous purpose away deliberately.

She bowed very deeply, humbly, almost before she could stop herself, and took the shame of failure. But as she stared down at the wet, grey concrete – she began to work out how to persuade her uncle to use his contacts to get this Major skinned.

Saito, meanwhile, took pleasure in demeaning the pretty little rich *okanemochi* he had been forced to take, probably because of someone with connections back in Tokyo, who'd landed themselves a job, in place of his highly-trained soldiers. He snorted in derision. A girl, and useless, even at seduction.

He looked over at the rest of the watchers. Time to finish the operation with a flourish. There were still half a dozen junior soldiers positioned in hidden vantage points on the warehouses, boats and even cranes, so the Major un-holstered his pistol and fired it once into the dark night sky, enjoying watching while Ayako hurriedly abandoned her pathetic bow and cowered, arms above her head – as a hundred sleeping seagulls launched themselves erratically into the dark night air with deafening cries.

DAN DIDN'T SLEEP that night. Not because the worn, yellowing *tatami* and thinning futon in the prison cell were uncomfortable, which they were; nor because of the raucous sounds of joy reverberating around the police station; he couldn't sleep because his mind wouldn't stop racing as he tried to make sense of a day like no other day he had ever experienced.

A day of snatched opportunities. While the city was celebrating, he had stolen their secrets. But there were other reasons he couldn't sleep. The danger of being a hated foreigner in an alien country entirely under their power caused him spasms of anxiety, with thoughts of being tortured, or facing 'the one-way drop'. So, to divert his neurotic mind, he daydreamed about Ayako, that they had taken the tuna boat and were together on a far-off fantasy tropical island with white sandy beaches, called Okinawa.

Ayako was happy, laughing as she cooked the famous Nagasaki delicacies she'd filled his mind with, wearing a loose-fitting silk kimono with long flowing sleeves in place of the robe she'd worn in her room, shimmering in perfect sunlight, her lips touching sensuously the mouth-piece of her *shakuhachi* flute. *Rule Britannia* slowly morphed into *Kimigayo*, before she laid the flute down and fell back on the soft, fine sand beside him, and he said, 'There has never been anyone like you in my life;' and she said 'I love you even more than I love my family… I—'

The cell door creaked open, and two young policemen marched in, barking out an order to stand, before escorting him down a long, winding corridor, into the main police reception area. And – there she was – HERE, in real life:

Her eyes glowed with fury. Now, in stark contrast to the image in his daydreams, Ayako was standing in front of him, enraged, forced by circumstance to dress once more in her *kokumin-fuku* uniform, with angry *Kempei* on either side, and several municipal policemen averting their gaze.

Why had Mr Lawrence come to this police station last night?

'A duty; a sense of insecurity caused by the announcement of war; for protection. Why does it matter?'

'It matters because… No, *we* ask the questions.'

But their red, sleepless eyes provided the answer. One of the junior policemen stood in the background with

Dan's tiny breakfast tray of rice, a bowl of miso, nori, a few pickles, and some kind of soy-broiled vegetable, and stared at Dan, smirking and sniggering to himself. Clearly, Dan was already notorious.

Only one memory would remain indelibly etched in Dan's mind – the look of hurt vengeance in Ayako's eyes when the trio departed, threatening a later reckoning – a look born on the day of Pearl Harbour – who knew what, when, who betrayed whom?

They would never know.

AT TEN O'CLOCK, Father Luigi had finished proudly showing two novice nuns round his beloved Church, when he popped into the tiny confessional to retrieve the racy novel that he kept in a vestment drawer, which he would read while waiting for sinners, or while penitents were composing themselves.

Under the novel was a large buff envelope which had not been there the night before.

'To Father Luigi,' he read, 'confessional material – private and confidential to the Church of Rome.'

He scanned the silent, empty Church and slid the door of the confessional closed behind him. Kneeling down, he ripped open the package, flicking through the document with shaking hands.

The Apostolic Delegate in Tokyo would be most, most interested. This material would go straight to Pro Deo at the Vatican and then to Father Morlion in New York. *The ways of God are mysterious, as are those of the strange British-American, but it is clear to see which side Our Lord is on.*

Father Luigi continued kneeling, praying for a speedy but just end to this terrible war – and did not emerge until lunchtime.

5

A WEEK BEFORE CHRISTMAS 1941, 'Daniel Lawrence-san', a celebrity prisoner if there ever was one, still languished in the Kanko-dori police station, comfortable in a Japanese way, strangely enjoying the peace and unexpected serenity of a thinly walled city-centre cell.

This lack of horror, and desperation at being forced into abject idleness came about because of a very small Sino-Portuguese doctor who attended to treat his leg. 'Was once in jail eleven years by the British in Rangoon, I tell you how to stand it. Hypnotise yourself. Yes, is possible. You focus on one thing you can do, only one thing and it becomes your life, your whole. Gives you purpose, gives you reason. Must be that nothing else matters. For me it was medicine. But in Burma that was in English, so I had to learn that, too – but only to learn medicine. Surrounded by prisoners, but from the moment I wake up, moment I go to sleep – medicine. It works. Becomes your life, all you ever want it be and the jail disappears.'

The doctor leaned in – he hadn't finished. 'Also, good way to forgetting about a woman.'

Though doubtful, Dan tried it, and the doctor was right. For Dan, it was learning Japanese, both the language and the people. The guards enjoyed it when he tried different words and phrases – the younger ones also wanting to practise the English equivalents. His favourite companion was the older municipal policeman, Sakai, who realised he was on to a good thing, lazing away the days babysitting the foreigner. Sakai would sit on an old *zabuton* cushion on the worn *tatami* mat in the increasingly chilly cell, picking thick, soggy, curly strands of tobacco from his twisted teeth, toying with the wood he'd found for the rusting metal stove, and smiling when Dan mastered a new phrase, as if he'd taught it himself.

And in a typical feat of discipline, Dan refused to think about Ayako even though she was still deeply embedded in his spirit.

Then one day the world came flooding back with all its frustrations and fright – along with Ayako. The day Dan knew he was leaving.

Nothing had been said – that was the point about studying Japanese culture as well as their language. Information is spread by stance and attitudes, or by what is NOT said rather than by words – the slight tilt of the head, the sucking of air through the teeth, the lengthy uncomfortable silences, or that old give-away, fanning the face.

So, when Inspector Takahashi came and looked in on him, without a word, with every shiny button of his uniform in place, Dan guessed he would soon be on the move.

Although no policeman ever said any such thing – it would be impolite – in truth, Dan was an embarrassment and a nuisance, albeit a refreshing one, to the Kanko-dori Police, who were more used to itinerants, drunks, and small-time gang leaders. They were not ashamed of their four holding cells, which though worn and yellow with tobacco smoke were kept clean, or the meals that came from the canteen across the road, it was more that they were not felt to be fit for the status of their Western 'guest.' In spite of the war, which seemed to be happening elsewhere anyway, Dan was secretly admired because he had outsmarted the hated *Kempeitai*, so it was with a heavy heart that Inspector Takahashi exuded, rather than specifically told, Dan the news.

And because he wasn't actually told, Dan didn't know when or where, he was going. As the junior delivered the breakfast tray, with the addition of a chunk of horse mackerel, he gave a particularly definitive bow, and Sakai left quite quickly after sharing a pot of green tea, bowing several times on his way out.

Then all was unusually quiet until, still quite early, he heard them marching down the concrete corridor.

His old friends were back, *Kempei*, and Dan's heart sank when he saw who wasn't with them. He thought to ask, but didn't – it would be giving too much away, and they wouldn't answer anyway. Instead, he had to put up with the official who'd been briefly in the next bed at the hospital, and who he had nicknamed the Pigeon due to his hideous English and incessant bowing when his superiors were present.

'Uh, you must… with us.'

Dan contemplated using his increasingly useful Japanese, but that might be giving another game away. Better to take their own unreadable road.

This was his first time in the open air since the fateful night of Pearl Harbour. It was a mildly beautiful day with muted colours and a misty, milky sun. The street outside was less busy than he remembered, fewer cars and lorries and people. The Pigeon pointed at a type-95 mini-truck with a canvas roof, where two older guards, with even older rifles, were standing to attention.

'You must here,' the pigeon said, and they half-helped, half-pushed Dan into the back of the truck. The guards sat at the opening, on wooden benches along both sides, with Dan on the inside. Despite having to share their journey with two barrels of fuel, he was pleased to see his trunk wedged between them.

'Can you tell me where we're going?' Dan shouted as the noisy engine whirled and started.

'Long time,' was all the Pigeon replied. Blank faces stared blankly back. End of conversation.

They drove for almost the whole day, now and again bumping violently over ruts in the road left by Typhoon Boca, with occasional 'comfort' stops by the side of the road or at various old, traditional wooden buildings adorned with fading metal advertising panels.

Just before dark they reached the ramshackle ferry terminal at Mojishi City in northern Kyushu – it had taken six hours to travel 190 miles, such was the condition of the roads. The ferry operators ordered the guards and Dan to leave the truck for the short journey, the Pigeon refused, threatening and bowing simultaneously, until the loader gave way with a guttural hoik, spitting a remarkable distance into the sea.

As the underpowered ferry swirled in the fast, choppy currents of the Kanmon Straits, for once the Pigeon smiled. 'Devil's Sea,' he chortled to Dan, waving his hand up and down. 'Many die.' Fortunately, the journey was only twenty minutes, docking at Shimonoseki in the dark, now on Honshu, stopping on the outskirts of the town because the single working headlight of the truck was flickering.

They bedded down under a travellers' awning outside a store that seemed to sell everything, most of it hanging from the corrugated sides. Dan asked to get cigarillos, the Pigeon shook his head, but allowed the toothless driver to bring them back with the rice and vegetables and bony smoked trout. As they lay on the *tatami* mats and ate, the Pigeon tied a rope around Dan's ankle, while he shared the cigarillos with the soldiers. It almost seemed like a party.

The Pigeon kicked them awake at 5 a.m., because he wanted to reach Nagoya by nightfall. The storekeeper brought more rice and soggy salted pickles, and at first light they were off. Although the roads were better on Honshu, the day seemed endless, and growing colder by the mile. The group had an early potato lunch at an army camp in Hiroshima Prefecture, then meandered the mountains and coastal roads to finally arrive outside a pleasant two-storey tenement in Nagoya at dusk. The Pigeon disappeared and came out with a rather nervous couple in their sixties – his uncle and aunt.

Once the bowing had finished, they were brought trays of a variety of dishes provided on the little yard at the back, including *saké*. The uncle and aunt stared at Dan with a mixture of hatred and embarrassment, until the five men bedded down under a hard tarpaulin to sleep off the *saké*.

The next morning, grey with drizzle, they joined what seemed to be a river of buses, tiny pick-ups, motorcycles with massive trailers, a few cars and a multitude of trucks, many of them in military convoys. The Pigeon ordered Dan not to look outside, while the guards held their rifles more firmly, as if at attention. Dan heard the word 'Tokyo' several times, although they were still thirty or forty miles away.

The small truck swayed and spluttered as larger vehicles, especially buses black with exhaust fumes, swept past, showering them with sleet and mud until the Pigeon shouted and the driver veered off the main road, through the outskirts of a dormitory town, with the Pigeon calling 'left / right / straight', and then they swung into the entrance of what appeared to be a school and stopped at a barrier – with a finality that suggested they had reached their destination.

Dan looked out of the back at a barren, barrack-style compound, with low buildings and huts dotted in the dirty slush. It was a High School surrounded by a towering fence of barbed wire, highlighted by searchlights.

As the Pigeon squeaked and snapped, a sentry asked the driver a series of questions and checked their papers. Dan tried to make sense of the chat with the guard, but the conversation was too quick to be clearly understood. Only one thing was certain – this was the Sumire Girls' High School of Home Economics, on the outskirts of Tokyo.

Dan shuddered, and not only because of the cold.

Once out of the truck and into the compound, Dan's reception was routine, brash, dehumanising and unpleasant. Having given him a large chalk board to hold, they stripped him to have his picture taken by a placid dumpy female charcoal artist. They poked every part of his person, gave him rough inner and outer clothing, sandals, one blanket, no pillow, a book of rules in schoolboy English, a metal pan and cup and chopsticks. They took away his money, his passport, the suit he'd arrived in, his shoes, and they tried to take away his Japanese phrase-book, at which point Dan put up a quiet, determined fight. 'The rules of war allow me to keep a book,' he said without knowing if that was true.

The man in charge, who clearly spoke some English, put his hand up at the staff member who had hold of the book, said something in Japanese, and nodded at Dan. 'We allow you to learn. But by Japanese rule, not your rule.' So Dan kept the book.

His billet was previously a girl's school dormitory, with twenty beds on both sides of a narrow, low-ceilinged hut. The wooden platforms that served as beds were each topped with a thin *goza tatami*-like mat overlain by a thin, lumpy mattress. Each of the internees had a small chest of drawers, and a Bible. As he arrived the 'residents' looked at Dan without interest. Most of them were older, sad, and shivering. Dan quickly realised that the enemy here was not the guards, but the cold. And then a surprise. The resident next to him, lying on a thicker tatami-style mattress, was Japanese.

Although asleep on his back, with knees held to his chest for warmth, the hair and face were so clearly Japanese that Dan immediately wondered what he was doing in a Western Internment Camp?

The moment Dan sat on his bed, the lights went out. Until then, not knowing where he was heading, his thoughts had been morose, morbid, terrified, wondering if he was facing a noose or firing squad. Now he was in a camp, surrounded by other westerners, the terror subsided, but so did the chance of the doctor's self-hypnosis – that spell was broken. Now he went back to his old mantra, a fantasy dream of that desert island, holding and being held by Ayako, because he couldn't get the feeling of her out of his mind. The imaginary dialogue was peppered with love and laments, and the joy that they were sharing this paradise and each other. It was a Hollywood movie of her rather than real life.

Whenever he woke, that first night in the Internment Camp, he used the dream as a sedative, until finally dull light seeped through the grimy windows, and the other residents woke and dozed fitfully, or read the Bible.

The beginning of the day was marked by the sound of a bolt outside being slid back to unlock the door. But everyone in the hut seemed too bored or too traumatised to take any notice. Dan counted the beds – two had not been slept in. He made a mental note of every face he could see and swung off the mattress, put on his sandals, and went towards the door.

'I wouldn't, if I were you.' An Australian voice, quite young, definitely working class. 'They leave you alone, if you leave them alone. Going outside takes you into their world. They like to throw snowballs, or rocks if it's warm, gang up and push ya' round, 'til you run back here, and then they won't let you in. It's against the rules, but that's their point. Shit on your colonial laws – we're in charge.'

'I'm Dan Lawrence,' he replied, but the Australian waved the introduction away.

'We stay together as a group, best way to survive.'

They were interrupted by a terrible coughing. An old man at the end of the hut, as far as possible from the draughts, was in a bad way. 'Pneumonia,' the Australian said. 'Dutch. Even more hated than us Anglos, said they ran out of pills. Maybe got a day.'

It was quite a lot worse than Dan had expected.

From another bed a man with a strong foreign accent also coughed, more lightly, and said, 'They think we should have joined up and be fighting for our countries – I tell them I'm from neutral Sweden, I'm a doctor, double why I fight nobody, but they don't listen.' He coughed several times more, spat into his cup, and started praying in Swedish.

As the group woke up and began chatting, Dan discovered they had only one hope – to survive, especially the older ones. Picked up, semi-randomly, many had lived in Japan for decades, some had Japanese wives and families, but as aliens were considered spies, or worse, cowards.

The fate of the Australian, a man called Arnold Smythe, was likely to be even worse. He was a Sergeant in the Royal Australian Army Engineers, attached to their Tokyo embassy as odd-job handyman and guard, arrested the night of Pearl Harbour at a bar in Shibuya, and 'disappeared'.

'Limbo is better than this,' he said philosophically. 'Didn't like the Japs before all this, now I 'ate 'em.'

More interesting than all this was the young man on the *tatami* mat next to Dan, Yoshi Davidson. Japanese mother, Californian father, studying at Tokyo University, picked up a week after Pearl. He'd been languishing here ever since.

'Just before I was arrested, my uncle in Berkeley sent a telegram to say my mother had been detained in San Diego, was somewhere in an internment camp in California, our house was burned, my father tried to stop it and he's in hospital, was tied to a tree by a mob with barbed wire – and he's American. Crazy stupid world.'

Arnie the Aussie had said, 'Be careful with 'im, could

be a plant,' a thought that had occurred to Dan. But as the first week morphed into a second, and became a month and then Easter, and their enemy turned from being the icy cold weather to the deadly monotony, Yoshi and Dan became friends. Yoshi taught Dan idiomatic Japanese, and Dan taught young Yoshi the ways, especially the tricky business ways, of the world, which Dan, even though young, understood like a veteran.

'Business is about trust,' Dan said. 'Trusting yourself, and no one else.'

This disappointed Yoshi. 'Isn't it about keeping your word?'

Dan shook his head. 'It's about surviving and profit.'

Yoshi was adamant in his denial. 'Nope, it's about caring for each other, about honour.'

'Ah, that's the Japanese half of you. A thousand years of honourable history – more like tribal arguments if you ask me.' He lowered his voice. 'Four different police forces, an army and a navy which battle each other, a dictator-led government that worships a divine ruler – add that to a festering sense of injustice at their place in the world, shortages of oil, metal, food – everything but fish – and when they're not at war with themselves, they're repelling all foreigners. From a business point of view, heading for bankruptcy.'

'Where'd you get that from? Not like the Japan I know. Educated, hard-working, family-centred…'

'Not united…'

'Sure, they are. They're taught absolute belief in the Emperor…'

Dan shook his head even more vigorously. 'The only thing that unites the Japanese is their hatred of Britain and America, and even that is undermined by their intellectuals' respect for our Western culture. Japan is institutionally divided – that's why America and Britain will win…'

'Like they did in Singapore.'

'Ah, well, Britain is in decline, I'll give you that – why I'm becoming American…'

And so the banter went round in circles, while life at the Girls' High School settled into a rut. There was no point in planning an escape, no news of the outside world, except what the Japanese wanted them to hear, nothing of importance happening at all – the only topic was 'when might we be able to leave?'

Dan soon learned to discount even that subject – because invariably the rumours proved groundless. They had been told they were leaving in January, February, March…

But then, in early May 1942, Dan was told to expect a visitor.

The Deputy Commandant called him forward after the usual breakfast of a cup of rice, watery miso soup and a few pickled vegetables and suggested he bathe himself.

Why? For whom?

The officer laughed. 'Lawrence-san, I cannot hurt the surprise for you.'

SMELLING OF CARBOLIC, Dan sat waiting in the interview room at mid-day. A very great surprise.

'I am in Tokyo for a week, visiting my father, so I asked to see you.' Bowing her head slightly, Ayako sat down.

Much paler than he remembered, and slightly dowdier, with a worried tiredness not there before. Her dark eyes had lost some of their sparkle, her black straight hair, wound into a tight bun, looked more traditionally Japanese, while the drab khaki *kokumin-fuku* she was wearing provided visible evidence of the increasing hardness of war.

Dan himself had lost fifteen pounds, his eyes were dimmed by boredom and bad diet, his hair uneven, cut under supervision by a Canadian inmate, his mouth peppered with ulcers.

'Miss Ayako, what are you doing here? I thought you'd been trying to have me arrested.'

'Mr Lawrence, if the Japanese really thought you were a spy, you go in prison, to be hang, not a comfortable internment camp.'

She spoke slowly, and carefully, almost without fault, almost as if her words had been prepared and rehearsed. What did she want – thanks? Dan stared at his hands on the metal table, unable to think what to say.

'I said them you are too clever to only be businessman, but they think I make excuse and they don't believe me.' She glanced up briefly to make sure she was being understood and then returned her gaze to her hands. 'They said you are only a coward – that is why you not try escape. They laughed and… "Ha, Okunaga – see, your love is weak." Well, I don't care they laugh, because I know you are spy!'

Dan leaned away from the bitterness spat across the table. No, she was not looking for thanks. 'Miss Ayako,' he replied frowning, 'whatever are you talking about? Of course, you know I'm not a spy.'

'Pah!' Snorting, she looked away. Silence fell between them. Then a change came over her. She had not come to insult or interrogate him, but to remember the good occasions, the friendship they had made. She took a deep breath and straightened her back. 'How is the camp? Can you eat and sleep?'

'Everything's fine, if only we could go home.'

'What, so you can fight the war "up here"?' She sneered slightly and jabbed a finger at, ironically, her own head. But once again the anger dissolved, because now that Japan ruled half the Orient, the Great East Asia War would soon be over, and everyone could go home.

'Home in England or in America?' she asked carefully.

'Either.'

'Which is your home?'

'Neither.'

'*Where* is your home, then?'

'Who knows – it isn't important.'

Ayako looked at him with pity. 'Home is very important to Japanese – most important ever, like family. It is home for our ancestors and our children. Japanese children. That is what we are fighting for.'

'Well, it's not worth it,' replied Dan, so irritated he didn't even attempt to tell the truth.

Ayako stared down at her hands again, silent for a long time. This argument was getting them nowhere, that was not why she'd come. She pressed her hands down together on the table and held them there, motionless. Dan opened his mouth to speak in an attempt to break the rising tension but something held him back. There was more to come. Her jaw twitched and for the first time in a long while she looked up, deep into his eyes. 'Maybe to you, Mr Lawrence, if the child half *Japanese*.' Then she bowed her head, sharply downwards, gazing at her hands on the table.

A moment of great awkwardness followed.

Dan stared at the top of her head with shocked realisation. He straightened up in the squeaky bamboo chair and, sliding it back, leaned forward and lowered his head as he tried to look into her eyes. She tilted her head down further in a bid to stay hidden.

'Miss Ayako, I think we'd better stop.'

To Dan's surprise, her head flicked up and she glared at him, furious at his rebuff. 'Why Mister Lawrence? Why we should stop? Tell me please. You think I am some kind of Comfort Girl? You think I am playing my job? You think I am to be dismissed for your pleasure?'

That is a line she had been rehearsing and rehearsing for weeks – now a strong sense of self-belief, pride, of what she had done for her country, a country now rivalling the best in the world, surged through her.

The full horror of her mixture of bitterness and resolve struck him. He sighed deeply. This meeting should never have been allowed. He sighed again, ran a hand through his greasy, chopped hair, then smiled, falsely, apologetically, and inquiringly, at her. 'Can we be overheard?'

She shook her now dignified head. 'No. My father know the Colonel.'

'Is that all he knows?'

Ayako was getting into her stride again, finding self-respect and purpose. 'My father know *everything*.' She smiled. 'Everything. All your tricks.' She shrugged. 'He said, "you-me"'—she pointed at him, then herself—'we both "victims".' Then she almost giggled. 'But, he is proud of me, what I do for my country, and he admire England. He say this is "very like Shakespeare, hope to make it all well in the end. Like Taming the Shrew." Do you know it?' Then another giggle.

Dan had no idea, and felt a stab of irritation towards this tricky woman, for invading his world and destroying the catatonic inner peace he'd found in the routine lethargy of the camp. What had happened to the innocent, supplicant, fiery-eyed girl, pure of body and spirit, the willing lover he still dreamed about every night, lying with him, caressing his cheek, as they drifted together in love on his imaginary desert island? What right did she have to come blundering into his life again, destroying the fantasy with harsh reality, brandishing her bitterness and pride with such arrogance? What good could it possibly do?

'There is really nothing I can say,' he muttered, finally.

Dan went to stand up to leave. Ayako put out a small, slightly swollen hand to stop him. 'Dan-san, please.'

'*Dan-san*.' The soft way she said his name, desperate, protective, loving, maternal, even if not for him… took him back towards the fantasy of the perfect woman… And then another reality hit him. HARD.

A wave of anguish at his own stupidity began to crash over Dan. He'd been too long in monotony-land, the camp, with no challenges, to keep his usually vibrant brain sharp. He was being a ridiculous idiot and breathed in deeply to steady himself. Her father was 'friends' with the Camp Colonel. Jeez. This required the utmost care; not too obvious, gently as she goes…

'You don't care?' she asked and, though disappointed, was neither surprised, nor convinced. 'I do *not* believe you.'

Dan shrugged his shoulders, don't rush this. 'Our countries are at war.'

'But we are still human persons, one day war will stop.'

'Look, I'm sorry. Maybe your father's correct. We are both victims.'

She looked at him, waiting. Would he ask? – the ultimate, selfish plea, the ultimate selfishness.

He looked at her – sad and hopeful and vulnerable – calculating. Finally, he decided. *Don't ask about her father influencing the Colonel, be silent, be Japanese. I'm family now, I don't* need *to.* Typical Dan, since the day he was born, with a deep self-serving survival instinct, always hidden, unspoken.

They stared at each other for perhaps twenty seconds, though it could have been forever. He was not going to ask, she could now believe Dan, soon to be a father, was not so entirely corrupt after all. She breathed out, relieved, then brightened.

'Do you ever think of me, Dan-san?'

'The whole time.'

'Good or bad?'

'Both. And you?'

'Only bad.' She laughed. 'You won, this hurt, so there is hate.'

Dan shook his head. 'Nobody won – except old men at war…'

'This you say Dan-san, like my father. But I think like my mother, this war is for good reason.'

They both sighed, isolated in their thoughts, with such different hearts.

'Soon I will go.' She placed a hand on her belly. 'In Tokyo this is very bad, so I will stay in Okinawa with my grandmother.' Tears welled up, she looked upset, but hid it almost instantaneously.

Ayako reached down into her cloth-wrapped *furoshiki* package and retrieved a carefully folded scrap of paper, which she placed squarely on the table and slid towards him.

For a moment they both stared down, as if the scrap was momentous.

'This my grandmother's name, and this is her address. Please promise to look after this forever. Okinawa is home, the best safe place for me and for…' She placed a hand back over her stomach again and sat in silence.

'Home,' Dan said. 'You're lucky. Don't really have one.'

Dan took the paper. He had heard about her father's Okinawan mother before, the night of Pearl Harbour. Could this whole meeting be a charade, another trap?

But, instinctively, he knew the treachery was over. Ayako might never forgive him, might even hate him, but she would not do anything to hurt the unborn baby.

She looked at him suspiciously and sighed. 'Maybe you will be good father one day, if you don't be wanderer.'

He half-nodded and half-shrugged, who knows what might happen in this crazy world? Then he couldn't help himself, his feelings for her took over, reaching forward and squeezing her hand.

'Say "*Hajimemashite*" to the baby from me when it arrives.'

In the dormitory later, Yoshi asked him: 'What was the meeting about?'

Even to a friend, Dan was reticent on personal matters, and given Yoshi's reputation, maybe even paranoid.

'A dream, a nightmare maybe, I don't know.'

The men lay side-by-side, Dan on his lumpy mattress, Yoshi on his thin *goza* mat, musing.

'Dan…' Yoshi turned to face him. 'The censors missed a couple or three sentences in my dad's letter. Was a neat code he used. OK to be our secret?'

Dan knew this would be good and nodded. 'Shoot.'

'Some of us are in line to be swapped. For Diplo Japs in Britain, the US, Canada and Oz.'

There had been rumours floating for weeks about secret negotiations, but Yoshi's letter was way better than gossip. 'Suppose the Swedish Doc won't make it, then.'

Yoshi laughed. 'Reckon not.'

'Or the Aussie soldier.'

'Nope. Swapping only Diplo. And my dad said students – something about Emperor's nephew. Sorry.' Yoshi knew that counted out Dan, who was only a businessman, not a diplomat, and on that basis wouldn't qualify for a swap.

Now Dan turned to face him, with the widest smile possible. 'Well, I guess it won't matter if I tell you what happened today. Turns out I got connections – have become part of the family of a friend of the Camp Colonel, and in your Jap-land, family always looks after family.'

Dan held up the scrap of paper with the Okinawa address. 'Abracadabra – this is my ticket out of here.' And he kissed it.

———

WHEN THE *ASAMA MARU* sailed three months later, on 2nd September 1942, Daniel Lawrence wanted to stand on the deck to watch Yokohama Bay, and the whole of Japan with it, fade sedately into his past, but the ship was to sail at midnight, with its somewhat shell-shocked human cargo already locked in cramped cabins. The Bay was said to be massively fortified and not to be seen by Western eyes. Ahead lay neutral Portuguese Goa, a change of transport via Lisbon, and on to the United States.

On that muggy Wednesday night, with such an uncertain future before him, Dan had no idea the tide of war had already turned against the Japanese, or that wartime America would provide the true base for his fortune.

Nor did he know that a thousand miles away, on the matted floor of a pretty, little red-tiled wooden bungalow in the village of Kakazu, Okinawa, Ayako Okunaga was gritting her teeth against a searing pain, determined to show her strength and resilience. The Japanese code did not allow women to cry out in childbirth, and with her grandmother and a neighbour in attendance such a bad omen would not go unnoticed. This child may have been forced on her, but she would do her duty.

As the evacuation ship finally slipped berth for the Indian Ocean, a tiny baby was wrapped tightly in a minute kimono and lifted onto Asako's futon. And, as it took its first breaths, and howled out, the deep horn of the liner blasted round Yokohama harbour, and a hundred dozing seagulls leapt skyward.

6

OCTOBER 1942, WASHINGTON DC

AFTER ALMOST A YEAR as a prisoner of one kind or another, in a country becoming increasingly rundown and threadbare because of a fanatical focus on military needs, Dan's first thought on glimpsing America was – *don't they know there's meant to be a war on?*

From the air, as the massive Boeing 314 Clipper lumbered over New York for the high-hog passengers from Lisbon to get a view, the city was not just vibrant – it exuded wealth, ambition, energy and plenty.

And as the seaplane skimmed the oily waters, landed and chuntered across to the billboarded dock on Staten Island, the very air felt free, in a way Dan had never imagined. But then he'd never been to America before. It seemed a free-wheeling 'let's do it now' kind of place, where the jetty boys who pulled the seaplane into the dock said, 'Howdy, sir,' and hauled his battered trunk up the slide, to where the greeters stood with cards and cheery waves.

On a warm calm day, in the mid-seventies, the contrast with the rigidity of Japan, their regimented discipline, was absolute. Dan stood back and marvelled at the purposeful bustle of individuals just 'getting the job done'.

And then, so welcoming, so strange, to see his name in big red letters, being held up by a cute lady in a light blue uniform that hugged her like a sailor.

'I'm Daniel Lawrence,' he said, unsure whether to shake hands or not.

She stepped back and saluted, her bright smile showing perfect teeth. 'Pleased to meet you, sir. Rating Dauser, I'll be your driver, Lieutenant Murphy's waiting for you in the Clearance Hall.'

THE CLEARANCE HALL turned out to be immigration for rich travellers. Lieutenant Murphy, the Navy's attorney in New York, who was, coincidentally of course, Abe Ford's nephew, was waiting there for Dan.

'If I may have your passport, Mr Lawrence, we'll have you through in no time.'

The Immigration Officer asked Dan just one question. 'Great Britain, huh. Where is your home?'

The Lieutenant and Dan exchanged glances, no need to be complicated.

'Henley-on-Thames, Officer, parents still reside there.'

The Officer didn't even mention that Dan had no visa, he just stamped an empty page and handed the passport back. 'Glad to have you on side, sir.'

'Who you know, eh?' Dan said to the Lieutenant as Rating Dauser turned onto the highway for Washington.

'And you're acquainted with the best,' Murphy replied, surprised that this legendary Brit was only the same age as himself. ''Course I shouldn't know, sir, but

Uncle Abe told me. You're a hero far as I'm concerned, and to the seniors further up the pole.'

As the Chevy purred on, Dan knew – *this is* home, *where I always belonged, fast, efficient, flowing, informal – shit even the sun lifts your heart.*

After flying for 42 hours at 145 mph in a bumpy but luxurious seaplane, he closed his eyes and tried to doze, but it was impossible. The *scale* of this country, the highways, the factories, the cities he passed heading south on the Pennsylvania Turnpike, simply had to be taken in, admired, digested – this land was in a different century from Japan.

As they swung into Washington, across the Potomac, the vista was even more enthralling, but it still did not seem like the capital of a country at war. True there were occasional armed policemen, but the shops were stocked and colourful, buses were crammed full, pedestrians had their heads up and seemed to be happy.

The DoD Navy buildings, still under manic construction with a dozen cranes, heavy trucks, and men in hard hats everywhere, were extraordinary in their scale, being built right alongside the Lincoln Memorial and the reflecting pond – a necessary land grab, symbolising that as municipal life went on all around, the war would be at the centre of the nation.

When the car parked up, and Dan stepped out to look at the frenetic activity, Murphy pointed at the cranes and found the words.

'Shows we're serious, sir, about winning this thing.'

And then it was down half a mile of echoey, bureaucratic corridors to meet the man himself.

'DAN!' Commander Ford cried, crushing his hand and slapping his back. 'We think you're a goddamn hero.'

'I'm just surprised it worked, that's all.'

'So are we. Enough to turn you religious.' Ford's large, fleshy face beamed – he'd been waiting eagerly for this moment. He buzzed his intercom. 'Daphne, bring in the package, please.'

As Dan unwrapped it, Ford winked at the other four men in the room who were sitting around a circular table. 'I thought of mailing it to you in Nip-land, but might have given the game away.'

It was a foot-high statuette of the Madonna. 'Present from Father Morlion, from Rome, unscrew the head.'

There was liquid inside.

'Whiskey – Irish – keeps the Cardinals happy.' And everyone roared with laughter.

Dan had been glancing round the room because he hadn't been introduced. Two men were in uniform, while the other two had on short-sleeved cotton shirts and suit trousers.

Abe took off his glasses and pointed them at the four grey-haired faces. 'Since you already briefed State in Lisbon, we're not going to pause for introductions, you can catch up later. We've got to get straight down to it.' Ford leaned back. The niceties were over, it was time for business. '"Logistical Supply"? Know what it is?'

Dan gauged the faces. *Be cool or enthusiastic? Unsure or knowing? Reticent or 'go for it'? British or American?* Through the window, he could see a crane swinging half an office across clear blue sky, to the accompaniment of drills, dozers, mixers and foremen whistling, so he went American.

'Sure, Abe. It'll be the challenge of Logistical Supply

that wins you the war across five-thousand miles of Pacific. That and the guts of Marines.'

Ford was biting a thumbnail, and glanced at the four grey heads with a gleam of 'this guy is smart, like I said.' '"Wins *you* the war," Dan? Don't you mean *us*.'

'Well, I'd love to help out, sir.'

'Don't you mean *do it*?'

The tallest of the men around the table, over six-six, in a new, immaculate navy uniform, which was deliberately unbuttoned, perhaps to signify his heart wasn't military, nodded at Dan. 'Three weeks ago, I was an attorney in Pittsburgh. Tomorrow I'm heading to Pearl, as ADC to an Admiral, will read up on naval regs on the flight down. Just no time to be anyway else.'

Ford slammed his desk in agreement. 'Ya nailed that, Phil. Gotta do it NOW.'

Suspicious, Dan wondered, had they rehearsed this? But inside he was thrilled to be needed, and he had an inkling this was the top team.

Ford waved his huge arm around them all. 'I wanted these gents to see your face, connect y'all. We ain't doing life-stories here, you only need to know ya work for me, and I work for the President.' He let it hang, most of them had heard this speech before. 'And the Navy, of course. Though it'd go better if the goddamn Navy worked for me.'

DAN FOUND himself housed in a sumptuous hotel, but without the slightest chance of settling down to sleep. Even though he'd not had even a vaguely comfortable bed since leaving Hotel Nagasaki almost a year ago, he was far too revved up to think about getting his head down.

This was too exciting, too challenging, too important – and an opportunity for payback on a gigantic scale. At two in the morning, he opened the hotel penthouse French windows that fronted onto the Potomac, breathed in the mild city air, and looked over the rooftops, across Pennsylvania Avenue, all the way to the White House. It was the speed of events here that made him feel giddy.

Adding Dan to the massive blueprint of Logistical Supply had taken Abe Ford and his team just six hours – to accomplish what it would have taken the British a week, and the Japanese a month, if ever. At supper Abe had explained *his* view of logistical supply, how to get American industrial power onto the beaches of the Pacific islands that would bridge their way to 'Hirohito's Palace, wherever that is.'

'The real job is politics. Raw and simple and mighty tough. If a door don't open, kick it in. If an Admiral gets in the way, shoot his ass. And when you've got the supply humming, send him a case of bourbon, and a new door. If I haven't had him fired. We don't have time for being palsy – chit-chat means dead marines, and any careerist that gets in the way'—Abe took a moment, chewing steak, talking about chewing ass, he wanted Dan to 'get it'—'we try to have our friends at the White House take down his office. Same day. That's owed to the guys facing lead. And I sure know—'

Dan was watching Ford devour a second steak – it certainly was a world away from a cup of rice and vegetables.

'—while you were still in diapers, I was in the port of Calais,' he sniffed at the World War I memory, not a good one. 'Twenty-two-year-old rookie, running hospital ships back to Hastings, south coast of England, with our dead and almost dead from the hell-hole trenches. Mostly it was arr-o-gant British generals got 'em killed, still fighting the last war, making goddamn stupid decisions. Hundreds of guys wasted.'

He threw back a slug of bourbon. 'Thousands, if ya count the Canuks and Australians.' Then another slug. 'Ain't gonna happen on my watch. Sheez. Asshole military careerists.' Abe pulled his wire-framed glasses down to wink at a couple of Congressmen dining with too-lovely secretaries, perhaps making a covert note for future use. 'Ain't gonna be unnecessary casualties, not on your watch, either, Danny, my boy.'

Having devoured what seemed to be half a cow, he waved at a waiter who darted across in a couple of seconds. 'An Irish coffee, with sugar…' He looked up at Dan who nodded. 'Make that two.'

Next came the Cubans, trimmed and lit by the concierge, and as they both puffed to the ceiling, Dan finally got to understand why he was at *that* particular dinner.

Abe opened his huge arms to the buzzing restaurant, as if in a wide embrace. '*This* is what we've got to get to the Pacific Theatre. *This*.' As he paused to puff, Ford's eyes misted up, he was talking serious stuff. 'The best of everything, that's what's gotta be on the transports, the tankers, the cargo ships, best of what our nation's got, for the best fighters we can find.'

He held up the cigar. 'I personally sent a thousand of these to Midway, after we beat the Jap fleet. Mrs Ford was not amused – and you know – they're still at Pearl. Held up by some dumbass Rear Admiral, who don't understand the meaning of morale, but went to Annapolis with King. Sheez.' Ford took a long puff and shrugged. 'Maybe son-of-a-bitch wanted them for himself.'

Dan knew all about Admiral King, who had served with Ford in World War I, while Roosevelt was Assistant Secretary of the Navy, visiting the trenches, getting a lifetime's experience of canvas caskets, and teenage amputees – while the British and French Admirals and Generals commandeered 5-star hotels and raged at each other.

The waiter arrived with the Irish coffees. Ford gulped his down in one. 'FDR says go round King, and I said "you didn't do that in 1918, you chewed them up and fired them," and Franklin winked. "I was young then, throwing weight around, I've learned the bypass works better than a battle. And luck is even better than that." He winked.' Abe let out a long sigh.

'Maybe you've guessed. That dumbass RA in Pearl made an inebriated remark about Mrs King, and he was on the next C-46 to Nantucket, to run our non-existent Navy there. Sometimes… jeez, FDR… ain't Irish, but sure has the luck of something.' He flicked his fingers for the check. 'Not rightly sure where the thousand Cubans are now, maybe you could chase them up.'

'In Pearl?'

'Yep. You're on the flight with Phil tomorrow. Figure a lawyer and a dealer will stir the place up just nicely.'

'Dealer', Abe had said. Whatever did that mean?

Which seemed to be it. But as he placed a twenty in the check-holder, Ford lowered his voice, leaned in and said, 'And Phil'll brief you about the Purple Channel in the C-47.'

Replaying this later, from the other side of his huge hotel terrace, away from the White House, Dan looked across the slumbering city. Almost dawn. He hadn't slept, but didn't care. He'd have the flight to Pearl for sleeping. *Home,* he was thinking. *When you know, you know.*

After just a single day, classless America was now his home and always would be. He sniffed and lit the half-smoked Cuban. There was a mist in the air, rising up from the river, reminding him of Nagasaki on a windless dawn. *What was it she said? 'Japanese fight for family and home'.* At the time he didn't understand, because he had neither. 'Family,' he muttered to the Washington skyline, still a fragile concept, although there was, somewhere out there, a being, though Japanese, a part of himself. He shrugged and blew a smoke circle that rose up in the still air. *But home, that was different – a base, to build from, to prosper, to become rich. Now I can go anywhere the wind blows, but I'll always be* here. The thought exhilarated Dan and made him burningly impatient. He wanted to get started, make a mark, be something, someone. Because now he had found a home, and coincidentally, a country to fight for. In his own way, of course.

Dan stubbed the cigar out in the pebbles of a hardy cactus plant, and, for the thousandth time *she* invaded his thoughts, her lithe, rangy figure, her hesitant lovemaking, the way they held hands afterwards, explored each other's skin, and feelings, talked of one day having a family, before he took her for the third time. 'Many Japanese women all they want, make home. Home is most important… you come Okinawa, I show you my home…'

He remembered how their eyes met, and she looked away quickly, and then his doubts that 'home' was real. 'I'm too much like my mother, to be a good mother', she once said. But maybe that was just to please him, because for Dan, home was only a base, a platform, to go outward – from which to take on and conquer the world. For Ayako, it seemed, home was a place to look inward – a place of family, ancestors, devotion, contentment, an end in itself. Perhaps. Or was that concept of 'home' part of her treachery?

He shuddered at the thought of being enclosed by such domesticity, a castration of ambition, but that was before being here in America – even the shadowy rooftops of the Washington homes he could see on the other side of the Potomac seemed to exude quiet strength. Though closeted within simple routine lives, Washingtonians had a competitive power that would now be focused on steady revenge, until the outrage of Pearl Harbour had been put to the sword, and decisively vanquished.

And yet, in spite of it all, he was still thinking about *her* and a baby. For the fiftieth time, Dan opened his wallet and pulled out the soft, worn sliver of paper.

Nishabaru House, Kakazu Village, Highway 5, Okinawa.
Mrs Asako Okunaga.

'Family,' he muttered again to the Washington skyline, 'who needs one?' But he carefully slipped the little scrap of paper back into its cherished place, before going inside to pack for Pearl.

IN EARLY 1943, Okinawa seemed to be a paradise.

A tropical, craggy island in the choppy, shimmering East China Sea, four hundred miles from the Japanese mainland, sixty-five miles long by seven miles wide, curved like a sabre. The terrain was dominated by hills and ridges above lowland towns and villages, with cliffs that terraced down to the rocky coast, pitted with caves and thick with fragrant screw pine trees, which crowded the windy, sandy beaches, offering shelter to the numerous hermit crabs scuttling in their roots.

The harsh landscape bred hardy natives, and young people who needed to get away for adventure, but who also needed to come back one day, to settle down in their island home. Mainly Japanese, partly Chinese, some darker-skinned *Ryukyuan,* the island had been invaded many times throughout its history, until 1879, when Japanese military forces planted their flags and annexed the Ryukyu Islands as Okinawa Prefecture. So, from the late nineteenth century onwards the islands were not just peaceful, they had grown to believe in themselves, unmolested and safe, in the middle of an empty sea, on the way to nowhere.

Shinju-wan had happened in another world, a parallel universe, but, by 1943, day by day, week by week, the military garrison had filled up with Japanese mainland forces, and two new airfields had been built over patchwork farms. Now the peasants and subsistence farmers took jobs for solid government cash, rather than bartering for paraffin, or swapping hard-earned homegrown yams, taro and goya to purchase second-hand school uniforms for the grandchildren.

But change was coming – accursed change.

Change was hated here even more than Tokyo. Change never brought anything but pain, sorrow and suffering. Like duty. And duty was as merciless as the tropical rainy season, and as unavoidable – better to endure duty, and the sacrifice of sons, than raise an impotent fist at gathering hurricanes.

The *Okinawa Shimpo,* the only newspaper the national Government now allowed as the result of the Newspaper Unification Policy, parroted how special Okinawa was, the island chosen by destiny to be in the forefront of the defence of 'our glorious homeland' – if the heathen westerners ever came, which surely, they wouldn't. Until then, island life meandered at horse-and-cart pace – although these days the horses were noticeably thinner, and there was little oil to dampen the shriek of the cartwheels.

What the Okinawans couldn't know, weren't allowed to know, was that the inexhaustible factories and machines and conveyor-belts of a vastly different country were blasting white-hot steel 5,000 miles away, supplying the US Pacific Fleet that was gathering full steam, hopping from defended island to defeated island, and, one day soon, heading their way.

Life might be increasingly harsh, but it was still to be lived as the ancestors dictated.

Such was the case of Mrs Asako Okunaga senior, in Kakazu village, squeezed into her cramped little bungalow along with Ayako and a surprisingly calm child. It had been an unusual year, and Mrs Okunaga did her best to put the obvious out of mind, let alone speak about it. Anyway, speak about it to whom? Who was there to tell that the baby was large, its eyes rather round, and that there was a distinct golden glow to the hair lying flat on its head? Such things might be noticed but should never be discussed. And then the mother, oh the mother, brittle but with such spirit, a spirit the old lady suspected likely born of anger, but Ayako never would say why, so that, too, would remain unsaid.

In actual fact, Ayako was bored, and furious, and deeply depressed.

While the world was blowing itself apart, and Japan had conquered most of East Asia, she was stuck in a rural backwater, marooned with a baby, albeit a good baby who watched a lot and rarely cried, but a baby who sucked and bit the very life from its slender mother – it was as if Mayumi had been born with shark's teeth. In the silence of her deepest heart, Ayako disliked this child with its needs and demands and horrid round eyes. She was a constant reminder of how she had been dismissed or betrayed – by the *Kempei*, by her father, by Dan. But Ayako didn't complain. That would not be approved, and anyway, breast-feeding was a given. The baby and only the baby came first. In theory.

With so many of the men away on military duty, or having died early from hard labour in the fields, Okinawan women had developed an almost catatonic forbearance. Ayako, from the big city, with pride and agitation bred into her through education, found their demeanour impossible to comprehend, and she began furiously to resent Mayumi as the source of her misery. The grandmother hid her outrage at such insolent behaviour by fussing over the baby even more than usual, until one evening, in the winter of 1943, the emotional dam broke.

There was no shouting, no tantrums, no harsh words. Instead, Ayako squatted down behind the oversized stone water-pot outside, and wrote a letter to her father.

Dearest Father,

I hope life in Tokyo is satisfactory and our family is safe.

Your mother has been most helpful, although her heavy breath has become more serious and I am required to take care of her as well, now. All is fine, the rainy season has ended, but the village supplies are now taken to the military camp, with little returned. The village chief, Higa, (his son was at High School with you), spoke to the adjutant, but the soldiers just laughed at him, and said it was the Emperor's food, and should not be wasted on old people who cannot fight. Grandmother says they slapped him, too, and called him a brown bruised-banana Ryukyu. *This is the name they use to insult islanders when soldiers march on the hills where we once played and that we are now forbidden to walk on.*

It is six months since I have been outside and I humbly ask if it would be possible to return to Tokyo so I can take up proper employment to help Japan's war effort. I have heard that many interpreters are required for work with westerners who are in prisons or are not allowed to leave Japan. Surely, I am needed to assist with this important work to help the glory of the East Asia victory.

I miss you terribly and am so sad not to be at home with you and mother. I miss Michiko, too, especially when I dream every night of all the strength the sons of our friends and neighbours have to show when faced by an enemy who shows no mercy.

Last night I read Henry Five *again and it made me miss you more.*

Papa, I'm straining like 'a greyhound in the slips,' please let me come home to do my duty for Japan.

Be sure to take care of yourself in these troubled times.

Your loyal daughter, Ayako

お父様

東京の生活にはご満足で家族の皆は安全なことと思います。お婆様には本当にお世話になっていますが、息切れがひどくなってきていて、今ではお婆様のお世話もしなければなりません。何事もなく無事で、梅雨も終わりましたが、村の配給は駐屯地に持っていかれて、その後ほんのわずかなものしか返されてきません。村長の比嘉さん（息子さんがパパと高等学校で同級）が副官と配給について話したのですが、兵隊たちはあざ笑って、天皇陛下のものだから、戦いのできない老人にやって無駄にしてはいけないと言ったそうです。お婆様によれば、村長さんは平手打ちを食らい、「茶色のよれよれバナナのうちなんちゅ。」と呼び捨てられたとか。これは高台の上を行進する兵隊が、島人のことをけなすときに使うあだ名です。今は立ち入り禁止になった、昔遊んだことのあるあの高台で。

もう六カ月間、村の外に出ていません。お父様、どうか東京に戻らせて下さいませ。お願いです。そうすればお国のためにきちんとしたお仕事に就くことができます。収容所にいる西洋人、あるいは、国外に出ることを許されない西洋人とのやりとりのために通訳が必要と聞きました。大東亜戦線を皇国の勝利に導く重要な仕事の担い手として、私が必要とされていると信じて疑いません。

お父様のお側にいられないのを恐ろしいほどさみしく思います。おうちでお父様とお母様と一緒にいられないのはとても悲しいのです。ご近所の勇敢な息子さんたちが、慈悲などみじんもない敵と対峙していて、それを毎晩夢で見る時、特に路子に会いたい気持ちでいっぱいになります。

昨晩はヘンリー五世を読み返しました。それで、お父様とよけいに会いたくなりました。

お話に出て来るレース前の競争犬のように、私はとても待ちきれない気持ちです。どうか、おうちに戻して皇国のお務めを果たせるようにして下さい。

この混乱したご時世に、くれぐれもお体をお大切に。

Your loyal daughter, Ayako

Intending to simply file her frustrations as she had done before, so many times now, Ayako realised that she had the opportunity to send the letter back home, in the care of the visiting education adviser, who was then returning from Tokyo in four weeks and might be able to bring back a positive reply.

But it was not to be.

My dear Ayako,

I always like to hear from you, but this time I found your words troubling.

Our duty is to our family, not the nation, which already has taken more than it is due. Although the circumstances of you being in Okinawa are not ideal, I feel that it would be preferable for you to stay, with my hope that this painful passage in our national history will be over sooner than Tojo and his military expect. I suspect these unkind wars will not end well. Do they ever?

As usual, your mother has a different view to mine. That is one reason I didn't share your letter with the family, but there is another reason, more profound.

Where is the mention of baby Mayumi? A baby might be born of despair, of trickery, of misunderstanding, but still it remains a child, the flesh from our being, the hope for our future, for a better and beautiful world. And a child's beauty is even more so when the hearts of mother and child are entwined, beating as one, and with an energy far more powerful than bombs and bullets and bayonets. Can you not see that? Have you missed out on the real purpose, the real journey through life that we must take?

I ask such questions neither to chide nor argue, but to point you in the direction love might be leading you

through life, the power of what you have made, the miracle of creation.
My dear Ayako, stop, please stop, and think of the baby, of how you will grow as Mayumi grows, with joy at seeing a being that you made blossom from seed to bud to flower. It is poetry, to which I dedicate my life. What is taking up arms, being part of a brutal machine in comparison? It is nothing. Nothing.

You know I have always loved you for who you are, the best part of fatherhood, you have provided so many surprises of the spirit that could not be expected. But sometimes the fork in the road comes from signs that point along the wrong path, directed by 'knaves' that lead us astray, who have feelings only to promote their hateful vision of our time. They stir to foment.
Remember Kipling?

'If you can stand to hear the truths you've spoken,
twisted by knaves to make a trap for fools.'

Please do not be Kipling's fool, my darling child. Stay with my mother, help them both, they need it more than our country, which has taken the wrong road. And love Mayumi as if she's part of your own heart, as I love you.

Okunaga.

文子様

文子からの手紙はいつも楽しみにしているのだが、今度の手紙の言葉には不安が掻き立てられる。わかってくれるだろうか。我々に課せられている務めとは家族のためのものであって、国のためのものではない。この国はすでに尋常ではない奉仕を強要している。文子が沖縄にいるという状況は理想的ではないが、沖縄に留まったほうが良いと私は思っている。我が国の歴史において辛いこの状態が、東條と軍が期待するほど長くは続かないという希望が私にはある。この残酷な戦争に良い結末はないと思う。戦争に良い結末などあったためしはないだろう。

いつものように、静子と私は意見が違うので、それがひとつの理由で文子の手紙は皆には見せていないのだが、他にもっと深い理由がある。

真由美のことが手紙にないのはどうしてですか。赤子というものはたとえ絶望や欺瞞や誤解などの元に生まれてきていても、それでも子供であることには違いない。我々の生命から生まれ出て、我々の将来において、より良く美しい世界を創るための希望を担う人間です。その子供の美しさは、母と子の心が一体となってひとつの脈を打つようになれば、さらに美しさが増す。その美しさは爆弾や弾丸や銃剣などよりはるかに力強いエネルギーを放つのです。それが文子には理解できないのですか。人生の本当の目的、我々が辿らなければならない人生の本当の道程を文子は見失っているのでしょうか。

このように問いかけるのは、叱責でも議論でもなく、愛が導く貴女の人生の方向を示すためです。貴女が生み出したものの力、創造の奇跡に目を向けてほしいのです。文子、今の考え方を止めてほしい。どうにか立ちとどまって、赤ちゃんのことを考えてほしい。真由美が育っていくとともに、種から蕾、花へと貴女が花咲かせた命を見ることの喜びと、同時に貴女自身もどのように成長するのかを感じてほしい。これこそ、私が自分の人生を捧げているポエトリーというものです。それと比べると武装することや、残酷なメカニズムの一部になるなどという事は全く何の意味もない。

私が文子の父になってから大方、いつもありのままの文子を愛してきたことはわかっているだろうね。文子には、何度も、予想しようもない精神の躍動で驚かされてきた。しかし、別れ道には、誤った道しるべが立っていることもあるのです。正道を外すようにそそのかす悪党は、この時代を憎しみに満ちたものとして誇張することしか念頭にない。彼らはことを荒立てるために動いている。文子はキプリングを覚えているかな。

『もしも、君が話した真実を、悪者が愚か者をわなにかけるために、ねじ曲げて語るのを聞くことに我慢できれば。』

どうかキプリングの愚か者にはならないでくれ。母のところにいて、両方を世話してほしい。母たちのほうが、誤った道を歩んでいる国よりももっと文子を必要としている。それから真由美を自分の心の一部のように、私が文子のことを思うように、愛してほしい。

父より

It took a month for Ayako to remove the dagger of her father's words from her heart, resenting Mayumi more and more. And worse still – every time she looked at the baby she saw that trickster Lawrence's eyes, eyes which mocked and now seem to imprison her. He was a double-crosser, so the baby was to be untrustworthy, the love she might have felt now twisted, making a trap for her. As the wounds from Dan, and now her father, festered inside her, she began to plan an escape.

A SCHEME BECAME CLEAR, one day in April 1944, while she was sitting in her favourite spot – a large, time-worn grey rock guarding a small winding path leading down to the cove, jutting up above the screw pine trees and looking out over the sea as it crashed gently on the rocks below.

Without her realising, a young, ragged lieutenant had come to sit on a rock nearby, also looking out to sea, smoothing the vivid red petals of a large hibiscus flower between his fingers, breathing in the scent of the restless waves and the ozone haze of the South China Sea.

For some time, though they were aware of each other, they did not speak, letting the magnificence of nature talk for them, speak to their souls. Until, that is, the young man found the courage and the words to reach out to her. His Tokyo accent caught her by surprise, out of place in such a wilderness.

'I have written a poem about this. Of how there is so much to live for here, and so much to die for, too. Would you like to hear it?'

To the lieutenant, this mysterious young woman looked perfect, adored and adorned by nature. The sea spray shone like diamonds in her long dark hair; her eyes glistened with misty droplets, her eyelashes like mini-rainbows, shimmering in the mist as she blinked her eyelids in the bright, salty air; her face, silkily wet, had the doll-like texture of a crystalised *Geisha* after the party make-up was removed – just before illicit love-making.

But for all the radiance of her ivory skin and dark innocent eyes, the beguiled lieutenant would forever remember her neck, swan-like, fragile but firm, teasing his gaze towards the sensuous paradise below her blouse and beyond. She was a picture-perfect, beautifully proportioned, *Ichimatsu* doll.

'Please recite your poem, if that is your wish,' Ayako replied, glancing at his open face and dancing eyes.

He turned towards the sea to gather himself, before swinging back to her, kneeling, hands on the knees of his wet uniform, now looking even younger than she had first thought.

'We were never asked what our lives are worth.
With the answer being 'nothing' to Razor Tojo's band.
The band that plays music as if they are the Gods on this earth.
So, I came here, more than often – forever to find peace.
And to ask the Gods of the sea and sky to speak for themselves.
'Why do you ask,' they say, 'when there is a God in your homeland to give
answer?'
'Because there is beauty to die for, and also hatred; should we die for that, too?'
He does not answer.
So, I answer for him:
'Only the God of beauty is worth to die for, to protect nature itself, to protect our land.'

The lieutenant stopped, tears in his eyes mingling with the misty spray, and waved his arms at the rocks and the sea. 'I could die for this, but never for hatred.'

Then silence. Strangely.

Even the sea seemed to hold its breath, at least in the lieutenant's mind, while he waited for his goddess to speak. But Ayako stayed silent, and so he demanded to know, misery and pain sharpening his voice. 'Does this make you angry? Do you think badly of me?'

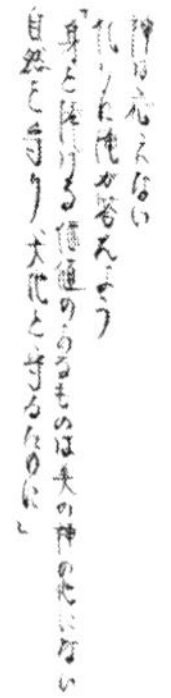

'I don't think of you at all, if that's what you say. It is the other nation's hatred we must fight against, to defend our land. If you don't do that, Japan will be lost to you – and to me. Beauty is within us all, but we must fight and sacrifice for our heritage, our ancestral land, destroy our enemy, fight and die to be honourable and happy.'

She was resolute in turning away from what the lieutenant offered, her face obdurate and full of disappointment.

That night, while Mayumi slept in the arms of her wheezing great-grandmother, Ayako scratched with her pencil on the shiny paper, a somewhat devious declaration of intent to put nation before family – and it was the hapless Lieutenant who had given her the idea.

Dearest Father,
Although I have been silent since your last letter, as you have been, my mind has been awhirl, finding my place in our time, which at present is not easy. Every day here in Okinawa, our ancestral home, is another day of waiting, a day of no consequence – perhaps it was once the same with you, before you won your scholarship to Tokyo.

And yet, while I wait, I know there is much to do elsewhere, and much that must be done. Soldiers are gath-

ering and although we are not told the reason, it is said 'the fires of hell' are on their way. This is not official, of course, but loose talk that is brought back by the locals working the bars in Naha, where the officers waste away the time. Many are here from Hokkaido, with their strange words and country ways, but they are also pleasant fellows who miss their families and sweethearts. I have begun to find a duty in serving such lonely warriors, who seek to show their gratitude by taking me for long walks in the mountains and along the coasts.

There is one who is particularly appealing, an officer with friendly eyes and good teeth. I am sure you would approve, although he is much more happy with General Tojo than I know you are. With your agreement I would like to introduce him to Grandmother and Mayumi and perhaps, if she agrees, the three of us might spend time together sometimes. As an officer, he has special privileges and his own small rooms where we can be in private. I have not ascertained his status, but Yoshi has said that he is familiar with children, so it may be complicated, though I know he would make a good father to Mayumi.

In your last letter, which seems so very long ago now, you asked me to dedicate myself to her, and I have tried, although I still believe my efforts would be put to better use serving Japan. There is talk about special prisoner camps for English captives, some in Kyushu, and I yearn to be of help. But if your instruction is otherwise, then I will do as you wish. I feel such a strong need to fulfil my duty, would you approve if I showed kindness to Captain Hayashi, to give back to my country in another way?

It seems I was born to serve like my honourable mother who was often absent from our family home while serving the Red Cross and the Aikoku Fujinkai, *and who I hear from grandma has now been awarded the Emperor's medal. I have discovered that I have a greater purpose as my mother's daughter, than as a mother to my daughter, which I hope you can understand as you did with mama.*

Your loving, loyal and obeying daughter, Ayako.

Two words did it. The word 'Captain'. Plus, cruelly provocative, 'a man being much more happy with Tojo'. 'Captain' meant an older man, and 'Tojo' meant supporting the fervent nationalists. Both words, she knew, would set her father's teeth on edge, and awaken his possessive, protective paternalism, and want to remove her from such influences. The fact that there wasn't a scrap of truth to Ayako's crude invention mattered little; from a thousand miles away, her guileless father had no choice but to believe, and then capitulate.

お父様

お手紙を頂いてから、ずっと返信しなかったのですが、お父様から追伸もなく、その間私の心は激しく動いておりました。この時代にどう順応していったら良いか考えるのは、現在では容易なことではありません。私たちの祖先の故郷、ここ沖縄では、毎日が待ちぼうけの一日で明け暮れるだけで何の発展もありません。もしかしたら、お父様も、東京に行く奨学金が授与されるまでは同じようだったのでしょうか。

なのに、待ちながらも、私には他でもっとやることがある。やらなければならないことがあることがはっきりしているのです。兵隊がどんどん増員されてきて、その理由は教えてはくれないものの、「地獄の業火」が来るそうです。勿論、公式な話ではなく、那覇のバーで働く地元の人達が持って帰ってくる噂話です。那覇では士官がバーで暇つぶししているので。北海道出身の人が多く、方言や田舎者のような所作が気になりますが、中には気性が良く家族や恋人を恋しく思っている人もいます。最近、そのような孤独な戦士のお世話をすることで私のお務めを果たせると考えるようになりました。そのお礼に、山の中や海岸沿いに私を連れていってのんびり散歩したいという人もいます。

中でも一人、特にすてきな人がいます。優しい目ときれいな歯並びの士官で、東條大将のことを、お父様より大切に思っていることは確かですが、お父様もきっとその人ならと思われると思います。お父様の承諾を得たうえで、お婆様と真由美にお会いしてもらって、お婆様さえよければ、その人と私と真由美でいつかどこかに行けたらと思っています。士官ですから、特別待遇されているので、よそから邪魔されない個室が与えられています。結婚していたかどうかは確認していませんが、子供には慣れていると言っています。複雑な関係になるかもしれませんが、真由美にとって良いお父さん代わりになるでしょう。

ずいぶん前のことのように思えますが、この前のお手紙で、お父様は真由美に身を捧げるように、とおっしゃったので努力しました。それでも、私は皇国に仕えた方が良いと今でも信じています。イギリス人捕虜のための収容所があると聞いています。九州にも何か所かあるとのことで、そこでお役に立てたらいいのに、と熱望するばかりです。でも、お父様が別のことをするように、とおっしゃるのなら、その通りにいたします。私は皇国に対する務めを果たさなければと強く思うので、お国のために尽くす方法として林大尉に親切に接することを承諾していただけるでしょうか。

お母様け、赤十字や愛国婦人会の活動でおうちを留守にされることが多かったのですが、私はお母様のように人に仕えるために生まれてきたように思います。お婆様によれば、お母様は天皇陛下から勲章を賜ったとか。私には、娘の母としての使命より、お母様の娘としての使命が強いことを発見しました。お父様とお婆様との関係に照らし合わせてご理解いただければと思います。

Your loving, loyal and obeying daughter, Ayako

A day later his reply: A telegram – not to her, but to Asako, his mother.

In order for Ayako to fulfil her broader duty in these difficult times, I must ask if you are strong enough to carry the burden of Mayumi. You must tell me if you cannot. I ask that you do not discuss this with Ayako.

Then his mother's tart reply, also by telegram:

The girl is less help than hindrance. She looks out at the sea with hope that she will not be here. It will be kinder to us for her to leave. I can manage, although life is not easy.

Finally, a week later, Ayako received a hand-delivered letter from a colleague of her father's who had flown in to work at the hospital, a reply she had eagerly anticipated since the telegram girl had visited twice, and her increasingly cold grandma pretended they were simply seasonal greetings.

Dear Ayako,

I have been saddened to hear that you have not been happy at our ancestral home but, yes, although my time in Tokyo is disappointing these days, the rural routine and lack of exciting career prospects were what made me want to leave. I expected that in retirement I would return to Kakazu, but many events will have come to pass before that can happen.

A colleague of mine from Keio University has confirmed there is a desperate need for interpreters in the Prisoner Camps at Fukuoka and has received word from the Commandant that they would be willing to recruit you in a probationary role. As you would be the only woman to be tasked that way, he was insistent on pointing out the dangers, because many of the prisoners behave like animals. Also, I think it's safe to say that the camps are not pleasant places to be, with many beatings and harsh practices employed to maintain control.

The position is probationary because the Commandant of the camp outside Fukuoka, himself an almost middle-aged man who is not fit to fight, will want to see how the prison works with a young woman translator. However, my esteemed colleague believes they may have little choice.

Please, darling daughter, be vigilant and careful. As you

know, I would have been pleased if you remained in Okinawa but, as is the case with your mother, I understand your spirit to contribute, and I will not stand in your way.

The military will arrange your transportation, but be mindful of the enemy submarines and take care of yourself. Good luck.

Your loving father

文子様

実家での暮らしが文子にとって幸福ではないのは哀しい。私も現在の東京の生活には失望しているのだが、田舎の代わり映えのしない生活や、仕事の将来性がない事などが故郷を離れたくなった理由だった。退官後は嘉数村に戻るものと思っていたが、それが実現するまでには色々な出来事が起こるだろう。慶應義塾の学者仲間が、福岡の捕虜収容所で通訳がいなくてたいそう困っていて、所長から文子を仮採用しても良いと通知があった、との連絡をくれた。文子はそのような役割に就く唯一の女性になるので、獣のようにふるまう者もいる収容所での危険を十二分に指摘するようにと言っていた。また、収容所は居心地の良い場所ではないのは間違いないだろう。殴打や厳しい処分によって秩序が維持されている場所なのだから。

この収容所は福岡郊外にあって、前線で負傷し戦えなくなった中年の方が所長をしている。この所長が若い女性の通訳を収容所に入れてうまく機能するかどうかを仮採用にして見極めたいからということだ。しかし、そんなことを言っている場合ではないだろう、と仲介してくれた先輩は言っている。

文子、くれぐれも慎重に、注意を怠らないように。沖縄にずっといてくれたら良いと思っているのは文子もわかっている通りだ。お母様の場合と同じように、貴女には貢献したいという精神がある。それに立ちはだかることはしたくない。

軍が輸送手段を提供してくれるが、敵の潜水艦に注意して、自分のことを大切にするように。無事を祈る。

Your loving father

Across the Pacific, the delivery of that letter coincided with Daniel Lawrence's thirtieth birthday.

He was at the Logistical Supply Forward Post on

Midway, a central base of operations for the massive US thrust towards the 'stepping-stone' islands and then, finally, the homeland of Japan.

Given the power and size of America's growing industrial might, supply wasn't an issue. The constant headache was logistics, or as Dan's team put it – 'who gets what, where, when and how?'

Most senior military administrators had avoided logistics as the hottest of hot potatoes, with the inevitable logjams seeming to be a personal affront to powerful Admirals and Generals – raging demiGods – who were always looking for someone to blame. But Dan saw it differently – as an opportunity.

'To be "blamed" is another way of saying we're in control, important, at the centre, where we're needed,' he would explain to his team – but being blamed didn't matter anyway. Abe Ford made sure Dan's 'political cover' was well known, and if an Admiral shouted too loudly, his supplies would '*dwindle*', a word Ford might offhandedly employ in a lawyerly call to the offending bully. So Dan's far-flung LS squad adopted the phrase 'to be dwindled' as a management verb – as in a Brigadier General would be 'dwindled' for chewing up a quartermaster, which meant that, while the essential munitions would arrive, the whiskey, coke syrup, candy and toilet paper would somehow have been left behind at Midway.

Dan's background in shipping, and his understanding of the nuts and bolts and rivets, helped, but his real genius lay in handling the massive airpower, what he called the special forces of immediacy, two thousand C-47s under the direction of logistics supply but not under their control, and that suited Dan just fine. His team directed them but the Army Air Force commanded them, the perfect balancing act to get the job done, a cover to taper the responsibilities for the inevitable failures.

As Dan said, no one knew who was in charge, but with two thousand planes carrying three tons a time, seven days a week, no one cared, so long as what was needed arrived where it was needed. It was among the greatest logistical feats in warfare history – ships, aircraft, munitions, rations, tanks, bombs, ack-ack, gasoline, uniforms, medicines, 'dozers, bridges, concrete, bedding, Jeeps, mosquito nets, flamethrowers, temporary roads, movies, field guns, rifles and people – mainly in the right place at the right time. And then, after the capture of yet another Japanese fiercely held island, the same in reverse.

In the empty flights returning to collect the next weeks' supplies, the heart-breaking injury evacuations, the letters home saying 'I survived', the ferrying out of exhausted Marines for R & R. And the more controversial, and therefore confidential, flights for senior officers to visit their families in Iowa or Missouri or North Carolina. All directed by LS, overseen by Dan and his team, responsible only to Abe Ford, who squeezed every last political advantage out of it, ultimately by the grace and favour of the President.

Dan's team was directing the biggest airline in the world, without timetables or limitations, all with a single purpose – to grind the nimble Japanese into the ground because of the overwhelming superiority of the world's now pre-eminent industrial power being focused precisely where it was needed.

And every single day when Dan woke up after just a few hours' sleep, he would remember Abe Ford's declaration as he made a sweeping gesture at the opulence of that ritzy restaurant in Washington DC:

'*This* is what we we've got to send them, the best of everything our nation can supply. Give 'em all we've got, and the Marines, GIs and dive-bomb pilots will give us all they've got back.'

———

DAN'S thirtieth birthday party on Midway Island was a surprise. He hadn't thought anybody knew, but military records of that kind are easy to access, and the team had done their homework.

Phil Denton, the lawyer from Pittsburgh who had become Dan's deputy, was an amateur historian, and provided an even greater surprise, with a rough drawing of a major moment in history. 'I discovered you were born same day the Archduke Ferdinand got shot in Sarajevo. Led to the First World War, guess it makes sense to keep that secret.'

Dan shrugged and smiled back, but didn't volunteer that Sarajevo was where he was born, too, before his parents trekked across Europe to settle in England. 'I'm focused on finishing this one first, Phil. Let's leave the Nazis and the Soviets to destroy each other.'

Later, in the tent they shared, Phil became philosophical. 'I was born in Pittsburgh, reared in Pittsburgh, went to school there, college with 4As, Masters in Jurisprudence, got married there, have three kids, senior partner in a Pittsburgh law firm. It's where most of the steel that's winning this thing comes from, and here I am, being bitten to billyo by every bug in the whole goddam Pacific, pumped up to kick every Jap butt that bowed to Hirohito, missing my kids and my dog, and Margaret, and yet, yeah, it really is, yeah, it really, really is, the best time of my life.'

Dan simply raised his beer glass because he knew Phil hadn't finished.

'And you. Been halfway round the globe, Mr Mystery, juggle 47s like on a string, swindled oil tankers from the French off Vietnam, have razor-chewing generals begging for bourbon, or the new drugs from Oxford England that only *you* can access, never did College, spent a year in Hirohito's prison and maybe others, never sleep, no commitments, half the nurses here catching your eye – at age thirty, you came from nowhere, going everywhere – hey, buddy, happy happy birthday – ain't it coming time for you to settle down and have a kiddie or two?'

Phil deserved more than the usual Dan impersonal brush-off, and Dan was in an unusually philosophical mood, too. 'Biding my time, sure, if I had a life-plan it would be family at thirty, but I'd have to settle down. And we can't do that with two thousand Goonies to look…'

Phil was about to reply when the tent flap flew open and most of Dan's raggle-taggle team were standing there, with half a dozen female Medics in slinky uniforms, and a case of Sicilian wine, just in by the miracle of LS while giving a Brigadier General a ride from the allied victory there. Once finished with the obligatory 'Happy Birthday', the whole squad crammed in, all talking at once about home and insects and how another battle was due now the casualties from Iwo Jima had been CASEVAC-ed to Pearl and California.

It became clear that one Medic, a brunette called Misty, had selected herself to keep Dan company, with a barrage of winks from Phil, who graciously opted for the overnight aircraft schedule duty, leaving Misty and Dan to finish off the dregs of a dozen bottles after the squad had drifted away.

'I'm not a fan of wartime romance,' she said, before the subject was raised. 'Seen too many "heroes-in-heartache", I call them, great guys with no arms or legs, talking about their childhood sweethearts, wondering…' She whacked a slow-moving mosquito, filled with someone else's blood. 'It's that twilight time, you got a net?'

They bundled onto Dan's mattress and pulled the net around, lying side-by-side, each with the dregs of a bottle, until Misty finished hers, and Dan leaned up on one arm, to guide his into her mouth.

'My Ma and Pa hate me being here. Too many men – had me down to marry a Princeton Grad, "happy-ever-after", like they *pretend*, but aren't. Mom has the money, her Pa's Pa, never gonna work, me don't want happy, want excitement, love being here, will you kiss me…?'

Dan didn't need to be asked twice, and though she stayed over, he was pulled from the tent because Admiral Nimitz had secretly flown in for an early morning briefing on the invasion of Saipan, a tricky island fortress, another stepping-stone closer to Tokyo, but more defended, more holy to the Japs as the Americans crept towards their homeland, more thunder and blood and casualty flights. Sitting across from him, General McArthur fidgeted and said, 'We're heading for the Philippines, too,' although Nimitz looked less than certain.

After the briefing, Dan went on the encrypted Purple Channel, bouncing from Midway to Pearl, to DC, where Abe Ford 'kinda-knew', and said FDR liked Admirals and Generals battling each other, and told Dan to keep close to Nimitz. 'He's the one who'll come out tops, until it becomes a land war.'

Back with his squad, while they leered at him because of 'the night before', Dan worked 36 hours straight, rearranging the support logistics of the massive Armada surrounding Saipan in order to focus on next-door Tinian.

Almost delirious through lack of sleep, he wandered the beach outside their camp with Phil and Haines, their head of transport, who'd been a railroad supervisor, and tracked every ship and aircraft as if they were trains on the East Coast railway in the '20s.

'You *know* the Nips,' Haines said to Dan. 'Now we're in gear, it's only a matter of time – why don't they surrender, so we can all go home?'

Dan had been thinking a lot about this and was not shy to share his view. 'They have to be beaten. It's in their spirit. The women are just as bad, won't let their men surrender. So, they'll fight to the death – for the honour of the nation and family.'

Haines laughed dryly. 'You've got to be kidding. I'm just fighting to win.'

Phil had stopped, struck by an odd thought. 'Do you mean Jap mothers are OK to sacrifice their sons?'

'I mean if we want to win this thing,' Dan replied, 'we'll have to go the whole way. It'll be dirty, no truces or armistices, they've got too much pride, the military has the emperor's nuggets, and he's got the nation's heart, like it's one big family. That's what I learned. And weirdest is – they're actually really nice people. Enjoy a laugh, get drunk, love their kids, polite and kind. And they admire us, want to be friends. And honourable – their word, their reputation – honour is all and everything.'

Haines and Phil had stopped walking along the beach, both fascinated and repelled by what Dan had said.

'But by our standards – our standards, the world has

lots of points of view – they're treacherous bastards. Tricky. Two-faced. And I'll tell you why. Because the glory of Japan makes everything legit. Any Jap will put another Jap first against any foreigner – *gaijin* they call us. It's a mild insult, bit like us calling them Nips, but it means they're all together against us and although they don't expect to win now, they sure won't easily accept losing. It's going to be bloody.'

Phil looked out at the sea, half-a-dozen C-47s were circling to land, more supplies, more American power, more Marines for the beaches.

'So, we're gonna have to bomb and burn the whole country to a wasteland?'

'Pretty much.'

'And you agree with that?'

'It's what's been happening to Germany.'

The three men stood in silence, feeling the beauty of the Pacific sunset, and the ugliness of mankind.

7

In the US the war only brushed with a light touch across the ordinary lives of at-home American families. In Japan there was now a stark shortage of every commodity except courage and forbearance.

The old and weary crawled out of their futon beds to scrape vegetables off scrawny smallholdings; school-children bent over paddy-fields between lessons, and wrote hero-gram letters to lonely, bereft soldiers; the factories, now largely staffed by women, worked all day, every day, attempting to turn pig metal into combat aircraft and howitzers; the towns and cities were overwhelmed by self-defence lessons and air-raid drills, every open space resounding to the shouts of '*Tenno Heika Banzai*' as the nation's homes became a future battleground.

The people endured misery as a national pastime, pain as a propaganda tool.

In Tokyo, Ayako's father woke up every morning in private despair, that his once beloved, rational country had lost its collective mind. But he told no one of this, especially not his wife, Shizuko, who was having what many people said was a 'good war'. The unacknowledged mistress of a senior member of the War Cabinet, she saw and thought little of her husband, although he still had powerful connections in the now underground liberal factions that used to govern before the nationalists and assassins and the military took over.

To him, none of this made sense. Japan should now surrender, apologise, pay reparations, open up to Americans, and start over. However, he knew that this would not happen, short of a catastrophe. Japan would continue to fight to the last man, woman and child, in a tragedy that even Shakespeare would not have dared to write.

The only personal bright spot was that, at last, Ayako seemed to be settled – if the tone of her recent letter was anything to go by. Camp 17 (Fukuoka), in Omuta, across the silty salt flats of the Ariake inland sea from Nagasaki, seemed to suit her well, to have given her purpose, and even status. Conditions were appalling and cruelty commonplace, but she saw this as the consequence of war, started by the blood-sucking sanctions of arrogant, colonial powers, whose soldiers surrendered rather than fought, and now expected to be treated with honour and respect.

The reason for her contentment, if not happiness, was not only the job she had been given, which was undemanding and routine, but the friendship she was enjoying with the camp deputy commandant, an older man her father most certainly would not have approved of – which now made him more, rather than less, attractive.

Major Ito had been severely injured in the early days of the war in Manchuria when a mortar round had exploded on firing, killing the artillery squad and removing much of the major's abdomen. Against the odds he survived to live a relatively normal life, albeit one with certain functions no longer working. This suited Ayako. Since her 'liaison' with the treacherous Daniel Lawrence, her self-pity and resolve had hardened into a nun-like emptiness that foreswore having sex with any man, yet allowed her to enjoy the warmth of the major's tender touch.

'Does it trouble my darling that I cannot be a full man to you?' he would ask, again and again, for reassurance, and she would reply, 'You are more than a full man, you provide my heart with everything it needs.' They would kiss, and she would say, 'Beyond everything.'

Ayako adored the Major. The tenderness and warmth she felt for him was enhanced by the increasing bitterness she felt towards the enemies of Japan. She watched the misery and inhumanity that surrounded them with sad resignation. For the purpose of discipline, the prisoners were required to be craven and subservient. If they didn't bow every time a prisoner passed a Japanese guard they would be forced to kneel and would be savagely beaten until unconscious.

But, as her father had said what seemed a lifetime ago, her feelings could not be a straight line when faced with the cruelties of the camp. Sometimes, when a British prisoner was tall in the way Dan was, or had a similar soft Southern England accent, old feelings would bubble up, and she would have to take a deep breath, make an excuse, go for an unscheduled 'comfort walk'. This conflict, between the evocative memories of their time together, or his voice, and the summary brutality surrounding her was so confusing, it gave her, perversely, yet another reason to blame him, even though she realised it was not his fault.

Her job meant that she should be at the Major's side almost all day, translating back and forth as he completed a daily round of the cramped dormitories, the sparse canteen, the septic medical hut, the frequent roll calls to ensure no prisoner had escaped and, most importantly, that all the prisoners worked hard in Japan's largest coal mine – the reason they were there. The allied prisoners were slave-labourers, required to work twelve-hour shifts for ten consecutive days, on a meagre mess tin of polished rice mixed with pigeon weed twice a day, and thin vegetable or seaweed soup.

The Mitsui mine was dank, dark, and dangerous. Prisoners were required to ignore safety rules and were not allowed to respond when colleagues collapsed from a rock fall or from the cumulative effects of exhaustion through malnutrition. They had to be left there until they pulled themselves up, or died.

The hardness this began to create in Ayako was a direct counterpoint to the childlike tenderness she felt for Major Ito. They shared a bitterness against Japan's enemies that they each found deeply satisfying.

None of the allied prisoners who were summarily sentenced had much understanding of the 'crime' they were alleged to have committed. Random accusations, obscure charges under the wartime powers act, a summary trial without legal representation, a hideous pre-scripted judgement, with the copycat façade of 'colonial' trappings – all sketchily translated by Ayako into English, even if the prisoner was Dutch, Russian or, in one instance, a captured Chinese officer. Most were Australian, English or American sailors or, increasingly, US airmen, who were subjected to the most barbaric treatment because of the growing fury at the perceived US atrocity of bombing civilian targets on the Japanese homeland.

Japan may have signed the Geneva Convention governing the treatment of prisoners in 1929, although they had not ratified it, and they'd agreed to be bound by its provisions in 1942, but those rules held no sway in Camp 17. Mock trials created terror among the prisoners, cowing them into working harder and harder, however malnourished or ill they might be.

When the progress of the war turned against Japan, the cruelties mounted. For failing to bow at the Rising Sun flag, a young Australian private called Runge, already emaciated by lack of food, was sentenced to kneel for days in front of the guardhouse with a bamboo pole held down by weights across the back of his knees causing excruciating pain, his howls ringing around the whole camp.

As Ayako and Major Ito lay side-by-side on their futon beds that airless evening, in the former mine supervisor's hut, both staring at the decayed ceiling, the sobs of Runge abruptly stopped. Either he had fallen unconscious or was dead, it did not matter – Ito shrugged – just another example of the wretched progress of this nasty war. And tomorrow the 'Hell Ship' *Akagisan Maru* was expected to dock at Nagasaki with another three hundred prisoners, who were by all accounts in even worse condition than the existing eight hundred.

Ayako swatted a mosquito, flicked its carcass away and asked, almost nonchalantly, the ultimate Zen question. 'Kazuo. Do you ever ask yourself what we are doing in this war, here?'

He looked at her for several seconds – how many ways were there to answer that conundrum? His eyes, usually carefully controlled not to betray a single thought, were at first piercing, challenging, but then twinkled. She was, after all, fifteen years younger, it's what his own daughter might have asked, if she hadn't broken off all contact after his injury. Ito leaned up on one elbow, reached out, and stroked her cheek. She was to be trusted, of course, so he faintly smiled.

'I have asked, yes, when I am engaged in *Mushin*.'

She liked his Buddhist calmness, and the touch of his hand, soft and soothing. 'Do you have an answer?'

'Not *an* answer, maybe several, but sometimes they change.' He enjoyed caressing her. 'I can no longer be facing the enemy in battle with a gun, so I face them here at the prison, making them work their hardest for our Empire. It is not as good, but it is satisfactory. I am content with the efforts we make, the discipline, necessary for high production and good order.' She twisted, wondering if his hand would move downwards, not wanting to suggest…

'The Mitsui mine, and the zinc smelter, may not seem to be winning our war, but the Fukuoka Prefecture says it is enough to produce thirty fighter planes a day, so production must increase and the new prisoners must know to work hard or be punished. Severely.'

As they lay quietly together, Ayako examined his tanned, lined face, the enquiring eyebrows, the sharp nose with a shrapnel wound on one nostril, partly hidden by the lavish moustache she so loved. She caressed his lips with a single finger and thought, *I love you*. She didn't say it, his rank meant that would not be proper.

But he knew, anyway.

And because she was young, and had a reputation for speaking her mind when silence would have been more sensible, or kinder, she said, '*Akagisan Maru*, I know this boat. Or one of very similar name.'

Kazuo was beginning to drift into sleep, the calm, contented sleep of a man who lay beside a young, devoted woman. 'Ah-so…'

'It once transported coffee from Brazil…'

'But it is a transport ship for criminals…'

'Is now. Prisoners in the hold where they used to have the coffee.' Ayako was beginning to have doubts, perhaps let him sleep…

Ito was struggling to stay awake, but cared about her. 'You know it…?'

'A long-ago story… not necessarily a good outcome…'

This prompted him to rise up on one arm. 'Please, I must hear it.'

'Very well.'

Where to start? Ayako *did* want to tell her beloved Kazuo about the most traumatic incident in her life but needed to tread carefully. His pride might be wounded.

'When I was attached by my father to the *Kempeitai* in Nagasaki, those monstrous idiots, I was commanded to visit the docks for translation purposes when the *Akagisan Maru* arrived with four thousand tons of coffee. Very important cargo, for Embassies and high Government in Tokyo, from Sao Paolo.'

'But would that not need Spanish?'

'Portuguese – but the owner of the cargo was British, my job was to translate, but also to accompany him, to see his purpose.' Ayako turned away from staring at the ceiling to face him. 'He was very cruel to me.'

'In what way, my darling?'

She did not need to say, silence was enough.

Now it was Kazuo's turn to tread carefully. The all-seeing Japanese bureaucracy had documented Ayako's 'service' to trap a spy, so he already knew about her acting as a man- trap, later being sent by her father to Okinawa. Although the 'facts' of a child were not specifically disclosed – they were there between the lines, a routine form of Japanese communication – the story was clear to an experienced reader.

As Deputy Commandant, Ito had, of course, read the file, he had read it many times in this very office, that they used at night as a bedroom, and he had hoped that one day she would mention it. He noticed she was trembling and tried to work out why. *Shame, for a humiliating memory? Anger from being so used? The pain of a mother missing a baby?* But before his analytical mind found the answer, Ayako told him anyway.

'It is a very bad memory but perhaps it may help if I can share it with you, Kazuo. Do you mind?'

This was everything he could have asked for. 'I will be pleased to hear.'

She nuzzled into his shoulder, pushed her slender thigh between his sturdy legs, and let the words, so long held back by a dam of pride, flow at last.

'I believe in family. My father and my mother, our ancestors. I always had thought that…' She trailed off, he stayed silent, to allow her to find a way. '…that the glory of Japan is not won on the battlefield, but in our homes, it is why I studied, to make my father proud. One day I, too, would have a family, children to grow and be proud of, it is what I dreamed of, sometimes still I dream.' Ayako sighed, looked away from him, so she didn't see the tears in his eyes.

'I hate this war, but I hate the British and Americans more, because they took my belief in family away from me, not by bombing, but up here.' She pointed to her head, her brain, her mind, the way that Dan had pointed to his, on Mount Inasa, what seemed like a lifetime ago. 'It is not possible, it will never be possible, to forgive.'

Ayako had been looking into the distance, now she turned back to Kazuo, saw the tears, leaned across and kissed them away. 'Because…' she trailed off, the anger becoming resignation, memories of abuse overwhelming her. 'Because, they…'

From outside the mine supervisor's hut came noises of commotion, a young Japanese guard yelling at a small detail of prisoners to pick up the body of Private Runge, indifferent to whether he was dead or clinging desperately to life. All that mattered was that he was tidied away. Ayako ignored the noise and continued. 'Because this was destroyed within me.' She pointed to her abdomen. 'In here. By making it putrid, unworthy of our great nation. As war destroyed that in you.' She was wracked by huge sobs, overwhelmed with misery, he tried to comfort her by belittling his own suffering.

'For me it was an accident, for you – not so.'

As Runge was hauled past their hut, they heard a plaintive cry of 'Please, help me, please…' It seemed he was not dead and the moving of his wasted body had awakened him from a coma, his cries receding as he was dragged away to the makeshift hospital. 'Please, please, no more…'

Lying together on their futon Ayako and Major Ito kissed deeply, the world outside the former mine supervisor's hut fell silent again, with only the shrill shrieking of the *banza katydid* crickets disturbing the quiet. She could feel the beating of his heart through the army-issue nightshirt, he could feel her thighs gripped around his hip, harmony had returned, but they were still troubled, Ayako especially, who was now whispering.

'Yes, there is a baby. As unwanted as this war. Except by my father, who sold himself to western ideas when young. I cannot want a child, when I think of it as an *invader*.'

Ito was thinking about his own ten-year-old daughter, Haru, who had only visited once during the year he was helpless in hospital, that she seemed to blame him for being a lesser father, rather than a wounded hero. But Ayako interrupted those thoughts.

'I know it is not the baby's fault that it has *his* eyes, the western eyes of our enemy. But each day'—she shook her head at the memory, now more with sadness than anger—'I would look and think "what's the use? I will never love this baby, better to be with her great grandma, who never will feel the pain of…"'

Ayako was interrupted by a knock on the door.

Ito tightened the tie on his pyjama top and stood across the threshold. Two orderlies bowed. 'Very many apologies, Major.' More bowing, backwards and forwards.

'And?'

'Sir, Prisoner Pavolopoulos has been reported stealing two bowls of rice, your order is required.'

'The "Greek"?'

'*Hai!*'

'Reported by whom?'

They bowed again. 'The American, Little.'

Ito swung around to Ayako, opened his arms in disdain, shook his head, as if to say, 'the shame of the enemy.' This was American Lt Commander Edward Little, who ran the meagre canteen, reporting the theft of a handful of food by a desperately hungry American Corporal. No Japanese would ever have betrayed another Japanese soldier to an enemy. The decadence of the west knew no bounds. Now he must carry out his duty.

'Have Pavolopoulos escorted to the underground starvation chamber with no reprieve.' A public, agonising sentence of death – by starvation.

The guard bowed again. 'Thank you, Sir.'

'And allow Commander Little an extra cup of rice for his cooperation.'

Later, as Ito and Ayako entwined towards midnight, enjoying the touch, the softness of each other, Ito basking in his power, he said, 'Western eyes? Do not feel so bad about not caring for the baby, my love. Like Little, Western eyes see only themselves.'

Ito went to kiss her goodnight, but was interrupted by the sound of banging and shouting, as Corporal Pavolopoulos was hauled from his billet and dragged to the starvation chamber cut through the whine of the *banza katydid*. He was murmuring '*Kyrie Eleison*' in Greek, over and over, until a corrugated hatch crashed down on his whimpers.

Ayako squeezed Ito's arm, he was only doing his duty. *War is cruel.*

THE FIRST TIME Daniel Lawrence truly understood the reality of war, in the early days of 1945, was when a drunken Marine Colonel demonstrated the power of a flamethrower on a Guadalcanal pig. The baby pig didn't even squeal, it was dead before it could take a breath. Dan was drunk, too, so he didn't care, but it was a lesson he didn't forget.

Having started the war as a Captain, that particular Lt Colonel, Bob Coherne, had already been at the forefront of five island invasions – Samoa, Kwajalein, Saipan, Guam and Iwo Jima. He'd been wounded twice, the first time in the butt in Cape Gloucester, when a Japanese booby-trapped bayonet sprang from a banana tree after he stumbled on a tripwire. 'Missed my vitals,' was his immediate response, as he urged the medics to get him back to the frontline, 'As-friggin'-Soon As Possible.' After which his nickname was 'ASAP Coherne'.

The second injury was at a forward command post in Iwo Jima after the terrain in every direction had been meticulously searched and cleared, when a full platoon of Japanese soldiers emerged from foetid tunnels they had been secretly hiding in for a week. 'All guns blasting,' was how Bob remembered it, preferring that memory to the fact he'd been hit by at least ten bullets, mostly in his legs and, yes, the butt again. And because he was such a huge man and didn't seem to feel pain, he was promoted and back on watch within a month, on crutches.

'And I'll tell you why we missed those pesky Nips, Mr Lawrence. Tryin' to save gasoline.'

They were sitting as close to a campfire as the hot humid night air would allow, letting the smoke wash over them to deter every kind of insect known to man. Although meant to be a high-level strategic supply meeting, alcohol was routine.

Dan had heard stories like this before; the army air force, the marines, the navy were always griping and lobbying for 'our kind' of supplies, rather than 'fancy stuff for guys in pressed uniforms'. And because of the casualties and horror of being in the firing line, they didn't hold back. Hence, incinerating a baby pig to demonstrate that gasoline is more important than 18" navy shells.

'If I'd had few hundred gallons more, we'd been able to smoke 'em out – you feeling partial to a flamed pork sandwich, Mr Lawrence?' asked in his Texan drawl twisted into the King's English, without irony or malice, though everyone knew it was meant to be an anti-Brit jibe at Dan's expense.

In spite of, or maybe because of, his brusque, direct manner, Dan liked Coherne, enjoyed this kind of crosstalk however serious the subtext, although other members of his team were more sensitive.

'Let me tell you about that special gasoline, Colonel.' Phil Denton would often play hard man to Dan's easy-guy. 'We're talking about a 9,000-mile round trip by C-47, which in turn needs refuelling and four stops each way. Barrel of that chalks up forty barrels to get it there.'

Coherne ignored Denton, both sides had made their point, so he continued with Dan.

'You're Abe Ford's man – yep?'

'Dan's his own man…'

'Not what I hear.' He pointed at Dan, who was waving insects away. 'Speak to *our Mr Lawrence* – and it's on the desk of "That Man in the White House" next day.'

Arthur Haines tried to cool the atmosphere. 'Guess you don't like The Chief.'

'Who does?'

Denton: 'You a Dewey man…?'

'Taft.'

'Double loser then.'

'If Taft'd won in '40, wouldn't need these…' Coherne gestured to the crutches.

This was a circular political argument that if the

Republicans had been in control and the US hadn't squeezed Japan into a corner by sanctions, the Japs wouldn't have bombed Pearl Harbour, and America would have stayed out of the war.

That moment coincided with the noisy arrival of half a squadron of C-47s landing one after the other on Henderson Field, the runway next to their camp.

Coherne cupped a hand to his good ear, the ear that hadn't been mashed by shrapnel. 'Always gives me a stiffy, Pratt and Whitney engines, sound of freedom, more supplies to beat the Japs with.' He shrugged with the only shoulder that still worked. 'You see, boys, down in Galveston, we don't admire blue-blood lawyers like That Man FDR, or let 'em tell us what to do – what to think – never will.' He held up his bottle of Southern Select specially flown in from Houston. 'Same guys who prohibited this golden nectar,' and took a mighty swallow. 'But I get it, we're on the same side. Jest don't ask me to *like* him.' He took another swig and threw the empty in the fire. 'Let's get down to business.'

'Business' meant discussing the next major offensive, which was meant to be a secret, but anyone with a brain had worked it out.

'The "Big O",' he said, as if giving an order to invade immediately. 'Now we've got Saipan and can bomb Jap mainland, we're gonna go *round* the remaining islands, let 'em stew in their own shit. Intelligence – if you can call it that – says Japs've shipped in an extra 120,000 of their best – fanatical, trained, ready to fight to the death, because, remember, they see the Big O as part of their blessed homeland…'

A Nurse had wandered into the circle around the fire with a first aid shoulder-bag, standing with hands on hips, above the receding sound of the C-47 engines, she shouted, 'I fix him, then he un-fixes himself.'

'Nurse Campbell…'

'Colonel, what have I told you about giving nature a chance…?'

'Mighty good evening to you, too. Meet the supply crew. These are the guys bring your lipstick from San Fran.'

'How 'bout some nylons then, boys?'

Arthur Haines pretended to write on his hand. 'On the list.'

'Eau de Cologne? I heard on Forces Radio we conquered the city.'

Denton tried his luck. 'Would I get a kiss?'

'Chief would. Which one's I/C?'

Dan had been quiet, more interested in the Big O, but they pointed, bringing him in. 'Name's Dan, Nurse, imagine penicillin is more important.'

There was an audible groan from the circle round the fire, too serious.

'Depends what disease you got.'

The guys looked at each other, this was one sassy nurse. She began changing a dressing on Coherne's foot, sitting on a log and resting his leg across her lap while she worked in the light from the fire. 'This Marine's had 'em all – I'm Peggy by the way, got any vodka?'

Of course they had, and passed over a bottle, from which she took a long slug, before up-ending it on the Colonel's wound, causing him to stiffen. 'This here's my only patient who doesn't yelp…'

'Gotta be like a waste…'

'Come all the way from Vladivostok…'

While still being treated, Coherne clapped his hands. 'Guys – the BIG O…'

The group fell silent. Should they be discussing this in front of the nurse?

'Oh, don't mind about Campbell. She sure can talk, but don't listen. An' she knows anyways. An' so do the Japs, ain't no secret, ain't that true, Campbell?'

'Well, it's been on Forces Radio we're headin' that way…'

'The secret's in the "*how*"?'

'Not on this leg Mister, that ain't no secret, not *any*-how. Island's got mountains.'

FROM THE AIR, it's easy to see that Okinawa really is shaped like a sabre, an island of rural paddy fields, rocky and forested, surrounded by turquoise coral reefs in the confluence of the deep blue Pacific and choppy China Sea. The North is mountainous and thinly populated, the South a patchwork of towns, villages and small holdings. At 33,000 feet the view at first suggested a peaceful, rural idyll, a land the world has passed by – but, on closer examination, it was clear that a different scenario was playing out.

Dan was looking down from a converted Boeing B-29 Superfortress, an F-13 version individually given the name *Over Exposed* by the crew, flying sedately, too high for anti-aircraft fire and too sudden for the Zero fighters that lacked advanced radar.

The aircraft had twenty-five cameras that could photograph a strip of land 3-miles wide. With most of the island being only six miles across it meant that an F-

13 could, in two passes, up-and-back, take hi-resolution film of the whole island and then rush it back to Henderson.

In the seat next to him, Coherne stared downwards, with apprehension, resolve and some excitement, watching the next invasion target flash by while actually licking his lips. Even as high as they were, you could see there were fortifications and armaments, wall to steely wall, all over the island. He mumbled to himself – the words inaudible under the throaty roar of the four engines.

'Colonel?' Although he couldn't hear what Coherne was saying, Dan knew from the serious expression on his companion's face, that this mumbling was important.

Coherne pulled closer, did his one-shoulder shrug, raised his bushy eyebrows and shouted in Dan's ear. 'I said, "*Remember the Alamo.*" All I can think of. Ain't sure why?'

Dan looked down at the glistening island, equally unsure, assuming it was a private battle cry, perhaps like a prayer. But then Coherne punched Dan's arm and nodded, now he had worked it out.

'I'm thinking place looks like a fortress, an' it's them Japs that's in the Alamo – never give up, fight to the last man.' Coherne's massive face was a tangle of contradictions, pumped up – unsure, worried – determined, ready for the fight. 'Yeah, the Alamo – that's what's ahead of us, and we're the Mexicans.'

Dan nodded, smart man this Colonel, and touched his wallet containing that little scrap of paper Ayako had given him, then mumbled the address to himself – 'Kakazu Village, Okinawa' – the nearest thing his sceptical heart could ever get to his own Alamo prayer.

Back at Guadalcanal, they gathered around the campfire for another bout of 'business and drinking', with the senior commanders, all in a more sombre mood. The reconnaissance flight had confirmed that Okinawa was bristling with garrisons, pillboxes and dug-in artillery, from top to bottom.

Coherne held up a card in the flickering firelight, with Kanji on it. 'Right boys. Know what this is?'

砦

A young Marine Lieutenant just out of Quantico jumped straight in. 'Is it Japanese?'

'Of course, it's frigging Japanese. But what's it say?'

Usually, Dan would not give away any unnecessary information about himself, but he wanted to up his status with the brass around the fire, and anyway, couldn't resist. '*Toride*. Stronghold. Fortress.'

They all turned to look at him, including the Navy Commanders, Army Air Force Colonels and senior Marines.

Coherne chuckled, his fleshy face lighting up. 'Mr Lawrence here is corr-ect. My spies tell me he spent a year in a Jap jail, guess you know a bit or piece about them, sir.'

Dan smiled. The 'my spies' was a nice touch. He swilled the last of the beer around his glass, then sure he had everyone's attention, sold his pitch. 'The Colonel's Kanji is right, Okinawa will be a fortress, we saw that overflying today, but it's not only a fortress of stone and armour, but of spirit. They won't give in, as the Colonel's legs attest, they'll dig in, tunnels, caves…'

'…we're gonna have to burn 'em out…'

Dan nodded, and addressed the whole group with authority. 'Bob – after your now legendary pig incineration last night, we found another dozen C-47s. So, today my unit, Logistical Supply, made plans to fly in an extra thousand barrels of flamethrower gasoline, and more by ship…'

The Navy Commander: 'What General LeMay does with bombers…'

'From the air…' Air Force Colonel.

The Army Brigadier: 'What we'll have to do on the ground…'

'Close up…' Bob finished off.

'Scorched earth. Literally.' That was the young Lieutenant, again.

Everyone rolled their eyes at him, as he now cowered. 'Well, it is, kinda…'

Later that night, after Nurse Campbell had climbed off Dan and they lay smoking and sipping tequila, he asked, 'What will you do when all this is over?'

'Become a dutiful, boring mother. What else?'

He blew out through the mosquito net and shook his head 'Has to be a lot else. I'm gonna dance all night for a month, watch movies again, buy myself a mansion in New York, make me a fortune, big world out there…'

'Not in Montana.' Peggy put her left hand in the air, showing a ring on her fourth finger. 'He's a farmer, good man, can't write, so his mother sends me letters, and reads mine back to him.' She laughed, with an odd combination of harshness and sweetness, the laugh of a lively woman who was happily resigned to a colourless, routine life. 'Walt said, "You go, serve our country, have a dose of high-jinx, get it out, then we can settle for what we've got".' She nodded, a good memory. 'An' that'll suit. Leave the adventuring to people that need to conquer the world, climb mountains. Like you. We're *eastern* Montana, like it flat…'

After she had gone, Dan lay awake listening to planes landing, one after the other, sometimes fifty planes an hour they said, wondering about Peggy's life, how a capable, robust woman would be content to waste away with a farmer called Walter. As always at such times his thoughts drifted back to those fiery eyes, that tiny room above the restaurant, and that little scrap of paper.

He didn't need to get the paper out – Ayako's scheming had worked – the contents were seared into his brain. *'Mrs Asako Okunaga, Nishabaru House, Kakazu Village, Highway No.5, Okinawa.'* His baby, a secret baby – for him alone to know about. Just as he liked it. Being a proxy father – one day, when this was all over, the child could be a special part of his life, a gift, like a medal to be cherished on special days, polished, loved. Dan wrinkled his nose. Maybe…

Another aircraft landed, screeching, heavy, that would be a bomber, maybe a B-29, just back from pulverising the mainland. Or had they started on umm… already…? With his baby there, Dan couldn't get himself to think the 'O' word, but he was interrupted anyway.

The side of his tent flapped back. Peggy had returned, now with a half of last night's vodka. She sat on the side of his camp-bed, the mosquito net between them, so with her weight on the net she could lean back against it, talking away from him, sipping the vodka.

'Was something you said: "Big world out there." Stopped me sleeping. And I wanted to ask – what about the kids? See'—she took another sip—'I've been having a ball out here, and I truly enjoy being a nurse – I mean, the broken guys is difficult, but you see past their wounds, the Doc says, "look into their souls," and you really can, maybe because they're pretty gone, most of them, can't speak for shock, you're so appreciated, and they're all kinds, we've had a Russian, Aussies, Brits like you, Dutch, so it's been a big world here, and when you said that, I knew you're right – but what about the kids? You go out discovering the world, you can't have kids, can't take them with you – but they gotta be the most important thing in life – I want three, at least – so what do you say, don't just tell me they don't matter, 'cause they do…'

She stood up, had a swig, put the bottle down, and climbed under the mosquito net, holding his cheeks in her palms and talking into his astonished face. 'So, that's my question, Mr Big Shot. Where are your kids gonna be, if you're out in your big world?'

Peggy cried and kissed him at the same time, holding him close, unfastening his pyjamas again. ''Cause that's your job, to protect them, which is why I'm headin' back to Montana, soon as this thing's finished, hey, do you even have kids? I should have asked ya.'

In a canvas tent smelling of disinfectant, on a lumpy camp bed, under a mosquito net more dirty than white, becoming excited again at her touch, he was never going to answer. But after Peggy left for the second time, having said her piece, now able to sleep – he lay awake as usual, because the little slip of paper had become a mantra.

'Mrs Asako Okunaga, Nishabaru House, Kakazu Village,
Highway No.5, Okinawa.'

Dan was thinking *what will happen when the bombs fall, bombs I probably helped send their way? And the navy shells? And the two billion bullets in transit from Detroit, Lansing or Independence Missouri? And the flame-thrower gasoline?*

The idea made him shudder, as he thought about the baby pig that didn't even squeal.

8

Leave the glory, the false heroics, and the sentimentality to the actors and sob sisters. War is simple: You've got to kill people, and when you kill enough of them, they stop fighting.'

Brigadier General Curtis LeMay

WHILE JAPANESE NEWSPAPERS and media still proclaimed the imminent advent of a glorious victory, the people, it seemed to Ayako's father, had fallen into an abyss of *shikata ga nai*, 'It cannot be helped' – a deadening, grinding acceptance that nothing could be done about it.

This was seldom spoken out loud, that would have been unpatriotic, but it was felt in all walks of life, across the whole of society – as if the entire nation was sleep-walking towards their own destruction. People went about their increasingly disjointed lives as best they could, trying to believe the censored news-sheets and scratchy radio broadcasts, while keeping their eyes down, away from what they could see all around. Especially ignoring the 'death visits' to neighbours about sons on islands they had never heard of, or the *hyosatsu*, the aluminium plate above the *genkan* door of a dead soldier, that read '*izoku no ie*', with a chrysanthemum symbol above it.

And that was before the bombing and the cruel use by the *gaijin* of 'dragons of fire,' lighting up the skies so brightly that no censor could conjure the vision away, nor lay balm on the burns. The progress was all in one direction now – '*warukunatte kita*' – 'it's getting worse, isn't it?' said with dour acceptance, as if it was a nasty rainstorm, always heavier and colder, with no sun in sight.

Until the 10th March 1945.

Japan's cities had earlier skirmishes with the devil of incendiary bombs falling from the sky, but on that fateful evening, the US Army Air Force General, Curtis LeMay, turned his ruthless attention to causing the greatest fire in all history, in the world's most densely populated city – Tokyo.

A special bomb, the model-E-46 incendiary magnesium-and-phosphorus cluster bomb, had been developed with Japanese wood and paper cities in mind, and LeMay decided it was time 'to stop swatting flies, and go after the dung-heap,' as Abe Ford had recounted to Dan later. The 500-pound E-46 had a particularly lethal modus operandi. Dropped at night from the bay of a B-29, when the bomb fell to 2,500 feet it released 38 napalm or phosphorus bomblets, which could penetrate roofs or explode on impact, discharging globs of flaming napalm over a wide area.

The flimsy Tokyo streets burst into flames, with whole neighbourhoods engulfed in a whirlwind of fire, burning everything in its path to ashes in seconds – with a single

E46 bomb, instantly igniting thirty-eight roaring fires across an area the size of ten football pitches.

LeMay had all the protective armaments removed so that each B-29 could carry twenty-four, 500-pounders, and there were 334 planes, adding up to 304,608 twelve-pound, phosphorus and napalm bomblets scattered across a city already crowded with families living in makeshift, ramshackle huts.

It had been called 'Operation Meetinghouse' – though Dan thought Melting House might have been a more appropriate name – and it led to the greatest loss of life in a single operation in history, with over 120,000 men, women and children incinerated, and double that severely burned. All in just one night.

At first, to those scurrying home on the ground, the raid of 10th March almost seemed routine, although until then most raids had been during the day. But that night, at midnight, the pathfinder B-29s tattooed an 'X' of fire across Koto and Chuo wards of Tokyo, so the fully-laden bombers which followed had an aiming point. Flying in at only 8,000 feet, to confound the city's air defences, the 'X' target was impossible to miss.

Ayako's mother, Shizuko, was with her regular, if forbidden, companion, Baron Kazushige Kido, First Deputy Minister of Home Affairs. They were on an ancient wooden seat lolling against each other, hidden in the leafy gardens outside the sanctuary at the Meiji Jingu, surreptitiously holding hands under his woollen Inverness coat.

It was late for a rendezvous, but his cabinet meeting had meandered on even longer than usual, and Shizuko had the excuse of taking the international boss of the Red Cross, Pierre Balou, to dinner at the fabled Ginza Aster, where her daughter Michiko worked while learning Chinese cuisine. Not that her husband, Junichiro, Ayako's father, would care, or even know – nowadays when she got home her impossible husband was usually in a whiskey- sodden coma.

Shizuko was briefing Kazushige about her Red Cross boss's suspicion of embezzlement. 'Pierre was not easily deflected, said there is evidence that Red Cross supplies and medicine are not reaching the prisoners…'

'What evidence...?'

'Witnesses of Red Cross stocks in warehouses – "stacked high," he says. And, of course, the prisoners…'

'He believes *them*?'

Shizuko shrugged, *yes, but does it matter?* '"Why would they lie?" Pierre asked. "So many prisoners are dying, for the want of medicine, and the camp doctors say the same." Perhaps he still trusts me, blames your Ministry – "Home Affairs are stealing Red Cross supplies," he said.'

Kido seemed unusually thoughtful. 'Did he mention me?'

She liked having so much of his attention. 'Pierre mentioned your name, but he can't know…' She was interrupted by the throaty drone of many Wright-Cyclone engines, the unmistakable sound of heavy bombers coming.

They both looked up, to see silhouettes in the distance.

'Those aircraft are flying low,' Baron Kido said, pulling her closer in the blustery wind, then, after two earlier, brief false-alarms, the sirens howled out again across the Tokyo skyline, calling on them to seek shelter in the nearest safe building.

'To the Ministry, I think,' he said, almost lifting her up in his urgency.

Shizuko shook her head while shaking free, 'Michiko will be finishing at Ginza Aster, I want to go there, to take her home.'

They set off across the park at a canter, Shizuko faster because Kido had a limp, an old Naval wound sustained at Port Arthur before the Japanese victory over Russia in 1904. As they reached the exit gate of the Meiji-Jingu Park, Kido's driver was waiting with the bodyguard. Still aware of the indelicacy of being seen with Kido, Shizuko held back, but he ushered her in saying, 'Not necessary now,' as a huge plume of fire erupted in the distance, almost dancing across the skyline – beautiful in a way, so long as you weren't in its path. Several seconds after the flames, came the roar.

'Bomb in Ginza,' the driver said, pointing at the flames.

Shizuko clutched at Kido's bicep – that's where Michiko was.

As they stood taking it in, another huge plume of flames exploded into the sky.

'That's in Chuo-ku,' the driver said, now shaking his head at what they were witnessing.

At last, Shizuko lost her composure.

'Michiko,' she screamed. 'Michiko!' and pulled away from Kido, beginning to stagger crazily towards the first explosion.

Kido pointed at the driver, 'Ginza Aster,' he barked, grabbing Shizuko and thrusting her towards his car. The driver looked doubtfully at the bodyguard, who stared back expressionlessly, opening the door, and helping Kido and Shizuko in, before climbing into the front, alongside the driver. As he started the engine, the heavens erupted – this time two B-29 bomb loads igniting ten thousand square metres of cityscape, somewhere out across the bay.

'*Hayaku!*' Kido shouted as the sound and blast of the explosions reached them while the driver edged warily out of Harajuku towards Ginza. Desperate to get to her daughter, Shizuko shook the driver's shoulder, '*Hayaku!*' Kido and Shizuko held each other tightly as the car swayed between terrified pedestrians running in all directions. A cyclist unexpectedly turned into their path and with a metallic thump they knocked him out of the way, picking up speed as the driver leant on the horn over the noise of the air-raid siren.

'Might she already have left?' Kido asked, partly sympathetic, partly to question whether they should be heading towards the bombs.

Shizuko shook her head, without logic. 'I am her mother,' she replied.

Then suddenly it didn't matter. The road ceased to be a road, it became a crowd, an impassable barrier of hysterical people, a massive tide of humanity pushing down the hill. Half an hour after midnight, with no trains now running, the throng that would usually be passing through Harajuku station had fled out onto the surrounding streets, moving as fast as they could, trying not to panic, trying to reach safety. Except nowhere was safe because no one knew where the next batch of murderous incendiaries would land.

The driver turned to Kido and put his arms up in despair. They were thoroughly stuck. And the air was becoming hot, stickily hot, fiercely hot. The very sky seemed to be alight. The bodyguard climbed out and opened the rear door, bizarrely holding his pistol along his right thigh as if it might help protect his employer.

Shizuko was clinging onto Kido, trying to stay calm, muttering, 'Michiko' several times to herself, and pulling him in the direction of Ginza. But as they looked down the hill, they could see, and now feel, an astonishing wall of flames a hundred feet tall, burning in a kaleidoscope of colours, as the small factories, chemical works and paper houses along the riverside roared in the heat.

Seeing this, the mood changed.

Michiko was no longer the focus – the instinct for personal survival took over. Oblivious to what anyone thought, Shizuko pulled Kido closer and kissed him lovingly, longingly on the lips. Kido then turned to the driver and bodyguard in dismissal, shooing them away, saying, 'Thank you for your efforts, now you must protect yourselves.'

The bodyguard was confused about where his duty lay, but the driver backed away, bowing, back towards the park, while Kido pulled Shizuko in the direction everyone else was jogging, away from Shibuya, away from the heat and the bombs. Except there was nowhere to get away. They were surrounded by flames, there was no way out of the walls of fire, with the wind – why had it now become like a tornado? – stoking the inferno, funnelling sparks and embers into them, and now the shop fronts were smouldering, such heat.

As they fled, yet more fire-bombs fell, creating higher and higher pillars of flames across Ginza and Chuo, falling on red-hot bare earth where factories and homes and humanity were already in cinders. Kido was beginning to flag, his heart never was strong, his metal-splintered leg was screaming 'please stop', but as he slowed, a store window exploded, firing molten glass into the air, which cascaded onto the galloping crowd, falling onto

Kido's head, burning his bushy hair. Shizuko stopped with him, to ruffle the flaming glass away, scalding her hand, giving up hope as his face began to blister.

At that moment, the loyal Ministry bodyguard came back to protect his patron. He pulled Kido up and shouted, 'We can find water at Futaba School, please, Sir, please…' and he began hauling his boss by the shoulder down a narrow side street, towards Kojimachi, away from the panicking crowd and the worst of the heat. Shizuko took the other shoulder and the odd trio, weeping in shock and anger and fear and outrage, limped across a dozen scorched alleys to the familiar sight of the domed, brick-and-tile clock tower of the Futaba Catholic School.

A small group of nuns, the Sisters of St Maur, had formed a chain at the regal entrance, swiping people with old scapulars and worn habits to extinguish flames on their clothes, singing '*Adeste Fideles*,' while shouting, 'This way, hurry, this way.' Then novice nuns guided them through the ornate entrance, across the rear courtyard to the massive swimming pool.

Kido, Shizuko and the bodyguard stopped on seeing there were a hundred people up to their shoulders in water in the pool, wailing and screaming, but as they hesitated another roar of heat and sparks and embers whooshed across the already glowing lawn surrounding the pool, so the trio took a deep breath and jumped in, still holding each other.

The relief of cool water on their scorched bodies was immediate, perhaps this would be their salvation.

Professor Okunaga woke up at four-thirty a.m. with a throbbing headache and a strange pattern of bright lights flickering against his eyelids. There was an odd smell, too, one he couldn't place. He lay for a while, confused and disoriented. Yes, there had been an air-raid last night and, as usual, he slept through it – if the bomb has your name on it, 'a man can die but once.' But what *is* that smell? Had he left something on? Gradually, gently, Junichiro dragged open his bloodshot eyes, first one, then the other. 'What is this flickering-flashing, Jun, why is it so bright, lighting the whole room?'

He turned over to look at Shizuko. *Why's she not there?*

He reached for his glasses to make sure, while attempting to remember. That's right, Shizuko was dining at Ginza Aster with the Red Cross boss from Geneva, and coming home with Michiko. He called out 'Micchan, are you awake?'

No answer, except now he noticed a loud, steady cracking from outside, like a massive bonfire, somewhere in the distance. *Cracking?* He really must get up to look. He slid the paper window open – and his life was changed forever.

Beyond the Hosei University buildings and the Imperial gardens, the whole city had burnt, was still burning, still exploding. The fires of hell. *What?* He looked for the quart of whiskey to steady his nerves. Empty.

He pulled over a wooden bedroom stool and sat, still able to see the devastation outside. Obviously, an air-raid, but how could so much of the city now be flat? All the way to the river only a few brick or concrete buildings remained – the rest is a wasteland. Eliot's *The Waste Land*. And the smell?

Professor Okunaga nodded to himself, becoming fully

awake, analysing the appalling scene. *Yes, all the way to the river.* His large head lolled to one side, eyes closed in thought. That's where they were, Michiko and Shizuko. He sat on the stool for a few seconds then suddenly burst into action, racing out of his 4th floor Hosei University apartment, climbing the central stairs, three at a time, shouldering open the wooden door at the top. To his surprise, a number of neighbours and colleagues were already on the roof, talking, several in tears.

'After *our* beginning, this is *their* ending,' announced the Dean of Hosei loftily, pontificating towards the ruins. 'Hellfire.' The group with him nodded in unison.

'"I never see thy face".'

They had not noticed Jun arrive, and now turned to hear him.

'Henry Fourth, Falstaff,' he said, as if that explained it. '"Hellfire, I never see thy face".'

'Ah, Okunaga, perhaps you slept through it,' he returned pointedly. 'As you see, "all is lost" – Anthony and…'

But the Dean was interrupted by his wife, Shizuko's best friend, crying out with pain and outrage while bowing. This was no time for scoring academic points. 'Is Shizuko…?'

Jun shook his head, vacantly pointing towards the devastated ruins of Ginza, 'Late dinner with the Red Cross…' Then stopped as he fully realised, turning on his heel and racing towards the stairs, with the Dean shouting, 'Come back, it's too late, don't be a fool, man.'

'Hellfire', 'All is Lost', *The Waste Land*, kept spinning in Jun's mind as he hurried around the Imperial Gardens in the dark on his way to Ginza, lit by the slowly dying flames in the distance, and the first rays of dawn. Incredible, he thought, as he came across the utter devastation from the Palace gardens onwards. Hellfire did not adequately describe it:

Where there had been trees were twisted sticks rearing up like crucifixion crosses.

Streets of houses were neat piles of ashes. Then, as he looked across towards Ginza, Jun saw the scattered bodies, some reduced to nothing more than charcoal logs, and he knew that the Dean was right – all hope was gone. He felt surprisingly little. Despair had taken hold, for the first time in his combative, successful life.

Nothing mattered, nothing would ever matter again.

He stood for a while with a few firefighters impotently watching the smoke, while protecting their faces from the extreme heat with the flaps of their headgear tied up over their mouths and noses as improvised shields.

'Ginza?' Jun asked of one who seemed to be the Chief.

'Gone. Nothing.'

'I should…'

'Go home, if you've still got one…'

It didn't help to be proven right about this idiotic war. Of course he had known that Japan should have thrown in the towel two years ago. Of course the United States and the British Empire would win. Of course carrying on fighting was futile, he knew, knew… and then an underground fuel tank and the world around Professor Okunaga exploded, and he wouldn't know anything for many days.

LYING IN HIS HOSPITAL BED, with bandages around his eyes, and only a few teeth remaining, it seemed surreal that he was listening to a driver, who had been sent by his Ministry to provide Professor Okunaga with information he neither wanted to hear, nor wanted to believe.

And this driver was a character, said to be forty-three, worked his way up after twenty-seven years at the Ministry to be the Minister's driver, so unused to talking that now he couldn't stop, rushing to get his story out to the important Professor.

'My father, may his soul rest in peace, told me always to take the path of the other direction in a crisis, and when all the people went down the hill, away from Harajuku, I went upwards, backward, back to Harajuku station. It was easier to run away from the crowd, back up to the gardens at Meiji Jingu. But before I went, the bodyguard he told me his plan. "If the flames become too hot, I will guide my employer and Okunaga-*sensei* to the Futaba School where there is very big swimming pool." And that is what he did, to save them from the heat and flames.'

Because of the bandages, Jun couldn't see the driver but sensed that he was shaking his head. 'Towards Futaba, I think that's the way everyone goes – not for me!'

Now he was definitely shaking his head.

'I know this pool, used to take the Minister's daughters. Sometimes Princess Atsuko would swim there. Very big. But so many people know this, too. I said to myself, "What you think?" and turned backwards to Meiji Jingu, the other path. My father was very wise, you know.'

Now a pause. He was coming to the point.

'That night the Meiji reached out to save me. Ginza, Chuo, was burned to ashes, but the park was not bombed once. And the fierce wind blew away. I could not visit Futaba School for one whole week, but when I did get through the story was bad. This is why I came to see you now.'

Jun understood that it would not be spelt out why his wife was in the Minister's car, but someone at the Ministry felt it was right and proper for her distinguished husband to know what had happened.

'They said that the heat became so strong, one-thousand degrees, that even the water in the pool was not enough.' The driver paused again, perhaps he should never have agreed to this. 'They said the water turned to steam, with everyone boiled and cooked and burnt, and it was not possible to recognise the bodies – all was ashes. Maybe, they say, eight hundred, now just a crust of scum.

How strange that this buffoon has provided calm by telling me how Shizuko met her death, Jun thought, but that isn't what he said. 'You have done your duty, as others see it. Now, please leave.'

Jun lay in bed for several hours after the visit wondering about war and passion, about how every generation has to learn all over again that attacking a neighbour rarely ends well. And the lies that all militaries tell to get young men to sacrifice themselves. Lies, maybe even more potent than guns and bombs.

Jun's musings were interrupted by an old doctor – the man must be in his eighties – lifting the bandages to shine bright lights into his eyes, murmuring to the Korean nurse so quietly that Jun couldn't hear, so he asked what the doctor had said.

'With care, it is likely that the sight in his left eye will be saved, he must remain in the bed for another week to be sure.'

Was that a lie? he thought, *but what would be the motive?* And did he want to leave the hospital, to go where? All he had left was Ayako – did she care, after the brutalities of this war? – with the censor's sharp eraser, did she even know of the Tokyo firestorm, that her mother and sister were… ashes?

Jun sighed. Not a weary sigh, but the sigh of a bedfast active mind – marooned in a hospital, marooned in a devastated city, in a beaten country. An inward 'call-to-arms' sigh, almost triumphant, a sigh of the refuse-to-be-beaten kind, the believer, the builder… building from the remnants of a smouldering pyre.

After all, he may not have many teeth, but he still had Shakespeare. Though the victor's poet, the Bard was a very good place to begin believing again. He chuckled to himself, seeing the words behind the bandages, almost delirious, thinking of a future Japan rising from ashes – rebuilding his Japan, not those childish idiot militaristic bastards. Rebuilding – what you do when all is lost. He began reciting, quietly at first, getting stronger and stronger, until almost shouting at the end.

'When we mean to build
'We first survey the plot, then draw the model;
'And when we see the figure of the house,
'Then we must rate the cost of the erection,
'Which if we find outweighs ability,
'What do we then but draw anew the model
'In fewer offices, or, at least, desist
'To build at all.'

'We will NOT desist, not desist.' Now Jun really was shouting. 'SO BRING ON THE BUILDERS.'

Ayako, like many others, guessed the fate of her family, deciding they were all dead, after Major Ito used his influence to discover that the true figure of the Tokyo deaths was far more than the censors admitted. The effect of this knowledge on Ayako was – silence. And, deeper than that, the erasure of her family from her mind – the easiest way, the safest way, the *only* way to cope. Ito went along with this in an unspoken conspiracy against feelings – as he said, 'The time for suffering is at *the end*, whenever and whatever that may be.' So, they drifted on in a cocoon of denial, a reflection of the life in Fukuoka around them.

The British doctor in Camp 17, diagnosed this with his forensic eye.

'Everybody's *waiting*. For what exactly, no one knows. Perhaps the end of the world, or perhaps the beginning of a new one.'

Given the direction of the war, the younger prison camp guards were even more on edge, crueller, like pent-up German Shepherds, waiting to pounce, while the older guards walked with perpetual bows, as if apologising, although still carrying a heavy staff for any prisoner who failed to mine the coal for twelve long hours, and especially for the arrogant British who melted the zinc.

Others, though, were more pragmatic, even cynical. Baron Mitsui, who owned the Mitsui Miike mine and zinc foundry, whose family had impeccable connections in Fukuoka and Tokyo, had become increasingly friendly with the British and American Officers, touring the camp in his open-topped car, bringing what he called 'step-up rations', which bore the unmistakable look of Red Cross supplies that had 'gone astray', albeit without the packaging.

However questionable, such 'gifts' were desperately

welcomed, given the malnourished state of the prisoners. The Baron was becoming a popular figure, in spite of the way in which he profited from their slavery, their emaciation and maltreatment.

Major Ito was now the de facto Commandant, as the Colonel had taken to his bed with terminal viral pneumonia, meaning that, in spite of her youth, Ayako was involved in some of the prosecutions, although not the cruel punishments.

One prisoner who came before Major Ito was executed for trying to learn to read Japanese. He was used as the target for a bayonet drill by the guard detail.

His body when examined showed over 75 stab wounds.

However, the random, sadistic beatings began to decline, to be replaced by quasi-judicial prosecutions under the Japanese Wartime Measures Act, which often had more serious consequences. The doctor observed this might be because, with the war moving implacably against Japan, the senior officers were beginning to consider war crime tribunals. Ayako had to attend the prosecutions as translator. Though the outcome of their judgements would be just as cruel, there was now a pretence that justice had been done, before severe punishment was to be carried out.

This surface accountability required that capital sentences were now subject to the supreme authority of the provincial court in Nagasaki, a rubber-stamp if ever there was one, but it did at least mean that the guards would have to use that ultimate sanction more sparingly.

Ayako was returning as translator from just such a court visit to Nagasaki, with an American prisoner and guards, on a steamy afternoon, when she saw him – before he saw her.

Professor Okunaga was sitting hesitantly on a bench made of wood and zinc, lingering in the waiting area outside the main camp gate, wondering if he was strong enough for the emotional outpouring he expected from his increasingly militaristic daughter. He muttered quietly to himself, trying to stiffen his resolve.

At first, Ayako wasn't sure. Was this dishevelled old man, seemingly mad, wearing a sweat-soaked winter cap on such a hot afternoon, with an ill-fitting patch over his right eye – really *him*? In the four years since he had awkwardly hugged her goodbye at Tokyo railway station, he'd aged twenty years, had lost his swagger, his authority, his fatherly-ness.

Still slightly uncertain, she gestured for the guard detail to go ahead into the camp and circled around the back of the bench, to sit primly on his right side, hands together on the lap of her dark pants, without a greeting or acknowledgment. When Okunaga felt the bench vibrate, he stopped mumbling, looked across awkwardly with his left eye and slightly smiled. Though he had few teeth, the full-lipped smile hadn't changed – it was him.

They sat quietly for several seconds, neither wanting to reach out, to hug the other, close but also distant, an unbridgeable gulf of belief between them. But they were still family.

'Did any survive?' she asked.

He shook his head.

'Even Michiko?'

He nodded.

'But not you?'

'As you see.'

Having been set from the start of this meeting, their chilly brittleness continued. During four years of war, they had become strangers, or worse, antagonists. This was as he expected, but she hadn't thought about it. Ignoring feelings, being numb, that was her dealing mechanism, and, though she held him to account, like her fury at Dan, Ayako knew deep down that her anger was neither true nor fair. She had become patriotic, perhaps even fanatical – and now she was embarrassed with his natty, academic, liberal, parasitic, old-world, military-hating opinions, and through that, her heart had hardened to him.

'Guess you feel vindicated? Japan's defeat is your win.'

'Not how I see it.'

Ayako sighed. This was so painful. Her mentor, the father she admired, believed in, loved beyond all else, had gone, utterly destroyed like their nation. She looked away fiercely. *What right has he got to do this, to hold me to account by his very presence, come back now, undermine the strong person I have become.* But he interrupted her self-absorbed introspection, unable to wholly extinguish the analytical, garrulous professor he used to be.

'My lion is dead. The roaring is quiet. Now even peace will not be enough.'

She sighed again, even more plaintively. 'Why have you come?'

'You are still my daughter, now my *only*. There is no other.' He chuckled, as he often did. 'I thought to come and save you.'

She went from irritation to anger to outrage. 'I do not need saving.'

'We all do.'

'You mean admit defeat.'

He noticed she was silently crying, and now thought

he should not have come. *What hope is there for her? The greatest atrocity of all, to twist a young, beautiful mind and destroy hope of simple family happiness, through nationalistic propaganda and hatred. That is the true war-crime.* But as had happened so many times in his colourful life, a diversion changed the course of his heart.

A hungry seagull swooped down, landed and walked towards them cawing, demanding food. What a noble bird. He thought of Shakespeare, and for no good reason it made him laugh. '"Enter yon gull Malvolio, a gull, a fool, a rogue, who goes to the wars to grace himself",' he recited, still giggling.

His laughter made her smile through the tears, seeing the lion was not wholly gone, even if it had few teeth and only one eye. But he missed his opportunity, like too many fathers, he didn't allow his daughter a voice, preferring his own.

'Embrace the future. And your daughter, who you do not ask about. Perhaps you are too much like your mother – sadly, *adieu, adieu, adieu*.' The seagull had now waddled away, to look for scraps elsewhere. 'I went to school with the doctor who attended Mayumi – said to be healthy and beautiful. So, there is much to live for, to take joy in. But we must shake off this tragedy, begin again.'

With this rebuff to her, and to her mother, he lost Ayako utterly. And in lots of ways, Ayako lost herself. *What is the point?* she was thinking. Perhaps the only way she could rid herself of him, expunge him from her life, was to twist a knife in his guts, and get him to leave – forever. A girl whose adolescence was to worship him, had turned full circle. She now needed to suicide him from her spirit. 'I don't see myself as having a father anymore.'

For a moment the Gods held their breath, but then he laughed, coldly. After a huge sigh, he rid himself of responsibility for her, or Japan. 'Thank you, Ayako. You have made me free. There are only ashes in your heart, like half of Tokyo. From that wasteland, I will build myself anew.' He turned to touch her shoulder. 'I shall start by finding a dentist, and then begin a future life.'

Jun stood up unsteadily, grabbed his grubby woollen hat and threw it at the prison fence, a symbol of moving on. 'It would not be fitting to only have two front teeth when I travel to Okinawa, to visit the remaining family I have.' He bowed, saluted her with a single finger to his wrinkled forehead, and staggered away.

But in his weakened heart, Jun knew it was a journey he never would make, that the United States' bombers and battleships were already pounding Okinawa, and the seas were infested with enemy warships and submarines. He would return to Tokyo, to his empty apartment, to read his books and contemplate what peace – when it came – would be like. And, yes, he'd get his teeth fixed. A lion without teeth would not be able to roar.

Shocked, but resolute, Ayako sat out there for a long time. So long that a guard went and got Major Ito, who escorted her back to their hut in miserable silence. As dawn spread across their bed, she felt herself re-emerge, re-energised, free. And so very, very, angry.

'There is much to do,' she said to Ito, although she knew he was asleep.

9

Nishabaru House
Mrs Okunaga's Okinawa lullaby

The moon is in mourning tonight.
Because the sky is alight with firecracker
trails,
Searing flames of red, white and blue into
the stars of heaven.
I have nothing to live for, save this tidy
bundle,
wrapped and wriggling under the shelter of
our rare oak table,
behind our family shrine.
This is my world, all my world;
there is nothing else now,
Mayumi crams every corner of my heart,
Which is broken to hear her cry.

Quiet, my child; your cries will not deflect

the bombs and shells which fly across
our land, to crash somewhere,
on fields and orchards and houses,
on babies and children, mothers
and fathers;
on people we don't know,
from people we don't understand.
Quiet, do not cry; make this a time of
peace between us.

Our village has so much explosion,
booms and bangs and fire – for what?
To flatten earth, flatten men, flatten
life,
to make an invasion.
Pah!
Men close their eyes, their minds,
Then go to battle, to fight, to kill,
Easy to do, if it comes not close to
their garden,
Easy to do, if it comes not close to
their children.
Easy to do if the button is pressed
five,
or five thousand miles away.
Pah!

There, my child, there, there – the
booming is over
Now quiet; great granny is with you.
In the morning you shall have
sweets,

今夜の月はお悔やみの月
それというのも夜空は花火のように
赤や白や青の炎が天の星まで舞い上がっているから

so try to sleep my little one, try to sleep.
The bangs are not meant for us,
and the Gods in the universe always smile
down on children.
Sleep, my darling, sleep…

— **ASAKO OKUNAGA**

Early on Easter Sunday, 1st April 1945, the American forces mounted a frontal assault on the undefended beaches ten miles north of Naha on the western coast of Okinawa. With surprise impossible, the U.S. tactics were simple – a huge naval and air bombardment, followed by a massive landing of marines.

The Japanese strategy was complex – let the Americans invade, then destroy their off-shore supply ships by naval action and *Kamikaze* attack isolating the beachhead before capturing the cut-off US marines intact.

In the event, the Japanese suffered heavy losses at sea, and the *Kamikaze* failed to destroy overpowering American air superiority. It was then that the American forces moved inland and began the bloodiest and most murderous battle of the whole Pacific war.

In the farming village of Kakazu, in her little thatched wooden bungalow, Mrs Okunaga had scraped the heavy oak table across the straw mats into the corner alongside the ancestral altar. Then she rolled and heaved the three traditional kitchen hearthstones to form the strongest possible battlements against flying shrapnel – once again relieved that she did not leave when the family evacuation ship had sailed for Japan last August. In spite of the censor, gossip had spread quickly round the Island that the ship was sunk by an enemy submarine and that all aboard had perished.

But now the American bombs and fires were terrible, and the Japanese soldiers just as bad, slinking stealthily through the villages like bands of robbers. Thank God she was far too old for their attentions and Mayumi too young. This filthy war – with so much to know, and so much unknown, and no safety anywhere.

But if Mrs Okunaga perished?

Then Mayumi, with handsome Eastern features around Western eyes, must live for them both. In any case, she was held in trust to grand-daughter Ayako – though what had become of that feckless young woman only God would know.

Mrs Okunaga sniffed the dank air and muttered another prayer to her ancestors. The makeshift shelter would provide protection against all but the most direct of bombs, with the thick stones of the cooking area behind them, her makeshift wall of furniture in front and the large oak table balanced on top. With a secreted box of Tokyo sweets from her son, enough hoarded rice and clean water for several weeks, perhaps the fighting would pass them by.

FOR FOUR DAYS, the American soldiers moved south from the beachhead. The Japanese army offered little resistance, sucking the Americans towards the fortifications stretched across the Island from Tanabaru to Nishabaru. On the 6th April the 96th Infantry Division took Cactus Heights with light casualties, moving up into position to assault Kakazu Ridge.

At this point, Okinawa was only a few miles wide, and nature provided a formidable barrier of gorges, tunnels, caves and ravines for the Japanese army to defend to the death. At five a.m. on the 9th April, two battalions of the 96th – the Deadeyes – began their attack.

When the Americans moved forward under cover of early morning darkness, no answer came from the heights, but almost every square foot of the scrubby ridge was infested with guns and mortars, zeroed-in on the peaceful gorge below. The Japanese held their breath. Still the Americans advanced, crossing the gorge, beginning to scale the ridge. The Japanese unclipped safety catches, smiling in anticipation, while the Americans crept unknowingly further in front of their supplies, reaching the crest of the ridge.

Just before seven o'clock that morning, their world exploded. Two whole battalions were caught in mortal surprise.

Machine guns spat a ferocious hail of death as the American soldiers were pinned to the steep, rocky slopes. Mortars pounded down on the gorge, cutting off the assault battalions from their reserves, and the usually patient Japanese infantry did not even wait for their mortar barrage to stop before charging fanatically down the ridge with bayonets drawn, screaming and slicing in hand-to-hand fighting which raged across the entire front line.

Fewer than 600 yards away, Mrs Okunaga gripped Mayumi with white-knuckled hands, alternately murmuring prayers and reassurance. The hell which she had expected since the Imperial soldiers had arrived a few days ago had now come to fruition. Just to live on Okinawa at such a time was pain enough; to be surrounded by fanatical soldiers was even worse; but to cringe and tremble on the very front line while responsible for a desperately loved, delicate child, wounded her more than death itself. Mayumi did not cry – the shaking, clinging pressure of grandma's hand dried the tears before they started.

From time-to-time spent bullets rattled the flimsy walls and thudded into the wooden roof supports, or occasionally zinged through the door to clatter among the pots and pans in the kitchen alcove fireplace. One stray round zipped between the hearthstones and skimmed along the table-top, to sheer off the nose of the *shiisa* lion-dog Asako had placed to stand guard behind them.

April 9th was a very, very bad day. But many worse days were to come.

Lt General Simon Bolivar Buckner Jr., had calculated two days to take the Tanabaru/Nishabaru line, perhaps a week for the entire Shuri heights. In fact, the final breakthrough took thirty agonising, murderous days, and reduced Kakazu Village to virtual rubble and matchwood.

The dusty road along the centre of the village became pock-marked with craters from dive bomb attacks, which were called up with ever more frequency as the American body count began to mount in the face of the hidden, cave-dwelling Japanese soldiers.

And then came the rains, turning Highway No 5 into a quagmire, the hills into marshes, the valleys to sodden graveyards, with floating, bloated bodies everywhere, unable to be picked up or buried because of the mud and the slime. Even the US Marines, who vowed never to leave a soldier behind, weren't able to retrieve their comrades.

In the humid, boiling air the smell of rotting humanity

was so strong, it reached up to what was left of Kakazu main street. Mrs Okunaga waved and waved her hand in front of Mayumi's nose, and prayed, and stroked Mayumi's hair. Perhaps one day there would be a world where men like her beloved, much-missed husband could die in their beds – rather than rotting on some pointless hillside.

With midnight, the firing died down, only an occasional burst from around the hills breaking through the dripping of rain from the trees. Mrs Okunaga was too exhausted from terror and anxiety to stay awake anyway, knowing that the next day would be the same, or worse.

On Tuesday, May 8th, after four ferocious weeks, the battle began to ebb south. The Japanese defenders melted away in the teeming rain, dodging tanks and lethal flame throwers through a network of tunnels and pillboxes, to re-group among the cliffs and ravines west of Yonabaru.

A sombre troop from F Company of the 2nd Battalion of the 96th tentatively crept into the outskirts of Kakazu in the middle of the afternoon. Of the twenty-six men remaining in F Troop, from the ninety-two who had started the battle, eight were walking wounded, three were being carried, and all were physically and mentally exhausted.

Inside the splintered remnants of her devastated house, Mrs Okunaga could hear the muffled commands and occasional clumsy clatter of the approaching American soldiers. She lay for some time under the table with her hand across Mayumi's frightened mouth, her heart beating almost as loudly as the distant crump of dive bombers.

She peeked through a bullet-hole in the boards of the outer wall. The *hinpun* wall protecting the front of the house had been destroyed and she could see soldiers running backwards and forwards, ducking in and out of the gateway of the house opposite.

Suddenly, a burst of automatic fire followed by a dull explosion made her jump and look away. When she glanced back, a soldier writhed in bloody agony on the muddy road, victim of a wild suicide grenade attack by the twelve-year-old son of her neighbours. Mrs Okunaga felt neither sorrow nor satisfaction – only a deepening desperation. What could she do to rid her beloved Mayumi of this terrible nightmare?

While treating their colleague, the soldiers seemed to pause for a while before continuing to comb the ruins of this simple, farming village. Now, though, they were more on edge, more lethal, much more likely to shoot at the slightest sound.

And they were coming ever closer.

Surely the soldiers would find them cowering under the table.

Should she shout out? Or just continue to hide?

Now they were only fifty yards away. If only her husband were still alive, he would know what to do, or if her son were here, or Ayako.

Twenty yards to go… two more ruined empty houses… no hope remained.

She looked into her great-grandchild's wide, frightened, western eyes.

'Mayumi,' she whispered, 'Mayumi, I love you. Now you must cry. Please cry.'

But all tears had been drained from Mayumi during the previous harrowing, hungry, horrifying, inhuman weeks cowering under that sturdy oak table. A two-and-a-half-year-old child could not be expected to understand. So, Mrs Okunaga committed a crime against her cherished beliefs of parenthood. She raised her wrinkled hand, and slapped Mayumi hard across the face.

Private First-Class Robert A. Bradley threw himself to the ground when he heard the stuttering cry. In the worn-out troop, combat training took over as a dozen, tired rifles turned on the shattered remains of Nishabaru House.

The soldiers waited, while the cry became a howl, and the howl turned into anguished sobs. *Is this another trap?* thought Bradley, whose usually steady nerves had been frayed beyond repair by the fanaticism of a Japanese army unable to consider honourable surrender.

Squinting down the rifle-sight, his shaking finger tightened on the trigger; then he grinned to himself. 'Heck, if it is just a little child…' He motioned the Sergeant lying on the ground ten yards behind.

Keep me covered, I'm going in.

The sergeant shook his head, rolling his eyes at such idiocy, mouthing a single word. 'Grenade.'

Bradley twisted on his side, reached for the armoury webbing and drew out a Mills bomb while the crying inside the house intensified. He glanced back at the sergeant, who now seemed undecided. The two men stared at each other in confusion, until the sergeant wriggled across the sopping rubble towards Bradley.

'Whad' yah think, Brad?' he whispered hoarsely.

'If it's a kid an' I lob this number – we're no better than the goddamn Japs.'

'Sure. And if it's not just a kid?'

Fifty yards behind, the whole troop was watching their conversation with mixed feelings; glad not to have to make the decision, and wishing they'd get on with it.

Bradley looked down at the grenade. 'We could warn them…'

'In English?'

'What about that Marine training film, the "useful phrases" – I can remember "surrender"…'

'Worth a try.'

The PFC cleared his throat and crawled forward to shelter in the rubble of the *hinpun*. '*Kosan Se Yo!*' he shouted. '*Kosan Se Yo!*'

The crying from inside was muffled, then stopped.

Both men looked at each other, nervous but intrigued, fingers hovering over the triggers.

'Try another, Brad.'

'Ok, "won't murder you".' Brad cleared his throat. '*Korosanai yo! Korosanai yo!*'

After a second or two a strange scraping sound rumbled from inside the house, followed by the wailing of a much older voice; then the rickety wooden door panel jerked forwards and slid off its rails, bouncing on the narrow veranda and clattering into the rubble-strewn courtyard below. An old grey head poked out from behind the remaining wall at ankle level, shrieking and sobbing hysterically.

For the first time in thirty-eight days Mrs Okunaga had crawled out from under her faithful old table.

'Thank God,' muttered the sergeant, then, 'Dawson!'

The Company linguist, a youth who had volunteered straight from Harvard, with a smattering of proper Japanese, crawled forward and began a faltering interrogation.

'Says she seventy-six, sarge.'

'Anyone else around?'

'Only her great-grandchild, still under a table. If we

spare her kid, the old lady will show us to the booby-traps.'

Mrs Okunaga was true to her word. Mayumi was carried out and feted by the whole troop, a rare moment of beauty in a miserable, nauseating battle. They called Mayumi 'Bradley's babe' – a reminder of their families safe at home in America, who would never face the danger and terror of being bombed.

And everyone agreed – Mayumi had sparkling, Western eyes.

That night, PFC Bradley, who was something of a troubled dreamer, tossed and turned in exhausted sleep, and when he awoke in the morning, two puzzling images twirled around each other in his mind.

First the Imperial Oath: *'The Emperor is sacred and inviolable, a living God to whom we give and owe our lives. Our death is nothing compared to the duty he provides us with. We are honoured to serve by our sacrifice.'*

And second the exultant look in Mrs Okunaga's eyes, when she realised her great-grandchild was safe.

A few days earlier Bradley had watched a wounded Japanese soldier cornered in a cave repeating, over and over, the Imperial oath, as translated by Dawson. For a few astonished moments he thought the soldier was surrendering, until the man reached inside his tunic and pulled the pin from a grenade. The soldier had a chance to lob it at Bradley, but instead, still mumbling the oath, he held the bomb to his stomach and waited. With a dull thud the soldier lifted several feet off the ground, spun head over heels in mid-air, splattering Bradley with entrails and blood, and when the soldier fell back and died, he was still staring at his enemy and murmuring that oath. The horrific memory of those dying, defiant eyes – the soldier's proud tinge of pleasure for a duty properly done – still made Bradley wonder.

And Mrs Okunaga had the same look. Why?

During a rainy breakfast, Dawson, who pretended to understand the Japanese, expounded a theory. 'Duty. And their attitudes to family,' he said breezily. 'The emperor is a God-like father figure; and in the crazy Jap world of the family, the greatest privilege for a son is to serve his father. The greater the hardship, the greater the service, and the greater the honour. Jap men are brought up to expect, and hope for, an unhappy ending. Men fight, men kill, men die – but men never surrender. So that look of exaltation means… "Emperor/Father, I do this for you. I am now a worthy son, because you do me the honour of letting me serve thru my death."'

'Crazy, huh?'

'Jap women are different. They see their duty as being to the ancestors, and to suffering and continuing life. The desires and ways of men take precedence, but the maternal code is still mighty strong. Women suffer – to give life; and suffer quietly, so the men feel free to do their thing. And deep inside women are committed to protecting and suffering for the children in exactly the same way as the sons are committed to serving their fathers.'

'So, there you have your exultant look; the Jap soldier boy had the joy of the ultimate service to the ultimate daddy, and the old lady had suffered in silence for five long weeks to protect a child of the family.'

'Crap!' The sergeant hated this intellectual talk by the over-educated, irregular wartime intake. Besides, it might be bad for morale, blunt the necessary, ruthless killing edge, if they talked about the enemy as people. 'Ask the old lady, she'll tell you. She was just pleased to escape with her arse intact.'

So, Dawson did ask, and her grudging answer astonished them all.

'It would have been a terrible crime if the child had been killed by American bombs or flames or bullets. Because Mayumi is half American,' he translated.

'That's all.'

THE STRAGGLERS of F Company stayed in the ruins of Kakazu Village for several days. Their instructions had been specific: 'occupy and hold village until relieved.' Exhausted to the core, the small troop were delighted to rest, sleeping on any dry *tatami* they found, washing in the large stone water pots, and sheltering in the shade of the rough limestone walls and the remaining thick-leaved fukugi trees in order to write letters home for the first time in a month. But on the Saturday a relief patrol filed along the pock-marked roadway.

F Company was ordered to merge with C Company and re-form for the eventual assault on the Japanese defensive perimeter along the Yaeju-Dake escarpment. Mrs Okunaga and Mayumi were herded away to the chaos and confusion of a huge refugee camp near Koza, to wait out the rest of the war at the occupier's pleasure.

The third week of June was a time of intense suffering and carnage on Okinawa, and as the massive American cordon tightened around the southern tip of the Island, the Japanese fought even more bitterly.

When the sergeant left his bivouac with a spade for his routine evening ablutions no-one noticed. Two hours later, when he hadn't returned, a nervous search-party set-off with torches into the coastal grasslands, fearing the worst. They discovered his body lying face down, half in and half out of a paddy field. He had been tortured – though why was anybody's guess. The rookie recruit called Reynolds, who had found the bound and gagged torso, was MEDEVAC-ed from shock.

The following day, the squad's linguist, Dawson, poked up his curious nose once too often, just as a shell exploded nearby, throwing a hail of shrapnel which turned his face into mincemeat. His helmet, with its signatures of the 'buddies' he'd fought with, was found two hundred yards from his decapitated body.

Of that trio in Kakazu Village, only young Bradley survived – but he lost both legs to his sentimental, reckless heart.

Just after dawn, on Monday, July 2nd (the day the Battle of Okinawa was officially ended) he waded out into his beloved Pacific near Mabuni Cliffs. The honey-comb caves along the Ocean side were said to be safe, all the retreating Japanese had been flushed out by flame throwers, or had committed *hara-kiri* in their final, cornered despair.

As Bradley bobbed on his back in the sea, he noticed a flock of seagulls cawing and swooping by the entrance of a coral-covered cave on the waterline. He allowed the waves to float him across, calling to his fellow doughboys who were playing water polo with an empty army canteen. The water lapped him through the opening into a gloomy cavern which widened out into a series of shelves that led to a room-sized, perfectly dry chamber.

Across the middle was a sight which made him gasp, then retch. Side by side, six almost naked Japanese soldiers, lay face down on mats; all had committed suicide in traditional style, their guts billowing out from their stomachs, their throats cut by a short ceremonial dagger. To judge by appearances, all were teenagers, one looked as though he were just a boy. On the left, an older man – perhaps the officer – sat cross-legged, upright. He would have been the last to die, without the comfort of a comrade to finish him off. But the serenity on his defeated face had been mangled by the pecking seagulls, and his entrails had been fought over by a thousand beaks.

Bradley stood there, dripping from the sea, and said a private prayer. His colleagues splashed up the tunnel. 'Oh my God,' they muttered, retching at the rank stench of death rising above the smell of the seaweed.

A trapped seagull thrashed around the cavern, finally flapping onto the squatting officer's head, perching webbed feet on caked black hair, with that pathetic, defiant expression of ridicule – as if the seagull now owned the man.

The squaddies turned to leave.

'We can't just walk away,' Bradley protested. 'I'm gonna do the decent thing.' Holding his nose he advanced towards the dead officer, shooing the seagull away, grabbing a dung-covered shoulder and pushing the body gently forward. At that moment he saw the wires.

Perhaps the Japanese officer set the charges to allow a choice of instant death, rather than lingering agony, perhaps he deliberately booby-trapped himself. Either way, it did not matter. The heavy explosion ripped fist-sized chunks of coral from the cavern walls and blasted them round like shrapnel. Two squaddies died instantly, the rest lost their hearing as the deafening roar rang round the enclosure. Bradley was catapulted over and over, crashing off the cavern walls like an animal carcass, slumping down in a bewildering twist of broken limbs.

Private Reynolds had just been discharged from hospital.

'Oh, my Jesus God,' he screamed hysterically, as Bradley landed at his feet.

AFTER HOVERING between life and death for two weeks at the military field hospital near Urasoe, Bradley was transferred by jeep ambulance along the muddy roads to the airfield at Kadena. The arriving passengers climbed from the medical C-47 and stood aside as PFC Bradley was wheeled out to the waiting plane.

Poor bugger, thought Daniel Lawrence, *losing both legs so late in this vile bitch of a war.*

Officially, The Chief of Logistical Coordination for the Pacific Theatre was on a visit to organise the supply systems for the occupation of Okinawa and the invasion of the Japanese mainland; unofficially, he was there to gauge the bitter divisions between the generals and admirals, and answer the burning question of the moment. Who will control the Okinawa military government – the US Army or the US Navy?

This was now a difficult question, because Roosevelt had died in April, and no one knew the new President Truman's mind.

Back then, Dan had been asleep at his desk on Guadalcanal when the PFC Comms Orderly quite roughly pushed his shoulder to wake him.

'You must come immediately to the communication hut, Sir, there's an urgent call from DC on the scrambler.'

In the Pacific it was 3:15 a.m. on Friday 13th April – what could be so desperate in Washington on a Thursday afternoon, especially as he'd gossiped with Abe Ford only on Wednesday?

'Daniel, my boy, serious news. It is being announced as we speak. President Roosevelt is dead, Truman is being sworn in right now. And, no, I can't say what it means, I hardly know the man. And the war in Germany is essentially over, all the focus is coming your way. It will be foolish to speculate but our new President is said to be a decent man, was already out of his depth as VP, and such men, in my experience, turn to their friends, of which I am not one.'

Dan blinked the sleep away. The formality in Ford's voice was a warning that their political cover was eroded and might be eradicated, and the lack of sentimentality about the death of his friend betrayed the seriousness. Dan could imagine Abe sitting at his desk in Washington with a couple of cronies, running through the angles, finding none of comfort.

To get the job done, Ford had made too many enemies.

'I fear we must all watch our backs and our fronts – the glory days may be waning.' And with that, Ford was gone.

Too much of a businessman to be interested in politics, Dan sat in the Comms hut for a while.

What difference would it make to the war? Not much, although with Germany defeated, the Pacific would become the focus.

What about Logistical Supply? Presumably the same petty arguments would carry on – probably be ramped up in the scramble for advantage in the vacuum of a new Commander in Chief finding his way.

And what difference for *me*? Without supreme cover can the job even be done?

In the constant turf wars between the army and navy, Commander Ford in Washington had been surprisingly even handed; 'Wouldn't trust either of them – neither could run my hometown P.T.A.'

Dan had to agree when he saw the unnecessary frictions and duplications. America was winning this war because of huge superiority in equipment and supply, and because of the intelligent fighting spirit of its enlisted men, but in spite of its regular senior military leadership.

Now in Okinawa, Dan could see the Island was in utter chaos. Rain clogged the roads, the harbours had been destroyed, the airfields were coming apart at the seams. Not only were virtually all supplies ferried in by air, but Okinawa was like a floating aircraft carrier, for bombing raids on Japan.

Add to that 12,500 American dead, 37,000 wounded, 110,000 Japanese soldiers killed and 160,000 Okinawan civilian casualties during the 81-day battle – and almost the entire population temporarily interned in giant refugee camps, where disease ran rampant.

Within a week of arrival in Okinawa, Dan had used the enormous power of demand for supply to construct a political base of some importance. Increasingly, Admirals and Generals referred to him for support; no request was ever refused, but those who offered the most cooperation discovered their requirements received highest priority.

The C47s, B26s and B27s arrived and departed with incredible frequency. In the third week of July alone, over two thousand sorties were flown from the United States mainland, a vital air-bridge which kept Okinawa alive; and when the harbour near Naha was re-built by engineers, the Island was ready to go on the offensive as a staging base for the up-coming invasion of Japan.

Dan sat in his prefabricated office on Kadena Airfield, drinking Scotch with Phil Denton, watching the tropical sun go down. It was time to face his real reason for being in Okinawa, one that had been gnawing at his heart every single day as news of the dreadful battles filtered back to his logistical supply base. What had become of his child, her mother and grandmother?

'Phil, I'm taking the weekend off to drive round the Island, see a sight or two.'

Denton almost coughed on his whisky. His boss had never taken a day's leave in two and a half years. A plan must be cooking in Dan's scheming mind, and – big on office politics – Phil fished around for a while.

'I've seen a site for an airport myself, by Ada on the north-east coast?'

'Yeah, that's what I hear,' Dan's non-committal reply.

'There's a beach at Okuma, perfect for swimming or coral diving…?'

'Thanks Phil – might take a look.'

'You'd have to admit, these Okinawan women are beautiful…?' A long shot this, but with Dan Lawrence you never did know.

Dan's eyes glazed over – a sign Phil had hit the spot. 'But half have got the clap.'

So that was it – a woman! Denton immediately relaxed; nothing to worry about.

A BLACK PAINTED, wooden ammunition-case lid had been hammered into the muddy ground as a road-sign.

Kakazu Village – Danger – Unexploded Shell Area. Uncleared.

Dan parked his Jeep and walked down the cratered dirt road into the ruined deserted village. He recited, for the thousandth time, the scrawl on the scrap of paper Ayako had given him.

Nishabaru House, Kakazu Village, Highway 5, Okinawa. Mrs Asako Okunaga.

It might as well have been on the moon.

The few houses left standing showed no sign of life, no clue to occupants or addresses. Houses had been left open to the elements, roofs were caved in, and sporadic fires had reduced many of the cottages to charcoal-covered heaps. Without realising it, Dan stepped across the flimsy wooden door which lay in the courtyard in exactly the place it had fallen when Mrs Asako knocked it off its rails. It might have provided a starting point for his quest. But after walking up and down the road a couple of times, he clambered up to the lookout post at the top of Kakazu Ridge, to make enquiries of the sergeant in charge.

'Taken by the 2nd Battalion of the 96th,' he said, chewing gum, surprised anyone could be interested. 'F Company, I did hear say.'

At the Divisional Headquarters at Itoman, the Colonel was somewhat offhand until he realised the function of his young questioner.

'Logistical Supply, eh? Cola syrup… sure, what can I do for you?'

F Company had indeed occupied Kakazu, but he believed the village was deserted when taken over. The sergeant had since died, as had so many of the other men, and the few who remained were now guarding the airport on Iejima Island. 'A fella called Reynolds is around someplace, I'll find him for you.'

Sadly, Reynolds – who'd just been discharged from hospital for the second time – had not actually been in Kakazu. He had joined the company a few days later. But he did remember PFC Bradley talking about an old lady and her grand-child, who'd sheltered under a heavy wood table in one of the houses.

'Something 'bout the kid having Western eyes. Bradley often talked 'bout them eyes and a grenade – meant somethin' special to him.'

'Where is Bradley now?'

'Hospital in Hawaii, lost both them legs, poor bastard.'

'A heavy wooden table, you say?'

'Yeah; Brad hoped to take the table home, 'til he lost his legs, that is.'

DAN ARRIVED BACK in Kakazu at dusk. The heavy rain pitter-pattered on the thick tropical leaves of the remaining trees, so he pulled on his military cape and picked up a powerful flashlight. He clambered down to the village, the ghosts of death and the rattling of the rain on ruined, rickety rooftops causing a nervous flutter in his heart. Perhaps he should return next morning? He stopped to watch a sodden rat-like creature skittling round the puddles on the potholed street, and then looked at his watch. Shit; tomorrow was Sunday, he'd need all that day to comb through the refugee camps – he'd better get this over with.

The houses were built inside a courtyard surrounded

by a thick limestone wall. Instead of gates at the entrance, each house appeared to have a small wall part way in, that obscured the house from the road. Almost all had been reduced to rubble but the thick walls were mostly intact. They were built on raised platforms about a foot off the ground and bordered by a narrow veranda. Passing from house to house, flashing the torch inside anything left standing, Dan was astonished at how delicate they seemed for a place so prone to typhoons, though it became increasingly obvious that the foundations were built to last. Each had its ancestral altar facing south towards the sun, each a tiny room that could only have been for sleeping, and a minute kitchen with a low, stone cooking area and a shiny earthen floor.

By the twentieth house, Dan felt a sense of intrusion on the domestic privacy of a proud, meticulous culture. By the fiftieth, the wretched homelessness of war plucked at his shaky emotions, causing him to give a heartfelt sigh of regret. War was only partly about killing or winning or losing, he decided. Perhaps the Japs were right – war is about families and people.

Well after dark, he finally poked his head through a raised open doorway, and the torch picked out the unmistakable shape of a large heavy table.

He clambered over the door, and climbed inside the house.

The sewer smell of five weeks of constant shelter still seeped through the floorboards from below. The scene was just as it had been left. Shrapnel-damaged hearthstones, a bullet marked altar, the scratches across the fading polished surface of a loved and cared-for table. Dan paused for a moment to consider. Somewhere, safe from fire, from snoopers – where would a canny old lady hide away her memories? Away from rain, away from bullets, blast and burglars. He went to the cast iron, log-fired oven in the kitchen alcove and opened the rusty, cream coloured door.

A neat package, wrapped in brown paper, tied with twine, nestled inside. He hesitated, uncertain about prying into the heart of an old lady. But he meant no harm – one day, maybe, he could meet her and explain. Laying the torch across the surface of the table to provide light, he examined the contents.

Most of the letters were yellowed and crumbling, written on flimsy rice paper in a scratchy Japanese Dan could not hope to understand. There was a locket with a miniature of a bearded, middle-aged man – probably Mrs Okunaga's father, or husband – several hallmarked certificates, a brooch, an ornate marriage-scroll, and there, in a thin cardboard box at the bottom of the package, the objects of his search.

Family photographs, perhaps a couple of dozen.

With shaking hands Dan picked up each sepia print and held it to the torch light. Most were studio shots with an address on the back of a shop in Naha. Groups of polite children smiled out at him with groomed obedience, tall young men posed in uniforms, in front of ornate buildings and statues. Then, halfway down the pile, a graduation photograph yielded a familiar face. At first, he was not sure, but the newspaper cutting underneath banished all doubt. At the top of the article was a passport-sized picture of Ayako.

LATER THAT NIGHT Recruit Reynolds was astonished to find the Colonel's batman pulling him from his bed and marching him to the HQ office, where a case of genuine Scotch whisky sat on the table like a vision in a dream.

The Colonel even poured him a glass, re-introducing that mysterious civilian visitor from the afternoon.

'Think, Reynolds, think!' the Colonel kept shouting, after each unsatisfactory answer.

But no – Reynolds didn't know for sure if the grandma or child survived.

No – he didn't know if the child was boy or girl.

No – he didn't know how old the child was.

No – he didn't know where they'd been taken.

BECAUSE BRADLEY HADN'T TOLD HIM.

SUNDAY WAS the first really fine day that summer. The wind had stopped blasting for a while, the regular rains had not arrived, the sun shone down from a brilliant cloudless heaven. And yet, Dan had never seen such misery.

In spite of almost superhuman efforts by their American occupiers, the Okinawan refugees suffered appallingly. The huge internment camps were, indeed, breeding grounds for disease, which quickly spread from the hospital tents of the civilian battle-wounded, across undernourished crowded compounds, killing literally thousands each week. On every guy rope, tree branch, even on the barbed wire perimeter fence, washing hung out to dry – as the fanatically clean Okinawans tried to scrub the diseases away. But still they died, whole families together, cursing the fate that had made their island the victim of constant conquests for five centuries.

The Australian Senior Commissioner for Refugees was frank to the point of rudeness.

'No, Mr Lawrence, I haven't heard of a Mrs Asako Okunaga, and to be straight we've virtually no record of names. More than half the Okinawan population of a million people are in a camp at present; their homes have either been destroyed or aren't safe. This is just one of sixteen camps, all the size of a town. One old lady, amongst this lot, simply can't be found.'

'What about a child of two-and-a-half?'

The bear-like Commissioner scratched his ragged, grey beard. He wanted to help, there were supplies he required. 'Sheesh,' he replied. 'You're still talkin' a thousand to one. If it's an orphan they are kept separately, do you know what the child looks like? Boy or girl?'

Dan shook his head; it was hopeless.

'Maybe the old lady will drift back home, Mr Lawrence, we're starting a rehabilitation program soon. That's if she survives, of course.'

Of course.

Dan had to leave that evening, after another scrambler call from an unusually subdued Abe Ford.

'My boy, I'm not used to getting orders, and then having to pass them on – but you have to relocate to Tinian, under the command of General Farrell, who I know from our New York State time together – he's an engineer, but a good man. They haven't told me to clear my desk exactly, but it's coming. It turns out that Mrs Ford has a friend or two who went to Kansas City Law School at the same time as our Mr Truman – not the sharpest knife in the drawer, they say. Didn't pass out. Decent, though. Her friend said it felt like the janitor becoming President, maybe the right choice to deal with Stalin.'

Dan didn't reply. He realised this was the end of Abe's proxy power, and a good time to show extra respect.

'Any idea of my role in Tinian, Sir?'

Abe sighed, the long sigh of a disappointed political operator about to be supplanted. 'Haven't told me that, either. Marshall called me himself, touch of the *bonjour-au revoir*, he wants you directing logistics from there. High priority. Ring-fenced, special op. Asked about your dealing with the press and politicians, I said you could deal with anyone and, no, I don't know what that's about either. In this town, when you're in the dark, it sure is dark.'

That was it.

Abe Ford never believed in saying goodbye, would be a waste of precious time, the line simply went dead.

THE NEXT MORNING, Mrs Okunaga heaved herself up on a frail elbow and smiled through her few remaining, scummy front teeth. The child was breathing better, the fever had passed, now the appetite would return. The days of shaking her fists at the heavens for being so old were over. Mayumi would soon be well. That child seemed to have the strength of a dozen Samurai, the will of a God. The old lady coughed, the racking, liquid cough of serious pneumonia. She smiled again.

Now I can go in peace, I have done what is possible.

'Mayumi,' she whispered, 'Mayumi, wake up.'

The young child opened sleepy eyes, blinking at the sunlight. 'You feel better now my darling, do you not?'

Mayumi nodded, desperately hungry.

'Here, see, your grandma has saved you some rice.' Mayumi sat up and reached across to cram a handful into her ravenous mouth. Mrs Okunaga grinned with pleasure – her task really was at an end. She held up a brown, leather purse.

'Please listen carefully, my child. Inside this purse is your certificate of birth, and a photograph of your mother; on the back is her name and her last address – and the name of your father. You must never lose it, because when the war is over you will see her again. But I'm afraid I'll have to sleep now – the kind of sleep where you never wake up. Wish me good sleep, and promise not to cry. One day we'll meet in another world. Do you understand?'

Mayumi was still shovelling rice, tears streaking down soft, smooth cheeks. She took the purse and held it tightly.

'Mrs Aragaki has promised to look after you, so be a good child. You know I love you, kiss me goodbye…'

Mrs Okunaga lay back breathing heavily, her duty fulfilled. Mayumi leaned across and kissed her on the forehead. The old lady let out a deep sigh and drifted into peaceful sleep. Mayumi was still kneeling tidily by her side, scooping handfuls of rice, holding the purse, half an hour later – when old Mrs Okunaga coughed and died.

10

General Curtis LeMay dominated Air Force canteen talk across the Pacific Theatre in the mid-summer months of 1945.

His megaphone orders cascaded down from Army Air Corps HQ in Guam into the whole region, gaining support or disapproval every night his lethal bombing campaign thundered into Japan. US Bomber Command ravaged sixty-six cities, killing many hundreds of thousands, destroying factories, schools, hospitals, breaking Japanese daily life and industry, but not their spirit, which held rigidly firm in the face of it all.

As the war in Europe wound down, LeMay ran wild. The full brunt of the enormous industrial power of the United States and the British Empire could be concentrated on a 'treacherous' nation of a hundred million increasingly desperate and hungry people, who still worshipped their Emperor, while held hostage by a militaristic Cabinet that simply wouldn't consider giving in.

After Okinawa there could only be one remaining target for invasion and occupation – the Japanese mainland itself, now ringed by hitherto unknown allied ports and airfields in the middle of nowhere, gradually, inexorably, twisting the knot.

Islands like Tinian, five miles from Saipan in the Mariana chain, which had the good – or, perhaps, bad – luck to be within B-29 bomber range of Japan's major cities. Mainly flat and built of hard Pacific coral, it was as if a million years of nature had prepared the perfect platform for the largest military airbase the world had ever seen.

Dan was astonished at what he found there.

Although only twelve miles by six, over the last couple of centuries Tinian had been conquered and occupied, conquered and occupied, conquered and occupied again and again – raped and ruined by a myriad of European and regional powers, including Spain, Korea, and finally Germany. Then, in 1919, the Japanese government was awarded the Marianas as a few desultory crumbs from the carve-up of German possessions after the First World War Versailles treaty.

Japan had dispatched many thousands of workers, planters and farmers, creating sugar plantations across most of the flat, porous, thinly-soiled land, beating or expelling native peasants until, in the early days of this war, the level ground and natural harbours allowed the Imperial Navy to build Tinian into a static aircraft carrier. But when its sister island, Saipan fell to the US Marines, it was only a matter of weeks before Tinian became yet another American 'stepping-stone' to Tokyo.

Back in those mid-summer days of 1944, the idea of such a tiny island accommodating six runways, two capable of dealing with fully laden B-29s, would have seemed ridiculous, but that is what the astonishing power of the United States war machine managed in a few frenetic months. From a pair of tiny Japanese 'dirt-and-dust' fields, that had been extensively damaged during the invasion by American marines, which had annihilated fifteen thousand Japanese troops, the US engineers provided an aviation miracle.

Built like a small city that reminded the construction engineers of Manhattan, the gridded avenues of billets, barracks, workshops, munition stores and canteens were named after their favourite streets and places in New York – 5th Avenue, Broadway, Upper West Side, Soho.

Tucked away from the main base of operations, on the Upper East-side of the island, at 125th Street, on Riverside Drive, was North Field – the address of the 509 Composite Group, named because it had gathered together the finest talent in the entire US Army, and was therefore disliked as a secretive elite by all the other squadrons on Tinian. Worse even than the 509 being in the front of the line for resources and personnel, they were not required to fly the perilous hundred-bomber missions over Japanese cities.

To his surprise, on arrival Dan was incorporated into the two thousand or so aircrew, engineers and scientists who comprised the 509, without explanation, simply told that 'the special mission' would be explained by General Farrell the next day.

In the meantime, because he was seen as a benefactor of what was called 'blind eye supplies' – the coke syrup, the chocolates, the perfumes, the pretzels, icebox hamburgers, the beer from everywhere, the whiskey, and the precious JD from Tennessee – on the evening of his arrival he'd been invited as a VIP guest to a B-29, *20-mission-accomplished* celebration, where several crews could write their own alcohol ticket on a raucous 'all-nighter', with a well-earned week of R & R on the horizon.

Informally, the Army Air Force took a lenient view of such parties, booking them into the corrugated briefing room, even encouraging the crews to 'let off steam, let it out, let it go', a kind of team therapy, to stop them bottling it up. In the early hours, as the party wound towards its conclusion, just before the hangover, one bomb-aimer, a lieutenant called Ed Phillips, after several quarts of his native Mississippi Mud, decided to tell his story of the Tokyo firestorm to a group of engineers and nurses, around a table full of empties.

'The memory I'm gonna have forever is not the flames or looking down thinking about the homes and factories we're blasting – no, it was the *smell*. Won't never forget that.'

No one spoke. Ed should be left to unload, let it out.

'Was when we opened the bomb doors maybe couple of minutes before dropping – it came in then. The smell of human flesh burning. Roasting. My parents live next to a steak bar in Southaven, kinda the same, but… Jeez… sweeter? Way stronger. This is up at 8,000 feet, weren't no expecting of that, and then it's me that has to push the button let our 24 babies go. 'Course I'm thinking, "if they been burned already, maybe it won't matter?" No choice anyway, army regulations, but it plays on ya, most nights.'

Ed took a few more swigs of Mississippi Mud, he wasn't finished.

'So we drop 'em, incredible buffering from the clouds of smoke and heat, incredible, and I close the bomb doors, but the smell is still in there. Could even be stronger.' He pointed to an older man – mid-30s - across the table. 'Major Fookes, here, comes on the intercom says, "Ed, you're gonna have to open them again, get that smell out, don't wanta be taking Jap aroma back to Tinian," and I do that – twice. First time, thought it was gone, but still hanging there. Second time, left them open for more than ten minutes over the sea, and that did it. Until on the next sortie, four days later – yep, still there. Way it is in my brain. Guess it's same as we've been hearing about folks being burned in those Jew camps in Germany.'

Major Fookes bowed his head, solemnly. 'Amen to that.'

Everyone lifted their glass. 'Amen.'

As the group broke up, a man in a T-shirt and shorts was standing next to Dan. 'I ain't with his crew, but know how he feels. Way better when you don't connect with down below. My name's Beahan, Kermit, sure do admire those provisions you bring in.'

'Lawrence, Dan. You're a bomb-aimer, then?'

'Very same. North Africa, Italy, Germany – bit of a veteran. Seems like you're sounding English, did nine months there, pretty women.'

Dan looked around, seeing the nurses. 'Like here. Might have to sign in sick.'

They both laughed, Kermit now intrigued by this Englishman.

'That'd work, mostly they have too much choice. Where're you billeting…?'

They were interrupted by two of Kermit's crew, arms across each other's shoulders, swaying, each holding a whiskey bottle in their free hand, which they raised to Dan.

'You guys in Logistics Supply – know the way to our hearts…'

'See you've met Captain Beahan, Honey Bee.' He went to nuzzle up.

Kermit pushed him affectionately away. 'Our radio ops, Abe Spitzer, don't never listen. And Mr Rear-Gunner Pappy Dehart. Couldn't hit a battleship.'

Spitzer held a drunken hand up, he had something serious to say, pointing his finger in Kermit's chest. 'This here man is called "The Great Artiste", the name of our aircraft. And people think it's because he can place a 500-pounder on a dime from 28 thousand feet – which he can. But that ain't the reason, is it Honey-B? Go on, tell him.'

Kermit twinkled and shrugged, too modest.

So, Spitzer continued. 'Because of his prowess – yeah, I went to College, know words – prowess with the *ladies*. Jeez, none of them are safe, because...'

The two of them chorused together, '...because he's the Great Artiste.' With that they swigged back a slug, and swayed away.

Dan shook his head and smiled. *Maybe that's another reason America is winning this war. Officers, Corporals, all working their own way in a team, hierarchy comes second.* 'You were asking. Haven't been billeted yet...'

Kermit nodded. 'I gotta a spare bunk, up near the nurses' compound. Best address on the island.'

THE MORNING AFTER HIS ARRIVAL, when Dan told Kermit that he was required to report to the boss of Tinian, Brigadier General Thomas Farrell, Beahan shook his head. 'Won't be available. You'll see Colonel Doyle, the ADC. Farrell's too high in the sky to speak to lowlife like us, Doyle's his gangster.'

Sure enough, when Dan turned up at the Nissen hut at Number One, 5th Avenue, Farrell was 'elsewhere', and Doyle wasn't the kind to stand on ceremony, emphasising every phrase with extravagant waving of his crisply-starched, uniformed arms.

'Mr Lawrence. We think your logistical work is finished concerning bribing Admirals and Marine Generals. *Kaputski. Roto.* Gone with that man FDR. God bless his scheming soul. We've now got bigger fish to fry. You're gonna be reporting direct to my team, here or in Guam.' Doyle paused, folded his arms, signifying he'd reached the nub. 'Now – what'ya' know about providing glitter for *VIP's*?'

Dan looked at this short, muscular, aggressive, bad-mannered Colonel and instantly decided he had done his time with the army. The days of fighting a war as victims of the Japanese were coming to an end, the military machine was becoming arrogant, a purpose in itself, cruel – time for a new life. But for the moment he would play the game.

'VIPs?'

'Congressmen, Senators, newsreels, radio stars, the press…' Doyle waved a hand with disdain. 'Story was, you an' Logistics know how to red-carpet people.'

This was, of course, a trap. Dan was being simultaneously side-lined and enticed into breaking regulations – set-up for a Military Police operation. The next step would be an escort to Guam to meet with the Provost Marshall. But Dan still had enough high-ranking friends, and levers of executive graft, to stand his ground.

'Congressmen, newsreels, the press? All I know is not to trust them.'

'But we need their nasty friggin' asses – here. Elsewise

Congress turns off the money tap.' Symbolically, Doyle now picked painfully at a mosquito bite on his cheek that had gone septic. 'Don't rightly know how we're winning this thing, so many enemies on the inside.' He sighed. 'How about I say your task is to keep 'em sweet, keep 'em happy, keep 'em under control.' He stopped picking. 'Trick Marshall reckons you did on the Brass for Abe Ford – with spies and bribery. Says you kept the lid on them Admirals talkin' stupid. Folks who know say you was admirable. Devious. Stand you good after this war.'

Clearly Doyle was a fast-talking conspiracy theorist, pre-war would have had connections with Tammany Hall, the well-known Irish political mafia that controlled New York through graft and coercion – until FDR became Governor, and ran them out of town.

Dan was unimpressed at this kind of coercive banter, with tricky compliments thrown in. 'In my experience, Generals and Admirals can't be bribed. Colonels, ah, that's a different matter.'

Colonel Doyle chortled at that – everybody had a price. But he realised that Dan was more self-assured, more Machiavellian than the simplistic military types he usually dealt with.

'Okay, Okay, have it your way, Mr Lawrence. Just don't get going high-horse about this. Gen Farrell wouldn't have got one bridge built in New York without some kinda'—he paused while a particularly noisy aircraft took off—'oiling.'

'So, Colonel, you want me to deal with these Congress and press people?'

'Control 'em, control what they see and hear.'

'About what?'

'Won't be telling ya, and you can't be asking. You'll

know when you know. But get 'em eating out of your hand, splash it all, the French perfume I've heard about, silk stockings for their wives, that lace from Venice, Cubans, real Scotch – hey, why am I telling YOU this, you're the expert.' Now Doyle punched Dan playfully on the shoulder, rather too forcefully. 'Would appreciate some Irish myself, with an "e", reckon you know what I mean.'

'Jameson or Powers?'

Doyle put both palms out and shrugged. 'Either – so long as it's wet.' And both men laughed, falsely, a treacherous bond created, even if only a bond of mistrust. 'Who you billeted with?' As if Doyle didn't know.

'A Captain Beahan, Colonel.'

'Ah, yes, sure, "The Great Artiste." Can hit a dime from thirty-thousand they say.'

'More like a dame.'

Doyle raised his bushy eyebrows acknowledging the joke. 'Guess it pays to keep a sense of humour when you're dropping bombs on folk.'

KERMIT LIKED DOYLE – well, Kermit liked everyone. Spectacularly good-looking, tall, jet-black pencil moustache, trimmed in Clark Gable style, a twinkle forever in both dark-set eyes, a caramel tan like a male model, it was not surprising he'd befriended lady camp-followers from Tunisia, through Italy, England, Utah, Cuba, and now the Marianas.

He wore his heart on his sleeve, but it wasn't to be found anywhere else. Romance was fun, but a man didn't know if he'd still be here tomorrow, so no point in Kermit making plans, however much a dame may want to. Almost a clone of Dan, with a moustache.

'Doyle say why ya' here?'

'Handle VIPs.'

'For what?'

'Didn't say.'

'Will be us. 509. It's coming to the boil. Too many high-flying guys outta tech college have arrived, scientists from all-over.' Kermit was where he liked to be, wearing only shorts, stretched out on his bunk, cool, though it was ninety-degrees-plus out there, smoking and tipping the ash into a navy crash-hat without the inners, philosophical, practical, at peace. 'The 509's been hauling an' dropping seven-ton pumpkins – told you've been cleared, don't harm to say.'

'Seven tons?'

Kermit leaned up on one elbow. 'Something's stirring. Been nine months of training, security everywhere, our commander, Colonel Tibbets', even tighter than ever been… and now you're Mr VIP. Reckon it's coming to a head.'

Dan was struck with a random thought. This wise-owl Captain, best bomb-aimer in the Air Force, was younger than him, maybe upper-mid-twenties, yet he could carry all the cares of the world on his muscular shoulders, calmly, comfortably. Kermit blew out a long trail of smoke at imaginary mosquitos, flicked the tip into the hat on his chest.

'And the Chaplain came by, an' not for the standard "respect dames" talk, reckon even he's spooked, needed cheering. "There be some things about which I can't help," he said. Reckon it's big, engineers call it the "gimmick", but that's all they know. "Gimmick".' Kermit laughed. 'But's gonna be soon.'

Two days later, on August 4th, Dan was ordered to make arrangements for an unspecified number of newsreel crews to fly over from Guam – 'maybe' – to be held in a facility house on Broadway he'd already sequestered, and kitted out and stocked with the 'best produce available', ready for a major announcement. And when he returned to their billet 'early-eyes' on the 6th, Kermit was gone, with a simple note scrawled on the back of a photo of Hedy Lamarr.

'Could be the day of the Gimmick'.

Dan waited around all that day, until mid-afternoon on August 6th, when a trio of B29s landed on North Field, accompanied by whooping and hell-raising from the ground crews who were breaking all protocol, even carrying the unusually smiling Colonel Tibbets high, shouting 'For he's a jolly good fellow…'

But this was interrupted by Tibbets and two other pilots being bundled on an immediate turn-round flight to Guam.

Doyle was at North Field to greet them, holding back, secretive as usual, not comfortable to be part of a jamboree, although puffing a Cuban. 'You won't be needed – not today, son,' he told Dan. 'Maybe not ever. VIPs are at Guam – LeMay wants to bask – but Truman will best him. Presidents always do. Farrell says it was the biggest darn bang in Christendom. City called Hiroshima. Guess mission went to plan, 'less you were looking upwards.'

As the Guam-bound C-47 with Tibbets and crew took off hurriedly, the yelping and hugging continued, with Dan still unaware of what had happened as the ground crews were breaking out cases meant for the VIPs, and racing around, pretending to be planes.

Even Doyle, sombre, tightly-coiled Doyle, was carried along with the moment. 'Thanks for the "with an E". Will go down smooth tonight.'

'You're welcome.'

'"You're welcome"?' Doyle's post-war recruitment game was already beginning. 'Guess we'll make a Yankee of you, yet, boy. Big political world waiting in New York.'

LATER, back at their billet, heading towards midnight – when Dan returned, Kermit was asleep, breathing angelically, the sleep of the innocent.

Dan stood for a while shaking his head at the calmness of this man. While everyone else had been celebrating the astonishing news of the massive atomic bomb over Hiroshima – seen as the end of the war – Captain Kermit Beahan, an official observer in *The Great Artiste*, an aircraft named after him, had gone to bed early, seemingly unexcited, untroubled.

At that moment, Dan's handie-talkie crackled, waking up Kermit, who muttered a sleepy, 'Hi.'

While switching it off, almost dropping half a quart of malt, Dan waved an unsteady apology. He'd been drinking. Kermit simply smiled, he understood.

'Guess there wasn't a nurse available.'

'What, Dan?'

Kermit seemed confused, then understood the joke and grinned. 'Oh, that didn't feel good, not tonight. Problem being in the Observation aircraft, see too much, nothing to do to take your mind off.'

Dan sat down opposite.

'So, *you* didn't drop it, "the Gimmick"?'

'Hell no.'

'They're calling it the "Cosmic Bomb".'

'Yeah. About makes sense, Dan. Real cosmic. If cosmic's purple, pink, yellow waves of dust, shooting thirty-thousand feet in the air, boiling. That'll stay with us, whole crew saying, 'well I'll be darned', we're thinking not something to celebrate, 'cept it has to be the war's end, ain't no one can fight against bombs like that.'

'They're saying equivalent of at least two thousand bombers.'

Kermit gestured – pass over the bottle. He took a long slug, nodding. 'How can a lone bomb do that? We saw it leave *Enola*, seemed big but normal, maybe like those British Grand Slams, seen them over the Ruhr, and they'd make a mighty big hole, but this gimmick was like hell erupting. At least two thousand bombers?' Kermit shook his head. 'I'd say five thousand. Jeez.' Now coming fully awake he took another slug from the bottle. 'What happened with your VIPs?'

'Didn't turn up. Remained at Guam. President Truman wanted the headlines, on a ship back after Potsdam, Germany, the conference with Stalin – Tibbets'll get the glory tomorrow.'

'Don't feel like glory. You should have witnessed. Was issued special arc-welder's goggles – brilliant flash still burned through.' Kermit sighed. 'Japs gotta surrender now, would keep their pride, can say they were beaten by scientists. Those gormy guys with rimless glasses, whose collars don't fit.'

THE SIRENS HAD BEEN SHRIEKING all night over Fukuoka, across to the west coast down to Camp 17, drowning out the *banza katydid*. Unable to sleep, Ayako was thumbing through a many-months-old trash magazine, filled with glowing stories and touched-up pictures of brave *Kamikaze* warriors.

While turning the pages, she was staring upwards at the circling mosquitoes avoiding the paraffin lamp outside the net, while the gentle breathing of Major Ito provided her the comfort that comes from sleeping with a secure, settled older man. Assuming the American aircraft knew this was an Allied Prison Camp and would not bomb their own men, Ayako felt safer than most Japanese, as if the prisoners were hostages, a thought that made her grunt with satisfaction.

The previous four weeks had been tough. The officers had eaten very little food except the unclean seafood fished out for them from the stinking harbour. A collapse in morale in the guards, especially the younger ones, was matched by a corresponding rise in the hopes of the prisoners, even though there was even less food for them, as they were uplifted by LeMay's extraordinary, multi-coloured 'fires from the sky' across Fukuoka, burning for days, with wafts of acrid incendiary smoke filtering down the coast. The prisoners knew they must avert their triumphant gaze, but the guards knew what they were thinking.

At last, the sirens fell silent, some other city was on LeMay's list to be pulverised. Away in the distance, the clock on the huge twin towers of Urakami Cathedral chimed midnight.

Still watching the mosquitos circling round, Ayako thought about the coming day's duty. Thursday 9th

August. She had been summoned to Nagasaki court to interpret for a disgusting Anglo-Australian prisoner, Corporal Robert Weaver, who had hit an elderly guard, breaking his leg with an ingot of coal. Weaver, of course, said it was a set-up, the coal had slipped from his grasp in the 110-degree humid heat down the mine but neither Ayako nor the officers believed that story one bit.

Ayako glanced at Major Ito, so honourable, so gentle. A kind man. A good man. That very day he had organised a delegation of prisoners and guards to go to the nearby local farmland and vegetable gardens. They had requisitioned any fresh produce and pickles for the camp staff – and some for the prisoners. Why did Weaver's attack on a guard need to go before a judge to rubber-stamp the death sentence? The prisoner was clearly guilty. Why should a cowardly man like that be allowed to bring dishonour on the camp, on Ito's role as Commandant?

Despite the quiet now the sirens had relented, she still found sleeping difficult. She sighed, reached under the edge of the net and turned out the paraffin lamp.

NEARLY TWO THOUSAND MILES AWAY, on the island of Tinian, a light switched on.

Kermit Beahan groaned as an orderly placed a coffee on his bedside table along with an envelope covered by lipstick hearts and a separate hand-written note. 'Eighteen minutes to briefing, Sir.' Kermit sat for a moment on the side of his bed, scratching himself in the pleasant, tropical night air. Two hours sleep, that's all he'd managed, two hours – the night before making history.

The next 'gimmick-run' had been planned for 11th

August, and they had been practising late last night, dropping a 'pumpkin' in the Pacific, but when they returned, sometime before midnight on the 8th, they were abruptly told to be ready again in two hours. The official reason given, '*gathering storms over southern Japan*', was probably less important than '*gathering Soviet Tanks on the Russo-Manchurian border*', following Stalin's declaration of war against Japan earlier that day.

Dan had been woken, too, by the orderly. 'This the *real* one?'

Kermit nodded. 'They say weather's closing, gotta pull it forward – I thought a second one wouldn't be needed.'

'Maybe isn't.'

'Yeah. *New York Times* science guy on the pumpkin run said, "I bet those weather forecasts came all the way from the Kremlin."' He pulled on his tunic and read the note, ignoring the lipstick envelope, unopened to one side. 'General Farrell says to meet me plane-side, before we start up, says he wants to sign the bomb.'

Most of the briefing was dull, routine. A surprisingly young senior officer stood in front of a series of blow-up photos and maps – being flipped over by a team of assistants while he spoke.

'OK. OK. Listen up. Special Bombing Mission 16 – Primary Target – Kokura City and conurbation – aiming point 104082, Kokura Arsenal. Secondary target – Nagasaki Urban Area – aiming point 114061, centre of city.'

Next the weather maps were turned over.

'Apart from a storm gathering off Iwo Jima, the forecast is good. Weather aircraft will be over both targets and radio back reports at 090915. This will enable the strike force to select either the primary or secondary target for best visual bombing. No radar drop has been authorised. Is that understood? Visual bombing only.'

He looked around the room and picked out the chubby pilot of the main aircraft, *Bock's Car*. 'Major Sweeney?'

'Visual drop, only, sir.'

The officer continued, 'Visibility is predicted excellent, so it shouldn't be an issue.' He pointed to the largest photo marked *Kokura Intelligence photo* to show the Imperial Iron and Steel Works at Yawata, and Tobata, the Kyushu Chemical Works, and the Kokura Arsenal. He tapped the blow up with his stick. 'Aiming point – factory chimney at Kokura, several hundred feet high.'

The whole room focused on the blurry photo of a circle, surrounded by rows and rows of low buildings. 'Gotta be one mile long, by one half wide. Be difficult to miss – Captain Beahan…?'

Kermit raised his arm, 'Photos on the aircraft, Sir?'

'Of course. Kokura's kinda flat, centre of biggest armaments industries in the Empire, conurbation six hundred thou' population plus itinerant labourers. Blast is calculated across a wide area. Nagasaki's smaller, hilly-to-mountainous, Mitsubishi factories and naval yards, population maybe downwards of one fifty thou'.'

The assistants changed the display to a large-scale map of the East China Sea.

'Your route is to the south of Iwo Jima, to rendezvous with observation and technical aircraft here – Yakushima Island, where you will proceed to target.'

Now a number of figures, for the engineers, navigator and pilot.

'Bomb-run will be upwind, and attack altitude 28 thousand feet – to prevent self-destruction. On drop, you will bank to at least 150 degrees. The bomb will have a very wide destructive area, but you should be ten and one-half miles from target on explosion. Thank you.'

No one in the briefing room moved – they knew what was still to come. 'Chaplain Downey – your mission prayer, please.'

'With hearts humble, yet somehow uplifted, we gird ourselves for the task which is set before us. Let no man give us stay; let no man hinder us in our appointed duty; for we have within our hands one of God's tremendous secrets. With Your grace may this special mission bring peace to the world, and help mankind find a new way to take your love. In the Lord's name, Amen.'

After a snatched breakfast, back at the Quonset Hut, Kermit put his affairs in order, asking Dan to keepsake a letter to his parents – 'reckon the Army would poke their noses in' – and stood for a while with the inventory of 'what's forgotten', before nodding. He was ready, and with Dan now ordered to Guam, both realised they most likely wouldn't meet again until back in America.

'What you gonna do when this thing's over?'

'Go back to making myself a millionaire.'

'You serious?'

'Yep. It's what I do. And you?'

'Army Air Force. Regular. What I do.'

After only a week, a quiet bond had been created, in two men who usually avoided war-time transitory friendships – a bond that would last for decades to come. 'Keep yourself safe.'

'And you. What we do.'

'Gonna miss this war thing.'

'Yeah, beats real life.'

They stood for another few seconds and, finally, Dan just had to ask.

'The envelope, scarlet hearts – aren't'cha gonna open it?'

'I know what it is, who it's from.' Kermit said with a shake of his head, then reached forward, hugged Dan hard, spun round, touched his side-cap with an index finger and left.

Dan looked down at the lipstick hearts, addressed to 'The Great Artiste'. It was irresistible and, heck, Kermit wouldn't mind. Inside was a hand-painted card:

'Happy 27th Birthday Honeybee –
From
Abe, Chuck, Donald Duck, Jim Van, Fred, Nails, Buck, Ray (with Mary Ann), Pappy.'

AT FIRST, General Farrell didn't look up when Kermit walked across carrying what he called his 'mission pillow', to help him sleep on journeys before his 'five minutes of action'.

'Captain Beahan, I'm about to be the last of fifty people to sign *Fat Man*, and I'd be glad for you to witness.' Farrell swung around to the half dozen aides who were standing with him. 'Gentlemen, space, please.'

The assembly moved out of earshot, which wasn't very far, given the pre-flight preparation noise. The doors to the bomb-bay were still open so the massive bomb was there between them, like a third person, already fused and live. Unlike *Little Boy*, the bomb that exploded over Hiroshima, *Fat Man* could not be armed in flight. The mechanism of fuses – four different kinds – had to be installed while the aircraft was on the ground, and only after then had the two sides of the massive round bomb been bolted together. That had taken place the night before. From that moment onwards, if *Fat Man* had unintentionally been set off, the entire Island would disappear into the Philippine Sea. As if to tempt fate, Farrell reached into his tunic pocket, twisted himself upward, and wrote on the side of the bomb.

'To Hirohito, with love and kisses. T F Farrell.'

He put the pen away, and turned to Kermit in a commanding, but slightly hesitant, way.

'So, Captain, let me tell you what that last signature means. Forget the usual rules of war, where the bombardier takes ownership when ya' get to the target.' He pointed at *Fat Man*. 'Way I see – it's *my* bomb. And while procedures and orders must be obeyed, reckon I'm allowed my say. Which ain't much…'

Kermit was entirely confused, unsure where this was heading, but he knew General Farrell was a thoughtful, humane engineer, co-opted back into the military in middle-age from a successful life in commerce. Since then, he'd built a solid reputation for getting the job done through understated organisational skill – rather than the bludgeoning style of Curtis LeMay.

'Of course, Sir,' Kermit replied, as if he understood.

'In your flight info pack you'll find optimal target focus – the factory chimney at Kokura, and estimated casualty figures. High for the primary – Kokura. Lower for Nagasaki'—he waved his hands about, the engineer frustrated at imprecision—'built across hills, ain't so specific…'

At that moment, the two men were interrupted by

another delegation coming from the cockpit of the B-29. Colonel Tibbets, Major Sweeney the pilot, and Kuharek the Engineer. Sweeney saluted with two fingers and said, 'Permission to speak, Sir.'

'Granted.'

'The auxiliary transfer fuel pump in the rear bomb bay bladder is malfunctioning. We've got six hundred gallons trapped.'

Tibbets and Farrell glanced at each other, and let the Major explain.

'Replacement will take at least three hours, Sir, and could be dangerous now the A-bomb is armed. But we'll lose at least five hundred miles, and the extra weight… guess still will be possible to make there and back, but gonna be tight…'

Tibbets patted Sweeney on the arm. 'Your call, Chuck.'

At that moment the bomb door clanged shut, as if the actual aircraft had made up its mind. 'Ah, the heck with it,' Sweeney decided. 'We'll go.'

Kermit stayed with Farrell as the others walked away. He knew the general hadn't finished.

'What I was saying, Captain Beahan. Do you know the difference between orders and intuition?' Farrell had a round, friendly face, topped by a shiny quiff of dark hair, greying round the edges, a lazy right eye, the glimmer of a smile, unusually engaging for a general, even more so for an engineer. But for all his friendliness, Farrell required an answer, even if the question left Kermit bewildered.

'"Difference between orders and intuition," Sir? Not sure I do. Guess I'd find orders easier to follow, Sir.'

Farrell expected such an answer from a Bombardier, even one as personable as Kermit.

'Well, let me tell you, son.' Farrell illustrated by

pointing with his hands. '*Orders* come downwards, from *people*, bosses, generals, Presidents. *Intuition* goes upwards, way of *God*.' Now he punched his own chest. 'Intuition. Up – from your heart, into your head, God pushin' your button.' He brightened – clearly intuition was far superior to orders, with all that double-dealing from humans. 'Intuition is personal, but belongs to God – like a prayer.'

Kermit tried to smile, to agree, but it wouldn't come. The weight of the entire world had been dropped on his usually easy-going, sturdy shoulders. Was he being ordered – well, cajoled – to use his intuition when dropping the greatest, deadliest bomb of all time? Or had he read this entire episode wrong? And now no wily Dan to discuss it with.

He glanced for the last time at the belly of the aircraft, the bomb doors closed, *Fat Man* hidden inside, with General Farrell walking away, shouting over his shoulder, 'Finest moments of my life have been intuition, Captain.'

It was far too early to be up, but Ayako still couldn't sleep, though now she had a reason beyond her usual anxiety. An urgent package addressed to 'The Commandant of Fukuoka 17' had been delivered to the camp by a despatch rider and the duty officer had thought it important enough to send over to Major Ito in the middle of the night.

> **TOP-SECRET**
> *The American and British Governments have developed a cruel, monstrous bomb, using which they are planning*

> *to destroy our cities, one by one, indiscriminately, murdering our families and loved ones, without recourse to civil casualties or the rules of war. Effective immediately, we order steps are taken to secure the prisoners of all camps so they can be moved into areas that will protect our home population.*

Ayako knelt on the *tatami* mat, becoming more and more angry every time she read and reread the order. *The Americans and British are cowards, bombing our homes, our defenceless old people and children. No Japanese soldier would ever attack civilians – maybe inferior races like the Chinese in the past – but not equal, civilised human beings, massacring everyone.*

And then, from nowhere, she thought about her father for the first time in many weeks.

That silly hat, the stupid eye-patch, his raggedness, waving his arms as they talked on the bench outside the camp, his bandaged feet not touching the ground, the way he shouted Shakespeare at the rushing clouds that evening, and – oh yes – the seagull that he stared down until it scuttled away.

She'd once read a book about why a woman should not have an abortion – because you never really rid yourself of the baby, part of them would remain with you, even if only a few cells, always there. Maybe it was like that with her father. Ayako started tracing his name across the order – what would he think? '*…monstrous bomb… planning to destroy our cities, one-by-one, indiscriminately, murdering our families and loved ones… massacring them all…*'

'What will you say now, PAPA?' she said out aloud. Ito

stirred, aware of her restlessness, reaching out by opening a single eye.

'What's wrong, Acchan?'

She handed him the order and then his spectacles and he read in the fluttering light from the paraffin lamp. It was as if the *banza katydid* held their shriek. By the time he finished reading, Ito was fully awake, still calm, but a steely determination had taken over his soul.

'Ah so, Top Secret, I understand.' He pushed himself up and used the order with its stiff envelope to fan himself while he pondered the situation. 'The prisoners must not know what we are planning. They're no use here if we can't work the mine any longer, so we must march them to Fukuoka and Nagasaki, hold them in prisons in the cities, use them as a shield to protect the citizens from these monstrous bombs.' He tapped the envelope and put it down, his eyes narrowing as he formulated a plan, fingers joined in a pyramid in front of his grey, tired face. She waited – he was coming to a decision.

'After overseeing the garden duties with the prisoners from Camp 11 at Nagasaki this morning, I will have them all marched to the jail on the hill at Urakami. The prison Captain was here, remember, he will release the Japanese criminals and will hold the Americans and British. Also, it is a place of execution, so you can bring Weaver there.'

'As you wish.' Ayako said this flatly, as if even the world now was betraying her.

'You seem uncertain.'

'There is little to be certain about.' Ayako began swaying forwards and backwards, murmuring, singing softly in English, more like a lullaby than a song… '"*I'll find a day to massacre them all. And raze their faction and their family…"'* She continued swaying. 'My father taught this about Imperial military, saying it means Tojo's army must kill every enemy or die themselves one day – Papa said it's Shogun meets Shakespeare. '*"I'll find a day to massacre them all. And raze their faction and their family… I'll find a day to massacre them all. And raze their faction and their family…"'*

Ito didn't understand, not the words, but he understood the meaning, the feeling – tragedy in a lilting voice. He swayed along with her lullaby, humming support, together forever, as one against the enemy, for eternity.

Kneeling there, as she hummed, Ayako bowed low to him and let the hum drift away. 'I love you,' she said, breaking all protocol.

He stared back and nodded, 'I love you, too.' He fanned himself again with the order. 'When all this is over, we must build a house in my family's hometown in Izu, somewhere overlooking the ocean, where we can dream again…'

11

On that early morning of Thursday August 9th 1945, very little had gone right with Special Bombing Mission 16 on its way from Tinian to the Japanese mainland, with *Fat Man* on board.

Needing every inch of the 8,500-foot Runway A, pilot Major Sweeney said a fiftieth prayer, revved the four Wright R-3350-41 engines, waited until the whole airframe was vibrating, gritted his teeth, shouted, 'Ready for take-off,' let go the brakes and the seventy-seven-and-a-half-ton plane lurched forward. On the intercom he told the crew, 'Some darn fool switched off the spotlight.' The light should have illuminated the ocean at the end of the runway, so he had to guess in the dark when coaxing the B-29 off the last scraps of mother earth. Had it crashed into the sea, the crew, the thirty-thousand air force personnel, and the entire island of Tinian, would have instantly disappeared forever.

With all engines straining, *Bock's Car* finally took off with just a few feet of runway to spare, wobbled, rose to fifty feet, dropped for a moment, steadied, then started slowly climbing – the observers on the ground who understood the destructive power of *Fat Man* took a huge breath of relief.

At first, Sweeney headed north at seven thousand feet, but had to climb to seventeen thousand to avoid storms and turbulence, because he didn't want the sudden dips and jumps to set off the 'sensitive cargo' sitting a few feet behind the cockpit. However, the increased altitude was burning fuel at a higher rate, adding to the problems caused by the six hundred gallons trapped in the rear bomb-bay bladder.

As usual, in spite of the terrifying take-off, the historic mission, the cosmic uncertainties of a plutonium chain reaction, the unprecedented responsibility – with the crew now fully aware of what was on board – they were calm, almost to the point of being bored. An eternal truth about bombing missions is that when the aircraft finally takes off, the fear of not returning, the anxiety of the briefing and, above all, the waiting, dissolves, as the team on board go back to being a family – the way of experienced aircrew everywhere.

Within half an hour, some were asleep, including Kermit Beahan, who was flat out in a back corner of the cockpit, nuzzling his beloved pillow, seemingly without a care in the world. Kuharek, the flight engineer, had his eyes riveted on the instrument panels, and especially on the fuel consumption. Navy Commander Ashworth and Lieutenant Barnes, in charge of the black box which was monitoring the bomb, were constantly checking read-backs from the fuses. James Van Pelt, the navigator, was recalculating the route to the rendezvous point with the two observation aircraft. All was peaceful, routine, so even Sweeney bedded down, handing over the controls to co-pilot Don Albery. And then, at seven am Tokyo time, as the orange sun was rising over the grey eastern horizon, the red warning light on the bomb's fuse monitor began flashing.

Ashworth and Barnes tried to stay calm, but their voices betrayed not just concern but a tone bordering on panic. Clearly it was not the primary firing circuit – if that, they would already have been blown to eternity; if it was a faulty barometric fuse, the one triggered by height, that would be OK so long as they stayed above two thousand feet – but what the devil was it?

Lieutenant Barnes opened the monitoring device. Inside was a jumble of wires and switches, any one of which could trigger the biggest explosion the world had ever seen. After what seemed eternity, but was just a few minutes, they discovered the problem. A technician back at Tinian had left two switches in the wrong position, causing the alarm. Barnes carefully, very carefully, flicked them back, and everyone could breathe again.

Having been woken up from a pleasant sleep by this extreme emergency, the second reserve pilot, Lieutenant Fred Olivi decided to lighten the atmosphere by singing a song through the intercom – '*Home, home on the range, where the deer and the antelope play, where seldom is heard a discouraging word, and the skies are not cloudy all day…*'

'Shut up!' shouted Abe Spitzer, the anxious radio operator, because there was a faint message coming through under the static and Japanese jamming. From the weather aircraft: '*Weather good. Primary target recommended for bombing*' – it would be Kokura. A minute later the other weather aircraft. '*Nagasaki reported clear, too.*'

'Good boy, Abe,' Sweeney said on the intercom, 'We're cooking with gas.'

By 9 a.m. they had reached the coast of Japan, flying over picturesque fishing villages, with orchards and forests terracing the craggy hills, peaceful in the morning sun, a world away from the ferocious bomb now heading for the heart of a bustling city.

The next misfortune, serious given the already depleted fuel reserve, was not technical, but entirely man-made. At the agreed rendezvous point of 30,000 feet over Yakushima in southern Japan, while one observation aircraft met up with *Bock's Car* as agreed, the other, piloted by Lt Colonel Hopkins, was inexplicably flying at 39,000, meaning that Sweeney and Hopkins could not see each other. After circling round-and-round for over half an hour, using up precious aviation gasoline, Sweeney shouted at Albury, 'To hell with it, we can't wait around all day,' and he turned to navigator Pelt and shouted 'Jim, give me a course for Kokura.'

Sweeney pulled out of circling, banked the aircraft, and began a straight run for the primary target. The attack had begun.

This is the moment when a crew ceases to be individuals, when teamwork becomes a cradle of trained concentration, and the world outside disappears.

Beahan crawled down to the bomb-aimer's position, lying flat under the cockpit, surrounded by maps of Kokura, Yawata and Tobata, with those sobering numbers of the population – Kokura itself 300,000, but a total in the wider blast area of 600,000.

Van Pelt told Sweeney, navigator to pilot: 'Two degrees right, one degree left.'

Buckley, radar: 'I have it in range. What's our true altitude?'

Beahan was calibrating his sights, comparing the

ground to his maps, with the order from President Truman – *visual* targeting required.

Van Pelt: 'Give me one degree left, Sweeney… Hold it; hold it. Fine. Good. We're right on course.'

Sweeney: 'Roger! All you men make damned sure you have your welding goggles on; I don't want any blind men on my crew.'

They adjusted their flight path and began the axis of attack.

It would soon be up to Beahan, when control of the aircraft passed to him.

On the flight deck, Major Sweeney looked cool, cocky and confident. He grinned. Three minutes to target now.

Buckley: 'Twenty miles out, captain.'

Van Pelt: 'Roger, Jim. Give me two degrees left, Sweeney.'

Sweeney: 'You got it, man.'

The bomb bay doors opened, the entire crew focused on the run in, no problems expected. It had been confirmed five minutes before by the US weather aircraft, *Bock's Car* was flying into less than one-tenth cloud – a blue sky.

Jim Van Pelt had routed them over the centre of the target area. Everyone could see down below – the factory chimney in the centre of Kokura, the Imperial Iron and Steel Works at Yawata, and Tobata, the Kyushu Chemical Works.

On the ground in Kokura, many workers on their way home from their night shifts saw the two planes flying high over the city, unusual because the air-raid sirens hadn't yet sounded.

One minute to go – Sweeney: 'It's all yours Beahan, over to you.'

One minute until Kokura would be obliterated, literally erased from the map, and one man with absolute control.

Those on the plane held their breath, the population of six hundred thousand below carried on as normal – the world had no idea – and then, from the bottom of the aircraft a shouted cry:

'GODDAMM TO HELL, NO DROP, NO DROP. I CAN'T SEE THE GODDAMNED TARGET, THERE'S A CLOUD OVER THE GODDAMNED, GODDAMNED TARGET.'

Sweeney gently banked the aircraft, to swing around, concerned about using up precious fuel. 'We're going again,' he said.

'Major, flak to starboard,' Albury said, 'Two thousand low,' as white puffs began to follow the aircraft over one of the most heavily defended targets in Japan.

The aircraft steadied again, with the sirens now shrieking below, and workers dismounting from bikes, looking up and pointing.

'Attack aircraft climbing, sir,' Pappy Dehart, a man of few words, shouted from his tail-gunner position.

'Yours, Beahan,' Sweeney said as the aircraft steadied on the target for the second time.

Again, the crew held their breath, waiting for Kermit's confirmation, but, again, at the last moment he shouted:

'NO DROP, NO DROP. CLOUDS STILL OBSCURE THE TARGET. NO DROP, NO DROP, NO DROP.'

In a cloudless sky this was beginning to cause confusion among the crew, but they would never question Captain Kermit Beahan, their crewman, their buddy, the 'Great Artiste.'

'Sit tight, boys; we're going around again,' announced Sweeney. 'One more try before we turn for home.'

Bock's Car circled round for another run.

With the sky still clear, they changed the axis of attack, partly to confuse the guns below, which were now finding the aircraft's height.

As they turned for a third time to make another run, the crew were becoming anxious and restless. Buckley and Van Pelt were getting excellent results with the radar, but the President's order was still for a visual bombing, although no one understood why.

Now from a third direction, there were puffy clouds, increasing, not decreasing. And so was the flak. 'What's wrong with Nagasaki?' the crew were asking themselves, but there was still one run to go, maybe third time lucky. But then, from Kermit:

'GODDAMN. GODDAMN. NO VISUAL. NO DROP. NO DROP. NO DROP.'

Then Dehart called out. 'Fighters below and climbing fast. Four of them.'

'Fuel critical, Captain,' Kuharek announced. 'Fifteen-hundred gallons, sir.' *Bock's Car* could not even reach the airfield on Okinawa if it had to carry *Fat Man*.

Major Sweeney made a fateful decision. There was just enough time for a single run over the secondary target 150 miles away – otherwise the bomb would be dropped in the ocean, an unthinkable disaster for the US Army Air Force. He set course to the southwest, towards the smaller, less populated, less murderous target of Nagasaki.

Man became God that day.

The population of Kokura had no idea of their lucky escape, because a bombardier 'couldn't see the ground.' As the aircraft sped away, three-quarters of a million

Japanese continued their routine life, tidying their neat and uniform houses, teaching their attentive children, wondering what to prepare for lunch, and when this bloody war would end, without knowing how close they came to Armageddon.

EARLIER THAT MORNING, Major Ito and a shabby contingent of guards had loaded forty prisoners from Fukuoka 17 onto a convoy of type-94 trucks and had taken them to a hillside seven miles from Nagasaki, as a gardening detail, ostensibly to provide fresh vegetables and fruit for the camp, without them being informed that they would, in fact, later be marched to the Urakami Branch of Nagasaki prison to be held there as hostages against air attack.

For the starving prisoners this was a welcome respite from the appalling conditions down the coalmine. There was even the possibility of real food, although they knew that if they were seen eating even a small scrap, they would summarily be shot. In the event, it was slender pickings anyway, although by mid-morning they had several bushels of sweet potatoes and mouldy corn.

As they worked in the hot, humid, cloudy weather, they could see the bay and the city of Nagasaki stretched along the twinkling coast, with the Mitsubishi armament factories in the foreground, now churning out personally-controlled *Kamikaze* 'human' torpedoes for a non-existent Imperial Navy. The prisoners were ordered to avert their gaze from the munitions factories, which was difficult while surrounded by such a lovely vista.

In the heat, Major Ito's war wound began to throb painfully, so a soldier pulled a bench from the lead truck, to allow the Commandant to sit, using his silver staff to swat away the insects.

———

HIGH ABOVE, still fifteen minutes out from Nagasaki, but in another universe, Major Sweeney ordered, 'Send Commander Ashworth up to the cockpit, Abe.'

A calm but earnest discussion began between Sweeney, Commander Ashworth and Captain Kermit Beahan, the subject of which would have been completely alien to those below: Whether to drop *Fat Man* using radar?

'This is the deal,' Sweeney announced. 'We've got just enough gas to make one pass over the target. Got that? If we don't drop it on Nagasaki we'll have to drop it in the sea.'

He let that hang, then continued, 'There's a slim chance we might be able to nurse it back to Okinawa, but dangerous as hell.'

'For God's sake,' said Ashworth. 'What in God's name does that mean?'

'That if you agree, we should do a radar run – if Beahan can't see the target.'

They stood there for what seemed like forever, as *Bock's Car* closed on Nagasaki at five miles a minute.

But still Ashworth was not convinced, saying, 'The President had ordered that the bomb MUST be dropped only when the target was VISIBLE,' and he 'did not have authority' to defy the President's order.

Sweeney tried another tack.

Nagasaki was a V-shaped port city with a population of 150,000, the designated target at the centre of the city, the apex of the 'V', would show very clearly on radar, there really could be no chance of a mistake.

'I assure you we'll be within a quarter mile of the target,' Major Sweeney guaranteed the timid Navy man in charge.

The Commander didn't immediately answer. He paced with hands behind his back, shocked to have such a momentous decision to make. 'Let me think it over, Chuck.'

Ashworth sat down in the corner, his face ashen, hands shaking, traumatised, in deep thought. Finally, he made up his mind.

'We'll have to risk getting the bomb back to Okinawa,' he muttered. 'Our orders were that we could not make a radar drop, I'll have to carry out orders.'

'Roger,' replied Sweeney, shaking his head, returning to his seat in the cockpit, unconvinced, but, as a good military man, compliant.

Well used to the madness of the Navy slavishly following orders, Beahan just shrugged.

Navigator Van Pelt was plotting the route to Nagasaki, while the entire crew stayed silent, considering their own thoughts – that the Navy man was mad. Commander Ashworth was twisting and turning in his seat, as white as a sheet, struggling with a truly momentous decision – could he defy the training of a lifetime in the navy and countermand orders, or, alternatively, quite possibly undermine the entire US strategy for ending the war?

The discussion went round and round in his head until, with five minutes to go, Ashworth, pale and trembling, crawled forward and touched Sweeney on the shoulder. 'I've changed my mind, Chuck,' he said, speaking slowly, deliberately. 'We'll let it go over

Nagasaki, visually, radar, or what have you. OK, to go with radar.'

'I could kiss you,' replied Sweeney, 'and maybe later I will.'

'Atta boy, Commander,' Albury said, as the crew cheered, and Ashworth 'thumbs-upped' back with a childish grin, and a huge sigh of relief.

The target would be the centre of Nagasaki – straight down the funnel of the port, with 150,000 people below.

Decision made, every member of the crew went to their designated places, put on their arc-welding goggles – in spite of the build-up of cloud outside, this time there was no doubt. *Fat Man* would definitely be dropped, each man was now alone with the steady, comforting, throaty drone of the Wright engines as the B-29 laboured towards the very heart of Nagasaki.

The bomb door was opened – the heavens held their breath…

AIR-RAID SIRENS WAILED over the Nagasaki skyline on a pleasant summer morning; across the shipyards, the concrete offices, the naval factories, the apartment buildings, the Nagasaki Grand Hotel, and the maze of pretty, narrow streets in the city centre.

In the old Dutch colonial-style Courthouse, Ayako paused for a moment to look at her watch – 10:53. Another false alarm, no doubt; everyone knew the American bombers passed over Nagasaki on their way from Iwo Jima to the rest of Japan, but the city itself had not been a target yet. In any event, the elderly Justice made no order to clear the Court. People would just have to accept the realities of war. He banged the gong – proceedings should continue without delay.

Ayako was in court to translate the evidence of a prisoner of war accused of assaulting a Guard, a capital offence. She had introduced herself formally to the court as Counsellor to Major Ito, the Commandant of War Prisoner Detention Camp, Fukuoka No 17, her thin, nervous voice adding to the monotony in the room. The ornate courthouse clock ticked away as two escorts prodded forward the tall, pitifully thin and shaking Australian POW.

'Name?'

'Corporal Robert Weaver.'

'Date of birth?'

'April 12th 1913.'

'Place of birth?'

'Southend, Great Britain.'

'Do you agree to tell the truth?'

'I do not recognise this Court.'

The Judge scowled at Ayako with irritation, because the Japanese words he understood had come from her delicate, dispassionate lips.

'Counsellor Okunaga, you should make the war prisoner understand the consequence of failing his duties to the Imperial court.'

Robert pulled his arms free of the grasping guards and smiled broadly at the carved wooden magistrates' bench.

'Nime, rank an' service number – that's yer lot, according to conventions.'

The Judge banged the gong once more. 'The war prisoner will be dealt with harshly – executed, by hanging – if he will not give evidence.'

When translated, this angry threat appeared to change

Robert's mind. 'Fine, I'll give yer a statement,' he mumbled.

Robert took his time, waiting for Ayako to translate each sentence, before continuing. He enjoyed himself, leering round the courtroom with a kind of juvenile glee.

'Well, they work you to the bone, down the mine, slave labour we call it, and on no grub, 'cept a cup of soup with a few leaves floatin' in it, past couple o' months nine POWs died of 'unger or 'orrible diseases, and there are rocks fallin' whole time. If the Japanese provided proper posts, or decent rations we'd be able to hold 'em – that's what happened. It slipped, fell on 'is leg, didn't mean no harm. Hiro was one of the best, weren't a cruel bastard, like most of them.'

By now, Weaver was into his lippy stride, with Ayako translating as best she could, realising that his testimony, in Japanese, would send the court into a paroxysm of outrage.

'The treatment in Fukky-oaka 17 is less than 'uman, and the people of Japan should be ashamed if they ever want t' be a civilised nation. Yeah, the Judge and the members of this Court should know that when the Allies win the war, as we will, Corporal Robert Weaver for one will make absolutely certain that their atrocities are against the Geneva Conventions, and decent rules of war, and will be properly and thoroughly exposed.'

While Ayako translated, an angry murmur rumbled round the courtroom. A stupid mistake – expecting an enemy soldier to testify. Why not just shoot him immediately?

The judge shouted for Robert to 'shut up'... the courthouse clock began to strike eleven... the distant drone of a single aircraft could be heard in between the chimes… coming in from the sea…

INSIDE *BOCK'S Car* all was calm, as the aircraft swept towards the city.

In the pilot's seat, Major Sweeney had no sense of making history, this was simply a job, one he was proud to accept, but unexceptional, although he was concerned at the fuel position, wondering if they would make the US air base at Okinawa. As if to concentrate his thoughts, Kuharek came on the intercom:

'Fourteen-fifty gallons, captain.'

Below the cockpit, stretched out in his bomb-aimer's position, Kermit Beahan was still studying the surveillance maps and comparing them to the terrain below, but as the aircraft swept in from the sea, Beahan shouted he could not see the city through the thickening clouds.

'Damn it to hell, I can't see it this time, either. I still can't see the target.'

'Look hard,' Sweeney shouted back. 'Keep your eyes open, Honey Bee.'

'No luck, not a bit of luck.'

'Okay, but check all your switches. We can't afford a hold up, not this time.'

'God no, no hold ups…'

Now flak was coming up, quite accurate already, as Ed Buckley and Van Pelt guided *Bock's Car* onto its target – the centre, the port of Nagasaki, but then Kermit Beahan shouted from his platform below.

'Bear right,' he called to Sweeney. 'A TARGET HAS BECOME APPARENT.'

Sweeney banked the plane to starboard, advancing on the much less populated suburb of Urakami, two-and-a-half miles from the city centre.

'I've got it. Believe it or not, I've got it. THE STADIUM. There's a hole in the clouds, I can see a target.' Kermit began laughing. 'YES, SIR, I'VE GOT IT.'

Kermit had discovered yet another technical glitch – the electronic button that controlled the delivery of the bomb was malfunctioning. So he had to release the bomb manually. Kermit reached up to an iron bar above his head, steadied, and then very sharply pulled down.

At 10:58, *Bock's Car* jolted upwards, as *Fat Man* dropped smoothly from her belly. 'Holy mother of Jesus,' Kermit said, still laughing. 'Holy mother of Jesus.'

The crew cheered and clapped with relief, as Kermit mumbled into the intercom, for everyone to hear. 'Never again,' he said. 'Never, ever again.'

The bomb drifted silently down on its four-minute-delay parachutes, heading for the tennis courts next to Urakami Church, two miles off target. The inferno would roar *over* the city because of Kermit's 'near miss'. Instead of an estimated one-hundred-and-twenty-thousand deaths, the official count six months later was 38,214 men, women and children.

Kermit's 'near miss' saved over seventy-five-thousand lives in Nagasaki – or compared with the carnage there would have been at Kokura, where 'cloud obscured the target on a sunny day'– over three-hundred thousand…

There are those who believe Kermit Beahan decided to twist that day, instead of sticking with Kokura on sixteen

---

On the hillside overlooking the city, some of the prisoners, taking a break and lying down with barely half a bowl of soggy overcooked rice, noticed the massive US aircraft and alerted the others. Ito had been in a foul mood all morning, so even those that still had the strength didn't dare to cheer, but when they saw a large object, carried by three parachutes, one large and two small, slowly drop towards Urakami, a low murmur ran through the group as they surreptitiously exchanged glances.

Major Ito, sitting on the truck bench facing the parachutes, pointed with his silver baton-stick. 'What's that?' he barked at his sergeant. 'Supply drop?'

The sergeant looked up and tilted his head, shielding his eyes with his hand, contemplating his answer. 'I can't see it's anything to worry about,' he replied. 'A lone bomber can't do much damage.'

Ito was eating lunch. Ayako had made her usual little 'patriotic bento box' – she had added a slice of 'safe' smoked trout from a mountain river, and some sardines and pickles next to the square of white rice with red Japanese pickle plum in the centre – and he nodded to his Sergeant, 'It'll be those leaflets: "*Your rulers are hiding the truth*"…'

'More pictures of Mr Truman…'

'"*Unconditional surrender does not mean enslavement*"…'

The prisoners looked on as the guards laughed. Ito sat staring, thinking about the long, hot march that lay ahead, wishing he had had some cool water with him. The Sergeant stood up to watch, as the three parachutes slowly descended towards the plateau of Urakami, four miles away.

'Could be Red Cross cigarettes. Kato will be quick off the mark. We should check with his unit on the way ba—'

As the Major and his sergeant laughed there was a blinding flash of a kind the occupants of the hillside had never seen before. The flash was so brilliant that it momentarily blotted out the sun, and the light it emitted was so intense that it held the eyes open for ten seconds, giving one eyewitness 'the impression of being dangled in hell and hauled out.'

It took twenty seconds for the shockwave from the blast to reach the hillside where Major Ito's POWs were working. They watched as four square-miles of factories and houses flew into the air, returning as dust and molten metal. The Mitsubishi steel works, the largest and most prominent manufacturing plant in the city, was razed to the ground, its metal superstructure melted in the heat. Later they discovered that railway engines, a mile from the explosion and weighing 100 tonnes apiece, had been lifted from their rails and thrown 300 yards.

And then there was the gigantic white cloud, that rose up from the massive explosion, the most terrifying sight of all according to later witness testimony from the POWs.

'About four minutes after the explosion a dense white cloud appeared over the target, a manmade cloud of incredible density, so dense that smoke from thousands of fires created by the bomb could not penetrate it, but arose in huge columns in outer extremities of this pure white cloud.'

A little later: *'Looking through a pair of common sunglasses at the cloud, colours appeared that have never been seen before; it looked like a giant Catherine wheel, only very slowly revolving and milling, green merging into purple and reappearing as blue as an Arctic ice pack, only to disappear and reappear as blood red.'*

And then such a silence that it seemed the world had come to an end. No crickets, no birds, no wind, as if life had stopped.

Sitting up on the bench, Major Ito put a hand to his face. His skin had already begun to blister. He touched his shoulder – it felt like severe sunburn. He opened his uniform. His chest was a strange red-mauve, like a bruise, mulberry in colour. He looked across at the prisoners lying on the grass, who were staring at him, this time without the usual deference or fear. Ito looked at them almost expecting answers, but they were horrified, too, even though they had been on the ground, hidden from the full force of the blast, the burn, and the shockwave, saved by a knoll on the mountainside. As the world's most lethal blast took its toll, though some were injured – inches mattered that day – many were unharmed.

Ito's loyal Sergeant, who had turned at the last moment, standing with his back to the blast, was enveloped in smoke, confused, until he realised it was the back of his hair smouldering, with little fires breaking out. For a moment he continued upright, then crumpled forward, as his cooked brain ceased to function.

'*Jigoku*,' Ito said, looking around, seeing that many of the prisoner escorts were reeling. Some had collapsed with their rifles, which had fired aimlessly in the heat, while others were kneeling or sitting cross-legged, unable to comprehend what had occurred.

The prisoners had no idea what to do, concerned about Japanese vigilantes coming for them. After years of cruel captivity, now faced with the chance to take control, to escape, they sat for a while discussing what they had seen, instinctively knowing the war was over.

Eventually, they pointed at Ito, who, still sitting on his

bench, stared straight ahead, shocked and increasingly in pain.

'Better 'ad take 'im back to Fuku 17,' the lead English prisoner said. 'What's left of 'im.'

CORPORAL WEAVER WAS ENJOYING his day in Court. 'One day yer'll pay for your atrocities!' he shouted.

Just before *Fat Man* changed everything, in the Nagasaki Courtroom, pandemonium had reigned. The Judge banged his gong, the Japanese escorts tried to stifle Robert Weaver's shouts with the palms of their hands. Ayako looked on in embarrassed dismay.

'You Japs 'ave tortured wimin and kids, now yer wanta 'ang me…'

Robert kicked and thrashed at his assailants, picking up an antique lectern and waving it around in an arc, smashing several heads in one crunching swing. Ayako tried to retreat, but found herself pushed back by Robert, down a narrow stone stairway which led to the cells below.

He continued to fight ferociously, his superior height intimidating the courtroom guards, until an agile policeman launched himself through the air, crashing into Robert, and tumbling in a heap onto Ayako, who had been cowering in the stairwell below.

At the very instant that all three found themselves at the bottom of the stairs, a blinding flash of brilliant white light drained all colour from the court.

In Nagasaki city, for many seconds, no-one was aware of anything.

Not of glass flying like lethal razors – slicing faces, and veins, and arteries.

Not of heads squashed in – like tin cans in a crusher.

Not of lungs exploding – like flimsy paper bags.

Not of a great roar – hurling full-grown bodies across rooms, gardens, streets, factories, houses, hospitals, churches; and smaller bodies across schoolrooms.

After some time – seconds, minutes, a lifetime – Ayako disentangled herself from the prisoner and the policeman, brushing white wall plaster off her formal clothes. When she staggered to her feet, a terrifying horror began to boil inside her.

Clearly, the Municipal Courthouse had suffered a direct hit. Bodies lay everywhere, almost everyone in the room was either dead or twitching or clutching their heads.

Between the low groans the odd, rasping call for help. 'Help me, oh please help,' they pleaded, reaching for anyone who might help. 'I'm hurt, I'm injured, I'm dying!'

Gradually, the few who could, struggled to their knees.

Standing next to Ayako, Robert also surveyed the scene, shaking his head in disbelief at the fragile façade of Courtroom authority in hideous tatters. The Judge sat slumped at the Magistrates' Bench, eyes wide open and blood spurting from the side of his neck. The court officials lay scattered on the floor, most had been hurled against the wood-panelled walls with unimaginable violence. The ornate furniture had been blasted into the centre of the Court and twisted into a splintered rubbish heap of debris.

Just then, Robert noticed flames licking along the ceiling beams.

It was a complete mystery. Robert had seen the effects

of bombing many times in his busy war, but never before had a blast set fire to anything – the impact of an explosion simply could not do that. For a long half-minute he doubted the evidence of his own eyes. His brow furrowed in confusion. How could a bomb cause ceiling beams to smoulder? His chest tightened as he realised that the window frames, the court benches – the whole room was very slowly, and for no apparent reason, beginning to burn.

Instinctively he tugged protectively at Ayako. 'Look, fire.' He pointed. 'We must get out – now!'

Outside, for the first time ever in summer, the *banza katydid* had stopped their high-pitched whine.

Ayako reeled under the impact of the view before her. The entire skyline was completely black, covered with thick clouds of soot and smoke. A sulphuric, dark yellow fog hung in the acrid air. Every building they could see was ablaze. Gutted street cars stood at crazy angles. Electricity posts were burning like matches. And all around, scattered amongst the dead, people were nursing their sizzling flesh. 'Help me! Oh, please help me. Help me.'

Tears of anger, of pity, of desperation burst from Ayako as she stood beside her prisoner, wondering what to do, where to go, whether this really was the end of the world. 'It is some kind of new American bomb,' she said to herself.

TEN MINUTES after the bomb exploded, the wireless operator, Abe Spitzer, sent a message to General Farrell at the airbase on Tinian.

'Results technically successful; but other factors make conference necessary before taking further steps.'

Those 'other factors' were Kermit Beahan's two-mile 'near-miss' – politically unfortunate, given militaristic characters like General Curtis LeMay's order to 'kill as many Japs as possible, to get this thing over with.'

But the crew did not care. After the aircraft survived the massive turbulence that almost shook the B-29 to pieces – at first Lt Olivi, and then the whole crew, broke out into a familiar song.

'Happy birthday to you,
'Happy birthday to you,
'Happy birthday, dear Honey Bee,
'Happy birthday to you…'

And the crew were all thinking, *what a way to celebrate your 27th birthday.*

THE BOMB actually exploded over the tennis court in the lush garden of 171 Matsuyama town, a bungalow belonging to a director of the Mitsubishi Company.

Urakami Prison, a hundred yards away, was wiped out, as were the two hundred Catholics, including Father Luigi, celebrating Mass in Urakami Church. A thousand doctors and patients died at Nagasaki College Hospital, and over two thousand five hundred workers died at their lathes in the Ordinance factory – still turning out the No 93 Torpedo for the virtually annihilated Imperial Navy.

But in spite of the deaths of nearly forty thousand men,

women and children, the densely populated heart of the city was spared. Fires raged for several days, people died in terrible burning agony, but as *Bock's Car* headed towards a semi-crash landing on Okinawa, with less than a minute's avgas left, Bombardier Kermit Beahan could have taken comfort from the fact that his humanitarian 'near miss' saved many more lives than it accounted for.

And in any case – Japan was already negotiating for Peace.

ALL AYAKO COULD SEE WAS litter and smoke. Fragments of freshly-baked roof-tiles, molten blobs of gutter lead, twisted skeletons of carbonised charcoal that had just before been people, were scattered like litter in the street.

The heat, the hell-like flash of heat, was beyond imagination, enough to ignite clothes into flames at three miles – enough to char the skin to a burning blister of roast flesh.

That was the smell – she remembered her father recounting the Tokyo firestorms, the odour of cooked meat.

The two of them stood in a doorway, off the main square, stunned. 'What should we do?' Ayako wondered.

'Dunno,' Robert replied. ''Spose I ought to escape.'

'Where…?'

The notion seemed ridiculous – everything seemed ridiculous, in the face of this monstrous Armageddon.

'Will we die?' Ayako asked the question flatly, as if she did not care about the answer.

'Don't see why, unless there's another of them things.' Robert looked up. Black clouds still obscured the sky.

'Jees, I never thought it'd come to this, never would 'ave. Them bloody Yanks in an 'urry again.'

A woman staggered blindly by, with a bawling baby in one arm and the other hanging limply from a smouldering piece of cloth wrapped over her back. They watched her go, powerless to help her.

Weaver glanced apologetically towards Ayako. 'Do yer 'ate us, Counsellor Okunaga, fer all this?'

She grabbed his tattooed arm and gave it a reassuring squeeze, that it wasn't his fault.

'Come; I am thirsty, we must go back.'

Walking along the remnants of the coastal railway that had been shielded by the bay from the blast, back to Fukuoka 17, they were surprised to see that some of the wooden railway sleepers were scorched there too, even at such a distance, bringing home to them the enormous satanic power of the explosion. By then the black sky had faded into a huge, grey-pink mushroom cloud, and the epicentre of the bomb blast could be seen on a hill near the remains of what used to be Urakami Church.

Lining up burnt sleepers with the source of the blast – and alternatively lining up those completely unaffected, they calculated how the wave of great heat had travelled in a perfect straight line, only deflected by solid objects or the contours of land in its path.

'So we were saved by being downstairs on floor,' she mused.

Robert laughed darkly. 'Me fightin' saved yer beautiful little body, Miss.'

In the early evening, back at Fukuoka 17, the prisoners cheered his triumphant return. Two Dutch POWs who were in the gardening contingent had been killed by the blast, a dozen others were 'serious', and some Camp buildings had been damaged by the fireball – but the inmates as a whole were buzzing with excitement.

'War's gotta end now,' they said hugging each other.

After Robert had told them about the carnage in the court, and the destruction across the whole city, a provocative chorus echoed over their rickety barracks, twisting the name of their camp.

'Fuok you over... fuok you over… fuok you over.'

None of the Japanese guards realised the crude meaning of this perversion of Fukuoka, except the Commandant and Ayako – the only two who understood idiomatic English.

Major Ito was laid out on a makeshift futon next to the camp shrine on the edge of the parade ground, shivering in spite of the hot, humid night. As Ayako cried bitterly against his broad, muscular shoulder, Ito bristled with murderous indignation. For him, this bomb was an atrocity, dropped by cowards from thirty thousand feet, on women and children, to kill using heat like poison gas. He winced as Ayako hugged him. This was the second uniform he'd worn that day – the first had fallen off his chest because he, too, had been scorched in that evil flash.

She leapt back in alarm. 'Shouldn't I send for a doctor?'

'They're all busy or dead,' he replied. Anyway, he wanted to deal with the prisoners first, especially that Australian trouble-maker.

'Promise me,' he groaned, pointing at Weaver, who was dancing a figure-of-eight reel with a group of chanting prisoners.

Ayako bit her thumbnail while sobbing, thinking about Weaver's kindness while guiding her back to the camp, divided by the love she felt for Ito, her duty towards him, and the hopelessness she felt in the face of such an unimaginable bomb. This war had left her so adrift, so scarred. And now she couldn't even nuzzle into her love for causing him more pain.

'Promise me,' Ito repeated, falling back onto a canvas bag that acted as a pillow.

His dying wish – yes, Ayako knew he was dying – could not be denied.

So, if Robert Weaver thought that Camp Counsellor Ayako would reward his kindness, he was mistaken. That evening, she squatted by Major Ito as he lay on the bloody futon, tending his burns, scheming his revenge.

Each time she heard news of the death of another friend, each time Major Ito groaned in pain, her fist clenched involuntarily, intensifying her desperation and anger. As the evening shadows lengthened into a starry night, Ito's injured chest, until then an agonising shade of scarlet, began to turn a deathly shade of black. Ayako fed him tea and salt-water, but his groans became gasps, and a little before midnight he thrashed wildly in a series of convulsions.

To Ayako it seemed so bitterly unfair. This good man did not deserve to die like this, roasted like a pig on the spit of American aggression.

She knew the prisoners thought Ito a bully, ruthless, perhaps even cruel – but he acted under orders. A real man, a Japanese man, would fight to the death, not expect his captors to nanny him.

In the early hours of the morning, a few guards gathered round smoking confiscated Red Cross cigarettes, asking Ayako to relay his orders. Ito lay hunched in a deep coma, his chest beginning to flake huge scabs of roast flesh. All across the camp, there were similar scenes – even more painful for the prisoners, because the wounds had been inflicted by their own side.

'Sergeant Suzuki,' she said, staring down. 'Find the Australian Weaver and hold him at rifle point until further orders.'

'*Ryokai*,' Suzuki replied, saluting, and went off to arrest his quarry.

Ayako dranksome *sakè* and watched her beloved's life slowly drain away. She felt curiously detached when the huge orb of a perfect sun rose over the surrounding mountains, and her lover finally died.

The actual moment was so insignificant – Major Ito simply stopped breathing. She shuddered, feeling suddenly lonely, as if a husband of many years had waved goodbye forever, leaving a clutch of memories unborn, unlived. His face muscles relaxed, and she studied it for understanding:

No, he was never unkind… whatever the prisoners might say.

No, never a monster… in spite of what he sometimes had to do.

No, never a sadist… the confinements and the beatings and the deaths hurt him just as much as they hurt the prisoners. She knew that as a certainty – alone together in bed, he'd often told her so.

When summoned to the dusty parade ground in front of the few remaining guards and prisoners, Robert could not understand it. 'Why me?' he kept asking.

Why indeed?

But bitterness and hatred got the better of her.

'You will die because of the death of our Commandant.'

This woman is crazy, thought Robert, and he tried to calm her.

'I didn't kill him, bomb did that,' he protested. 'We were—'

'Keep quiet,' she ordered.

Sergeant Suzuki, acting on cue, kicked Robert on the shin.

'*Uruse*!! You shut up when lady talk.'

Ayako could have told Robert so more if things had been different. How she had been brought up by a father who admired the West, and had taught her to speak their language – a father who was now disgraced and estranged, dead to her, maybe even actually dead. Her mother, who had betrayed her father and flaunted her lover, was definitely dead, as was her little sister, murdered by Western incendiary bombs during the Tokyo firestorms of March. And worse – the Japan that she loved, beyond even her closest family, was also dead.

A numbness filled her. *Our brave men will soon surrender. Not because their courage has died, but because Western cowards are bombing their families – a callous atrocity that is worse than all the torture tools put together. So, for the love of their fathers and mothers and children, the warrior men of Japan will endure the unendurable – and bow their heads to a conqueror.*

Her only remaining family, baby Mayumi, had probably perished, too. The memory of that moment of Western decadence made Ayako tighten her fist again. And now Japan, her country, would meet the same fate – abused and defiled by a brutal Western culture, inconsiderate Western manners, its young women falling prey to tall Western men like Mister Daniel Lawrence.

Robert looked at her, dry-mouthed, hope dwindling, taking in her bitterness and hatred.

'Counsellor, please, yer really must listen. I 'ad nuffink to do with 'is deaf. Nuffink – an yer know it. An' remember, if ah'd not fallen on yer, well, yer might be a gonna too.'

She did not hear him. Her head was clear, her voice firm. She had duty to carry out. The guards and prisoners were watching, she must act decisively.

'Sergeant Suzuki. Just before the bomb exploded yesterday, Judge Kawano passed a sentence of death on this prisoner. Can you carry out his orders, please?'

Robert did not understand a single word, but he knew the meaning, as did all the men around him.

The few seconds' hesitation before Suzuki grabbed his arm and screeched, 'Lady said to come!' The nervous, voyeuristic look on guards' and prisoners' faces alike – trying to read his condemned eyes – as Robert had tried to read so many eyes before, and the miserable, funereal silence – all added up to one outcome: execution.

Robert shook his head at Ayako.

'The war'll soon be over; I've done no 'arm, no 'arm at all. Why me?'

She looked straight through him, and this time did reply.

'Because you brought dishonour to Commandant Ito on his last day alive.'

'What, the rock were an h'accident, I liked Hiro.'

She looked towards Ito's blanket-covered body. Then she swivelled back fiercely. 'Your end does not matter. It is duty.'

Robert shrugged, it was clearly useless to protest further. The only course left was to go down fighting.

Swinging round on his heel he smashed his elbow into Sergeant Suzuki's mouth, feeling teeth splinter under the force of the blow. As the guard raised his arms to protect himself, Robert grabbed at the rifle. . It happened in a matter of seconds, and none of the other guards could stop him now. He reached for the trigger.

The first shot tore through Suzuki's backside, and ricocheted out into the chest of a guard standing opposite. The second shot, fired at Ayako, flew straight between her legs.

The third shot, fired at point-blank range by a panicking guard, hit Robert in the neck.

Robert coughed once, coughed twice, then muttered a final testament. 'Yer'll swing for this, when we've won the war, just yer see.'

Then he spluttered a final time – and was dead.

Ayako looked down, her duty carried out. 'I don't think so,' she said.

EARLY ON THE morning of Wednesday, August 15th, Ayako took a small square of rough green cloth and wrapped up the very few things she still owned. Having tied it securely across her back, she set off for the main square of Nagasaki, not far from where she had lodged above the Namihei restaurant.

Nearly four years earlier, the crowds there had ecstatically celebrated *Shinju-wan* – the sinking of the US Fleet in Hawaii – with firecrackers, flags, singing of the national anthem, a special *go-gai* edition newspaper with pictures of the valiant Japanese forces, and speeches. Now, though a crowd was gathering, the mood was desperate and sombre.

Many of the tiny, boarded houses had no roofs, blown away by the blast from the atomic bomb, still more had fire or burn damage, scorched by the massive, radiant heat. Others were surprisingly unharmed, protected by Kermit Beahan's 'near-miss'. None had glass in the windows or doors.

Ayako stood for a while, without expression. How life had changed since those days of celebration, since watching from the top window of the restaurant as Daniel Lawrence walked away, surrounded by cheering crowds. Now there were homeless families stretched out on the narrow pavements, delivery men squatting against their bicycles, old ladies in threadbare dresses leaning against broken doorways – while exhaustion hung in the still acrid air.

Gradually, the square was filling, gathering around a barrage of loudspeakers that were wired to the side of an army truck in the centre. Something was going to happen, though no one knew what, or how, but the word was out – it would be at 12 noon.

Ayako made a decision. She walked across to the shattered front of the restaurant and, jostling the stiff sliding door half open, edged inside. The owner, Mrs Matsuo, was still there, sitting at a glass-strewn dining table, her grey head bowed, wishing neither to greet her, nor be acknowledged, sad but strangely exhilarated. She had her hands across the table, palms up, as if in prayer. Ayako bowed, but let her be, before stepping between the empty tables and climbing the familiar stairs, now bare of boxes of food, up and along, to the room she had lodged in a million lifetimes ago, now looking so different from the room where she had been with Lawrence. The desolation matched her mood.

Just before noon, she changed into her favourite scarlet kimono and knelt on the floor next to the blasted window overlooking the square, fearing the worst. Her usually silky skin was covered, like so many others', with mulberry-coloured boils, and she had been vomiting lately.

At twelve o'clock precisely, the high-pitched, lilting, ceremonial voice of his Imperial Majesty, Emperor Hirohito, living God-King, never before heard by his subjects, crackled across the city from the loudspeakers.

'After pondering deeply the general trends of the world, and the actual conditions obtaining in our Empire today, we have decided to effect a settlement of the present situation by resorting to an extraordinary measure. We have ordered our government to accept the provisions of our enemy's joint declaration…'

Ayako sat, stony-faced, taking in his words.

'…the war situation has developed not necessarily to Japan's advantage, while the general trends of the world have all turned against her interest. Moreover, the enemy has begun to employ a new and most cruel bomb, the power of which to do damage is indeed incalculable, taking toll of many innocent lives. Should we continue to fight, it would result in the ultimate collapse and obliteration of the Japanese Nation.'

She began to sway backwards and forwards on her haunches, nodding her head, as if a momentous decision had come to pass inside her.

'The thoughts of those officers and men, as well as others who have fallen in the field of battle, and all their bereaved families, pains our heart night and day. We are keenly aware of

all of you, our subjects. However, we have resolved to pave the way for a grand peace for all the generations to come, by enduring the unendurable and suffering what is unsufferable. Let our nation continue as one family, from generation to generation. Unite your total strength to be devoted to the construction for the future. Work with resolution to enhance the innate glory of the Imperial State and keep pace with the progress of the world.'

The crackling stopped as the hollow speakers fell silent.

A different sound now echoed up from the square, the wailing sound of hundreds of men and women weeping. Japan was beaten, Japan was humiliated, Japan would be occupied, Japan had surrendered. But mixed in with the bitter tears of misery, were also tears of relief. At last, the war was over.

Upstairs in the bomb-blasted room, Ayako reached for her cloth bundle and, pulling at the stiff knot, took out a photograph of Major Ito in his military uniform, staring sternly at the camera.

After several moments' thought she slid out another – of her father – smiling up, with a Shakespeare play on his lap. She propped both pictures on the skirting board facing her.

On the floor to her right, she laid out a final message of goodbye, scrawled on the back of the only paper she could find – the US propaganda leaflet.

She had written:

'WE HAVE NOT TRIED HARD ENOUGH.'

She put it next to a handwritten copy of a poem by Yoshida Kasshichi, about the Battle of Guadalcanal.

Gadarukanaru-sen shishu

Our rice is gone
Eating roots and grass
Along the ridges and cliffs.
Leaves hide the trail, we lose our way
Stumble and get up, fall and get up.
Shoes have torn, toes cracked.
Unable to bear my backpack's weight,
I discard all my kit.
Alone I retain my short sword
And a pistol with the chrysanthemum crest.

Covered with mud from our falls
Blood oozes from our wounds
No cloth to bind our cuts
Flies swarm to the scabs
No strength to brush them away
Fall down and cannot move.
How many times I've thought of suicide?

負い来し米はつきはてて
名もなき草を喰いつつ、
辿れる尾根や、断崖や、
つもる朽葉にふみまよい、
幾度かまろびし、つまずきし。
靴は破れぬ、踵裂けぬ。
背嚢遂に負いきれず、
装具もなべて捨てはてぬ。
残くはわずかに短剣と
菊の御紋のつきし銃。

泥にまみれつ、にじむ血に
纏くべき布もなくなりぬ。
血による蠅を追うことも
ものうくなりしたおれ伏し、
幾度自決を想いしか。

She sat for in silent meditation before reaching inside

her bag for a crimson silk scarf, and Major Ito's ceremonial short-sword. Slowly, she tied the scarf tightly around her knees.

Ayako looked out of the window at the bare, burnt branches of the trees in the square, at the weak sun dribbling through the haze… and was interrupted by a gentle knocking on the thin bedroom door.

Who could it possibly be? Not now, not any time. After a few seconds, another knocking, firmer, more insistent.

'It is not convenient,' she called out, partly sobbing, partly outraged at the interruption.

She could hear below, passing on the narrow street, a gaggle of men talking in reverential terms.

'…enduring the unendurable…'

'…as one family, from generation to generation…'

'…enhance the glory of the Imperial State…'

The flimsy door slid open, Mrs Matsuo stood shaking, tears across her tired, wrinkled face. In her hands was a cup of miso soup. 'Masaichi is alive…' she announced with a wail, exultant, but also furious.

'But his picture was on your family shrine.'

'They told me he was dead, but Masaichi was in a Chinese prison hospital, four years, the censor in Fukuoka held his letters, but now they are released. He has no legs…' she trailed off, seeing the crimson silk scarf, the photos. She shook her grey head, understanding Ayako's desperation, but not approving.

'Masaichi will be honoured to endure the unendurable…' She pushed the bowl of soup forward, forcing Ayako to take it. 'And he will need a good wife.'

In the distance a string of firecrackers exploded, whether in mourning or celebration for the Emperor's speech, Ayako could not know. In a daze she took the bowl but turned away without thanks, mildly outraged that a lowly restaurant owner would presume to see herself as family to a Professor's daughter.

Mrs Matsuo sighed, reading her mind. 'All will be not the same, very different,' she said and shuffled away along the corridor, leaving Ayako with her knees still tied by the crimson silk scarf, the photos of Ito and her father, the poem of despair, Ito's short sword on her scribbled note.

Across the city, as if the Emperor had commanded them along with his subjects, the *banza katydid* restarted their shrill whine, the first time since the atom bomb. Ayako joined with her own wailing, quietly at first, gaining strength and intensity as a howl, then almost a scream, the huge tears salty in her moaning mouth – the sound of the coming heartbreak and effort and shame of having to bow down and give in to create the Emperor's new beginning.

Still sobbing, she untied the crimson scarf, using it to wrap Ito's short sword; she looked again at the poem – it now seemed self-pitying, shallow; she folded the note, keeping Truman's propaganda words on the outside; she stowed all the objects in the bundle and was now alone with two photos, staring at her. The defeated warrior on the right, the smiling, kindly academic on the left.

Her howling, the sobs, the tears had stopped, though the pain continued.

Japan had chosen the warrior, and had failed. Terribly so.

Her eyes moved to the academic – her father. Why had the song of the *banza katydid* become like violins? His favourite – Vivaldi.

Ayako bowed at his picture, once again the dutiful daughter.

Perhaps when strong enough she might go to visit him in Tokyo. *If he has survived.*

IN ALL, that week, 526 Japanese committed *hara-kiri,* an astonishingly small number in a country where the code of honour sometimes requires that act to clear a name or to reinstate a memory.

The Emperor had taken the lead in his ceremonial speech, so the 'honour' demonstrated by *hara-kiri* was felt to be an indulgence to 'hate' – even in a proud country which had lost independence, its most important treasure.

The women still wailing in the square, the men banging their heads on walls, and fists on pavements, were preparing their hearts and minds to fight for that future. Japan might have lost the war to the inexhaustible production capacity of America's industrial heartland, its creativity and ideas, but it would now try to win the peace by copying the victor's methods.

As the sun dipped slowly into the sea, the crowds in the square dispersed back to shattered homes, to care for their radiation-sickened families, and to reach inside their aching hearts for the resolution to continue.

The sun, they decided, would rise another day.

12

'DID YOU KNOW, when Japanese women commit suicide, they tie a silk scarf round their legs – so as not to expose the inside of their thighs as they die?'

Dan admitted he didn't.

'Some women,' his companion went on. 'Some people, some nation; heck, who can compete with that? No race on earth I know. We'd sure better watch them in the future.'

On Sunday, September 2nd, three weeks after *Fat Boy* exploded, Dan sat beside a breezy naval surgeon who had droned on, like the C-47 they were in, all the way from Tinian. 'Course, it ain't the blast injuries'll be the problem now, those'll have died. Gonna be radiation. Yep, worse than poison gas, gets you from the inside out.'

'Jes-sus!' the man exclaimed, as the Dakota banked on its final circuit towards a small tar-and-scorched-grass airfield; for the first time, the devastated city could be seen through the portholes.

Below them was a grey-black wasteland, flattened and

burnt by a gigantic fist of heat; a thousand small campfires dotted the city in the drab, drizzling dawn.

The C-47 bumped along the runway to park by a line of army tents. When Dan climbed down, Phil Denton strode out from behind a long row of aircraft to greet him.

'Welcome to the end of the world.' They shook hands, with none of that military saluting. 'A storm centre's headin', Dan, just so you know, you'll be grounded here for a couple days.'

'What's the city like?'

'Biblical description of hell,' Denton replied. 'Tell yah over breakfast.'

Within an hour the drizzle became torrential rain. All unloading squelched to a halt; fourteen C-47s stood saturated in the downpour, as did the Nagasaki homeless in their dug-outs and lean-tos. To the putrid boils, the bleeding gums, the bloody excrement, the loss of hair, the nausea of radiation sickness was added the aching chill of a two-day tropical storm. But Dan could not wait; he used what was left of his dwindling influence to commission a Jeep. He knew where he had to go.

The ancient stone facade of Kanko-dori police station was still standing and, even more surprising, Sergeant Hanazono, looking much older and greyer, had survived and still remembered Dan.

'You man of "special operation", yes? With *Kempei*?'

Hanazono was visibly ill at ease. The hierarchical Japanese system had not yet settled on how to treat conquering foreigners; after all, Japan had never been conquered before.

Dan looked down at the old policeman.

'The young woman, the interpreter – Ayako Okunaga; where is she now?'

Hanazono rubbed his eyes; he wanted to be helpful but he had no idea. Anyway, what was the fate of one girl in the face of the devastation of his city? He leaned forward, hands on the wooden counter, and shook his head.

Back in the Jeep, Dan drove through the pot-holed roads to the Nagasaki Grand Hotel. From the outside it seemed deserted, having been closer to Beahan's near-miss than the city centre. The front steps were even more rickety than before, but the inside had survived almost unscathed. The mounds of glass and splintered oak and bamboo that used to be the reception area had been swept into neat piles. Dan couldn't resist visiting the ballroom, where in the corner by the stage, the elderly manager was sitting to attention reading a book behind a desk that had been pulled from the back office. To his side were a rolled-up *goza* mat and simple futon bedding.

The manager smiled, still wearing tails and bowtie, though creased and torn. 'Mr Lawrence,' he said, standing up and bowing. 'Welcome back.'

They stood awkwardly grinning at each other, the manager correct as always, Dan reticent about his reason for visiting the hotel and not sure what to say.

'I flew in this morning before the storm…'

The manager nodded, and bowed again. 'What we have is yours to command, Mr Lawrence, but…' he gestured with a gloved hand to the forlorn ballroom with no windows, the lashing rain creating pools of water on the grimy dance floor.

'Guess I'm here for old time's sake,' Dan heard himself say.

This emboldened the manager to venture beyond his customary reticence, although still choosing his words carefully, to say. 'There are many matters to consider, Mr Lawrence, it will be a long journey.' He folded his gloved hands in front, unused to being personal. 'I shall stay here until the Nagasaki Grand falls or is taken down.'

'Like the captain of a ship.'

The manager nodded, 'just so.' He began pouring from a flask of water into a spotless cup and handed it to Dan. 'This I told to Mistress Okunaga, not past six months ago.' He looked up, a gleam in his wise eyes, instinctively knowing that was the reason Dan was there. 'She was visiting a prison in Urakami, as translator for prisoners. It is no more.'

That was the centre of the bomb. 'Visiting?' Dan asked quickly.

'For the justice in Nagasaki.' The manager shook his head slowly and sighed. What was an educated young woman doing in such company? 'Yes, she was in *Nagasaki*.' He emphasised that word not to cause alarm, but to let Dan know she had been nearby. 'She visited hotel for same reason as you – "*Mukashi no koto o omoideshite kudasai*." Old memories.' The manager had misted up; beginning as a bellboy, it was his fiftieth year at his beloved hotel, in his heart now a metaphor for Japan. Built for service, once magnificent, now destroyed.

'Six months ago?' Dan prompted.

'We can have only hope.'

LATE THAT NIGHT, in the flapping shelter of their army marquee, Dan decided to tell Phil Denton about his child, and for the first time in his life Phil actually listened in silence until he had finished.

'So you don't know if the child is alive?'

'Correct.'

Or the mother.'

'Correct.'

'Or where they are?'

'Three ticks.'

Phil stroked the stubble on his chin. 'Guess I'd wonder, if the child survived, 'bout if it looked like me…'

Dan took a swig of beer. 'It's a strange thing, Phil, but in spite of all the battles we've been through, all the supplying, the thousands of people, there wasn't really a day I didn't think about them.'

'"Them"?'

'Mother, too. And you're gonna ask me why, aren't ya?'

Phil shook his head. 'I know.'

'You do?'

'Yep.' Phil leaned over and clinked Dan's bottle. 'Normality. What keeps us going in these crazy times. Keeps us sane, caring, *motivated*. And that's a word I hate.' He took a deep breath. 'Those Marines aren't killing machines, they maybe have to act like it sometimes, they're doing it for their families back home. Why a letter is worth a thousand mortar rounds. We're the same.'

'I don't have a family,' Dan said sourly.

'Didn't.' Phil threw his bottle into an empty ammunition case and opened another one. 'War gets us like that. Distance, makes us fonder, you know. We can pretend not to care, but it don't work.'

Dan was quiet for a while, then reached into his tunic and brought out his wallet, carefully pulling out a little piece of paper.

Nishabaru House, Kakazu Village, Highway 5, Okinawa.
Mrs Asako Okunaga.

PHIL WHOOPED. 'MRS OKUNAGA – THE GRANDMOTHER?'

'Great-grandmother.'

'So that's where you disappeared those two days. Always wondered.'

'Was a long shot.'

Phil nodded. 'Would've been in some refo camp.' The storm outside was beginning to calm down. 'And you've got one day to go find the mother before we leave. If she survived. If she's here…'

It was whiskey time. Phil poured them both a long glass.

'Sounds like the end of the road to me, Dan.'

'But the hotel manager said she'd been around Nagasaki six months ago. So what would you do?'

Now the storm had blown through, the tent was an oven. Phil opened the flap and tied it against a tentpole. From their pitch on the hill near where the Mitsubishi factories used to be, they could see the arc of the port sweeping around the bay. The torrential rain had dampened down much of the surface bomb damage, thin green shafts of goose-grass were poking thru the sopping ground, and seagulls had started swooping again.

Phil turned back. He had already swallowed half a tumbler of whiskey but poured another. It was their penultimate night of being with the military, of service, before heading home forever, and going back to civilian life. A time of celebration, but also contemplation.

'You wanna find the mother, right? You gotta.'

Dan shrugged.

'Hey, don't be so tight-lipped British, don't kid a kidder.'

They were standing by the opening of the tent, Phil thinking about his family back in Pittsburgh, Dan about Kermit's controversial near-miss, already an unspoken 'weather cover-up' story, knowing that the badly fragmented view could have been a whole lot worse.

'Tell you this, Dan. And I sure ain't accustomed to giving you advice. We have a Denton family rule: If we get separated, become lost, don't know where we are, where anyone is – the rule is – go back to the last place we were physically together.'

'That's a jail near Tokyo, Phil.'

'Round here?'

'Another jail, went there this afternoon, cop didn't know.'

'Before that?'

Dan went cold as the memory of the room above the family restaurant came flooding back.

'Hit a bullseye, have I? Or a bruise?'

They fell silent again; a silver half-moon peaked through clouds above the port, the twisted cranes hanging in the dark water. They were looking at the now historic, battered and beaten Nagasaki view. Down in the docks the Prefecture clock, a quaint survivor, struck a plaintive midnight, almost overwhelming them. Phil sighed, sad but, heck, now they'd be going home.

'The guy who dropped the A-bomb was a friend, yeah?'

Dan nodded.

'Did a good job.'

'Not what the Air Force think, Phil.'

'Air Force didn't ever know shit.'

They took a deep breath of the cool, fresh air. The rain had washed the radiation away. Denton punched Dan's shoulder.

'Guess you'll be taking the Jeep tomorrow, then.'

Downtown Nagasaki was both how Dan remembered it and so very different. Gone were the bustling people, the children running around, the handcarts and rickshaws, the street-sellers, the gossiping labourers, the outdoor cafés. Although still summer, no trees had leaves, few houses or shops had glass, though some had thin-paper coverings; the inner city was still intact, but traumatised, ravaged.

Dan drove into the market square where a few old men were sitting playing cards, watching as he parked the jeep, wary and inscrutable.

Walking across the square and along the narrow street, Dan marvelled at how changed this was to the last time he was there, when the whole city was having a Pearl Harbour party. He paused to let a family with their heads bowed pass, seeing them glance at him obliquely, respectful. He had the fleeting impression this might be how an Ancient Roman soldier, after conquest, felt wandering around the beaten tribes.

Going on down the narrow, cobbled street off the square he reached the Namihei restaurant, the outside battered but much the same as four years before.

This was a long-shot, but what if she *was* there? Why had he come? Yes, he had to try, but why? He flattened his hair, took a deep breath, and opened the door.

The ever-present Mrs Matsuo looked up from arranging cups on the serving counter. Their eyes met, for a moment she was too shocked to even blink, then she looked down at the cups, her lips trembling. Dan hardly noticed because standing in the corner, over by the stairs, was Ayako. She had been wiping a table, but now froze in mid-wipe.

She had often dreamed of meeting him again but it was never like this – not with radiation boils, which were healing, true, but scarred the edges of her mouth; not with hair hanging down in clumps, hair that hadn't been cleaned in a month; not wearing a ragged cloth day kimono, with no socks or shoes and dirty feet; not being so shaken that she couldn't think, let alone speak.

And he – bright and sparkling, clean and tall.

It was not fair.

Mrs Matsuo broke the silence.

'Why's he come back?' she wailed. 'Isn't there enough trouble in the world?'

Dan understood, even her guttural Japanese, but took no notice. He had found Ayako, but now she existed, he had no idea what to do.

'We don't want him here!' Mrs Matsuo shouted, even louder.

Ayako slumped down on an ancient wicker stool, looking at her cloth on the table.

'What do you want?' she heard herself say in English.

'Perhaps we could have a coffee.'

'Coffee! We have none.'

Dan kicked himself. Stupid, stupid, stupid. Of course. From behind, he heard Mrs Matsuo bark, 'Tell him to go away!' but neither took any notice.

'Tea?' he asked, a self-deprecating grin on his face.

They looked at each other for the first time in three years. There was something. What was it?

'Not here,' she replied.

THEY WALKED in silence down towards the docks, which were buzzing with engineers, American and British military, in khaki or navy-blue shorts, trucks everywhere. Dan was used to such activity, but Ayako held back: here along the dockside the occupation was complete. He bought them green tea from an opportunistic hawker who had set up next to the port entrance.

Ayako set her face away from Dan, looking across at the seagulls. 'Why have you come?'

'To see you.'

'Why that?'

He nearly said, 'unfinished business,' but caught himself. 'What you said last time, at the camp. We have a child.'

She almost spat out 'Pah!', but stopped herself and instead looked away for a long time, then gestured to the port, the allied military, the bomb demolition clear up. 'It is easier for me if the child is dead. Don't make me tell you why.'

'Sorry, I have to ask.'

She shook her head slowly. it should be obvious.

'Because the child is half me, yes?'

Ayako turned to look at him at last, calmly, almost as if not judging him, although in her heart she both loved and despised him. A Western man, kind and giving in his way, but making everything in the world about himself. Not because of pride or duty, which would be a Japanese man's way, but because of selfishness, the Western way, of needing to control everything around them, in order to possess their own lives.

But why – why - did this make her love him? Because it was strangely exotic, brave even, and so different from the men she knew, who crushed the individual in themselves. But for those same reasons she also despised him.

And yet she still found him handsome, now with more muscle than before, and still a gentleman, in that English way. Her father would have loved him too.

He interrupted her thoughts. 'Have you seen a doctor?'

'They are very busy, but the one from the camp in Fukuoka who is now helping the Americans said the radiation will become less but make my life not so long. He did not know how…'

'I could find treatment for you.'

'There is none. It is done.'

'Perhaps in America…?"

They both let the thought hang. Was this an invitation? even Dan wasn't sure, but before he could make up his mind, she shook her head, kindly, not to reject him, but because she had a different future in mind.

'I am promised.'

'To whom.'

'To duty. To help the fallen warriors, to make Japan strong again. This is, perhaps, one more reason why I don't want to know the child. I have other purpose, for as long as I am strong. Mrs Matsui's husband was killed by glass from the A-bomb, her son Masaichi is returning from Manchuria, with no legs. That is my duty.' Ayako smiled, lop-sided because of the healing sores. It reminded Dan of the Geisha doll from the first time he had seen her.

He turned away to hide his wretchedness, more in love with his interpretation of her than ever. Of course, he would let her go, not that he had a choice; as in eternity, the woman would grow as she needed to, away from him.

She leaned forward and gently squeezed his arm, a maternal gesture, loving in its way, presaging the life she was beginning.

'I don't want my heart to be an occupied zone, Dan-san. I want to live and die as a wholly Japanese woman, in peace.'

THE ISLAND-HOPPING C-47 was bound for Honolulu, then on to Washington and Pittsburgh. As Dan buckled up, Phil Denton asked him how it had gone.

'It occurs to me, Phil, that you're an evil genius – perfect for an attorney.'

'Shoot.'

'She was there.'

Phil howled in triumph. 'The Denton Family lost-and-found system wins again.' He looked out of the porthole: the engines were starting. 'So, how could that be evil?'

'Turned me upside-down. Before, she was still a girl. War has made her a woman, knows what she wants…

'…and it ain't you.'

'Ain't America.'

Phil nodded. 'Look, Buddy. You had to try. Elsewise, she'd have haunted you forever.'

They were taxiing on the crushed-down grass and cement which served as a runway. The Pratt and Whitney engines roared, and they were on their way, soaring over the burnt remains of the city, and then the flattened hill that was once the suburb of Urakami, and the crumpled remains of what had been Japan's biggest church. They undid their belts and lit cigarettes.

'Boy or girl?' Phil asked, mainly for conversation.

Dan took a long draw on his cigarette and shrugged. He didn't know.

'Did you even ask?'

'Nope.'

Denton shook his head with resignation, then reached over and slapped Dan's thigh, the most affectionate gesture he'd ever visited on him. 'Hey, daddy, keep the faith. You gotta a long life ahead of you. These things usually work out.'

EPILOGUE

August 5th 1955.

Bradley's Garage,

Buffalo,

Springfield, Missouri.

Dear Mr. Lawrence,

I hope you do not think it impertinent of me to write you on this matter, and I hope you are the person I think you are.

I saw you on the Springfield TV news and it reminded me that when I was in the Navy Hospital at Pearl Harbour after the Japanese war, the Colonel of the Dead-eyes told me that you wanted to ask some questions. Concerned some old lady in some village in Okinawa we captured.

If you are ever in these parts I would be glad if you came on over. I surely do not know much, but there is plenty of room for you to stay.

I am mighty pleased to see your business is doing so good.

Regards,

Robert A. Bradley (Bob)

TEN DAYS after the letter was mailed, the phone rang at Janie's General Store and Bar on the wide, empty drag which was the sleepy centre of Buffalo.

Janie went running up to 'Brads' with a message.

'They're phonin' back in thirty minutes. Long distance…'

Bradley wiped oily hands on oily overalls and hobbled along beside her.

'Sure strange, don't remember givin' anybody your number…'

He sat drinking draft and swatting flies until, right on time, the phone sang.

The personal assistant to Daniel Lawrence thanked Mr Bradley kindly for his unexpected letter and wondered if he'd be prepared to fly to New York. There was a flight on Thursday from Springfield, through St. Louis, and the ticket would be waiting in his name. All expenses paid, a vacation if he'd like it, and Mr Lawrence would be much obliged. If Bob needed time to think, or would like to journey later – well, he could come whatever date would suit.

'Nope,' replied Brad. 'No siree.'

'What, you won't come?'

'Nope, I don't need no time to think. Thursday'll do perfect.'

As he told Janie, over a celebration draft. 'It's his money – an' heck, I wrote him I didn't know much.

Never been to New York before. Have to get me a haircut.'

In August 1955, New York was the centre of the financial world – maybe of the whole universe. The city hummed with energy, which was the main reason Dan was there, to build an international trading company, and one day maybe own America.

When Bradley was met at Idlewild Airport by a driver holding a bright red card with his name printed in black, a sense of panic gripped him – maybe he shouldn't have taken this hot-shot's money.

Then there was the uniformed ex-Vet doorman standing like on parade on Broadway, the receptionists in suits, the tall black lady who walked him across to a bank of elevators, accompanying him to the penthouse, no less – where the boss himself was waiting to greet him.

'Mr Bradley, I'm Dan Lawrence, how do you like New York?' he said, and a moment later he was being led to a leather-buttoned sofa, facing a desk big enough for one of those new executive jets to land on.

'It's fast, real fast.'

Dan did not stay behind his desk but came around and sat down opposite. The gangly man in his early thirties blinked back uncomfortably. Janie at the Buffalo store understood, but maybe these business tycoons had heavy ways of dealing with folks who wasted their time and money.

Though that kind of money didn't much count to Dan, he didn't like to waste time. 'Mr Bradley, tell me about Okinawa.'

'Not much to tell, of course. Terrible fightin', plenty medals, the Japs were murderous, we won, lost a lot of friends. What you want to know?'

'An old woman and a young child?'

Brad swallowed hard. It was all he had, so quick.

'Kakazu Village, our orders were to flush it out, an' in this house, under a big table an old lady comes out…'

'Big table?'

'Oak – wanted to bring it home.'

'Which house?'

''Bout three-quarters way down from the top… this old lady comes out shoutin' an' weepin' – 'Save my baby.' Heck, I nearly lobbed…'

'What sex was the baby?'

'A girl. Thought yah knew.'

Both men sat back in their chairs. Brad relaxed, instinctively knowing his fare was now repaid. Dan was turning mental somersaults, picturing the still clear memory of Ayako's defiant, beautiful face. He snapped his eyes through fourteen years into the present and onto the man across from him.

'What did the girl look like?'

'The funniest thing – she had Western eyes…'

As Brad said the words, his Midwest twang faltered. Maybe he should've flown first class.

Dan shook his head. 'A friend of mine, a really close friend, was the father. Before he died, asked me to do what I could.'

'Oh... sure… well… heck… yeah… not much more to tell yah. They were marched off to a refo camp, and the baby girl 'peard strong and purtty.'

'Know which camp?'

'Nope. We were ordered to Mabuni. Rest yah know.'

'Like losing both legs?'

'Don't notice much, do it?'

Dan tapped his fingers on the side of his chair. 'Mr Bradley, you've been an enormous help. If I can assist you, at any time in the future, don't hesitate to ask. In the meantime, enjoy yourself in New York. Stay a week – we're paying.'

Brad cleared his throat, 'Well Mr Lawrence, sir, there's one thing I'd be mighty glad of. Your tyre factory in Springfield…' He hesitated – would this hotshot throw him out? 'Well, since your company took charge back of May, they won't supply me with honest-to-goodness tyres, sir, they say I'm kinda too small for it to be worth their while. Heck, I am small – don't I know it. But, well, sir, your tyres'd be… Well, I'd pay the extras for them to deliver.'

So that was the real reason behind Brad's letter. Dan reached for the intercom on his desk.

LESS THAN A WEEK LATER, Margaret Murai of the Japanese Private Enquiry Bureau crossed her long legs and munched on a cracker.

Dan glanced round the cocktail bar of the Waldorf Astoria. As usual he faced the entrance lobby with his back pressed against the early evening tinkling pianist, so he could see but not be overheard.

Margaret shook her head, a sceptical large-boned lady, with a reputation for telling it direct. 'Mr Lawrence. I gotta be straight with you. Best way to proceed is to insert a small classified ad into the *Ryukyu Shimpo*. Could be the newspapers would push a story on your search. Gotta be –

if the girl still resides there, she would hear and come forward.'

Blasted woman, Dan thought. *How come so many clever people in New York can't listen?*

'Miss Murai, forgive me. It has been made abundantly clear to your agency that the girl must not know.'

'Sure thing, buddy, guess it's your dollar.' Margaret Murai did not like secretly spying on a minor; you never did know the client's motives. 'You are a businessman and will understand the importance of statistics. On Okinawa, there are 139 junior high schools and 68,326 pupils.'

For a long time, perhaps even a minute, Dan didn't answer, a strange hiatus in a city where people interrupt the whole time. Margaret was not surprised – she'd been briefed about Lawrence, how he wouldn't be hurried, didn't fill a gap in a conversation, often stayed silent, how you simply had to wait for him to respond. She crunched a few more crackers. Then he leaned forward and mumbled confidentially, 'The girl means a great deal to me, Margaret, but I do not want to interfere with her life.'

'Oh sure... you're just going through all this effort for her sake. You don't know her name, don't have a photo, know her domicile, or know what school she attends, and you won't even say why you want to find out. Forgive me for being so sceptical but we get all kinds of kooks in our line of work.'

Dan smiled back with hidden excitement. In his world of business no-one had dared to be quite so poisonously rude for too many years.

'I can see you need reassurance before taking this job. Well, her father was a very good friend.'

'That's not reassurance, buddy – that's crap.'

The smile froze on his face. Deep inside, Dan was

churning with rage. What right had this woman to interrogate and judge him like this? His money was as good as anyone's, and better than most. Who the hell did she think she was, playing high and mighty priestess to mankind? With typical control he leaned back and gave her his most powerful negotiating stare.

But she just crunched another cracker.

'Why, huh?' he said, keeping calm.

Margaret nodded. 'The big three-letter W.'

After eight years in the Private Eye business, Margaret had learned – some cases take a week, some a couple of months, but they stay with you forever. Sometimes, when her car was stalled in traffic or she was running a bath, she'd suddenly wonder about a person she tracked down, a husband she found out, a life she rearranged. And over the years she'd come to realise that she could only be really effective if she knew the honest reason for her investigation. The client's confidences gave her confidence, and made her try that little bit harder.

The rendezvousing diners came and went, and the post-Broadway theatre-goers were drifting in for nightcaps.

'To be honest, Dan, you don't know why you're doin' this?'

'She's family, I guess. Physically at least, I'm her father.'

That made her laugh. 'Family's not physical, family's spiritual – or so I'm told.'

'No kids?'

'No-oope. I'm sure you've noticed that I'm half Japanese, but not the family half. We were interned in California during the war and my Jap daddy just took off on release and hasn't been heard of since. Ma's remarried, and we don't miss him.'

'Not at all?' Her anti-father statement had disappointed him.

'Not one crummy bit!' But the bitterness in her answer reassured him.

'So we have a deal?'

'Guess we do.'

As they stood up to leave, she kissed his cheek platonically, and said, 'I guess 139 junior high schools and 68,326 pupils ain't so very much. I'll just have to try that little bit harder.'

Sure, she'd told him that, but not this hard.

After sharp-talking herself onto several bouncy Air Force rides, she discovered Nishabaru House was still derelict, like so much of the Island – and nobody, but nobody, had heard of old Mrs Asako Okunaga.

Simple things would help – like the exact age of the girl. 'Conceived the day of Pearl Harbour,' he'd said, so twelve – but twelve and what? If she was nearly thirteen, she might by now have left junior high, because the girls on Okinawa enrol at five and leave after seven years and eight months.

But the worst aspect of her search only struck two weeks after Margaret checked into her room at the Grand Castle Hotel and looked out on a tropical evening, across the busy skyline of Naha. Thirty-two schools checked so far – only another hundred and seven to go. Suddenly a ludicrous thought occurred to her: she didn't even know who she was looking for.

Just an orphan girl of twelve, with Western eyes.

Amazing. To think she'd agreed to this madness. But she *had* agreed – and spent a tidy sum already.

So Margaret did what she always did at such moments. She went on the town to get blind, obliterated drunk.

Naha was a good choice of venue. The vibrant city buzzed with helpful male companions, mostly G.I.s from the big US bases, with money to burn and no Western women to burn it on. The drinks were cheap, the company passingly attentive.

In the morning, as the captain knotted his military tie and Margaret lay frazzled on the bed, he asked the most inspired question of his sheltered life. 'What theatre did ya' say you're with, baby?'

'What?' she replied, blinking from last night's vodka, only remembering briefly saying she was 'employed in the theatre of life.'

'Theatre. Youse said you're with a theatre and you're lookin' for a girl…'

'I did?' As she rolled away from the early morning tropical light, she had a typical investigator's idea. Not honest, but not quite dishonest, either. And… justifiable. Maybe.

'Twelve to fifteen-year-old Okinawan girl with Western features wanted for exciting role in theatrical production. No experience necessary, snacks and pop supplied.'

The adverts had run in both Okinawan newspapers, followed by the date of the auditions. But the proper selection took place afterwards, over the Pepsi and pretzels, with the detailed questions on the application form.

Name…? Mother…? Father…? Address…?

If ward of a guardian – very common on Okinawa at the time – *real mother's name…? Real father…?*

Each evening, after the girls had sung their folk songs and recited their poems, Margaret would gather with Mr Konishi, the Okinawan schoolteacher hired to help her out, and each evening the search would seem more hopeless.

After half a dozen sessions, Mr Konishi silently understood what was required. He had stopped pointing out the acting talent on display or the beauty of the Oriental/Western faces – instead, he spent more time on the details on the application forms. In truth, he'd given up on this peculiar quest – until, in a barrack-like schoolroom in the Central Okinawan town of Nago, a particularly tall girl out-performed all others.

As Margaret watched the girl, a thrill swept along her skin, akin to the excitement a director feels on discovering a genuine new talent. This girl did not perform to be judged – everyone in the hall felt she was judging them – and if there had been a play the girl would have been hired immediately. Mr Konishi asked the girl to stay on until the end of the auditions, and Margaret was surprised that she could speak some English.

'What is your name?' she asked.

'Aragaki Mayumi.'

'Is that your real name?'

The girl paused for a moment, for the first time unsure of herself. 'It is not.'

Margaret could feel her whole body shaking. 'What is your real name?'

'Okunaga Mayumi.'

Okunaga. Okunaga! – the name from Daniel Lawrence.

Margaret looked down at the form.

Real mother's name...? Real father...? Both were still blank.

'Why have you not filled in all the form?'

Mayumi stared back fiercely. 'Do I get the part?'

FROM THAT DAY in September 1954 onwards, Okunaga Mayumi was never alone again. Silent, distant, controlled eyes watched her attend senior high school in Nago and progress to a degree in engineering at the recently established University of the Ryukyus in the rebuilt war ruins on the heights of Shuri.

Then in August 1964 Dan received an alarming message that Mayumi had disappeared. Neither the University, nor the carefully cultivated neighbourhood spies in Nago knew where she had gone.

THREE DAYS BEFORE CHRISTMAS 1964, Dan trod gingerly across the icy morning sidewalk from his limousine into the lobby of 100 Park Avenue. The guard at the desk was reading as Dan swept towards the private elevator to the west of the central shaft.

He turned his personal key and the doors slid open, but before they could close a fur-hatted young woman slipped in beside him.

'Sorry, this is a private elevator,' he said politely, holding the doors open. 'I'm afraid it only goes to the penthouse.'

'I know,' she replied.

Then he saw her face properly, smiled, and touched the elevator button.

'Welcome aboard,' he said. '*Hajimemashite*.'

She nodded with approval. 'You know the right word.'

He smiled. 'I had a great teacher.'

Astonished at the joy he felt, Dan wondered how he could ever have thought a child would weigh him down. And the doors closed on them both.

—END—

AFTERWORD

HISTORICAL NOTE FROM THE AUTHOR

What is truth and what is fiction? The eternal conundrum for a novel based on history, which – like truth – is subject to judgement and interpretation. Even official documents lie, often deliberately, to justify the unforgivable, or sometimes, in modern parlance, to protect an institution's ass. For instance, the invention of clouds, or smoke across the target by the US Army Air Force, because they didn't kill enough people.

Further, the dropping of the world's biggest-ever bomb created generations of prejudice, based on morality or points of view – it was very different for those on the ground, for those in the aircraft, very different for the Japanese, and the Americans who sent the bomb. Tricky terrain to navigate.

And, as always, special personalities play a great part – in this story, US Army Air Force Bombardier, Captain Kermit Beahan.

The key facts are incontrovertible. After three runs across the primary target through a clear sky over Kokura, Beahan did not drop the bomb. Had he done so, at least three hundred thousand people would have been killed. When they reached the secondary target, Nagasaki, in spite of now being authorised to drop using radar, making a bullseye simple, he chose to drop *Fat Man* on a hill two miles short, so the massive blast largely flew over the city. Instead of an estimated one-hundred-thousand-plus being killed, six months later the toll was only thirty-eight thousand.

I say 'only' because that's what modern warfare is about – relativity, numbers, cold statistics. Which wasn't the book I wanted to write.

While Beahan's 'near miss' hadn't hitherto been explored, it was the story in people's hearts, good and bad, afraid and heroic, which reached out beyond basic facts towards a different kind of truth, that was most interesting; and because we can never know those motivations, the safest form of expression is the novel. Albeit, with all the risks and inventions that involves.

So fact and fiction evolve side-by-side, real people and imagined characters, which imputes a particular discipline – one might say obligation – on the author to play fair, especially when hard reality takes over, because the material and history require it.

For example, the dialogue on the atom-bomb run from Tinian, across Japan to Kokura and Nagasaki. Kermit Beahan's son gave me what amounts to a transcript of intercom chatter on the aircraft. The words were written down by Abe Spitzer, the radio op on *Bock's Car*, and include Kermit Beahan shouting, over and over, 'No drop.'

Perhaps even more important, Kermit's son, (also called Kermit Beahan, and also an Air Force officer), told me that, as a professional soldier, his father would not have acted on his own volition, would only have obeyed orders. If true, that must bring a wholly different speculation to the 'near miss'. There was, it has been said, an alternative chain of command, bypassing Head of US bombing, General Curtis LeMay in Guam, like a back channel, and there are rumours that President Truman was deeply appalled at the carnage of Hiroshima – but as author, eight decades later, I cannot know if this had bearing on events.

So, the dialogue on the ground at Tinian between Beahan and General Farrell is imagined. Yes, I took liberties with history. However, I do know they met each other while *Fat Man* was being signed by Farrell, and by all accounts Farrell was an unusually politicised officer, directly recruited by Groves for the Manhattan Project, and reported to be more humane than most.

While investigating, it became obvious there is not just *one* single truth – save that in the final act of the cruellest war in history, 27-year-old Captain Kermit Beahan dropped the most destructive bomb in history well short of the secondary target, and thereby saved hundreds of thousands of lives.

Bernard Clark
February 2025

ACKNOWLEDGEMENTS

Japanese Dialogue and Advisor: Alex Scotcher Fukuda
Japanese Artist and Calligrapher: Eliichi Fukuda
Text Editor: Sarah Williams
Layout: IdleWilde
Cover Design: Mark Peters
Editorial Advisor: John Lawton

ABOUT THE AUTHOR

Bernard Clark was born into a British military family, spending his formative years in a dozen different countries, before joining the BBC.

After spells as a reporter, presenter and foreign correspondent, he began making documentaries and factual series in the UK and the US, then launched a London-based independent production company in the mid-1980s, which is still thriving forty years later.

Bernard began his relationship with Japan in 1988, with the award-winning 'Japan Season' for Britain's Channel 4 – 53 hours of programming across five weeks. Since then he has worked for every Japanese TV network, and won the coveted Japan Prize. His company TVT KK has translated and transmitted BBC World News in Japan for over thirty years.

Bernard has written several books, including *A Mother Like Alex,* the story of a woman who adopted nine special-needs children, primarily with Down's Syndrome, which was a best seller.

He lives with his family on a farm near Newbury, England.

Printed in Dunstable, United Kingdom

66262664R00202